Praise for Jean Thompson and *City Boy*

"What's most intriguing about her tale of exploded love and painfully acquired self-knowledge is the balance Thompson achieves between inner turmoil and outer chaos. She charts the ritualized psychological skirmishes of marriage with uncanny accuracy . . . Thompson not only understands our need for stories that take us to the edge of the abyss, that enable us to witness rage and wickedness, she also understands our subsequent desire to be rescued from this forbidding place."

—Donna Seaman, *Chicago Tribune*

"Jean Thompson is a writer of extraordinary intelligence and sensitivity."

—Vince Passaro, *O, The Oprah Magazine*

"Jean Thompson is one of the rare contemporary writers who have earned their credentials as card-carrying members of the literati while addressing the delicate, ineffable business of ordinary family happiness. . . . Thompson's prose is crisp, slangy, staunchly unpretentious."

—Lisa Zeidner, *The New York Times Book Review*

"Sweetly smart, irresistibly urbane."

—*Elle*

"Thompson's ability to create a swirl of the strange and the familiar is why [her] novels work on both heart and head."

—Erica Sanders, *People*

"Thompson has written a sharp, painful book about emotional destruction that progresses at the speed of a thriller yet retains the convincing reality of a documentary."

—Dail Willis, *Baltimore Sun*

"Mesmerizing . . . *City Boy* abounds in mordant wit and keen psychological observations."

—Judith Wynn, *Boston Herald*

"Like Maxine Chernoff and Joyce Carol Oates, Thompson, a stellar stylist, offers unexpected twists, piercingly insightful descriptions, venomous dialogue, and unfailing empathy in a galvanizing novel of hazardous love."

—Donna Seaman, *Library Journal*

"Thompson has created a compelling portrait of young love beaten down . . ."

—Elizabeth Weinstein, *The Columbus Dispatch*

"Thompson dissects the breakup of a marriage in cool, convincing detail, capturing the fraught day-to-day dynamics of conjugal life. . . . The gradual unfolding of motive and shifting of sentiments reveals much about the mechanics of love, betrayal, lies, and jealousy."

—*Publishers Weekly*

"Jean Thompson is a writer worthy of [our] trust."

—Robin Vidimos, *The Denver Post*

"What is both terrifying and oddly reassuring about *City Boy* is how slowly and irrefutably the façade of normalcy disintegrates, how the crimes committed in the name of love begin to pile up until they topple, how much these characters—even as their lives spin entirely out of control—resemble you and me."

—Pam Houston, *O, The Oprah Magazine*

Also by Jean Thompson

NOVELS

Wide Blue Yonder
My Wisdom
The Woman Driver

COLLECTIONS

Who Do You Love
Little Face and Other Stories
The Gasoline Wars

City Boy

A NOVEL

Jean Thompson

Simon & Schuster Paperbacks

New York   London   Toronto   Sydney

SIMON & SCHUSTER PAPERBACKS
Rockefeller Center
1230 Avenue of the Americas
New York, NY 10020

First Simon & Schuster paperback edition 2005

SIMON & SCHUSTER PAPERBACKS and colophon are registered trademarks
of Simon & Schuster, Inc.

For information about special discounts for bulk purchases,
please contact Simon & Schuster Special Sales at
1-800-456-6798 or business@simonandschuster.com

Designed by Jeanette Olender
Manufactured in the United States of America

10 9 8 7 6 5 4 3 2 1

The Library of Congress has cataloged the hardcover edition as follows:
Thompson, Jean, date.
    City boy : a novel / Jean Thompson.
        p.   cm.
    1. Chicago (Ill.)—Fiction. 2. Married people—Fiction.
3. Marital conflict—Fiction. 4. Apartment houses—Fiction. I. Title.
PS3570.H625C58 2004
813'.54—dc21   2003057257
ISBN 0-7432-4282-3
    0-7432-4283-1 (Pbk)

In memory of a city boy

Sergio Garcia

1985–2003

City Boy

One

They had a bad neighbor. Bad in all the usual ways, and difficult to ignore. Music, noise on the stairs, carelessness about the disposal of garbage. Above their heads, he carried on wrestling matches with the furniture. His uncarpeted floors were a soundstage. He dropped and bumped and scraped. Jack and Chloe called him Hippie Pothead Rasta Boy, or sometimes just H.P.R.B. Being witty made them feel better, although not for long. Pot smoke wafted down to them along with other alarming vegetarian burnt smells, brown rice flambé or tofu gone wrong. A perpetual low-grade party reigned upstairs. There were muffled shrieks, more of the furniture wrestling, comings and goings late at night. When, after a time, they complained, they got nowhere. The kid was too stoned, his life already too full of mess and distraction for anything they said to register. The landlord was no help, nor were the police, unless they wanted to get him busted for the drugs. Even under the circumstances that seemed like a crummy thing to do. So eventually they learned to live with annoyance, grievance, and the sense that an unfairness had been done to them.

Their building had only four apartments, two up and two down. One in three odds of getting a rotten neighbor. Or no, that was figuring wrong but the odds didn't matter, they'd still lost out. The building was seventy years old, faced with mellow brick, located in one of those near-north Chicago neighborhoods that was in the process of changing from bad to marginal to good. You had to put up with the occasional street crazy or filth pile, but that meant the rents were more affordable. They intended to be tough and savvy about city life, although neither of them had much practice with it.

When the realty agent had first shown them the apartment, Hippie Pothead Rasta Boy must have been out of town, or sedated. The kitchen was small, the plumbing arthritic, the baseboards had been painted muddy brown. But Jack and Chloe fell in love with the expanse of front windows and good light, the hardwood floors the agent promised would be sanded and refinished, the sense of cozy space that allowed for a vision of smart urban living. They went out and drank martinis to celebrate signing the lease. The future had the same bright jolting perilous taste as the gin. They were young and just starting out, and every decision felt momentous.

The remaining two neighbors were old, remnants of earlier migrations that had in turn been succeeded by other ethnic tides. Jack and Chloe's apartment was first-floor front. Mr. Dandy was first-floor rear. Little Mrs. Lacagnina was directly above Mr. Dandy. Jack and Chloe were conscientiously nice to them. Or tried to be. Mrs. Lacagnina was entirely deaf, a fortunate thing given her proximity to H.P.R.B.'s antics. Jack and Chloe waved and arranged their faces in welcoming expressions as she staggered past with her trolley of groceries. Sometimes she allowed one of them to help her get it up the stairs. More often she brushed past them, her lips shaping soundless prayers or imprecations, wrapped in Sicilian widowhood as she was in her head scarf and old wool coat. The coat was rubbed slick with wear, a dark, boiled green, although it gave evidence of having once been black. Perhaps it had been bought new for the funeral of the anciently dead Mr. Lacagnina. She wore the coat even now, in the blooming warmth of spring. Her skin, what Jack and Chloe saw of it, was flat, chill white, like a milk carton. They hadn't lived there long enough to know how she managed in wintertime, or if she now remembered she'd had another life before she'd taken up mourning.

Mr. Dandy had more conversation in him. He was the first one they met. The day after they moved in, they found him out in the lobby, scrutinizing the names they had newly posted on the mailbox. "Orlovich," he said. "What's that, Jewish?"

"Christ," Jack said, but only loud enough for Chloe to hear. He felt her warning fingertips against his arm. Then she took a step past him and the light fabric of her dress brushed his knee.

"Hi, I'm Chloe Chase and this is my husband, Jack Orlovich."

Jack watched the old man absorb the full impact of Chloe, Chloe being charming. His loose and mottled face seemed, for a moment, not young, but as if there might be a young man somewhere behind it. God he loved seeing that look on other men's faces, even a creaking ruin like this guy, and knowing that he was the one who had Chloe. Not them. The old man pulled his stomach in and introduced himself as Seamus Dandy. Seamus! What's that, Irish? Jack wanted to ask. They all shook hands. Jack made sure he gave him a wrenching grip. Mr. Dandy scowled. "You two are putting me on. You aren't really married, are you?"

"Really and truly. We just have different last names," Chloe said in her pleasant, humoring tone.

"Well that's a bunch of hooey. What's the point of getting married if you aren't even going to sound like man and wife?"

Jack had missed his chance back there with the Jewish remark. The thing to do when people asked belligerent questions designed to put you on the defensive—Are you Jewish/gay/gaining weight—was to say, heartily, No, are you? In this case the true answer was more complicated. Yes, by ancestry, his father, which was probably all Mr. Dandy cared about. No, by inclination and practice and by the way it's none of your goddamned business. But he hadn't been quick enough and now all he could do was stand there while Chloe did her usual swell job of handling things.

Chloe laughed, as if Mr. Dandy had said something agreeably witty. "Oh, there's lots of reasons."

"Huh," said Mr. Dandy. "I'm a bachelor. It's made for a long and happy life."

Chloe deflected Mr. Dandy's further opinions on the married state by asking him if he'd lived here very long. Mr. Dandy said if she meant Chicago, he was Chicago born and bred and never lived anywhere else except for when he was in the service. If they meant this exact spot, he'd had the same apartment for twenty-three years last November.

"Then you must like it here," Jack said, making his official, inane entry into the conversation.

Mr. Dandy looked as if he was trying to remember who Jack was. Oh yeah, the Jewish guy. "It suits me."

Chloe said they thought it was a great building, so much more character than their previous cookie-cutter suburban complex. The construction was much better also. They didn't skimp on materials back then; there was a big difference. She made it sound as if she was paying Mr. Dandy a personal compliment. Mr. Dandy said, "Well, they don't let the colored in. That's something. There was a Mexican gal once, she was in your place. That was only the one. Which ain't bad, considering how they're thick as fleas everywhere else."

Jack and Chloe didn't dare look at each other, though a current of disquiet passed between them. Jack thought that Chloe was probably a little sore she'd wasted all that niceness on the old coot, maybe even chagrined that she'd courted him so transparently. Transparent at least to Jack; Mr. Dandy was as dense as the famously well-constructed brick walls. Chloe was good at getting people to like her, agree with her, do what she asked them to do. Diplomacy, they called it. Jack was the impatient one, while Chloe was better at negotiating with the world, smoothing the way. At least this was how they had come to think of themselves, one of the ways they had agreed to be a couple. Chloe had perfect pitch when she wanted something from people, knew how to read their high and low notes, say or do or be what was needed to harmonize. There are some beautiful women who stand a little to one side of themselves, gauging the effect they have, adjusting, stepping back or bearing down. And that was fine, except, perhaps, for those occasions when the mechanics showed a little too obviously.

Neither of them quite knew what to say next. They were embarrassed for Mr. Dandy because he was too oblivious to be embarrassed for himself. Jack considered making some black friends for the express purpose of inviting them over. He thought this was funny, in an awful kind of way. Later, when he tried it out on Chloe, she threw a pillow at him.

Mr. Dandy said, "I grew up in Back of the Yards. That's all Mexican now. There's whole churches they took over that's nothing but Spanish. Padre Armando. Padre Jorge. You ever hear anything so silly? At least the colored keep to themselves that way."

The longer you listened to such talk in silence, the more complicit you became, and the more likely Mr. Dandy was to move on to other races, creeds, and nationalities. Chloe hurried to invite Mr. Dandy to tell them what line of work he was in.

"I'm a railroader. Retired. A union man. I worked on the Burlington Northern longer than you been alive, young lady." Mr. Dandy winked gallantly. He had puffy, prominent eyelids, like a frog, Jack took pleasure in noting. "So what is it you folks do?"

Chloe spoke the name of her employer, the famous downtown bank. "Jack's the creative one. He's a writer."

"Part-time schoolteacher," said Jack. He wished Chloe hadn't come out with that. If you said you were a writer, people wondered out loud why they'd never heard of you.

"Part-time what?"

"Substitute teacher," Jack admitted.

"Writer, like, books? Which ones?"

"I'm just starting out," said Jack stonily. Damned if he was going to tell Mr. Dandy anything else that could be used against him. He was already pegged as the Jewish guy who didn't even have a real job and wasn't man enough to be ashamed that his beautiful wife was the one supporting him.

"*Angela's Ashes.*"

"Excuse me?"

"That's the book you need to read if you want to be a writer. That guy's rich now, you know. They turned it into a movie. And the best part is, he didn't have to make anything up."

Jack murmured that he had indeed read *Angela's Ashes,* and admired it. Mr. Dandy said, "It's full of all the great Irish themes. Tragedy. Suffering. Innocent little children stricken dead. You get some suffering under your belt, young fella, so's you'll have something interesting to put in your book."

I'm suffering right now. Activate flight plan. Outta here. Jack sent telepathic messages to Chloe, willing her to receive them.

"Hey, you get stuck for ideas, you come talk to me. Thirty-seven years of railroading, I bet I got enough for two, three books. The glory days of rail, when you busted your hump and did a man's work. Winters when the lines froze solid and summers when the wheels put out sparks and set off twenty miles of grass fire. Amtrak was a bad idea nobody'd thought of yet." Somewhere inside Mr. Dandy's yeasty flesh he was muscling an engine around a sharp curve, or some other legendary lie. His eyes kindled and his knuckles cracked. "I can tell you everything you need to know, all you got to do is write it down."

Which would be worse, Mr. Dandy looking sideways at you, glowering and mistrustful, or Mr. Dandy waylaying you with scrapbooks and memorabilia, a runaway train on a collision course? Jack imagined timing his exits and entrances, furtively skulking in and out of the apartment so as to avoid Mr. Dandy, the legion of imaginative excuses he'd need in order to explain why he wasn't writing about the glory days of rail, *Chloe, help.*

Chloe said, "Oh, Jack never runs out of ideas. You'd probably have to wait a long time for him to get around to your book."

"Decades," agreed Jack, deadpan, for Chloe's benefit.

But Mr. Dandy was already losing interest in him, reverting back to his original glum disapproval. "Ah, whatever. Write a book, don't write a book. Either way it don't keep the world from spinning."

A blast of amplified music startled them. It came from upstairs, loud but distorted, as if it originated inside an agitating washing machine. Reggae music, set on spin cycle.

Jack and Chloe looked at each other, then Mr. Dandy. He said, "That's something you better get used to. This guy." He jabbed his thumb at the mailboxes. Jack craned to read the name. Berserk? No, Brezak.

"Does he—" Jack began, but it had become difficult to make himself heard. He tried to pantomime questions, who and what the hell. He shrugged at Chloe, who shook her head and looked unhappy.

Mr. Dandy waved his hands around his ears as if shooing gnats. He raised his voice to bawl, "It's enough to make you curse the invention of electricity, ain't it? Nice meeting you folks." He stumped off down the hallway, pursued by island rhythms.

Jack and Chloe retreated behind their own door. Through some trick of acoustics, the music wasn't quite as loud, but it was clearer, jumpety jumpety jump, a singer carrying on about his no-good woman. Jack thought it was Bob Marley, but then, Bob Marley was the only reggae singer he knew. He said, "I didn't think anybody was still big on this stuff."

"This could really be a problem."

"Wasn't there some old Eddie Murphy reggae skit, 'Kill de white people, kill de white people, yah yeah.'"

Chloe said, "Seriously . . ."

"Give it a minute." Chloe would expect him to go up there and complain, threaten, whatever. It was man's work, the opposite of charm. It was nothing he looked forward to. He sat down on the couch with a magazine and pretended the loopy music wasn't making his foot pat in syncopation.

From the bedroom Chloe called, "It's worse in here. Like it's traveling through the heat register."

Hell and death. He put the magazine down and stood. Just then the music stopped and someone upstairs took a running start, raced across the floorboards, and collided with a heavy object.

Silence followed. Chloe came out of the bedroom and the two of them gazed at the ceiling. Jack said, "Maybe they killed themselves. Death by reggae."

"Is there a noise ordinance? We should find out. If it's as bad as he was saying."

"I hope it doesn't come to that. The calling 911 part."

"Wimp."

"You gotta admit, it would be getting off on the wrong foot."

"Well you have to work here. You decide if you can take it."

"Yeah. My work." He watched Chloe pick up a lamp without a shade and put it down again in the same place. They were still unpacking and everything was scattered and disordered. "Speaking of which . . ."

"I'm sorry honey, I had no idea he was going to pester you like that. What a character. I bet you money everybody calls him Jim Dandy. What."

"Nothing."

"Not nothing. What."

"Just don't go around introducing me to people as a writer."

Chloe was messing with the lamp again. Jack thought they were both waiting to see if the music would start up again and force them to do something about it. Chloe frowned at him. "Really?"

"Yeah, really." There were times when Chloe tried to charm her way past him as she did other people; Jack always called her on it. He didn't want to be other people to her.

"You think I'm trying to make myself more interesting by bragging about you."

"No," said Jack firmly, although he might have believed something of the sort. But to admit the possibility would be to open the door to one of Chloe's morbid self-criticism sessions.

"I can't even tell normal people, like the ones I work with? How come? I want to brag about you."

"Wait until I do something worth bragging about."

Chloe made a face that was meant to express forbearance in the presence of long suffering. "Not this again."

"Not the pep talk again, okay?" He'd published a few poems and two stories, all in magazines whose names were known mostly to the other people who published in them.

"I love 'The Joyride.' It's a great story. Can't I brag about that?"

"Do me a favor, say I'm an English teacher. Everybody knows what that is, you don't have to answer a million questions."

He didn't feel like a writer yet and he wouldn't until he had more to show for himself. Only in the last few months had he attempted to go about it in any organized, full-time fashion, although he'd always written things, had always vaguely imagined doing something that messed around with books and literature. Teaching English to high school kids had been the path of least resistance. One night, after he'd again complained, whined really, about the things he was always whining about—students who were dull or rude or semicriminal, small-minded colleagues, administrators whose names were synonyms for incompetence, the daily round of frustration, tedium, and outrage—Chloe said, "Maybe you should quit."

Jack stared at her. "Gotcha," Chloe said.

"Quit and do what?"

"I don't know, whatever's going to keep me from listening to you be miserable every night of my life. Unless that's the fun part for you. You know, the hopelessness and all."

Over the next few weeks they planned it out. Chloe was going into the bank's management-training program. If he substituted even a few days a month, the money would be enough, barely. It was understood that this was a chance for him to make the writing work, one way or another, within a finite but unspecified period of time. They agreed that Jack might feel dependent, beholden, etc., that Chloe might come to feel burdened, resentful, and so on. They resolved to be clear-eyed and up front about these and other possible issues, talk things through. It pleased them to be arranging their lives this unconventionally. Chloe's job, the only real job now left between them, was downtown. It made sense to move into the city, and besides, no one expected a writer to live in the suburbs. What were you supposed to write about, shopping malls?

So now it was all up to him. No excuses. It filled him with dread. There had to be writers out there with titanic egos and monumental, obnoxious amounts of self-confidence. He wasn't one of them. Maybe if he stumbled onto some unforeseen, high-profile success, he'd be transformed, maybe that was what happened to people. But this was difficult to imagine when he sat in front of the computer, that expensive, obedient, superbly engineered machine that had been chosen for its ability to effortlessly reproduce and transmit his every written thought, and felt like a goddamned fraud. At his lowest ebb he felt himself to be devoid of ideas, talent, taste. He wasn't fooling anyone. He didn't have what it took. Whatever it was. He tried to imagine the words he wrote at this very desk making their way out into the world, catching on fire in the minds of people he would never meet. It seemed absurd.

Yet he knew that all this was to be expected, even the dopey, puerile, self-hating parts. It was what he'd signed on for, a process that might still lead to nothing, but there was only one way of finding out. And when he seized on something he'd written, a page, a paragraph, even a single word, and thought it was good, more than good, it allowed him to keep going until the next such time. As long as he kept going, he was allowed to take himself seriously.

These were in a sense the most private moments of his life. He didn't always feel like offering them up, even to Chloe, who sometimes, in her solicitude, sounded as if she was encouraging a slow child. He usually settled for saying that his day had been "not bad" or "not terrific." Sometimes he fell into the easy pose of exasperation, since there was always something to be exasperated about in writing. But always there was what he held back.

Chloe let a silence settle. Then she said, "They did a nice job on the floors, didn't they?"

"Yeah." Floors. He recognized another Chloe tactic, a statement you were meant to agree with. But he was ready to be softened up. He didn't like being out of sorts with her, especially when it was due to his own gloomy, backward pride.

"It's a selfish act, isn't it. Writing. I mean it's supposed to be all about communication, but it's actually very self-involved."

Of course they'd been over this ground before. "Yup," Jack said. "Damn near misanthropic."

"My name is Igor. I assist Dr. Frankenstein in the laboratory. His genius is far beyond me. I can only gape and marvel."

Jack raised himself off the couch just far enough to grab Chloe by the waist and pull her down on top of him. Her legs beneath her skirt were bare and he ran a hand behind one warm knee.

"What are you doing?"

"Don't worry, I'm a doctor."

He pulled her dark hair away from her neck and kissed his way down to where he could feel her heartbeat. He waited to see if she would protest or pull back, but she didn't. They had been too tired from moving in to make love last night. It felt like something they should do in this new place before much more time passed.

Chloe stood up and took his hand and they slow-walked into the bedroom. Jack kicked his shoes away. Chloe's dress had a zipper in the back and she presented herself to him so he could help. He loosened the zipper, then pressed against her from behind, spreading her legs and making her stagger a little, until he gripped her around the waist and steadied her. "Let me get this off," she murmured, trying to twist around to face him.

"Not yet." He wanted her clothes tangled around her, wanted to push them aside and see her breasts and flushed stomach and perfect ass revealed in all the ways he could imagine, imagining just moments away from happening because his hands and mouth were full of Chloe and her breathing was damp and rapid and now he had to hurry to get his own clothes off. Chloe was on her back on the bed and he was leaning over her when the music started up in mid-growl, as if the volume control had been yanked hard right. Again it was reggae. Boom da boom da ya ya, hey mon, talkin boom da boom da ya ya.

"I don't believe this."

Jack tried to carry on for a while as if it wasn't happening, had to give up. "Shit."

Chloe rolled away across the bed. "Maybe now you'll want to go talk to them?"

"Not this very minute." With an effort, he reclaimed his body.

"You still want to . . ."

"Why not. It's a cinch they can't hear us."

So they went ahead, determined not to get chased out of their own bedroom. It felt as if they were trying to race the music to the end, boom da boom da ya ya, boom da boom da ya ya.

It was another couple of days before they had any face-to-face encounter with the upstairs neighbor. Sometimes the noise level dropped off and they actually found themselves straining to hear the music. They let the weekend pass without complaining. After all it was the weekend, people stayed up late, carried on. It sounded as if giant mice, giant Jamaican mice, were loose upstairs, bouncing and tumbling and smoking weed. There was at least one girl up there; they heard her giggling and shrieking. But they saw no one. The inhabitants seemed to have entombed themselves, although it was fine spring weather and people were crazy to get outside, the way you were in a northern city once winter was behind you.

On Sunday Jack and Chloe bought Italian ices and walked along Belmont Harbor and watched people launching their boats into the blue water. They explored the less threatening portions of their own neighborhood, went to a pizza place on Clark and drank a bottle of red wine. They walked home with the streetlights just beginning to bloom. The air was warm and scented with something that might only have been the right mix of pollution and automobile exhaust, but which smelled sweet anyway. A maple tree in an apartment compound was sending hundreds of kamikaze seedpods rattling to the ground. People were sitting out on their front steps in the twilight. Jack and Chloe exchanged greetings as they passed. They felt again the promise of the city, a place that might be ugly in its separate parts, but was beautiful in its whole.

Chloe had to get up early for work the next morning. The people upstairs seemed to have no such imperatives. At ten-thirty the music was still bouncing merrily, and voices were cheering it on. Chloe sighed and looked at Jack. He gave her a mock salute, closed the apartment door behind him, and climbed the stairs to the second floor.

Since it was inevitable that he'd be making this trip, he'd more or less rehearsed it in his head. He wished he was someone who flew into righteous rages and made threats and scared people. Once only had he gotten into it with a guy in a parking lot outside a bar, his first fight since he was a kid. They'd both been drunk and the other guy went down after a few sloppy punches, knocked off balance more than hurt. A crowd had gathered to watch. Now they began backing away. Jack, who was tall but not built so as to intimidate anyone, had laughed incredulously and spread his arms to show how harmless he was, and just then the other guy had risen up and tackled Jack around the knees and they both went down again.

The upstairs hallway was a narrow corridor running the length of the building. It wasn't hard to figure out which door was the problem. The wood fairly vibrated. Jack knocked, then pounded.

The door opened. A girl with short hair dyed Raggedy Ann red peered out through a crack. "Hi, I live downstairs—" Jack began.

The door closed. Now what. He raised his hand to knock again, and it reopened. This time it was a kid in a wrinkled gauze shirt, with a tuft of beard on his chin and an expression of droopy suspicion. "What's up," he said. A statement, not a question.

Jack was only five, maybe six years older than the kid, but already he was at some age-related disadvantage. "What's up" didn't invite you to respond in any way that moved the conversation forward. It was some kind of hipster code or beer-commercial-speak, layered with irony. Jack settled for mumbling "Sup," feeling stupid, then launched into his speech. "My wife and I just moved in downstairs . . ." The noise was making him shout. "Hey, can you cut that music down?"

The kid turned to give some instruction to Raggedy Ann, who was probably busy spraying Ozium into the clouds of reefer smoke. The music subsided. Jack imagined Chloe downstairs, listening.

"Hi, Jack Orlovich."

He extended his hand. The kid stared at it as if it were a piece of machinery that came without instructions. They weren't doing real well at the greetings thing. Finally the kid shook, a vaguely sticky, squirming grip. "Rich."

"Nice to meet you. Look, you have to keep the noise down. Especially when we're trying to sleep." Screw diplomacy.

"Oh . . . Okay." The kid—Rich—leaned into the door. Beyond him Jack could see some grimy wood floor and an ugly couch that looked like you'd get a rash from sitting on it. "So when do you guys sleep?"

"Right now."

"Yeah?"

You wouldn't think it was a hard idea to get across. Jack couldn't tell if the kid was belligerent or just way stoned. His hair was long and pulled back into one of those rat-nasty ponytails. He looked shifty as hell, but not really dangerous.

The kid turned his back to Jack and had some sort of conversation with the girl behind him. Then he swung around again. "Does your plumbing work?"

"I guess. Sure." Now what.

"Mine's screwed up, we got no water pressure. You know anything about plumbing?"

He didn't, and Chloe was waiting downstairs for him, but the kid was opening the door wider, beckoning, and Jack stepped inside. How could he not? Three days of listening, he wanted to see where they kept the trampoline and the pipe organ.

The apartment was laid out like his and Chloe's, same-but-different enough to make him feel as if he was the one who was stoned, or had followed a white rabbit down its hole. The kid was leading the way back to the kitchen, loping through the rooms with a sturdy gait that Jack well recognized. The music was still damn close to loud, and Jack took the opportunity to turn it down a few notches without the kid noticing.

He had an impression of walls painted in bright, inflamed colors, turquoise and purple, and blinds drawn across shut windows, and curtains on top of that, and too much lamp light, and stale, overcooked air, a total effect of hectic claustrophobia. The television and stereo and their attendant cords and clutter took up one entire wall, like an altar to noise, or maybe to Bob Marley. A poster of him, his brooding silhouette edged in bands of rainbow, hung on the wall where, in his own apartment, Jack would have seen a newly hung print of Monet's water lilies.

There were stubs of melted candles in jar lids, paperback books, clothes hung on doorknobs, scattered newspapers, mail, drinking glasses abandoned with an inch or so of suspect liquid in the bottom, plastic forks, towels, a pair of ancient, peeling cowboy boots, magazines, a couple of empty jugs of supermarket wine, a Halloween mask of a green and melting-faced monster, a bag of foil-wrapped chocolate Easter eggs, a paddle racquet missing its tethered rubber ball. This and more was piled or strewn on floors and tables. He told himself it was just like the way he'd lived when he was the kid's age, though he didn't really believe it.

When Jack reached the kitchen, the Raggedy Ann girl was there too. "It ran out right in the middle of doing the dishes," she said, an aggrieved housekeeper.

The kitchen wasn't worse than the rest of the place, or at least it wasn't exponentially worse, as he might have feared. It smelled of curry, and some other spices he couldn't put a name to, something dank and weedy that he associated with countries where people died of plagues.

The kid said, "I think maybe it's the water line, the whole line coming into the apartment, because the bathroom doesn't work either."

Jack pretended to examine the faucet, even made a show of opening the cabinet beneath the sink and fiddling with the valve. How dumb were these people? "Well, for whatever reason, it looks like your water's been shut off."

"No way."

"God, Richard, weren't you supposed to call them? Wasn't there some kind of big deal deal with the bill?"

"Shit, man."

The two of them looked incapable of formulating any sort of response besides staring longingly at the sink. Jack said, "There was probably some water still in the pipes when they shut it off, so you couldn't tell right away. Tomorrow's Monday, you can call the water company in the morning."

"This just sucks," said the kid, peevishly. "I mean, we can't even flush the toilet."

Jack only wished it had been the power bill. "Well . . . ," he said, preparing himself to leave before they asked to come downstairs and use the bathroom.

"Why do they even charge you for water, what kind of rip-off is that? It's like charging for air."

"Or food," Jack couldn't resist, which made the kid give him that sullen, cross-eyed look again, before he decided it was funny, and laughed.

"'They belly full.' Yeah man, some things just don't change."

"Yeah." He must have uttered some Rastafarian password without knowing it.

"Hey, you want a drink? Look and see what we got." The kid nodded to the girl, who opened the refrigerator and began rattling through the shelves.

"Thanks, but my wife's got to be wondering what happened to me."

"Tell her to come on up and party," said the kid cheerily. He was sloshing a bottle of undrinkable wine into not entirely clean plastic glasses.

"Work tomorrow," Jack reminded. "Maybe some other—"

"One drink. What the hell. No water, plenty of wine. Come on, don't be a total killjoy."

He was exactly that, he was the King of Killjoys, and he didn't want to get too chummy because he guessed, correctly, that this was only the first of many occasions when he'd be up here trying to get the kid to do or not do something; nevertheless here he was, taking the glass, sitting down on that ugly couch, not passing up the joint when the kid sent it his way.

Or no, it hadn't happened quite that fast. They were still in the kitchen when the girl, whose name no one had thought to tell him, shrieked without warning, "Mouse! Mouse!"

She was squawking and pointing to the floorboard next to the refrigerator. Jack caught a disappearing glimpse of something gray and frantic. "Oh *God*," said the girl. "Rich, we have to set some traps."

"What are you so scared of, you're only what, five hundred times bigger than it is? It's a living creature, it has a right to exist."

"I don't care, I don't like the way they sneak around on their sneaky little feet. And they're dirty." She appealed to Jack. She had some kind of dire stuff on her eyelashes that turned them into dark blue spikes, and a number of tattoos peeking out of her clothing like glimpses of underwear. "Don't you think mice are just vermin?"

CITY BOY   17

Jack was struck by the notion that the times they'd thought the people upstairs sounded like mice, it might have been actual mice. No, a bigger concern was that the mice might begin commuting downstairs. He said, "Well, killing mice isn't any worse than frying a chicken or—"

"Exactly," said the kid, happy to launch into this. "That's why I don't do that shit. Eat flesh. It's unnatural."

Jack, who could never keep himself from meeting an argument with an argument, said, "Animals eat other animals. That's pretty natural."

This stopped the kid for a moment, but then he kept right on coming. "McDonald's isn't natural. Antibiotics and hormones and brain and bonemeal in cattle feed isn't—"

"Okay, forget McDonald's. We're living creatures too, we're allowed to exist, take up space, eat. You know, survive. We don't have to apologize for being here." By this time Jack was drinking the wine, which was so sharp and metallic, he found it necessary to get a great deal of it down, so as to anesthetize himself against the taste.

"Survive, yes, not trash the planet so corporations can make big piles of money for their stockholders. The white man's Bible spells it out, page one, where the Lord gives man dominion over the fish of the sea and the birds of the air and every living thing that moves upon the earth. It's a fucking business plan."

He must be one of those white guys who went around pretending they were black. It seemed like a really tortured way of going natural. At the same time, Jack couldn't entirely disagree with the kid's sentiments, although he himself might put it in some less simpleminded way.

The kid said, "Come here," beckoning him through the dining room —at least that's what it was in his own apartment. Here it was harder to determine function. In the front room the kid shoveled through a pile of books and came up with a frayed paperback, *Triumph Over Babylon*. The cover showed a city skyline, Babylon, presumably, skyscrapers and power lines and traffic signals, the works, everything wavering and crumbling. "This lays it all out. The roots of the struggle against the death culture."

"Oh. Sure." Jack sat down to open it. The first chapter was called

"The Black Jesus." He wondered, not for the first time, why he bothered writing fiction, inventing things.

He looked up to see a lit joint under his nose, the kid waving it so the curl of smoke scribbled back and forth. "Coming at you," said the kid, in a strangled, trying-not-to-exhale voice, and Jack reached out and took it.

He sucked in a mouthful of smoke, felt it rising in him like an elevator. Lungs, bloodstream, brain, top floor, everybody out. The kid's stuff was excellent. No wonder he always looked so slack jawed. Not that Jack was feeling entirely crisp and articulate himself at the moment. Chloe didn't like him smoking, and over time he'd pretty much given it up. It wasn't anything he'd promised her never to do, so technically he wasn't going behind her back, what the hell, she was probably already pissed at him for staying up here, which in some stoned way seemed to make everything all right.

"You're not a cop or anything, are you?"

The kid was sitting on the floor with his back against an armchair that was the mate of the wretched sofa. The girl had come in and draped herself across him and was rubbing one hand in slow circles above, below, and over the kid's crotch.

Jack was too stoned to pretend not to stare. "No, I'm not a cop, I'm a writer."

Damned if he knew why he said it. He felt pointlessly embarrassed.

"I really didn't think you were, I just had to ask, you know?" The kid had only heard the not cop part. He was safe. "Because cops'll sit right down with you and smoke your shit, but they have to tell you who they are if you ask them. It's the law."

Jack was pretty sure this was not the case, but he nodded, Uh-huh. His head felt like it was full of syrup.

"Oh, this is perfect." The kid jumped up, spilling the girl in a heap, and bent over the stereo, turning the noise up to painful levels. The song was "I Shot the Sheriff," the kid accompanying it on a spirited air guitar.

"Whoa, whoa," Jack flagged him down. "You can't play it that loud. Wife. Work. Sleep. Remember?"

The kid shrugged and looked sulky, but lowered the volume. Jack said, "Headphones. Quiet hours. We've got to get something worked out here, Rich."

The kid said Sure, okay, but in the moment before he did so Jack caught the knowing look that passed between him and the girl. It was plain to them he was some hung-up fussbudget fixated on tiny decorum, an inhabitant of boring squaredom. They had their own absorbing world of sex and music and intrigue. He wasn't any part of it. When you were under twenty, the boundaries were clear. He could hang with them, smoke their herb, groove to their music or pretend to. He would still amuse them.

Maybe it was just his brain on drugs that made this rankle. Hey, wiseass, you're the one who's the joke here. Let's get that straight. He hated having his insulated bubble of smugness punctured, wanted to believe, in the face of all evidence and history to the contrary, that he was the only one capable of insight, observation, judgment. It was always a shock to realize that someone else was peering back in at him, that he was himself horribly visible.

He was ready to get up and leave, he was through with these people, but before he could get his hands and feet and all his other balky parts in motion, the door buzzer sounded.

The apartment building had a security door and a buzzer for people who wanted entrance. Also an intercom that was supposed to let you ask who was there, but this was broken, and looked as if it had been for some time. It wasn't a problem for Jack and Chloe, who would only have to open their front door to see who was standing outside. But the kid would have to go downstairs. He and the girl looked at each other.

"Randy."

"You think?"

The kid jumped up and hit the entry buzzer. Now it really was time for Jack to leave, but he lingered, just to see what new sort of oddity might walk through the door, and also to administer a few more cautions about the music.

There were feet on the stairs. The kid opened the apartment door

then made an effort to close it again, too late, somebody he didn't expect already half inside, the kid giving up and walking away, the girl
leaning forward with her lips pushed into a pout—all this happening
in a second or so, as Jack struggled to get upright in the sagging couch
cushions and brace for whatever menace was on its way into the room,
vengeful drug lords or some other bad trouble he'd just larked his way
into the middle of—

But it was only another girl. A narrow-shouldered, narrow-faced girl
with a hitch in her step and pale, damp blond hair. She didn't say anything, nor did anyone else. The kid resumed his seat on the floor. The
Raggedy Ann girl hunched up close to him and got her hands busy
with his shirt buttons.

The blond girl closed the door behind her and surveyed the room,
Jack included, with an expression of haughty disinterest. She took a
seat in a corner that put her in everyone's line of sight, although the
three of them were careful not to make eye contact. Jack was actually
grateful for the music. Without it there would have been only glowering silence. Raggedy Ann was playing up to the kid for all she was
worth, pressing and squeezing and carrying on voluptuously. The song
ended and another song began. It seemed to be a contest among them
to pretend that no one else was in the room.

The blond girl maintained her cool, scornful pose. She took a pack of
cigarettes from the pocket of her denim shirt and studied it critically,
then removed one and reached across the coffee table for the lighter.

Her sudden movement startled the kid, who had been lying back
with his eyes half closed as the redhead fondled him. He'd been pretending the music was so compelling that he wasn't noticing anything
else, a supreme, almost yogilike act of concentration. But the way his
eyes shot open and his head jerked gave him away.

The blond girl lit her cigarette, allowed herself a small, meant-to-be-
noticed smirk, and tossed the lighter back on the table.

Jack thought he could guess what all this was about, although the
notion of anyone fighting over the kid's scrawny ass seemed ludicrous.
Without meaning to, Jack was examining the two girls, comparing
them, as if he were the one who got to choose. Raggedy Ann was, if not

prettier, at least more decorative, had gone to more effort with her eye makeup and silver rings and bright green blouse. The blond girl was less obtrusive, less costumed. Her clothes were drab and her hair hung flat and straight around her shoulders. She didn't have much of a figure, at least as far as Jack could tell from all her flapping layers of cotton. She had on a patterned skirt of the sort of material that was usually made into cheap bedspreads. It was hiked up around one knee and when Jack tried to get a peek at her legs, she caught him at it and withered him with a look.

Jack sank back into the sofa. He felt like an idiot in so many different ways, there was no use in trying to sort them out. He wished there was a lever he could pull that would drop him through the floor and into his own living room. The blond girl spoke up above the music. "Who's the big asshole?" Meaning him.

The kid was pretending he'd just noticed her. "Him? He's . . ." It was clear that he'd forgotten Jack's name. "Neighbor."

"What did you tell him about me, huh?"

"Nothing. Christ."

"Because he's looking at me like he heard something really choice."

"God, you are so paranoid. Like everybody's supposed to care about you and your crazy psycho-bitch routine."

"Right," said the girl, sending smoke through her nostrils. "I remember how much you used to hate it. And all the different interesting ways."

The redheaded girl lifted her mouth out of the kid's neck for long enough to say something utterly vulgar.

Jack got to his feet. "Just leaving. Take it easy."

Nobody said anything, although the kid raised his hand in a half-hearted wave. Don't let the door hit you on the butt on the way out.

Jack paused in the hallway. He no longer felt the pot, at least not in the way he had before, but he was still addled and unsteady and uncertain about what had really happened. He stared at the closed door, shook his head as if there were someone there to agree with him about the strangeness of it all, then made his way downstairs.

The music was a low growl overhead. He supposed this was the best you could hope for. He saw how quickly they would come to accept all such unacceptable intrusions and annoyances.

Chloe was asleep. She lay on her side with the covers drawn up to her waist, leaving her arm and shoulder bare. The arm was long and graceful and as insubstantial as a bird's wing, and like a wing it was bent at the elbow as if tensed for flight. Her face was in shadow but the line of her throat was clear and the dark mass of her hair spread across the pillow with that same look of arrested motion. He wanted to wake her up, tell her everything, get her to laugh and marvel and exult in how lucky they were to have each other and the life they were building together, a life the freaks upstairs would neither know nor appreciate. What had happened tonight would be incomplete to him until he told her the story. But tomorrow was a workday, and he let her sleep.

He had only gone into the bathroom for a minute and when he came out he paused, listening to what was going on in the bedroom over-head. It was not the first time he had heard these sounds, although never this clearly. On other occasions it had been possible to at least pretend they were something else. What unsettled him now was not so much the sounds themselves, but his absolute certainty that no one had come downstairs from the second floor.

Two

When Jack was a kid growing up in the boring perfection of the southern California suburbs, he longed for all the places that were not southern California. From television and movie screens, magazine covers and billboards, he took in all the bright and dark, slick and grainy images. They jumbled together like a giant commercial for the world: wheat fields, tornados, barns, eagles, coal mines, Graceland, Christmas tree farms, Mayan temples, subways, Bedouins, windmills, flagpoles, manholes. Amazing stuff, all of it. Indiana seemed as foreign and exotic as India. And always there was the feeling that life, real life, was going on somewhere just beyond his reach.

His father was a surgeon who specialized in sports-related injuries. His mother made stained-glass artifacts in a studio attached to the pool house. His older sister was serious about riding horses. Jack grew up with his parents' expectations, although they did not weigh on him very heavily. He was meant to go to medical school, prosper, buy real estate of his own. His mother worried that he didn't join enough group activities. His father was always telling him to get his nose out of a book and go outside and *do* something. Karate, soccer, Little League, cross-country: he moped his way through all of these before he was allowed to give them up. A bit of a loner, a kid who looked out from inside himself.

He experimented with all the commercially available forms of rebellion: motorcyles and angry music and marijuana. He was smart enough to get through high school without much exertion, smart enough also to stay beneath the radar when it came to troublemaking, or for that matter, achievement. Camouflage and dissembling came naturally to him. His real self was in hiding, waiting to emerge in the same way he felt his real life was waiting for him.

His college entrance exam scores and grade point were good enough to get him into the California schools, but he wasn't having any of that. His mother's brother had gone to Northwestern, and that allowed him to enroll there, where his parents couldn't possibly keep an eye on him.

Jack loved it from day one. He loved the deciduous trees igniting with autumn, and the stiff lakeshore winds, and the enormous, souped-up city just beyond the borders of campus. In the beginning Chicago shocked him with its purposeful shoving crowds and the sheer size of its raw and blighted parts. But it was the world he'd been denied, and he was in a hurry to make up for lost time.

It only took him a semester to change his major from premed to English. Because he wasn't blond and didn't talk about surfing, people at first refused to believe he was from California. He found he could use this to his advantage. He stopped telling friends that his family lived in Sherman Oaks and instead said Los Angeles, or if he wanted to make a flourish, "You know, the City of Angels." He broke up with his long-distance high school girlfriend. He joined the campus chapter of the ACLU. He and his friends made weekend excursions to the Art Institute and Blackhawks games. A number of times they went to a particular South Side blues club, where it thrilled them to have the bartender nod at them in recognition. Jack was pretty sure that his real life had started, but he wasn't yet as confident that this was his real self.

When his parents asked him what he was going to do after college, he said he would teach. At that point it was only an answer designed to put them off.

Of course he took poetry writing classes. Writing was both easier and more difficult than it would become later. Easier because he was ignorant of all the mistakes he was making, harder because he wasn't used to the way writing could jerk you from high to low and back again. He loved the workshop classes, he sometimes wished you could make a living going to poetry workshops, well, you almost could, if you stretched grad school out long enough. At first he wasn't confident about speaking up in class, but he made himself pretend to be confident, and, amazingly, it worked.

In these classes students gathered together to encourage each other's writing in productive and positive ways, and sometimes this actually happened, but everyone knew the classes were also about showing off. Jack enjoyed the competition, the first time in his life he could say that about anything. His writing was good enough to cow his fellow students, who were reduced to quibbling about things like the way he used capital letters. When it was time to talk about other people's poems, he developed a habit of holding back his comments until the rest of the class had spoken. If he felt the poem was bad, he said so more in sorrow than in anger. If it was good, he was generous with praise. Even the professor sometimes seemed to be waiting for him to declare himself and pull the discussion one way or another. And even in the intense atmosphere of the workshop, where many of the students were further agitated because they were sleeping with each other, or failing to sleep with each other, or had already slept with each other and were no longer on civil terms, Jack was someone everyone agreed to admire.

Privately he believed he was one of the best writers on campus, but then his heart sank as he thought about the universe beyond the university.

It was the start of spring semester of his junior year. "Spring" was a bad joke. The weather was sleety January. The classroom on this first day smelled of wet wool and radiator heat. It was an advanced class and most of the students filing in knew each other, knew the professor, knew where they stood in the pecking order. There was an atmosphere of weary professionalism in the room, like soldiers who have been through a number of battles and know what the next campaign will bring.

Jack arrived late and was annoyed to find the seat that he thought of as his, the far corner of the back row, already occupied. The girl who had taken his place looked as if she was accustomed to sitting exactly where she wanted to. She had black hair looped up on top of her head and held there by two ivory chopsticks. She wore a white ski sweater and ripped blue jeans and beneath the jeans were black fishnet stock-

ings. The stockings just killed him. He sat down a few seats away and
tried not to look at her exposed knee, or the long rip along the inside of
her thigh, but then he found himself looking at her face, which was
every bit as disconcerting. She was exactly the kind of girl who young
men wrote poetry about. She might have been sitting there for just that
purpose, like a model in a figure-drawing class. The arch of her eyebrows, slant of her cheekbones, soft chin, and full mouth were rendered in clear, pure lines. It was an intelligent face, its expression a bit
severe, perhaps from a long experience of being stared at.

Many weeks later Jack would write his own poem about her. It said
that the human eye was like a seed that sent its roots through light, that
at the sight of her face something had grown up inside him, a living,
restless tree with blood for sap and a constellation of singing leaves. He
didn't turn the poem in for class. It was too formal, he decided, too
much a working out of a conceit, and besides, he was afraid that someone would bring up potatoes and the fact that they also had sprouting
eyes.

That first day the professor went through the roll. Jack didn't have
long to wait to learn her name. She was a C. Ms. Chase. Ms. Chase
opened a green notebook and began tracing elegant spirals across the
blank page as the professor gave his up-and-at-'em speech. He did this
at the beginning of every semester. The professor was one of those
melancholy men who compensated for it by being especially antic and
vivacious. He talked about observation, how poets must be passionate,
accurate observers of the world. Yes, passionate, by God. How they
were to make use of technique, but they were not to become a slave to
it. How they should each strive to find their own true, unique voice.
How they should be honest with each other in their criticism, even
though this might be painful, and that honesty, both of feeling and of
expression, was to be the primary aim of their writing.

Ms. Chase raised her hand. This was unusual, it caused a mild stir.
The professor's speech was not meant to be interrupted. You were not
really even meant to listen to it. The professor said, "Yes?" in an over-
polite tone that indicated he was a little pissed off.

Ms. Chase had a sweet, rather dusky voice. "I was just wondering . . . can you really assign a value like honesty to language?"

"I would certainly hope so. I hope, at least, that we could all agree there's such a thing as dishonest language, and that it has no place in poetry."

This was a rebuke of sorts and Ms. Chase's lovely profile flushed, but she carried on. "I mean, you're assuming that language has these fixed and immutable values . . ."

"Instead of . . . ?"

"You can't assume anymore that language is merely representational. It's a self-referential system with its own burden of social and political constructs. Assigning values to it isn't just subjective, it's naive."

The class gaped. Such talk was like an evil spell. None of them was entirely sure what it meant but they knew it was an attack. They looked at the professor, who had turned stone-faced. Jack, dismayed, wondered if he was going to be forced to hate her, if she was like one of those cursed fairy-tale princesses who spat out snakes and toads.

After a moment the professor said, "I guess I'd begin by asking you if everything you just said is unreliable and has an arbitrary meaning, or are you exempt from all that?"

"You have to use language to investigate language," said Ms. Chase, still sweet voiced, but with an edge of stubbornness. Jack had to admire the way she was able to carry on an argument even as those fishnet stockings did their thing.

"Which theory class did you take? This all sounds very familiar. This," he nodded to the rest of the class, including them as he excluded Ms. Chase, "is the way academics tell us that poetry doesn't matter. The currently fashionable way."

"I just don't think you can write without an informed self-awareness." Her pen was moving across the notebook page even as she spoke, the spirals coming faster and tighter.

"Critical theory's a virus. It sends out legions of little jargon-spouting spores that infect everything they touch. How did you get into this course anyway? Did you take the beginning workshop?"

"No, but I've written—"

"If you had, you would have learned that poems aren't logs that exist just so they can be gnawed down into little piles of toothpicks."

The class sensed something new and dangerous, a situation that might get genuinely out of control, and not for any of the usual reasons, such as students sneering at each other's poems. The professor was no longer acting like their Scout troop leader, breaking up quarrels and leading sing-alongs; he was actually being mean.

Jack raised his hand. He wasn't sure what he was going to say, but he couldn't let things go on any longer in this unbearable fashion. "Jack," the professor said promptly.

"I just wanted to say . . ." He filled his lungs with air as if this would fill his head with brilliant thought. "I'm thinking about why people write poetry in the first place, or at least why I write it. And it's not really about language, even though language is the medium and it's what we're always arguing about. You write a poem because you want to communicate something with absolute clarity. All the nuances and contradictions and complexities, the whole nine yards. I have to believe you can do that. I have to believe that two different people can read a poem and come to the same understanding. That people can understand each other."

He stopped, feeling like an idiot. But what he'd said had been just vapid and heartfelt enough to calm the room down and bathe it in a wash of good feeling, a warm soup of good intentions. Understanding and communication, they were all for that. They were once more united. The professor, no doubt embarrassed by letting himself carry on so, began talking briskly about deadlines and reading lists.

Ms. Chase was silent for the rest of the hour. She closed her notebook and gazed out the window at the gray clouds dropping ice on the empty sidewalks and lawns. She had the sullen expression of someone who knew she was being watched. Jack swore at himself for being so obvious. He was communicating with perfect clarity all right.

He was going to say something to her after class, explain himself or apologize, but as soon as the bell rang she positioned her oversized shoulder bag, rose, and stepped out the door. A girl Jack knew from

last semester claimed his attention and kept him from following. By the
time he left the classroom with that girl and another friend, she was
gone. "What was all that about?" the friend wondered, and Jack said he
didn't know, he guessed the professor had just gone off because of some
professor thing. "Who's that girl anyway?" he asked, but his friend
didn't know. No one remembered seeing her before.

Ms. Chase was not in class the next time it met, nor the time after
that, nor any other time, and the workshop closed seamlessly around
her absence. The professor returned to his usual merry self. Jack looked
her up in the student directory. She was Chloe Chase. C.C. There was
a campus address and a phone number and the information that she
was a graduate student. That seemed to explain something; only a graduate student would pick such a dauntingly wordy fight with a professor.
He dialed her phone number twice and hung up before anyone answered. She seemed entirely beyond his reach. He told himself to just
forget it.

Then a couple of months later he went to a party at somebody's
apartment, somebody he didn't know. You didn't need an invitation for
such parties, you only had to know where they were. There was blast-
ing music, and people jamming the balcony in spite of the cold. By the
time Jack and his friends arrived, most people were drunk and getting
drunker. It was the kind of party where the next day the hosts were
obliged to go through the rooms to make sure that strangers weren't
still passed out on the furniture.

The keg was in the kitchen. Jack rinsed out a plastic cup and filled it,
then stood around wondering if there was something wrong with him
for not having a good time at parties anymore. He said hello to a few
people he knew, but it was too loud for much talking. The idea was to
drink a lot and stumble around in an alcohol-induced blur and hope
you came across a willing girl or some other adventure. He had just
broken up with a girl he'd met at another such party. They'd had a
spotty few months together before deciding that the convenience of
sleeping with each other wasn't worth the mutual boredom and irritation. Now it seemed to Jack in his gloomy state that his only options
were to call his old girlfriend, who would probably let him come over

in spite of everything they'd said about being through with each other, or to go home to his own solitary and miserable bed.

People were dancing in the living room. Jack stood in the doorway, a nondancer trying to strike a pose of being too serious and preoccupied for noticing anyone hopping around to amplified music. Which would have served him well, if Chloe Chase hadn't been one of the dancers.

He didn't know how he'd missed seeing her before. She was dancing with a guy Jack couldn't take seriously, a skinny kid with buzzed hair and a white shirt and narrow black tie, like a parody of a Mormon missionary. Chloe Chase was dancing up a storm. She rocked and sweated. She was an entirely different being from the postmodern princess of the classroom. Her black hair was loose and it whipped across her shoulders. A strand of it caught in her open mouth and she teased it back and forth with her lips. The sight of this caused Jack actual physical pain.

If only, if only this were a '30s movie and he was Fred Astaire but better looking, and she was Ginger Rogers in one of those filmy movie star dresses, and he could cut in on her partner because everyone in the audience knew they were supposed to end up together. Since it wasn't a movie, he had to stand there for another fifteen minutes watching her and the missionary carrying on. Jack didn't think he was her date, just one of those weird-looking guys that beautiful girls palled around with sometimes.

Finally they stopped and Chloe leaned into the missionary and said something in his ear and turned toward the kitchen. Jack followed her. She was taller than he remembered. The black fishnet stockings were not in evidence, but she was wearing a pair of high-cut leather boots that led the eye upward to the crotch of her jeans, well, his eyes would have ended up there in any case. In the kitchen she opened the refrigerator, pondered, and retrieved a bottle of water, which she drank greedily.

Now or never. Jack stepped in front of her. She regarded him over the upended bottle. "Hi, I don't know if you remember me—"

"Oh God, you're from that awful class."

She didn't say it in any making-a-joke way. He guessed the good news was that she remembered him. He said, "Yeah, sorry about that, things got a little—"

The music took another jump in volume and she shook her head, meaning she couldn't hear him. Jack bent closer, realized he'd run out of things to say. She was staring up at him as if looking for another reason to dislike him. He said, "Your eyes are blue."

"What?"

"I thought they were but I wasn't sure."

She said something he couldn't catch, pointed to her ear. He positioned his mouth over it. "I said, I quit writing poems and I'm changing my major to landscape architecture."

She didn't want to smile at that but she did. Jack asked God for just another couple of sentences, enough to let him continue impersonating somebody clever and winning. She spoke next. "Who are you anyway?"

"I'm Jack."

"Chloe." She didn't offer her hand. "I mean, who are you, one of those guys who works on the literary magazine and wishes *On the Road* didn't exist so you could write it yourself?"

Jack fell backward, clutching his heart in mock dismay in order to hide his actual dismay. He did, in fact, envy *On the Road*. "That's me," he said. "Callow to the core."

"I'm sorry, that was rude of me. It's just, the writers I've met here can be so predictable. The same books, the same tired old poses. Always responding to past forms instead of creating new ones. Art has to be a revolutionary process, it can't be content with stasis. That's what I was trying to say in class when that asshole mugged me."

Jack noted that she must not have drunk much, to be able to jump right into an argument this way. He could have volunteered his own thought, that new forms were always a response to past forms, but that really wasn't the direction in which he wanted to steer things. "I felt bad about that. He shouldn't have lit into you. It was pretty hostile."

"I thought about staying in the class, just to force him to confront his totally regressive thinking, but I decided it wasn't worth it. He's obviously happy there in the poetry museum."

"Actually, it's a pretty good class. But it would have been even better if you'd stayed."

It was the first mildly flirtatious thing he'd said to her, or at least the first one she'd heard. She didn't answer, just flattened her lips in a perfunctory smile. Jack reminded himself that she was a girl who heard her share of come-ons and cheesy lines. He felt he'd lost ground and didn't know how to regain it. The party still surged around them with its noise and commotion. He was trying to think of a way to ask her if she wanted to go somewhere quiet and talk, without actually using those words.

The Mormon missionary guy came bounding up then. "God, it's getting ugly here. There's a girl in the bathroom trying to scrub off a tattoo with Comet."

"What did the tattoo look like?" asked Jack, but the missionary had decided to ignore him.

"So if you've had enough fun for one night—"

"It could also be kind of important just where the tattoo is. Because there's some body parts you really don't want to treat with Comet."

Chloe said, "Dex, this is Jack. Jack, Dex."

"How ya doin," said Dex, indifferently.

"*Mucho gusto.*"

"I'll get the coats, meet you at the front door."

"It was a genuine pleasure," Jack called to his retreating back, then, turning to Chloe, "Who's he?"

"A friend."

"Uh-huh." Dead end. Jack watched her getting ready to take her leave, and just as she said "Well . . . ," he said, "how about I give you a ride?"

"To where?"

"Wherever you're going. Dex too. I wouldn't want him to feel left out or anything."

He waited while she made up her mind. He tried to see himself in her eyes. This tall boy with the hopeful, foolish smile, willing himself to be brave. Yes, brave, he'd forced himself to be so, as if this was his true self at last and she had called it forth. She could just as easily dismiss him and send that self back to where it came from but she didn't, she said, "Sure, thanks, we could use a ride."

Forty minutes later Jack was sitting at a table in between Chloe and Dex in a Chicago bar of the fancy sort that his old self would not have had the nerve to enter. He ordered a beer and didn't get carded. Sooner or later he was going to have to cop to being barely twenty years old but not, thank God, tonight. Tonight he was on a roll. He felt like a spy who'd bluffed his way into the palace. He studied Chloe's hands on the blond wood of the table. They were restless hands, shredding a paper napkin, tapping, tracing those invisible spirals. Her nails were blunt and the skin was stretched tight over the small bones and knuckles. Warm hands or cold? He decided it was even a good thing Dex was there; it took the pressure off. And he was able to listen to the two of them talking in a way that she would not have talked to Jack alone. Dex asked Chloe how the new life plan was going and she said not bad, not bad. By this time next year, everything was going to be back on track.

Jack nursed his beer and pretended he was a turnip, deaf and dumb and incurious. Dex said, "Good for you, honey. You deserve a lot better." Jack wondered if Dex was gay. He didn't know any straight men who called people "honey."

Chloe said, "He's wondering what we're talking about but he's too polite to ask."

"Who, me? No, actually I'm kind of slow-witted. People are always saying things I don't understand."

She laughed at that. Jack smiled and hoped he could keep his streak going. So far, attractive silence broken by witticisms was serving him well. Chloe said, "We were talking about this guy I used to be engaged to. I call him El Beefhead. Enough said."

"And the new life plan?" Jack ventured, all spy casual.

"Oh, I left the Ph.D. program in English and started over in business school." She seemed a little embarrassed. "I've taken a vow of pragmatism."

"Nothing wrong with that."

"No, there's not. It's just different. Grad school that actually trains you to earn a living."

"That can be important."

She leveled her eyes at him. They were as blue as the impossible skies in a child's storybook. "Yeah. Especially if you don't want to depend on some total prick to support you."

Dex said, "You gotta lay off the rich boys, Cece. There's always hidden costs involved."

"So this guy," said Jack, not wanting to dwell on the topic of rich boys, "is he in school here too, do you have to trip over him all the time?"

"He's not in school," said Chloe, in a way that was meant to close off discussion, but here was that damned Dex winking at him, either because there was a good story that wasn't getting told, or— He didn't want to think for what other reason.

"So the poetry class," he said. He knew he was asking too many questions, like an interview. "How did that fit into business school?"

"Oh, that was just like a last fling. My little humanities fix. And you know how well that turned out. Okay. Why did you say what you did that day, were you trying to shut me up?"

"I was trying to shut both of you up."

"Ooh," said Dex, appreciatively.

"Seriously. You were both getting your feelings hurt. I didn't want that to keep happening."

"*His* feelings," Chloe snorted.

"Sure. You were telling him he was irrelevant and fusty and out of it."

"Oh, let's get off it. Let's put it behind us." She looked at her empty glass and Dex rose obediently to go to the bar. When he was gone, Chloe said, "So you think I was mean to him. I'm a mean person."

"No. You had an opinion and you were very articulate in expressing it."

"You think I'm opinionated."

"I didn't say that either. What do you care what I think, anyway?"

"It's not really about you. El Beefhead used to tell me I was a smartass. That I was too competitive."

"You mean, you were smarter than he was."

"Yeah, I guess."

"Why do you care what he thinks either? He's not worth it," said Jack. He thought this would be easy enough. A few cheap shots at the old boyfriend. Girls liked that kind of thing.

Chloe gave Jack another of her appraising looks. He was more used to it this time, but it was also from closer range, and it made all his ignorant gallantry cleave to the roof of his mouth. She said, "It's just a confused time for me right now. I probably shouldn't even be allowed out in public."

"Sure." Jack nodded, as if he knew what she was talking about. She was drinking faster than he was and he wondered if she was a little drunk now. He was trying to take it easy himself, which was a change from the way he and his friends usually operated, getting drunk enough to abdicate responsibility for anything they did. He wanted to keep a semblance of a clear head in her presence.

"So you're some kind of undergrad."

"That's right."

"Jack."

"Right again."

"Well, let's just have a good time tonight. Let's forget there's any such thing as intelligent conversation."

"Sounds fine to me." As long as she let him stay, he'd agree to anything. Dex returned with her drink and she downed a good portion of it in short order. It had never occurred to Jack before that beautiful girls had the capacity to be unhappy.

They stayed at the bar until nearly closing. Jack remained on the edges of their talk, which was mostly about people he didn't know, history he had not been a part of, the inbred feuds common to graduate students. He kept his mouth shut, kept listening. He was beginning to form a new, or more shaded, impression of her. The part that was sharp edged, that was glib and argumentative, was also brittle, like a crust, something of a deliberate effort. In much the same way, she laughed and carried on with Dex and from time to time her gaze lifted to survey the room, as if inviting people to observe just how bright and carefree she was being.

Every so often Chloe or Dex asked him a question or lobbed some joke in Jack's direction and he smiled and said something in return. He was trying to imagine how the night might end, just what configuration it might take, everything he was capable of imagining. He guessed they wouldn't stay in the bar much longer. Dex was showing signs of wear. He laughed with a kind of whinny, and he kept rubbing his eyes. Chloe was increasingly silent. Cunning Jack kept smiling and doing his turnip routine. "Okay, I've had it," Dex announced. "Shit faced."

"Shit Faced 'R' Us," agreed Chloe.

They straggled outside. It was always disorienting to find yourself on the sidewalk in the darkness, with the city coming at you from all different directions, and even Jack, who had been cautious about his drinking, took a moment to get his bearings. Chloe and Dex were giggling and holding hands as he led them to the car. There were some real advantages to being gay, he decided.

"Where to?" Jack asked, once he was behind the wheel. As if he didn't know exactly where Chloe lived. They gave him directions back to Evanston. Chloe was in the front seat but she kept turning around to talk to Dex. She both was and was not sitting next to him. If only Dex boy would get himself dropped off first.

Praise the Lord. Dex said, "Take a left here and go down to the end of the block. See that light? That's it. My man Jack. Chloe darlin'." He made a couple of passes at opening the car door but couldn't figure out how the handle worked.

"Are you gonna be all right?" Chloe asked, concerned.

"Tip-top."

"Because I could come in if you need me to."

Jack gritted his teeth and prayed a small, ugly prayer. Dex gave the door handle another whack and it popped open. "Le voilà."

"Good night, then." Jack waited until Dex got himself out on the sidewalk, gave him the big wave, and sped off. "Why does he dress like that?" he ventured.

"He thinks it's funny."

"I guess it's a grad student thing."

"I guess."

Without a third person in the car, she seemed to be receding from him. "Where am I going?" Jack asked after a space of silence.

"Oh, sorry. Go down to Ridge, turn right, then straight for a while."

For all Jack knew, she'd already planned her exit strategy, had it all timed down to the second how she was going to escape him. He wasn't going to push anything, he decided. Wasn't even going to ask for her phone number. He knew the damned number, he was just going to wait a couple of days, then call. He was already practicing his own good-night speech, how he was glad to see her again, maybe something else about the class, or even about poetry, nah, deadly. He pulled up in front of her apartment building, on one of those tidy, tree-lined streets that were thought to be beyond the reach of students. "Come on in for a little if you want," Chloe said, and let herself out of the car without waiting for his answer.

"Can I park here?" he managed, and she said over her shoulder that he could. She was up her front steps and had her keys out while Jack was still trying to get one stumbling foot in front of the other.

The door was standing open when he approached it across the wooden porch. It was one of those old frame houses that had been divided into apartments. He registered antique details like carved fret-work and white wood trellises supporting the remnants of last sum-mer's vines. "Hey, Chloe?"

A narrow entry hall, and a room beyond it, both empty. He heard a toilet flushing, stopped where he was.

She came out still tugging at her clothes; Jack looked away. "Come on in. You want a beer? Oh never mind, I don't have any."

"That's okay. Really."

She sat down on the couch and after a moment of stupid hesitation, Jack closed the front door and sat down next to her. It was a small room and there wasn't anywhere else to sit or anything else to do with him-self. Everything was middle-of-the-night quiet, except for an occa-sional car passing outside. The couch was low and soft and just sitting on it made them sink toward each other. Jack tried to lift himself up, discreetly put some space between their hips. He was afraid she was going to come to herself, realize she didn't know him, start screaming and slapping him away.

But she only said, "You don't talk a lot, do you."

"Oh, once you get to know me, I'm a babbling brook."

She looked up at him, a touch of a frown between her eyes. He had the disconcerting impression that from moment to moment, she actually did forget who he was. If he leaned back slightly, he could see down her shirt. He was attempting to disassociate from his body, will it into dullness. Should he start talking, was that what she wanted? "So where are you from?" he began.

"You know that guy I was talking about, my ex?"

She waited until he said yes, he did, and still she looked at him suspiciously, as if he'd said something wrong.

"I wasn't going to marry him because he was rich. That was totally, totally not important."

"Of course not."

Again, that look of heavy disbelief. She was on the edge of a quarrelsome drunkenness and anything he'd say would be a mistake and he was something other than sober himself. He shut his fool mouth.

"It started off perfect. It was perfect for the longest time. Is that supposed to be bad? Is it some kind of tip-off? Hey, I didn't know that, I just thought it was all perfect. Sex too. You mind if I say that? Or I guess I already did."

She was arching her back, trying to get herself turned around to face him, and here was one leg in its black leather boot wriggling open so he could see without effort up the length of her blue-jeaned thigh. "It's okay."

"Then all of a sudden, or no, not sudden, more like a faucet that starts to drip. There's all these things wrong with me. I laugh too much and it gets on his nerves. I was taking these elitist classes. I spent too much time with my friends and they were elitists too, and what did I do to my hair, it looked like crap, and I better let him drive because I was such a lousy driver. Get the picture? When I'd ask him what was going on, what was the matter, he'd say, Nothing. I was just overly sensitive."

"Well good riddance. He sounds like a tear-down artist. Somebody who was just so insecure and threatened—"

"Yeah, I know how it works."

"Sure. I'm sure you—"

"Everybody thinks if you talk about something enough you can make it go away. Therapy is such a total, total . . . Oh, goddamn him. Know what I'm gonna do. I'm gonna write a poem about him that'll clean his clock. A hate poem instead of a love poem. Can you do that?"

"I'm pretty sure you can."

"Forget it. A poem. He'd laugh his ass off. Steal his money. That's what gets to guys like him."

"We can do that," said Jack loyally. Robbery didn't seem like an unreasonable thing to consider.

"Great. Steal it all."

"Or you could just write him off. Move on. You know, living well is the best revenge. Have a little fun. If there's things you like to do for fun. So are there?"

Silence. Her eyes had closed, she had fallen off the edge of drunkenness and into sleep. As quietly as he could, he eased himself off the couch and made his way to the bathroom. The combination of desire and having to piss made him hobble.

She was still asleep, passed out, maybe, when he returned. Jack looked around him, tried to fathom something from her books and pictures, but he felt as circumspect as if he was in a doctor's waiting room. He supposed he should leave, get himself home, call her later and hope she remembered him in some vaguely positive way. He knelt down in front of her. "Chloe?"

She didn't stir. Her lips were parted and a tiny whistle of breath drew in and out. Her forehead was damp and her hair clung to it. Jack reached out and with the tip of one finger touched a strand of it.

Her eyes opened. Blue floodlights. The lids drooped but she focused in on him and said, "What?"

He drew his hand back. "You okay?"

"Sick."

Her skin was pale and sweated and Jack thought she might throw up. That didn't seem disgusting to him, rather, almost a kind of intimacy. "Can I get you anything?"

"Water."

"Hold on." He went into the kitchen and ran water into a glass, found two frozen-solid ice-cube trays in the freezer, forget it, hustled back to her. It amazed him that he was here at all, much less that she might turn to him for any sort of help, that there was anything in him she might find of use or value. "Here you go," he said, offering the glass.

She spilled a little but got it down. "God, I'm a mess." She sounded both more sober and more distressed.

"Nah. You're just kind of drunk and on the way down."

"I've been whining all night. Sorry."

"A shoulder to puke on. Everybody needs one."

"Please don't say puke."

They laughed at that. It was a relief to laugh in this weary, comradely fashion. Jack was thinking it was turning out all right. They would be buddies, or at least start off that way. In his mind he was already working it out, how they would get to know each other, the way that might progress. He was still leaning over her when she reached up with both arms and although he had not planned or foreseen it, they were kissing.

They staggered, trying to find a balance. Then Chloe pulled him down on top of her. He landed with his knees on either side of her, still in danger of falling over completely while she was rising up to meet him. He put one arm around her shoulders, which were thin and tense, tasted the inside of her mouth, still cool even through the alcohol bitterness, and then it no longer mattered what he had or hadn't planned, he wanted her.

They kissed for a time, until that began to seem unsatisfactory. Jack tried to work her shirt loose. She allowed this, and allowed his hand to burrow beneath the fabric to reach her breast in a way he hoped did not seem entirely desperate and adolescent. Everything was happening in a blurred, hasty fashion, with too much clothing and furniture in the way. Their weight sank into the couch even as he got her shirt open and groped around at her waistband. She allowed this also, she seemed cooperative, if not enthusiastic, in a way he didn't want to admit was faintly disappointing. It was difficult to get her jeans slid over her hips, he didn't want to think about those damn boots, but he finally managed it all, pulled her panties down too and cupped his hand over her pubic hair, his fingers exploring and prodding. She put her hand on top of his and bore down hard.

It was what he'd been waiting for. He wanted to be inside her that instant. They were going to have to get up and find the bedroom, or at least stand to get rid of the last of their clothes, or maybe he could manage to get himself out and open her legs enough to enter her. That was what he was attempting to do when she said in an unnatural, high-pitched voice, "Wait a minute, wait a minute," and pushed him away.

He stared at her, confounded. She shrank back and tried to cover herself. "I'm sorry, I can't do this. I'm really really sorry."

Jack had stopped himself, in some conscious sense, but his penis hadn't gotten the message and was still straining to get at her, dragging the rest of his body along with it. She rolled away from him; one of her boot heels caught him in the ribs. "I *mean* it."

"Jesus Christ." He managed to get himself untangled from her, sat down on one end of the couch. "What the hell's the matter?"

"I know this is crummy, I'm sorry."

"Yeah, you said that." He could hardly believe what was happening, that it wasn't a bad joke, or a notion he could talk her out of. "Wasn't this all your idea, did I miss something?"

"I know, I thought I could, I wanted to, but I can't."

"'Can't,' what's that supposed to mean?"

Her head drooped. "Can't." Very quiet.

She sniffled, but Jack wasn't buying it, wasn't in the mood to feel sorry for her. He sat glumly. She said, "It doesn't have anything to do with you—"

"Gee, thanks."

"I mean I'm a horrible messed-up person. I'm completely toxic to be around."

"Well you could have told me that up front. That you were a total flake." He was angry and humiliated, he didn't care what he said.

"I'm just not . . . really in my body right now."

She sounded wistful, even a little puzzled. Jack dismissed it as more theatrics. "Sure, I get it. Nobody's home."

"I don't blame you for being mad. I absolutely understand that."

He didn't want to be understood, at least not by her at this moment. "I have to go." He got to his feet. She had pulled her pants back up; her shirt was still open and her bra straps were down around her elbows. Although she was sitting up primly, one small breast stared back at him, its nipple a blind eye.

"Please don't feel like this is anybody's fault but mine. I mean you seem like a really nice person," she offered.

"Yeah, you did too." He picked up his coat without putting it on, got himself outside, and made that car go. He drove and drove, sped down the empty streets, jammed his brakes, daring the cops or anybody else to get in his way so that he could wind up in some genuine trouble, but that seemed as stupid and sad as everything else that had happened, and finally, after a trip to the lakeshore, where there was nothing to do with the thick gray cold water except throw yourself in, or decide not to, he simply went home.

He woke the next morning feeling a complicated shame, both for himself and for her. When he was able to think more coolly, he computed the amount of alcohol involved and soberly—that was the word—was almost grateful nothing more had happened. She had been drunk, and although he knew that girls sometimes got drunk so that they could permit themselves to have sex, he didn't want to imagine how things might have gone if she'd had her second thoughts a few minutes later. She might even have called the police, had him arrested for rape, and he would have had a hard time trying to get anyone to believe otherwise. Things like that happened, you heard about them. He told himself he'd been lucky, but he didn't believe it, and in spite of the deep wound to his pride he was sick with wanting her.

What, if anything, should he do now? He could call her or write a letter, demand an explanation or pretend that he understood. Or stay the hell away, give up on her this second time. He had been badly treated. Maybe she hadn't intended to goad and frustrate him, but in the end she had not been afraid to do so. Maybe she'd only brought him along for the evening, brought him home, because he was someone she judged she could get the best of, dismiss easily. He didn't really believe that of her, although thinking that way satisfied his darkest moods. She had only been unhappy. Unhappiness made people heedless of anything or anyone else, made them cruel.

Since there was nothing else he could do, he wrote a lot of poetry. In one sense this made him feel better, but it also rendered Chloe and everything that had happened between them more distant and fevered, and less real.

A couple of weeks passed. Jack couldn't have been said to be avoiding her, since he didn't know where she spent her time, but at least he'd kept himself from calling or showing up at her door. He was standing in line at a coffeehouse when Dex came up behind him, scanning the menu.

Jack nodded to him. He didn't know if Dex remembered him. He had an equal, if contradictory, fear that Dex knew everything that had happened that night. "Oh, hey." Dex said. "You're the guy from the party."

"The limo driver."

"Yeah, how you doing?" Dex wore a red plaid cowboy shirt with shoulder seams shaped like arrows. He was so skinny, he looked like a little boy dressed by a mother with a bad sense of humor. Jack had to wonder about the rest of his closet. He paid for his coffee and moved away. But he wasn't fast enough about adding cream, which was where Dex caught up with him. "Say, you talk to Chloe lately?"

Jack said that he had not. Dex opened three sugar packets, spiked his coffee with cinnamon, dumped in enough 2 percent milk to turn the whole mess gray. "She had to drop out of school, she had herself a little bit of a breakdown."

"A what?"

"Nothing meds won't cure. Poor girlie. Always tries so hard. She's one of those people who thinks if you just make a plan and stick with it, if you're very *intelligent* about it all, you get what you want."

"Breakdown, what, she's in the hospital?"

"Oh no, Mister Party Man, excuse me I forget your name. She went back to her folks in St. Louis."

"But she's all right?"

"Well sure. It was just a little episode. I honestly don't know if she'd like me talking about it. It was sort of messy. She's fine now. Good as new. Or will be."

Jack was having trouble separating Dex's prattle from what the words really meant. "What's she doing there, St. Louis, she's going to stay there?"

"For a while, I guess. Do Mom and Dad things. Take a little mental health break. Get away from El Beefhead."

"The boyfriend . . ."

"That big sack of poop. He is so not helpful. I called him, I left messages. Nothing. What does it take to get some people's attention? Girl takes a stomachful of pills and aspirates her own vomit and all that other good ER stuff. Oh shit. You did not hear me say that."

If they'd been somewhere more private, Jack could have strangled Dex to get the real story from him, or maybe punched him out just on general principles. The worst he could do here would be to spill Dex's coffee. "She tried to kill herself with pills?"

"Kill, I don't know what she was trying to do. It could have been one of those cry for help things. I had, honestly, no idea. I mean sure, she was sad and all that, but I wasn't thinking *fragile*."

The person he really wanted to hit, Jack realized, was himself. "So the beef guy . . . ," he began, hoping he was someone everything could be blamed on.

"Don't get me started. Definitely not worth killing yourself over. Bout of hives, maybe. He owns that bar we went into the other night, or part of it. Wheeler-dealer. He owns a lot of stuff. I don't know why she kept going back there. Scene of the crime."

"Was he there that night? At the bar?"

"Na. Probably out with some new lucky girl. It must be hard for somebody like Chloe, you know, Miss America, when things don't work out. She's not used to it. I mean if you're beautiful and smart and you always brush your teeth and do your homework, why shouldn't you live happily ever after?"

Jack asked if Dex was likely to see or speak to Chloe and Dex said he guessed so. Would Dex tell her that her friend from the poetry class was sorry to hear she was having troubles? He made Dex repeat it. He didn't feel any confidence that Chloe would remember his name, just as Dex had not, or even if she'd known it to begin with. One more reason having sex that night wouldn't have been up at the top of the good ideas list. He walked away in a fog of dread and guilt and sweat. Even though what had happened to Chloe had not actually been his fault, he felt at least complicit as a witness. There was nothing he could do for her now, besides hoping she had friends other than Dex.

That was all Jack heard of her for some time. She did not reappear on campus, or at least he didn't see her, nor Dex. The semester ground to a halt in May and he went back to California for the summer. He got a job umpiring kids' park-district softball, just to get out of the house and away from his parents' increasing fretfulness about his future. Four years of tuition at Northwestern was a lot of money, even for the doctor. Jack was going to be a bum. He could have stayed home and been a bum, it would have been a lot cheaper. Jack said he'd pay back the money, if it was so damned important. (Ha, his father remarked.) Jack said he didn't care about money, he just wanted to do what made him happy. Well Christ, his father said, terrific, son, but you don't really seem happy, and Jack had no answer to this.

It was a relief to go to work and arbitrate disputes among eight-year-olds. (The adults involved were another story.) He was soothed by the green and manicured playing fields, and the moment when the sunset crossed over to twilight and the lights came on, and the simplicity of the game itself. He liked the kids and their kid-sized sorrows and problems, which, now that he was older, seemed easily solvable. He wished he was a kid again just so he could go back and do it right. In the same way, softball, which he'd been largely indifferent to as a child, now appealed to him as a great way to avoid anything more complicated. His life seemed to be taking place in slow motion, like the arc of a ball thrown high for an easy catch.

He drove home from the games with the radio turned up loud. Sometimes he stopped at a friend's house and watched movies, or they might head down to Santa Monica or Venice and hang out on the beach. They met girls there and on occasion the girls knew about parties or somewhere else to go, and they'd spend the night together. But even this felt like killing time. He didn't tell anyone about Chloe, though he and his friends traded war stories about sex. There was no way he could turn her into a joke or something to brag about or even an episode with a definite conclusion. California, his life there now and in the past, seemed much the same way, something left hanging, a ball that never landed, a place where there were no real events, only beautiful surfaces refracted through the glass of car windows. Whatever else happened, he decided, he wouldn't be coming back here.

In August he returned to school. Although it was a relief to be in Chicago again, he had no enthusiasm for classes. He was only practicing things he already knew, papers and tests and sitting in chairs. He was simply waiting until he got his degree and would be expected to enter what was archly called the real world. He had used up all the available poetry classes and started in on writing fiction. It was the only part of school he enjoyed. And you could at least pretend fiction would make you money someday, although he didn't announce it to his father as a career move.

He might never have seen Chloe Chase again, he wasn't one to believe in fate or destiny or anything more grandiose than good or bad timing, if he hadn't agreed to go to a campus lecture with a friend. It was a women's studies lecture, not the kind of thing he usually went in for, but the girl who wanted him to go—the *woman*, come on, Jack—told him not to be a total pig, it wouldn't kill him, he might even learn something. Besides, he never went anywhere anymore, just stayed home wearing a hole in the couch, which Jack had to admit was true. But, he argued, he'd probably be the only male there, he'd feel stupid. "Jack, it's not lingerie shopping," his friend said, and he gave in.

In fact there were a number of men there, looking not at all uncomfortable, but earnest and engaged, like the devout at church. Jack gave up being apprehensive and settled in to be bored. The speaker had a lot of severe things to say about gender roles and acculturization. Her tone was not accusatory, but still Jack felt accused. He listened glumly. There were words like modality and praxis and polysemous, as if to pile enough weight on the subject of sex to immobilize it. Maybe things were better back in the good old pig days, when the war between men and women must have been jollier, or maybe he only felt that way because men got away with more then. The speaker reminded the audience that male dominance was an insidious and pervasive thing, established and protected by powerful economic and social forces. Jack couldn't decide if he preferred being a mindless pawn or an insensitive boor. It was a relief when the speaker switched to talking about the plight of women in India, in Africa, in Guatemala, places he could hardly be held responsible for.

After the lecture there was a question and answer session. Jack was amused to note that two of the questions came from men, who were either anxious to demonstrate how enlightened they were, or because, being men, they couldn't keep themselves from trying to run things. One of them asked if conventional linguistic systems privileged the penis. "Can we go now?" Jack groaned.

The speaker took a question from the back of the room. The question was scholarly, involved, hedged, and buttressed with serious terms. The voice was Chloe Chase's.

Jack edged around in his seat to make sure. The room was an auditorium with seats that rose toward the back so that he was able to see her face in profile, like a cameo. It was her, although she was too far away for him to tell much else about her. His face felt muddy, stiff, as if the blood had congealed in it. His heart flopped around in his chest.

There was another question, and then a sense of stirring from the audience that marked the end of things. "I have to go talk to somebody," Jack told his friend, who said, Please don't tell me you came along just to pick up chicks.

He was worried that Chloe would get out the door before he could reach her, but she had hung back to talk to a group of people. Jack waited at the entrance and when she finally turned his way and saw him her face was, he imagined, the mirror of his own: blank, frozen, braced as if to absorb a blow.

She had to pass by him. Her mouth tightened and her eyes skittered away. Jack opened the door for her and bent down so that his voice wouldn't carry. "Look, I know I'm probably the last person in the world you want to see—"

She tried to brush past him. "Please," she said. "Just pretend you don't know me."

"I want to make sure you're all right."

"If I say yes, will you leave me alone?"

"Yes. No, not unless I believe you."

The crowd behind them was pushing them both out into the hall. Chloe walked ahead but allowed him to catch up. Her voice was low as well. "Why do you care how I am?"

"Come on."

"I was horrible to you."

"You were having a tough time."

"I was a lunatic. I try not to think about it."

"You don't think I feel bad too? Hey, you want to go back inside and get a discussion group going? 'When gender games go wrong.'"

She bent her head to root around in her purse, as if there was something in there that could render her invisible. Her hair was pulled tightly back from her face with a clip. She wore a long black sweater, big and shapeless, the cuffs unraveling. She gave the impression of trying to hide inside it. She was still beautiful, she would never be anything else, but her new, subdued aspect hung over her like a veil. He hated that she had been unhappy, hated that he'd had any part in it. She murmured, "I'm sorry about what happened. I said it then, I'll say it now."

"I'd like to get beyond sorry. There's gotta be a way."

One of Chloe's friends approached, then veered away, sensing trouble. She was on the verge of flight, he knew he had only one chance to find the right thing to say. "I know you're sorry, let's, you know, stipulate that. I'm sorry I didn't behave better myself. But you know what,

ever since, it's like my whole damned life's been in suspended animation. I can't even say what's supposed to happen next with you and
me. But if I'd never seen you again, I'd spend the rest of my life wanting to. So kick me in the head or whatever you need to do so I can just
get over it."

He waited, as he had once before, for her to make up her mind. What
he'd said was true, although he hadn't known it until he'd heard himself speak. His life had stopped, she'd stopped it, he was waiting to see
if she would start it up again, give it back to him. He felt almost serene,
balanced there between one possibility and the other. My heart was in
my mouth, people said, but his heart had come out of his mouth and
floated free.

Chloe said, "You don't even know me. You don't know me at all."

"Not a problem."

"If I started acting like a normal human being, you probably
wouldn't recognize me."

Jack smiled and shook his head. She sighed. "All right, so what do
you want to do? Is there some kind of plan?"

"I hadn't thought that far ahead," Jack admitted.

"Well . . ."

"We could have ground rules," he suggested, and when she looked
alarmed, he added, "No poetry."

"Good thinking."

"I don't write like a theorist. You'd have to accept that."

"I'm not really attached to that stuff anyway," she admitted.

"All disputes to be arbitrated by a panel of prominent feminist
scholars."

She giggled. Oh lovely sound. "Coffee," he suggested.

"It would have to be some other time. I really have to get home."

This was slightly disappointing, but Jack told himself it was a part of
normal courtship. Normal, that was the ticket. He wasn't even going to
hold her hand without informed consent. "Uh, phone number?"

"Hold on a minute." Again she dove into her purse, came up with a
pen and a scrap of paper. "Here. Let your fingers do the walking."

They both looked away, perhaps remembering where his fingers had been walking the last time they met. Then they laughed, covering it up. "All right then," Jack said briskly. "I'm gonna go for the clean exit here. Good night, nice to see you again."

Chloe said good night also. She seemed relieved. He was too, he had to admit, he didn't think he could have talked another thirty seconds without catastrophe. He was already walking away when he stopped and turned around. A milling crowd of women took up the space between them, and he had to shout. "Chloe? Do you remember my name?"

"Why, did you forget it?"

The crowd goggled at him. He saluted Chloe. Good one. "You're Jack," she said. Smiled sideways and waved good-bye.

Jack's friend had been watching from a distance. "All right, who is she?" she asked, once they were outside.

He told her everything. From shame or discretion or both, he hadn't told anyone before, but now he felt as if a curse had been lifted, as if he'd grabbed hold of the world and beat it in a fair fight. "Go ahead, tell me I'm nuts," he concluded.

"You're nuts. She sounds like a real piece of work."

He was annoyed, he hadn't really meant her to agree with him. "Hey, she was in crisis."

"You are already so whipped."

"Give me a break."

"You know one reason I wish I was really really good looking? People are so much more willing to make excuses for you."

"And to you I say, phooey." He felt dangerously happy. He wanted to drive a car too fast or swim for miles in a cold ocean or at the very least stay up all night thinking about her, which was the only real available option. Nothing had happened between them yet and nothing might, he knew that. It was almost beside the point. He was in that exalted, engulfing phase of love and possibility, where hope was just as good as actuality.

Jack called her the next day. The hell with playing it cool. Her voice on the phone was cautious and a little amused. "So you're not going away until I go out with you?"

"Stalker, that's me."

They agreed that they should do something low-key and nonalco-holic. They met at Lake Front Park and walked among the joggers and promenading golden retrievers and Taiwanese soccer players and any-one else lucky enough to have free time on this blazing-warm October day. The air was hazy and the high-rises that lined the shoreline to the south receded into the shimmering distance, resembling some science fiction cityscape on another, less complicated planet. The lake was flat and calm and as they walked they occupied themselves with gazing at it, relieved to have something to look at besides each other. But perhaps because of their history so far, they soon began talking in a way that was nearly intimate.

Chloe said, "You should have just gone ahead and done it to me. What a miserable girly trick."

"'Done it to you,' what kind of talk is that? Not to mention all the ef-fort of having to make bail."

"I wouldn't have told anyone. I would have felt too stupid."

Jack squawked out a laugh, too surprised to be hurt, but she said quickly, "No, God, I didn't mean you were somebody . . . I meant I was the idiot."

"Thanks, I guess."

"Of course I liked you, or I wouldn't have . . . Look, I wouldn't be here now."

They both sighed, as if they'd gotten past some important point. Jack turned to look at the blurred horizon of the lake. If you squinted at it hard enough, it resolved itself into separate bands of color, shades of gray, azure, steel blue, black. He tried to comprehend the enormity of it, three hundred miles of water that led you into still other waters. He said, "This is the first time I've known I was going to see you. Every other time was a surprise."

"Maybe you'd like it better that way. I could just sort of materialize, pitch a fit, then disappear."

"No," said Jack. "I like it like this. Knowing just how long I'll have to wait."

She gave him a blue and startled glance. For a moment he thought he'd gone too far. Then she tilted her head, as if he might make more sense viewed sideways. "Just who are you really, Mister Stranger?"

He began to tell her. Some of it he'd just figured out himself. He was a man willing to dive in over his head. It didn't matter where the current led him. And perhaps this was what Chloe sensed about him, that willingness. He talked, she talked. They tested the waters. In the days and weeks and months to come, they could be forgiven for believing the hardest part was behind them.

Three

Mrs. Lacagnina had a married daughter who lived in Berwyn. Every Sunday she arrived to take her mother to church and then out to dinner at a cafeteria. The daughter was stout and fiftyish, with black hair polished to a hard shine, and a wardrobe of pastel trouser suits. Jack had seen the two of them negotiating the stairs, the daughter coaxing, overhelpful, Mrs. Lacagnina still bundled in her rug of a coat and head scarf, still wary and silently mumbling. They seemed a perfect representation of the Old World and the New, or how within one generation the antique and wizened might be transformed, might gain flesh and bloom with color. Jack had said hello to the daughter a couple of times but nothing more, hadn't given her much thought aside from feeling relieved that Mrs. Lacagnina had someone to take care of her, until the daughter arrived at Jack's door to introduce herself.

Jack had been having a difficult day. It was a Friday, and Chloe was at the office, and there was nothing but his own contrary self to blame if he didn't get any writing done. He'd sat down at eight o'clock with his coffee and the newspaper for the half hour he allowed himself. There was still something fresh and promising about the morning before the clock reached nine and sent the whole world to work. After the paper, he indulged in another of the stay-at-home's guilty pleasures, checking CNN for Breaking News. Assured (and faintly disappointed) that there were no hostage situations or terrorist attacks in progress, he looked out the front window. Nothing he saw gave him any excuses to procrastinate. Across the street was an apartment building nearly as old as their own but less well maintained, showing signs of slatternly neglect about the awnings and tuck-pointing. Next to that, a yellow brick four flat with a tiny yard fenced in wrought iron and twin urns of geraniums on each side of the front walk. So it went on down the length of four blocks, modest blight next to modest gentrification, until you reached Clark Street and its commercial traffic. It was June, and Jack guessed it was going to be a fine warm day, although the sky was the familiar Chicago no-color. Particulates. You had to wonder just how much you shoveled into your lungs in an average day.

Finally he picked up his manuscript and began to read. He had thirty pages of a novel, a bare start. The novel was about childhood, childhood being the one stage of life that Jack felt he might have sufficient credentials to write about. Sometimes this seemed like a good idea, other times, like today, it seemed, well, juvenile. Or at least unambitious. He'd heard an artist on a television program say that design was more important than execution. If a bad orchestra played Mozart, it was still Mozart. This was what worried him about his novel, that no matter how he shined up the writing itself, no matter how elegant insightful vivid, etc., it would still be in the service of a mediocre idea.

It was after lunch, he'd written only a few crabbed sentences, he was trying to decide if he should put the work sadly aside for the day or allow himself a tantrum. The problem with computers was that they were too expensive, too much of an investment, to simply pitch them out the window in a fit of pique.

The door buzzer sounded. As badly as the writing was going, Jack was still unhappy at being interrupted. He wanted to sulk in peace. Looking through the peephole, he saw the broad face of Mrs. Lacagnina's daughter, her lips painted apricot to match her blouse. He opened the door, said "Yes?" in a tone of polite exasperation.

"You know who I am, right?"

"You're—"

"Because you shouldn't go opening your door if you don't know people. Toni Palermo. My mom lives upstairs."

Jack spoke his name, asked what he could do for her. "If I could have two minutes of your time," Mrs. Palermo began. Jack surrendered and invited her inside, either from some reflex or good manners or so as to have a better excuse for accomplishing nothing. He couldn't decide

which. Mrs. Palermo stepped across the threshold, took in the apartment at a glance. "Nice," she pronounced. "What's that, is that what
they call a distressed finish? You know how long it'd take me to trip
over some little area rug like that? About two seconds. You're married,
right? Your wife has taste. It's always the woman who makes the house
a home. This is all very classy. Spacious. My mom's place has too much
junk in it, I'm always after her to throw things out. You got an ashtray?"

Jack told her they really didn't care for people smoking in here, and
Mrs. Palermo reluctantly put her cigarettes away. The orange lipstick
had an unnerving fluorescent quality. She sank into the couch. She was
so fleshy, it gave the impression of one piece of furniture sitting on another. "Bad habit, I know. Nerves. I just took my mom to her doctor's
appointment. Everything's out of whack with her. Blood pressure,
heart, arthritis, you name it. And she won't move out of that apartment.
Believe me, I've tried. She could go to the care center that's six blocks
from us and talk to other human beings and have all her meals served
to her, but no. She'd rather sit here by herself and eat soup out of a
can."

Mrs. Palermo seemed as talkative as her mother was silent. Or perhaps this was what Mrs. Lacagnina would sound like if she were audible. Jack said, "You must worry a lot about her."

"I call her twice a day, what else can I do? I have my own house and
family to take care of. My brother lives in Wheaton, do you ever see
him come around? You have kids? When you do, have daughters, not
sons. So anyway. I wanted to ask you a favor, if I give you my phone
number, will you call me if you notice anything going on with her, you
know, a problem."

Jack hesitated, not because he was unwilling to be helpful, but because Mrs. Lacagnina's life on a daily basis seemed problematic. How
could you differentiate a crisis from her usual crazy-lady routine? "You
mean, she falls down the stairs or something?"

"God forbid. Or you don't see her around for a couple days. I mean I
call her, I ask if she's got food in the house, if she's able to get out, but it's
always the same answer, she's fine, leave her be. She's got one of those
special deaf telephones, I still don't know if she can hear me."

Saying yes, Jack realized, would mean taking on a certain responsibility for Mrs. Lacagnina's comings and goings, maybe even pounding on her door and trying to rouse her out of her deafness. But there was no way to refuse and feel good about himself, so he said he'd be happy to keep Mrs. Palermo's number on file.

"Thanks. That's a big relief. I didn't want to ask that old what's-his-name, he's half dead himself. And for sure not the drug addict." Mrs. Palermo gave the ceiling a meaningful glance. Metallic scraping sounds were coming from upstairs, an industrious, wincing noise, as of someone trying to retool a bicycle into a lawn mower.

It had been a few weeks since Jack's initial trip upstairs. In that time he'd been forced to climb to the second floor on a number of occasions to request that one thing or another, one commotion or another, cease and desist. Each time he was greeted with the same genial, stoned incomprehension. Once Chloe had made the trip herself when Jack was busy on the phone. She came back looking pensive. "Is it a health code violation to keep mice as pets? You know, regular mice?"

Twice when Jack went up to talk to Hippie Pothead Rasta Boy, the redheaded girl was in residence. On two other evenings, the blonde smirked at him from where she lay draped across the sofa. But never again did Jack see the two of them occupying the kid's apartment at the same time. He began to wonder if that night had been something he'd imagined, some drugged and muddy dream. He couldn't comprehend how these people arranged their lives.

Now Jack said to Mrs. Palermo, "No, I don't guess you'd want that guy in charge of anything. Let me get something to write with." He went to retrieve a pen and pad of paper from his writing desk. Mrs. Palermo was looking around the place in an interested fashion that made him anxious to send her on her way before she began making any more intrusive comments. To distract her he asked, "Did you grow up here, you and your family?"

"This place? No, we lived over on Waveland Avenue. Mom came here after me and Rocco, that's my brother, got married and moved out. My dad was already dead. He passed away, what, almost fifty years ago."

Jack waited while Mrs. Palermo wrote her phone number in careful, florid digits. "Fifty years," he repeated. "That's a long time . . ." He supposed he meant a long time to be dead, but that would have been crass. "I'm sure that was hard for your mother."

"Yeah, they were only married for six years. Six years a wife, fifty years a widow. He drowned. My dad."

"Oh, I'm sorry." Stupid, to offer consolation for something that happened before you were born, but what else were you supposed to say. Mrs. Palermo waved it off.

"That's all right. I was just a little kid, I don't remember that much about it. Or him. Sometimes I think even what I remember's only what they told me. Dad drowned on Lake Michigan. Him and some friends went out on a boat fishing. It was the one guy's boat and he was supposed to know what he was doing. October 1953. They hit a squall. You know about storms on lakes? They're bad because lakes are shallow and the bottom kicks up easier. Anyway. Here comes the sad stuff. The two other guys washed up a week later. Fish ate parts of them. You don't want to know which parts. They never found the boat. Never found my dad."

"Wow," said Jack, inadequately.

"Maybe that's why Mom, you know, lost it. Not ever knowing. She still keeps his shoes in the closet, his clothes on hangers. I think she even still sleeps on the one side of the bed. Like she always expected him to come back. It's a little nuts. She could have married again, the church lets you, and she was still a young woman. But she just stopped her life where it was. When do you cross the line between love and crazy? I tell my husband, you disappear on me, I'm selling your golf clubs. That's a joke, after a while you have to turn it all into a big stupid joke. Well I'm off. I need my cigarette, or else I just keep talking till I use up every word in the English language. Then I start in on Italian. That's a joke too. Very nice to meet you, and thanks for helping me out."

Then she was gone, leaving Jack to ponder yet another neighbor and the life lived behind closed doors.

When Chloe came home that evening, she was tired from her week at work, so they planned on staying in, eating take-out Thai food, and watching videos. Jack thought of telling her about Mrs. Palermo, offering her up as something interesting in the course of his boring day. But Chloe could be impatient with what she called Jack's weirdness museum, his accounts of different pathetic or grotesque events. Death by fish was likely to make her shriek in disgust. And besides, it would have shamed him to turn Mrs. Lacagnina's half century of grief into dinnertime chatter.

They were finishing up their meal and drinking red wine in the balloon glasses they'd gotten as a wedding present. Chloe said, "This is the good stuff, isn't it? I'm drinking and drinking but I don't feel drunk."

"You will."

"You know what the big power thing is now? No casual Fridays, and everybody tries to dress to the max. It's supposed to show you're more cutthroat than the next guy."

"Well you are, aren't you?"

"Oh you are so amusing, have you ever considered writing comedy? What it means is heels and hose five days a week. You try it sometime. I don't mean that, you know, literally."

"Maybe it's what I need. A career wardrobe. For motivation."

"What?"

Jack shook his head, sorry he'd allowed himself one of his usual sadsack comments about writing, the ghastliness of it. Chloe didn't need to hear such talk. This was her time to unwind, crow, complain about her job, even if it left him feeling a little dull and housewifely by comparison. "So how many million dollars did the bank make today?"

"I'm not going to tell you, you'll just go off on your corporate-greed thing."

"I can't afford to anymore. A corporation pays my rent."

Chloe reached across the table and speared a forkful of Jack's prawns with basil. "You know what? I think I'm not bad at this stuff. Business. It's like a board game you play with real money. I never thought I'd be good at it, I just didn't want to be another bright girl who couldn't get a job. But I'm actually doing okay. You should see some of these guys who think I'm only somebody to hit on when I clean their clocks in a review."

"What guys hitting on you, exactly?"

"'Hitting's' probably too strong a term. I misspoke."

"Chloe."

"Forget I said it. Delete. No biggie." Chloe took another gulp of wine and smiled in a way Jack imagined she'd been practicing since childhood. By now he'd seen it often enough to be skeptical.

"Which guys."

She sighed, the alcohol making her elaborately patient. "Once in a while one of the suit boys gets an idea. That's all."

"What do you mean 'an idea,' are we talking flirtation or assault here? What do they do?"

"Oh you know perfectly well the kinds of things men do. Skip it. I can handle it. Women have to everywhere, it's not just me."

"Then you should file a complaint or something."

"Wrong wrong wrong. That is so naive. Then you're poison. Then you're a whiny bitch. Not a team player."

"Then what you're saying is, workplace-harassment laws are only good against men you don't work with."

"Yeah, pretty much. Sucks."

"That's ridiculous. Somebody's molesting you and you can't—"

"'Molesting.' Oh boy. You're really getting off on this. Next you'll probably ask me if I enjoy it."

Jack stared. Chloe stared back, flat and challenging. He said, "Whoa, I only said—"

"See, I can't talk about stuff like that with you because you immediately make these *assumptions*."

"Well that was a pretty big one right there. Did I ask you that? Did I even mention the word 'enjoy'?"

"No, but I detected this little proprietary—this little, I don't know, nasty curiosity."

"This whole thing is stupid. You can't drink, you never could."

It was the wrong thing to say. It was how their arguments started, with words getting off track, then the tracks going haywire, looping and doubling back, ending up somewhere that shocked you with its ugliness. They didn't argue often, but Jack could remember every time.

He hated their fights, hated being different people who no longer liked each other.

Chloe reached for the wine, poured another sloshing glass and set the bottle down with a thump.

Jack said, "All right. Great. Drink as much as you want."

"You think this is about me drinking?"

He did, but it seemed unwise to say so. Drinking gave every argument that extra, snarky edge. "I'm sorry I made you talk about things you didn't want to. I just don't believe you should have to deal with a bunch of crap at work. It's a bank, for God's sake, not a garage. Are you gonna keep being mad?"

"Let's just watch the stupid movie, all right?"

They cleared away the dinner plates and settled in on the couch. Jack had picked the videos: *Mission: Impossible* and *American Beauty*. He asked Chloe which one she wanted to watch and she shrugged and said it didn't matter, she'd seen them both. At least she'd stopped drinking, probably to demonstrate to him that she was indifferent to it. She looked muzzy and glowering and still spoiling for a fight. He put on *Mission: Impossible,* figuring that shallow and unreal was better right now than dark and obsessive. They watched in silence as the snazzy secret agents wheeled and dealed. Chloe said, "It's really just the one guy."

Jack held his peace and waited for her to say more. On the screen Tom Cruise, master of disguise, peeled off yet another rubber face.

"Or the others are just minor and stupid and harmless, they say things like hubba hubba, what a dress, okay not hubba hubba but you know what I mean, and maybe they go back to their desks and talk dirty but that's just pathetic. You can tell these are guys who go to bars and try to come up with clever pickup lines and think they get shot down because the line wasn't sharp enough. But this other guy. Promise me you won't say anything until I'm through. He's in the same training group as me so we end up on projects together. Kind of guy who's always working angles, it's not what you know it's who you know, that kind? You know what I'm saying?"

She seemed to want him to answer. He ducked his head in a nod and
Chloe gave him a measuring, scornful look.

There were times when he simply had no idea what she wanted of
him, what was required of him to be her husband.

After a moment she went on. "I'm not telling you this to get you mad
or jealous or get you anything. It's so you'll know. This is how I have to
deal with people sometimes. All right this guy. Right from the start I
could see him calculating. Oh boy, I've got the radar for that. He starts
out like we're pals, comrades. You know he's really got a five-year plan
that includes giving me and everybody else in the place orders someday. He doesn't get slimy until you remember that all-day conference
thing we had? Up in Barrington? He wanted me to go home with him
and have sex. Those weren't the exact words. No, I won't tell you. He
said I could always say the meeting ran late. It's not like he didn't know
I was married, it's not like I don't talk about you! I said No thanks. I
guess I didn't sound torn enough for him."

She'd been talking fast and now she stopped, stared at the movie,
perplexed. "I know I saw this before but I don't remember this part
at all."

"That's it?"

"Well, it brings us up to the present."

Jack was beginning to see there might be a reason for the whole
draining argument, a reason that was coming up now. "Go on."

"He waits till I'm getting ready to come home, he tries to get on the
elevator when it's just me and him. He always starts off talking about
work, some question I have to say yes to. I know that trick. But whatever he says, you can feel the slime oozing out between the cracks. If
we're together long enough, he says other stuff. He asks about you
sometimes."

"Me? What the hell does he say?"

"You know. Sex stuff."

"I will kill him."

"No you won't. This is him trying to get me rattled. It's a power
thing. If you come in and fight my fights for me, I lose."

"Chloe, shit, this has been going on for how long? You're stuck be-tween floors with this slime devil, talking about our sex life?"

"I really don't like that term. 'Sex life.' It's so prissy. People should just say 'fucking.' It's the express elevator, by the way, I've never known it to get stuck. You always exaggerate for dramatic effect."

"So that's what you talk about. You and me . . ." He couldn't bring himself to say fucking. He got up from the couch and stood over her. He didn't know how much worse this was going to get, how much longer he was going to have to listen to his wife relating, in a thought-ful tone of voice, things that should be treated as outrages, and which seemed specifically designed to render him an impotent fool. Upstairs the bass track of the kid's stereo beat against the floorboards like a pile-driver.

"Oh I don't tell him anything, do you really think I'd do that? He in-sinuates. I evade."

"Couldn't you just not take the elevator, don't they have stairs, huh? Insinuates what?"

"You know. That married sex is boring. Like he would have the slightest clue."

She gave him another appraising look, then rubbed her eyes with the back of her hand. The alcohol wearing off into fatigue. Jack had a sud-den sickening doubt that things had happened the way she'd said. But it was crazy to start thinking like that.

"Look," he said, trying to approximate calm. He wanted to take her to bed, reclaim her with everything he could put into his lovemaking, he wanted to unhear everything she'd said. But he knew there was more to come. "You'd better tell me what else."

"Jack, honey—"

"Just lay it on me. Let's get this over with."

Chloe shrugged, suggesting that she was humoring an unreasonable request. "I went out for a drink with him the other night after work. Now don't jump down my throat. It wasn't anything. It was only to get him to back off. Gunfight at the OK Corral."

"Where did you go?"

"What difference does it make?"

"I'm curious. Where people go to do things like this."

"I'm going to ignore that insinuation. We went to Bandera. If that's really important. Nothing happened, you are so paranoid. I'm telling you so that everything's completely transparent. He's not going to bother me anymore. I worked it out. Problem solved."

Another unhappy thought visited Jack. "You're telling me this because somebody might have seen you out with him and it might get back to me."

"Well if it did I knew you'd do exactly what you're doing now. Not understand. I had to show him I wasn't scared of him. Everybody thinks things are so easy for me, all I have to do is smile and show a little leg and I get whatever I want, well, it's absolutely not like that! It makes me feel stupid and horrible and worthless. Maybe I shouldn't even try to do anything serious, I should just be some dim-bulb slut like everybody thinks I am anyway."

She was blubbering now. Her face was growing red and heated, like a child's. Part of Jack thought, unkindly, that she might be expected to start crying once he'd cornered her, part of him was concerned. "I don't think that, come on."

"I'm such a chickenshit. I know I shouldn't get sucked into some little jerk's power trip but I don't know how else to do things, isn't that pitiful? You want to know the truth, all I know is hitting on and not hitting on. Fucking over and getting fucked. That's pretty much the way my world shakes out. Yes sir."

"Now don't get carried away."

Immediately he regretted saying it, since her voice turned shrill and hateful. "Carried away. That's rich. Like when you rant and rave about how nobody appreciates your great, stupendous writing, is that getting carried away? I'm sorry. I'm sorry. That was really crappy. I didn't mean it. I bet you're sorry you ever met me."

"You know that's not true." He spoke as if trying to coax her down from a ledge.

"Yeah, but I don't know *why* you're not sorry. Poor Jack, you probably thought I was a normal person and here I'm a huge boring mess."

"Don't, Chlo."

"I didn't fuck him. You didn't ask. But I know you want to know. So I'm telling you. Whether you believe me or not."

"All right. We're through talking about this."

"I ruined everything. I made you think about it happening."

"You aren't responsible for somebody else's bad behavior. You don't have to hate yourself because sleaze boy—"

"I hate myself for being the fuckee, don't you get it? God listen to me. Could I possibly be more vulgar?"

He pulled her up from the couch and let her cry weakly against his shirt. Crying was better than talking right now. She was still trying to get words out. "I don't deserve you, why are you so nice to me when I'm so horrible? Why do you even put up with me?"

"Because I love you, dummy."

"But why. Why do you love me?"

"There doesn't have to be any why."

They stood there, rocking, until Chloe inhaled through the mess of tears and said she was beat, she was just going to bed. Well he was beat too, not just from the argument, but from the effort of trying not to say some wrong thing that would make her distress ratchet up another notch, a doomed effort since there was never really any right thing to say. He could feel the weariness in all the stress points of his body: jaw, shoulders, gut. He tried to remember when it had become his part in their marriage to talk her down from ledges.

Chloe went into the bathroom to blow her nose and rinse her face, came out looking clean and small and subdued in an oversized T-shirt. Jack lay down on the bed with her. It was only nine-thirty and he knew he wouldn't sleep, forget about sex, but he also knew his presence was required to soothe and console her. Perhaps this had always been his role, one he'd taken on freely. And perhaps it was inevitable that whatever you signed on for began to assume weight and shape.

Chloe fell into a wan, exhausted sleep after a few minutes. The music upstairs was as loud and obnoxious as ever; he was probably going to have to threaten the kid again. Chloe must have been truly spent to sleep through it. When Jack was certain she was breathing regularly, he got up and closed the bedroom door behind him.

This wasn't the first time. Tonight might have been the messiest and most prolonged of Chloe's meltdowns, but he'd seen them before, you could argue that he'd seen them almost from the beginning. There were times he thought they were just a method of getting attention, in the way that women always seemed to need attention, and maybe that was part of it. Maybe drinking too much and feeling overwhelmed at work had been part of tonight's episode. But Jack was mindful of her history, of the suicide attempt that she always brushed off as "just a big mistake." And always, at some point, she rolled out her litany of self-hatred, her intractable insistence on how unworthy, disgusting, etc., she was. It all struck Jack as ludicrous, so demonstrably untrue that it must function as a kind of ritual self-abasement or false front, designed to mean the exact opposite of what she said. Then again, there was always the possibility that she believed it.

Now he was faced with trying to decide what, if anything, he should do. Chloe would wake up in the morning cheerful and apologetic and disinclined to discuss, or even remember, anything she'd said. He wasn't going to let her off that easy. He was going to insist she go back to the therapist she'd seen in school. Or another therapist if, as he expected, she argued it hadn't done her any good. It made him feel better to have a concrete plan. Going to a shrink was what people did, after all, when there was a problem. He knew she'd taken Prozac for a time, although he didn't see that in itself as alarming. Back home in California, everybody from his soccer coach to his mother had been on Prozac. Maybe she just needed to go back on it. He wanted to believe that whatever was wrong could be set right, and that somewhere out there was the right shrink or the right dosage.

As for the creep at work. Jack had gone to a reception a couple of months ago for the bank's new management-training class, where he'd shaken hands with a number of near-identical junior suits. He had trouble remembering anything distinguishing about their faces or conversation, let alone imagining any one of them as some Machiavellian seducer. They all seemed young and stiff and self-conscious. They held on to their wineglasses as if someone might come along and try to take them away. They hadn't found much to say to Jack, either because he was outside their business orbit, and therefore of no consequence, or else they veered away from him because they had in fact been talking dirty about his wife. There were two or three other women in the program besides Chloe, but they dressed like Soviet-era bureaucrats and were, if anything, more brittle and anxious than the men. It wasn't hard to imagine Chloe attracting attention, both good and bad. It was all too easy to imagine.

Jealousy was something he'd had to come to terms with in his young marriage. It roosted on his shoulder like a molting raven, dropping its occasional hideous, scabby feathers. Jack knew, as you knew any fact of nature, that there were plenty of men out there who'd lust after Chloe and make fools of themselves in the process. Chloe had a habit of referring to these men lightly. It was no big deal, she seemed to be saying, it was only to be expected. Jack didn't find this reassuring. He didn't like thinking these were routine happenings. He didn't like that tonight she'd been the one to bring up, however backwardly, the word "enjoy."

The dour bird on Jack's shoulder dug its claws in. He wondered if Chloe's keeping secret this new problem for so long—for how long, exactly? Shut up, he told the raven—meant it was something worrisome. Then he told himself it was his own goddamn problem if he was this wretchedly insecure.

Sooner or later you reached the end point of this sort of thinking, and there was nothing to do except put it aside, or start the cycle all over again. He was too tired for that, so he rewound the movie and straightened the kitchen. He was aware that the music from the kid's apartment had stopped, thank God, but now there was some commotion on the stairs. This was typical: the kid and his entourage were on their way out, and the party was moving right along with them. He listened to the voices, it was hard not to, since they seemed to be stuck at some midpoint on the staircase. This happened often enough that Jack suspected they got too stoned to remember if they were coming or going.

The kid was laughing his head off, a loopy, braying sound. "You oughta get that tattooed on your ass. 'My strength is the strength of ten because my heart is pure.'"

Male voice: "Fuck you, Brezak."

"It's not like you don't have enough room back there."

"And the horse you rode in on."

"Yeah, if I had a horse, I could see which of you had the biggest—"

"God," said the male voice, adopting a new, disgusted tone, probably because he was getting the worst of the slam contest, "another intellectual evening."

Jack guessed the redheaded girl was out there: she had a recognizable, smutty giggle. And he thought he detected at least one other girl's voice in the general commotion of talk and yahooing and whatever heavy objects they were dragging behind them. One of the girls said, "So are we going to Cosmos or what, I can't believe you guys don't want to go."

"How much is cover, ten?"

"Ten, no way, eight."

"It's ten, it's Ghostface Killah."

"No way, it's Viper."

"Uh-uh. Ghostface."

"Well whichever, it's ten."

"Eat me. Eight."

"I don't wanna go if it's Viper."

"Are you kidding? I love Viper."

"Eat your mother."

"You guys I need the keys, I have to go to the bathroom."

"Grab my smokes, they're on the TV."

"You owe me for those. I got them when I got the beer. I don't have the keys, you do."

"You have to have them, you're the one who locked up, shit-for-brains."

"I gave you three extra bucks, that was for smokes."

"How do you figure it was extra, the beer was fifteen and you only gave me seven."

"Eat me. I gave you nine. That's six for the beer, fifteen minus six plus three."

Jack had had enough. He stepped out into the lobby and looked up the staircase to the landing, where the kid, Raggedy Ann, and a couple of other skanky characters were camped out. "Hey, Rich?"

A single old-fashioned light fixture with a yellow bulb lit the stairs. The landing was in shadow. A long, skinny arm emerged, raised in greeting. "Oh hey, man, we were just about to leave." Although the group didn't look as if they were just about to do anything, except possibly hunker down further and play cards. "You ready, guys?"

Raggedy Ann had adorned her face with glitter. When she leaned over the darkened railing to peer down at Jack, it had the unnerving quality of a mask. The other girl—Jack hadn't seen this one before, a chubby, moon-faced underaged-looking girl with large breasts squeezing out the sides of her halter top—whispered something urgently.

"Well go ahead but hurry up," said Rich, standing and shaking out his legs, producing the keys from his pocket like a magic trick. He was doing a new thing with his hair, some sort of home-cooked dreadlocks involving a lot of red and green yarn. He looked like a Christmas ornament produced in a shelter workshop. "Here. Jeez. Friday night," he said to Jack, by way of explanation for—the noise? the gathering? Although to Jack this explained exactly nothing, since the kid didn't punch a time clock and hardly needed to blow off a week's worth of stress. He'd once told Jack that he "helped out" at a health food store.

"Great, just keep it down, okay?"

Jack went to close the door when the kid said, "Everything all right down there?"

"Excuse me?"

"Thought I heard somebody hollering a while back."

The kid was far enough away in the shadows that Jack couldn't read his expression. He assumed, from the solicitous tone of voice, that it was smart-alecky. "Everything's terrific," said Jack. "You know. Friday night."

He stared up into the gloom, then went back inside and shut the apartment door. After a little time he heard them making their way down the stairs, a caravan of whisperings and snorted giggles. Then the outer door opened and a slice of street noise mixed with their sudden laughter.

Jack was asleep, a light, dream-flecked sleep, and when he awoke he knew from his own alertness that it was still early, perhaps midnight, and he'd been asleep for only an hour or so. The buzzer from the street had been stabbing into his dreams.

Chloe raised up on one elbow. *"What?"*

"It's nothing," he told her. "Go back to sleep." She rolled over into her pillow, never really having woken up. Jack rolled out of bed and hopped around to get his pants on. The buzzer sounded twice more. He couldn't imagine who would come to see them. They didn't have friends who dropped by after hours.

When Jack looked out through the lobby to the street, he didn't at first recognize the small figure hanging back from the light. He was still trying to run through the catalog of people he knew. Then he came fully awake and saw it was the nameless blond girl, Rich Brezak's some-time girlfriend, now cupping a hand against the glass to peer inside.

He wasn't inclined to let her in. He advanced until he stood opposite her on the other side of the glass. She looked up, gave a good imitation of being surprised to see him. "Oh, I guess I hit the wrong button. Sorry." The glass blotted the sound of her voice.

Jack didn't believe that for a minute. "He isn't home."

She knew that already. "Yeah, I'm really sorry." She didn't look sorry. She shuffled her weight from one foot to the other.

"He isn't home," Jack repeated. "Believe me, I can tell."

"Can I just talk to you?"

"Better you should stop waking people up and go home."

"What?"

In order to be heard through the glass, she was half-shouting, but Jack didn't want to wake Chloe. He put his mouth up to the narrow space where the doors joined. "Go home."

It startled him when she put her mouth close to the same spot on the other side. "I need to get in there."

"Yeah, sure." You shouldn't go opening doors if you didn't know people.

"I have to leave him a note."

"Try the post office."

"You know what Rich says about you, huh? He says you ought to loosen up, quit kissing your wife's ass."

He took a step back from the glass. The girl tilted her head to look at him. The streetlight above her turned her hair lurid, ghostlike, and left her face featureless. "Oh come on, I was just messing with you. What do you care what he thinks anyway?"

"Why do you need to come inside if he's not here?"

"I want to be here when he gets back. It's important. Come on. I won't ring your bell anymore but I'll stay out here all night. Me and the muggers."

He bet she would. She was that kind of nuts. He might have gone back to bed, let her take her chances, if it wasn't for his own disquiet. He'd thought the night was over, and here it was still in process, as if he was now dreaming the fight with Chloe in some different script or permutation, and whatever he might do now was important.

The girl seemed to know he was wavering. "What are you afraid of, you think I'm going to shoot him or something? As if. Wouldn't waste a bullet on him. Trap him, maybe, like the varmint he is. God, I'm kidding. You really do need to loosen up."

From somewhere down the street came a commotion of screeching car tires and voices braying. They both looked toward it. "Are you gonna open this or what?"

Jack worked the bolt and held the door for her as she slipped in beneath his arm. "Thanks," she said with enough of a sarcastic edge to indicate that it was about time. In the fuller light of the lobby she no longer looked menacing or hallucinatory, just an ordinary girl, something less than pretty, with a swagger and a smirk as self-conscious as a monocle.

They didn't know how to manage looking at each other or not looking, talking or not talking, now that they were standing in the same space. The girl recovered first. "Right. I'll just make myself at home."

Jack motioned her away from his apartment door, down the hallway that led to the back door and alley. They passed Mr. Dandy's door, closed and silent, though for all Jack knew she'd rung his buzzer too, and the old man was awake and listening. "What are you . . . ," she began, but he shook his head and pointed. She rolled her eyes, either exasperated or pretending to be, and walked ahead of him. She dragged one leg; he remembered her limping. She wore another of her long, droopy skirts, and he wondered briefly if that was for some purpose.

There was a backyard of sorts, a pocket-sized square of grass enclosed in a high board fence. Somebody, Mr. Dandy, probably, had planted hostas and lilies of the valley and a row of seeding lettuces around the borders. There was a cement walkway, a broom, and a hose neatly coiled on a reel. Two white plastic chairs were set out to enjoy the meager view. "Sit," Jack told her.

She did so, although with no very good grace. "What did that crack about my wife mean?"

She shrugged. "I didn't say it. Rich did."

"Rich should mind his own goddamn business." As always, he didn't care to think about other people peering in at him, forming judgments.

"Yeah, he can kind of get to you, can't he?" She lifted her head to gaze at the back of the building. Both Mr. Dandy's and Mrs. Lacagnina's darkened windows were crowded with half-seen objects wedged onto the sills and wadding the curtains. An electric fan, a vase empty of flowers, stack of newspapers, television antenna, pair of socks spread out to dry. All the debris of long tenancy pushing at the seams of their apartments.

The night was cool and the girl shivered inside her denim jacket, although she didn't seem aware of doing so. "I don't know, he thinks it's funny that she's always sending you up there to complain, it's always she has to sleep, she has to work, she has a headache. He says she runs you."

He didn't respond. It served him right for asking in the first place. The girl leveled her stare at him. "My name's Ivory, by the way."

Maybe it was and maybe it wasn't. It sounded too much like a made-up name, one of those things girls did to glamorize themselves. "It is," she insisted. "God, I hate it when people get that look. Like Doreen or Heidi are supposed to be normal names?"

"I'm Jack."

"I know. I saw it on the mailbox."

"You're a pretty observant bunch upstairs, aren't you?"

"Look, I'm just going to sit out here, and if you're gonna be hostile you can leave."

It would have made sense to go back inside, lie down next to Chloe, and let this odd girl lurk in the dark, if that was what she wanted. He was so tired but there was a tough knot of muscle lodged under one ear, the start of a headache, and enough irritation and unease to keep him from going back to sleep anytime soon. There wasn't anyone he could tell about Chloe. He didn't have those kinds of friends anymore, friends you could unload on about anything, or maybe he did, a couple of them, except they lived in different time zones and anyway, there would be something ungentlemanly and disloyal about making such calls. Pretending he was concerned about Chloe when what he really wanted was to rage and complain. She ran him. She ran him and he couldn't help but let her. He said to the girl, "You want something to drink, wine or—"

"Yes."

Chloe was still so soundly asleep that she didn't stir even when he sat down on the bed next to her and touched her shoulder. "I'm going out back for a while. I'll be right outside." He could at least say he'd tried to tell her in case she woke up and missed him and there was some further scene. He doubted it; she was snoring into her pillow. It was either the alcohol or perhaps she'd taken one of the prescription sleeping pills she wasn't supposed to take if she drank, and now he'd have to worry about that too because she couldn't be trusted to take care of herself.

There was an opened bottle of red wine on the kitchen counter, the wine in it level with the bottom of the neck. Jack stared at it, unable to remember when this second bottle had been uncorked. He found two plastic glasses, his sweatshirt, and in the front closet, an old striped blanket.

When he went back outside, Ivory had positioned herself so she could see the length of the building's hallways, and whoever might come through the front door. Jack handed her the blanket and she gave him a sharp, suspicious look, which Jack was later to interpret as disbelief that anyone might do something nice for her. "Thanks."

"Welcome." He poured out the wine and gave her one of the glasses. She sniffed at it, tasted it by extending her tongue, like a cat drinking milk. "I can't ever drink a whole lot. It makes my face turn red, I'm allergic or something. But I need to take the edge off, you know?"

"I don't guess you'd care to tell me . . ."

She was busy draping the blanket around her knees. "What?"

"Never mind."

"About him? Rich? He's a little shit."

Jack said nothing. He wondered if she meant it, or if it was just the kind of thing girls said when love turned inside out on them. Ivory took another tiny sip of wine. "Is my face getting red?"

"I don't think so. I can't tell." It was unevenly dark in the yard. The sky above had the fizzing quality of a television turned to a blank channel. Its color was a dulled, meaty pink. It was never entirely dark anywhere in the city. There was always the reflected light of a thousand thousand mercury vapor street lamps, of car headlights and searchlights and skyscrapers. Babylon. He couldn't remember the last time he'd seen stars, or even the moon. In his present state of mind this seemed sad, even desolating, a sign of how wrong his life had gone without his noticing.

Ivory was prattling on. "Maybe it's only the cheap stuff I'm allergic to, would that make sense? Those big jugs of cheap stuff? Once I swear my tongue started itching. But this isn't bothering me, I think because it's quality. You guys have money, I bet." She waited. "So do you?"

Jack roused himself. "That's really kind of nosy."

"Well so is asking me about my love life, don't you think?"

He said, neutrally, "We can buy a bottle of good wine now and then." In fact they both were and were not wealthy. When they'd gotten married, Jack's father had transferred over to him some Treasury bills and bonds, with the understanding that they were meant to hold on to these assets, be prudent, reinvest the dividends. In time, as life events, that is, children, accrued, there might be additional gifts. Down the road, an inheritance. But for now Chloe had her school loans to repay, and they had a budget like anyone else. While it would be embarrassing to ask his parents for money, and his father would say sour things about it, there was money available if they really needed it. He'd never known it not to be, he had never had to live without its presence backing him up. He guessed that to someone like this girl, the things they took for granted would be beyond reach. He felt irritated, as if she had accused him of something. He said, "Okay, I'm sorry if I asked you a personal question. I thought you might want to talk about it. My mistake."

"You mean you wanted to know the horrible details. You were hoping they'd be horrible."

"Just one thing. If you hate him so much, why come around here?"

"God you are so clueless," Ivory said. "You should go on game shows, be the one who makes everybody else feel smarter."

"And you can go on and make them feel nicer."

That stopped her. They sat in silence long enough for Jack to think they were through talking, and sooner or later one of them, him, probably, would get up and leave and that would be the end of it. She said, "It's so he can't pretend I don't exist."

"I'm sorry if that's what he's doing."

"I don't understand how people can all of a sudden shut you off. Shut themselves off. It's unnatural."

No, it was entirely natural. He understood it perfectly. When he was younger he'd done it himself more than once. You got tired of a girl for whatever reason, or sometimes for no reason. And because you didn't want to admit you were fickle or irrational or shallow, you simply ignored her. At some point there might have to be a conversation. Often enough the girl figured it out on her own and ignored you right back. It was a crude system but it got the desired results. At least as long as everybody played by the same rules. He said, "I don't suppose you want any advice."

"No, but you're going to give me some anyway."

"Find something else to do. This is a waste of your time." As far as he was concerned, the kid would be a waste of anyone's time. Love, go figure.

She muttered that it was her time to waste. "Fine," said Jack. "But I guarantee this isn't going to end up the way you want it to."

"Well maybe you don't know what I want."

That sounded like bravado to him, shaky bravado, but he let it pass. He heard tears in her voice, and beneath that, a layer of something stubborn, fey, reckless that might break through to the surface and produce crying or worse. "How old are you?"

She consulted her glass of wine. "Twenty-one."

"Uh-huh. I mean really."

"Nineteen. Not like it's any of your business."

"Don't you think that's a little young to be so caught up in the whole hopeless romance-stalker thing?"

"No. I think it's exactly the right age."

He tried again. "You have a home? Somebody who might be worried about you being out all night?"

"Look, I've got my own place. Maybe you'd think it's a dump, but it's mine. I have a job, I pay my own bills. I take care of myself. So you don't have to act like I'm some *waif*." She took a pack of cigarettes out of her jacket and lit one.

"You shouldn't smoke."

"If I get cancer, I get cancer."

"Nice attitude."

She blew smoke in a thin stream, ignoring him.

"What's the matter with your leg?"

"What?"

"I noticed you had a limp."

"Yeah, my pelvis is fucked up."

"Oh, that's—"

"I'm real used to it. I was in an accident when I was a little kid, it never healed right. There's this place on my hip where there's no bone and the skin just hangs. You want to see? It's kind of interesting, in a gross way."

"No thanks."

"You were trying to that first night. Remember? You were scoping me. But hey, that was before you knew I was a cripple."

"Cripple, what kind of talk is that."

"But you were, weren't you."

"All right, maybe so. But I don't think it means I should be doing it now." He felt embarrassed, he wanted some logical exit from the conversation, wasn't finding one.

She seemed to feel she'd caught him in some squeamishness that gave her an advantage. "Yeah, my whole leg is real gnarly. But you know what, you learn to stare stuff like that right down. My nickname in school was Swamp Thing. Because I walked crooked, worse than I do now, and I was dorky anyway. You get so shit people say doesn't bother you. It rolls right off. So don't think you can lay your Big Brother wisdom on me that's supposed to make me behave like you think I should. 'Cause all I hear you saying is Swamp Thing, Swamp Thing, Swamp Thing."

"It's a pretty name."

"*What* is?"

"Ivory."

Another round of silence. Jack shifted his weight in the chair. His brain was still sending out sparks of static and agitation, but his body had begun to melt down into a deep, muscular tiredness. He said, "I had a big fight with my wife tonight."

Her cigarette flared as she took a last drag and stubbed it out. Her light hair turned toward him, a milky spot in the gloom. "Care to say what about?"

"I don't know what it was about." Or it was about the fear he'd always had but refused to acknowledge, his own crippled part that he stubbornly pretended was invisible: that he loved Chloe more than she would ever love him. He stood up. "I have to go to bed. Will you be okay out here?"

"Sure."

He hesitated. "Promise me I won't be sorry I let you in. That you're not going to set the place on fire, anything like that."

"Don't worry." She sounded tired also. "I probably won't even talk to him. Thanks. For the wine and all."

"If you're not going to talk to him—"

"I just need to be here. I can't be anyplace else. It doesn't have to make sense to you. No offense, but I think I want to be alone right now."

Jack left her sitting there and let himself into his apartment, and into his bed again, where Chloe turned toward him in her sleep and pressed herself against him. She was warm from the bed and sleep had soothed the unhappiness in her so she breathed calmly, and her hair smelled clean and he thought he understood the girl outside better than she would have imagined. If you were sad and in love, there was only one place you had to be.

He woke up early, the morning still gray, and walked out to the back-yard. The grass was dank with dew and a rag of spiderweb in a corner of the fence was etched in dripping silver. The striped blanket was folded neatly on a chair and the girl was gone.

Four

Today Jack was teaching social studies, the Westward Expansion, to a class of South Side junior high schoolers. O Pioneers! O Sacajawea and the Gold Rush and the Alamo! Like they cared. It was summer school, make-up classes for kids who had already sunk to the bottom of the heap. None of them wanted to be here, why would anyone? Only the Alamo excited any interest. It had drama, and teams you could root for. The Mexican kids in the class were all for Santa Ana while the black kids thought Jim Bowie was pretty cool on account of the knife. Yeah, but Santa Ana capped Jim Bowie's ass. Yeah, but they was so lame. It took thirty or forty of em. Ol Jim cut em up. Bullshit, he was just hidin in the house. Want no house, was a fort. He was hidin, he was pussy. Was not. Was too. He dead pussy. Santa Ana took him out. Well Santa Ana be dead too.

Jack intervened, steered them back to maps and border disputes, and the class resumed its listless inattention. He was just another white guy come to tell them things they didn't need to know. What use was the westward expansion to them? The gold was long gone and the land claimed, with no place in it for them. What use was history itself, since everything had been decided before they were born?

The weather had turned hot and the classroom had no air-conditioning, only a couple of fans stirring the heat and making enough noise that Jack had to pitch his voice at a half shout to be heard. The students slumped over their desks or stared out the windows. The playground outside was sun-blasted asphalt that could have served as the pavement of hell, surrounded by chain link. Beyond that, cars moved slowly through the glaze of heat, past the ordinary ugliness of laundromats and check-cashing stores and whatever it was they sold behind those barred and grated storefronts. Billboards advertised Empleo Avisos and Fast Credit. Gardens of broken glass grew in the vacant lots. Some catastrophe had left a single wall of a brick building standing like one of those desert-rock formations that are given picturesque names. Children died on such streets. You read the newspaper stories, you were shocked by them, except that it happened too often to be truly shocking. Jack thought, If I was one of these kids, and this was what I saw every day, would I care that there was such a thing as Manifest Destiny, or the Northwest Passage, or anything else I read in a book?

He didn't know and he wouldn't have the chance to find out. He was only a substitute, here for a week to replace some luckless woman who'd broken both feet getting out of a bathtub, an accident he didn't want to try and visualize. He wouldn't be here long enough for any of these kids to learn, let alone remember, his name. He wrote words no one read, he stood in classrooms and spoke about the dead past to children who had already stopped tracking their futures. He felt disconnected from some important part of life itself, or perhaps it was only from his own life. He said, "Getting back to the Alamo . . ."

That evening he asked Chloe, "Do you want to start a family?"

"Now what brought that on?"

"I don't know. Does it have to be something? Can't it just be biology? Like salmon spawning."

"Salmon."

"Well do you?"

"You picked a funny time to ask." They were in the car, driving to dinner with friends. Traffic nudged along. Radiators labored. The temperature that day had reached ninety. By now it had slipped back a couple of notches, but a layer of gray humidity had settled in. Chloe had her compact out and was trying to put on makeup. The air conditioner blew a thin, inadequate stream over their knees.

"Just think about it. We can talk later."

"I thought we decided this already. I thought we were going to wait five years." Chloe scrutinized her lip line, made some tiny adjustment, then snapped the compact shut and gave him a skeptical, I-dare-you-to-impregnate-me glance.

"You know why I'm bringing this up now? So you have to listen. Unless you want to get out and run through traffic."

"Very sneaky."

"We didn't really decide, we said we'd decide later. Five years. I don't know where you get that."

"Because in five years I should have a track record at the bank, or wherever I end up working. I can take a leave without doing a lot of damage. I'll be thirty-one, that's not so old. What's the big rush?"

A car pulled up next to them at a light, speakers turned up so high that even through the sealed windows they heard boom and feedback. The glass rattled. Jack supposed they should be glad that H.P.R.B. wasn't into rap. He couldn't explain to Chloe why the idea of children had struck him with such force. There was some need or lack in him he hadn't suspected. He was a little embarrassed, but secretly happy. He waited for the rapmobile to pull past them before he answered. "I just want to be able to talk about it. I really want kids, I want to make plans. Buy little rubber footballs, things like that."

"What if we have a girl?"

"I'm still getting her a football."

"You don't even like football, dope. I want kids too. Just not next week, okay?" Chloe reached over and took a swipe at his hair. "This is really kind of cute of you. Daddy."

"Mommy."

They smiled at each other, then Jack turned his attention back to driving. It was a few days after their quarrel. Things were going better. They were both making an effort. Jack had brought up therapy, in a tentative, roundabout way, hedging more than he'd planned, but at least he'd come out with it, and Chloe said maybe it wasn't a bad idea. She was under a lot of stress at work, she could use somewhere to dump it besides on him, poor old Jack. Poor old Jack was glad she'd been receptive, although he didn't think she'd actually gotten around to calling for an appointment. In the new, sunny atmosphere of the last few days, it didn't seem quite as urgent. He supposed Chloe was right, there was nothing urgent about children either, except that he wanted to try on the idea, imagine his life opening out into this new country.

He merged onto the Eisenhower and pointed the car westward, squinting against the sun, which was balanced on the horizon like an elongated red egg. The people they were going to see lived in the suburbs, in Elmhurst. They were Chloe's friends, a woman she'd been in the M.B.A. program with, and the husband. Jack supposed that no matter how long he and Chloe were married, they would always be her friends, not his. Like certain pieces of furniture, some friends resisted joint ownership.

The woman's name was Frances and her husband was Reginald. Fran and Reg. Fran worked for American Express in some corporate capacity. Reg sold air-purification systems, fancy, hi-tech machinery that pulverized odors and used electrostatic filtration and ionization to zap bacteria, dust mites, and anything else that you'd been breathing all your life and which hadn't killed you yet. Chloe had been Fran's maid of honor at their wedding, as Fran, later, had been Chloe's. The two of them gossiped on the phone and met for lunch downtown and compared notes about their jobs and, Jack was sure, husbands. That was all fine except that every so often the women felt it necessary to mount a full-scale dinner offensive between the couples. Jack was resigned to this even though it meant he spent a lot of time paired off with Reg, watching off-brand sports like hockey or auto racing, or hearing about high-energy, virus-killing fields. Tonight was the first time since Jack and Chloe's move to the city that they'd all gotten together. At least it was a weeknight and they couldn't stay late. Jack had encouraged the idea of a weeknight.

Fran and Reg had bought a small but actual house. Some of the dinner inviting, Jack figured, had to do with showing it off. When they pulled into the driveway, he noticed evidence of new, aggressive landscaping—skinny trees held upright with staking, meandering flower beds that, at this point, were growing mostly wood-chip mulch. A straw wreath with a clutch of pink flowers and pink ribbons hung on the front door. Jack wondered how long it would take for Chloe to say something complimentary about it all.

Not long. Fran opened the front door before they could knock, and she and Chloe hugged. "This is so cute," Chloe said, meaning the wreath. "We could never put anything like that on our door, it'd be gone in fifteen minutes." Sometimes Chloe liked to maintain the pose that they lived in an urban combat zone.

"Jack, darling." Fran held out her arms for him to embrace her. She liked to flirt with him by making a show of pretending to flirt with him. Jack went along with it, he supposed he didn't mind the little bit of a feel that came his way, perfumed arms, breasts, mouth on his neck, all of it timed and executed to get the most for her money before she pulled away and beamed fondly at him. Jack actually liked Fran; she meant no harm and she was pretty, in a toothy, corn-fed blond fashion. But it was such a sad, strangled way to get a little of what she needed, or thought she needed. All the desperate energy that went into finding some safe, small channel. He was glad that Reg wasn't a hugger.

Reg was out in the backyard, priming the grill. "Shakespeare!" He and Jack shook hands. Jack smiled gamely at being called Shakespeare. It hadn't been funny the first time. Reg waved at Chloe, who was still in the kitchen with Fran. Reg asked him what he wanted to drink and Jack said Was that a martini there and Reg said It was, it was. Jack could count on there being martinis at this house, looked forward to them. They went along with the sweet expanses of lawn and the calming views of actual sky, the sifting leaf shadow and carriage lamps and mailboxes and swing sets and purple-martin houses set on poles and sparkling garbage cans and well-stocked garages, all the fond, absurd equipment of suburbia. Jack had to admit, he still felt a certain affection for such things, a comfort level he couldn't deny. This was what he'd grown up with after all, or something very similar, even as he was sure he would never live this way again.

Reg went inside and returned with a cocktail shaker and a glass for Jack. "Here you go. I don't know where the girls went. Probably upstairs, going to the john together. Why do they do things like that?" Reg shook his head. Clearly, he was satisfied to have a wife he could make such ritual complaints about. It meant that life was going along in ways he expected and understood. Reg had sandy hair already thinning on top, although he wasn't yet thirty, and small, handsome features. Or at least, Jack supposed he was what women considered handsome. It was a salesman's face, pink, well-barbered, the face of a professional smiler.

"How's that martini?"

"Perfect. Hits the spot."

"We're having shish kebab."

"That's great."

"Fran got these contraptions, special skewers that are supposed to keep your mushrooms and shit from falling off."

"Always a problem."

"I said we should do steaks but she wanted something fancier. Company food. Wait till you see the salad." Reg got up from his lawn chair and ministered to the coals. The grill was one of those heroic, oversized models, suitcase shaped and mounted on a sturdy trolley. It had its own hinged hood and carving shelf and hooks for utensils. Jack was mildly surprised that they hadn't yet traded up to gas.

"So, how's the book coming?"

"Not bad. Slow." It was what he usually said. Reg might not be Mr. Dandy, but Jack still kept his responses guarded. The physical process of writing was dull in a way that people couldn't square with their notions of the glamour of it all. He had told Reg that his book was about California, growing up in California, which he hoped carried hints of trendy decadence and exotic sex, more interesting than anything he was actually writing about, let alone had experienced.

Reg said, "Well great, keep it up. There's got to be some pretty good money in the book game."

"Not usually."

"Come on." Reg looked at him expectantly. He thought Jack was joking.

"No, really. Some people get big money, most everybody else gets chump change." If you ever got your book published in the first place. If you ever finished writing your damned book.

"You mean, only the best-seller guys clean up."

"That's right."

"When you say big money, what are you talking, a million? I'm asking because I really don't know."

"I guess there's one or two who might make a million dollars writing the kind of books I write." By which he meant serious, nonfluff books, literature. "Of course celebrities do all the time, you know, movie stars and politicians who get big contracts for their memoirs." He hoped he didn't sound too snotty or dismissive. For all he knew, Reg might enjoy reading the wit and wisdom of Monica Lewinsky.

"How long does it take to write a book, a year?"

"Or longer," Jack said cautiously. He wasn't sure where Reg was going with this.

"Say it took two years. You've still got a shot at making half a million bucks a year."

"No, Reg. Not even close."

"Oh, I get that it wouldn't be for your first book. You have to build up to it, get name recognition. But there's always that potential, right? The big score."

"In theory." Jack gave up trying to make disclaimers. From now on, he supposed, Reg would regard him as a millionaire-in-waiting, and an inevitable disappointment when none of it happened.

Reg said, unexpectedly, "At least it's something you really want to, you know, devote your life to. Nobody gets to do that anymore, I sure don't."

"Hey, I thought you liked your job." Reg was always talking about it in droning detail. The Healthy Home. The unremitting vigilance against the menace of mold and spores.

"Aw." Reg waved a hand. "Sure, it's a great job. Good money. A real growth market, the technology gets better all the time. Boss is kind of a hard-ass, hell, you can find that anywhere . . ." Reg was mumbling a little, his chin nudging the rim of the martini glass. "But it's just a job, you know? It's not a passion. Two different things . . ."

His voice trailed off. The coals simmered redly. Jack wondered if he should say something hearty and reassuring. He was trying to imagine what Reg meant by passion, if he had secret desires to sing in musicals or be a NASCAR driver or start his own brewery or something even more unlikely. Reg wasn't a guy you suspected of passionate depths, or rather, even his depths were ankle deep. But maybe (probably), Jack was just being a snob again . . .

After a moment Reg shook his head, hoisted his glass, drank. "Ah hell. You gotta have something to bitch about, right? Hurry up and get that book between two covers so we can have a big party for you."

Jack said Sure, that would be great. Trying to reflect some small portion of Reg's enthusiasm. Through the sliding glass door he could see that the women had come back into the kitchen and were getting busy with the food. Fran came out with a tray of stuffed mushrooms, little plates and napkins and forks. "How about something to munch on? How's those coals doing, chief?"

Reg said the coals were getting there, just give him twenty minutes' notice before everything else was going to be ready. Jack balanced his plate and glass. "Careful, those are hot," warned Fran, just as he sizzled his tongue on a mushroom. He nodded, ducked his head to try and work the thing between his teeth, since he didn't want to either swallow it down or spit it out. Luckily, Chloe came into the yard then, and he was able to worry it into a napkin while no one was looking.

"Hey, Reg." She patted him on the shoulder. "How's the Clean Air King?"

"Hi, beautiful. I'm great. Hunky-dory. When you going to leave this sorry guy and run off with me?"

"Not until after dinner at least," Chloe said lightly. She looked terrific. She was wearing a black sleeveless shirt and white shorts and her bare arms and legs gave her the startling impression of nakedness. You forgot how much of a woman you could see, once they switched to summer clothes. She had done her hair in a heavy, complicated braid. There were fine, clean lines in her scalp where the hair crossed and recrossed. Chloe was always complaining that she had small breasts, always standing in front of mirrors and pulling her shirt tight to demonstrate how inadequate they were. He could see their pretty curve at the neck of her blouse. He wouldn't have changed anything about them for the world.

Chloe saw him watching her and smiled in a way that was meant for him alone, and which tightened his groin. Whatever foolishness or social contortions they went through on such an evening, her smile told him the two of them would leave here, resume their real selves, be together again in their bed.

Fran had gone back inside and now returned, balancing a heavy pan. Jack stood. "Here, let me get that for you. This really looks good." It was the shish-kebab skewers, which in Jack's opinion always looked better than they ended up tasting. Something always charred or turned up raw. Chunks of green pepper or onion bumping through your gut.

Reg said, "You know what we could do, bring everything out here. Eat at the picnic table."

Fran, who was flushed and distracted from the cooking, gave him a weary look. "It's not picnic food. It's rice pilaf and Tunisian carrot salad and sesame asparagus."

"I bet the Tunisians eat outside all the time. I bet it's more authentic."

"Oh you don't know one thing about them, Tunisians, who cares, there's a million mosquitoes out here."

"The tiki torches. Light 'em, we can sit here and laugh at the little devils."

"I do not want you dragging out those ugly torches. They are revolting. They are *National Geographic* TV special."

"Okay, how about mosquito repellent?"

"Forget it."

"I will take personal responsibility for the mosquitoes."

"Reg."

"You could humor me, you know? Just this once. You could say it was kind of a kicky idea."

"Except it's not."

Reg wouldn't give it up. He was still joking, or pretending to, in a heavy alcohol-tinged fashion, but his bottom lip was curling in a babyish pout. "Well what good's having a yard if you never use it?"

"What good is a dining room if you don't eat dinner in it?" Fran's voice climbed a notch. Her throat was hot crimson.

"Okay, I got it. How about we take a vote." Reg nodded to Jack and Chloe, potential allies. Jack thought briefly about turning the hose on Reg, or maybe feeding him a mushroom.

"How about when you bother to plan a meal, shop for it, prepare it and serve it, you can decide where we eat. I already have the table set inside, so shut your face."

"Ooh," said Reg, falling back on wordless sarcasm, but Fran had already gone back into the house.

Jack and Chloe avoided looking at each other. Reg said, "She's just jealous because mosquitoes never bite me."

Chloe got up, saying she would go help Fran. Jack, left on his own, said, "It is pretty nice out here." An insipid remark that he supposed was his attempt at taking sides, showing guy-type solidarity.

Reg stood and poked at the shish kebabs. "Am I supposed to put these on or what? She didn't say. How the hell am I supposed to know?"

"Want me to go ask?"

"No, I'm just gonna sit here like a big dummy and wait for somebody to tell me what to do."

"Women always kick up a fuss about their cooking," Jack offered. More of the guy stuff.

"You want to know something? I don't even like shish kebabs. You get everything off the skewers, it's so full of holes it looks like it's already been chewed."

By the time they sat down to eat, everyone was cheerful again, in a way that was only partly false. You had to get around and get over such minor unseemliness. Jack understood entirely how irritation surfaced between two people who occasionally forgot they were lovers. It happened, no big deal. But he also had a private unease, as he held up his plate for Fran to dish out cubes of beef and pineapple and wizened vegetables, as he went through the process of eating and praising the food, that had to do with his own equivocal position here, his sense of being a target for his hosts' separate discontents. Reg imagined Jack living out some high-finance, über-author dream, while Fran rubbed and nuzzled him and imagined, well, he didn't want to imagine and so become an active participant in her fantasy.

He didn't really find himself thinking about sleeping with other women, or at least, not in any detailed, organized way. He took note of women, registered their faces and bodies, lingered for a time over the stray erotic urge, then passed on. He had a troubled sense of how such thoughts would invade you if you allowed them to. Now he was made aware of the roundness of Fran's breasts shifting beneath her knit shirt, the jut of her ass as she leaned over to retrieve a platter, then a sudden vision of her body arched and working beneath his . . .

Throughout dinner he was scrupulous about not meeting Fran's eye directly, or letting his hand linger next to hers as she passed him plates of food. No under-the-table kneesies. Damn the woman for setting off this commotion in him. Then he made an effort not to worry about either her or Reg, since it was only some accident of proximity that forced him to have anything to do with their problems.

The meal was quite good, once you steered around certain of the skewered items. There was red wine and white, also good quality, though Jack, mindful of driving later, took only sips. The others drank and laughed, drank and laughed, and Reg and Fran seemed to be friends again, and the hyper-filtered air blessed their lungs, and Chloe was next to him, one bare shoulder within grazing distance of his mouth. Fran brought out coffee and a lemon tart for dessert and Jack began to calculate how soon they'd be able to express their thanks and regrets and escape into the night. He tried to get Chloe to look at him but she was intent on her wineglass, staring into it and agitating it in those familiar tight spirals.

Fran said, "I wish you guys lived closer. We could do this more often." Although she looked weary and even untidy from the effort of mounting the evening. Her yellow hair was pushed into a crest at the top of her head and her makeup had smudged around her eyes, making black fishhooks at the corners.

Jack said, "You'll have to come in to the city, see our place. We'll have us a night on the town."

"That'd be sweet," said Reg. "Anytime. I'm your boy."

Chloe said, "It's a dump. Our place."

The others looked at her, waiting for her to make a joke out of it. Chloe lifted her gaze from her wineglass. Her braided hair seemed to pull at the corners of her eyes, lengthening them. "I mean, we fixed it up some, but it still screams, 'Let's live in squalor and pretend we like it that way.'"

Fran said, "Oh come on. I saw it when you were moving in. It's really a cute apartment. All those windows."

"It's what you get to see from the windows that counts. You know, the gang wars and such."

Jack said, "I haven't seen any of that, and neither have you."

Chloe shrugged. The expression in her narrowed, heavy-lidded eyes was one of bored disagreement. "Fine. Whatever you say. Then there's Rastaman upstairs, I told you guys about him, didn't I?"

Fran said, "Oh, you can run into that sort of thing anywhere." Glanced at Jack. She was trying to help him out, she wanted him to see that.

Reg said, "No shit, gangs? You gotta watch out for that. Bad news."

"There aren't any gangs where we live. Chloe's just into telling war stories."

"Like nothing like that ever happens."

"It's a perfectly safe neighborhood. The realtors have a statistical—"

"Jack's just into acting like he knows more than anybody else."

"Cut it out, Chlo."

She finished off the wine in her glass, raising it delicately, since she knew the others were watching. "I speak the truth. *In vino veritas*. It's a dump."

"In which a lot of people would be happy to live."

"Yeah. Stupid people."

"Put a lid on it."

"Uh-oh. Now he's working up to a manly anger."

Reg and Fran had gone entirely silent. Settling down the misbehaving spouse not their job, just as he and Chloe had hung back earlier, when Reg was trying his damnedest to be a jackass. In fact, if you considered Fran sleazing all over him, he supposed he was the only one of them who hadn't yet acted badly tonight—all of this passing through his mind in an instant, along with some calculation of how much Chloe had been drinking before he decided, enough.

He stood. "Time to go."

"Am I embarrassing you? I'm embarrassing him." Chloe turned to Reg and Fran, nodding.

"The only person you're embarrassing is yourself."

"I'm being indiscreet. Too bad. Or, as the French have it, *Tant pis*. It bothers him. Living in a crappy little apartment because he can't bring himself to find a real job, now that doesn't bother him."

Fran said, "Oh, Chloe."

"It's an artist thing. Romantic failure. The reason nothing he writes sells is because it's actually too good for anyone to read."

"We're leaving. Or I am. Suit yourself."

"Joking! Joking! He has no sense of humor about this stuff," Chloe said, confidingly, but she did push her chair back from the table and looked around her, as if there was some further process required to get herself gone but she'd forgotten what it was.

Jack lifted her up by her elbow. "Thanks for dinner. It was really very nice. Thanks for having us."

"It was great seeing you," said Fran, only too relieved to fall back into hostess mode, even though her eyes were skidding around in her face and she had to be wondering if anything worse was going to happen before she could get rid of them.

"Reg. Always a pleasure."

"Sure, guy. Anytime." Reg made as if to shake hands, but Jack had both of his on Chloe's arms, steering her ahead of him. Her shoulders tried to squirm away but he kept his grip. At least she was quiet, though she raised her chin to look back at him in a smug, knowing way.

When they got to the front door, Fran said, "Chloe, your purse." She scooped it up from the hallway table and presented it.

"Thanks, hon. I love you."

"I love you too, Chloe. I hope you feel better."

"I feel fine. I feel a remarkable sense of clarity. I'll call you. Lunch."

"That'd be great."

"Reg. You're my hero."

"That's swell, Chloe. You're a swell girl."

"I always think that a man should have a career, I mean, it makes them so much more interesting. Gives them something to make conversation about."

"Good night," Jack said, propelling her down the pathway, to the car. Chloe shook herself loose from him and walked with mincing care to the passenger side.

Jack started the car and pulled away, leaving Reg and Fran standing in their pink-wreathed doorway. They would go inside, look at each other, secretly excited by the ugliness of it all. He imagined the things they would say, how they would both feel better satisfied with each other, at least for a time.

Chloe settled back and half-reclined in the seat, her knees braced against the dashboard. "Go ahead, say it."

"What am I supposed to say."

"Your righteous, pissed-off . . . you know, how much you hate me."

"There's no point in talking to you when you're like this."

"Chick-en."

"Is this just a drunk thing? Or do you always think I'm not worth shit, and it only comes out when you're drunk?"

"I thought you weren't going to talk to me."

He shut up. Chloe sank deeper into the seat, turned her head away from him. He only wanted to get home, not be here with her. His eyes were having trouble with the freeway darkness. He was afraid he might missteer in traffic, send them crashing into one of the cars that floated past them with only a shimmering rush of sound, then he was afraid they might not crash, and his furious heart would propel them all the way, and he would have to endure this and more. The city approached and unrolled around them, the El stops that always surprised him with their crowds of people waiting for trains in the tinny yellow light, as if each of them had some perfectly reasonable reason for coming and going this late, well they probably did, they weren't standing out there just to make him feel lonesome and menaced. Then the vacant, tenementlike factories, or perhaps they really had been tenements, which stood at some distance in their no-man's-land of rail sidings and burned-over ground. Then the grand downtown buildings filled the windshield and it was time to look for their exit, and Chloe said, "You know we really can't think about having children until you bring in an actual income."

She had not previously sounded sloppy or slurred, the way you thought of drunks, and she didn't now. Instead she was calm, matter-of-fact. Whatever poison the drinking set loose in her was of some other sort.

Although Jack knew better, he couldn't keep himself from answering back. "So it's money. That's the important thing now."

"Well don't tell me you don't need to have money around if you want to do the kid thing."

"Fine. You've made your point. Everybody tonight was enlightened."

"You know what's totally, totally unfair of you? The way you make fun of Reg."

"Reg? What the hell does Reg have to do with anything?"

"I respect Reg. He gets up in the morning, puts on his shoes, and slugs it out in the real world. Sells them air cleaners. Brings home the bacon."

"I make fun of him? You told me Fran only married him because she wanted to play house. Never mind. No point arguing with a drunk."

"Oh right, that's the answer to everything. I'm drunk."

"Why don't I take you back to good ol Reg, see if he wants you on his hands."

"Yeah, that way maybe you'll get to fuck Fran like you want to."

He was startled enough to let the car slip away from him before he bore down on the steering wheel. He barked out a laugh. "That's not even drunk talk. That's just crazy."

"Sure." Her tone was absent, as if she no longer cared, or perhaps had even forgotten what she'd just said. An image of Fran, her offered breasts and mouth, seized Jack like a spasm, *What the hell was happening to him?* He wasn't going to fuck Fran, he had no intention of doing so, but the two of them had made him want to.

Chloe roused herself. "At least they have a real house. When are we going to be able to afford a house? Oh, forget it. What's the point."

"We have enough money. If you want some yuppie fantasy life, that's too bad."

"Sure," she said again. This time her tone was drawling, lazy. The mocking stranger inside her who felt only contempt for him.

"You know, never mind about kids. Probably not a good idea."

"I always knew I was going to have to do everything myself. Earn the paycheck. Have the children. Arrange the social life—"

"Like you did tonight. Thanks."

"—but I thought you'd have more pride than to *let* me do it. Put up more of a fight."

"You don't know what you want."

"Oh, but I guess you do. You know everything about everything in the entire, absolute world."

Once more Jack gave up on talking. He concentrated on navigating the streets. He was tired beyond fatigue now, wondering how he was ever going to be able to sleep and get up again, drag himself into to-morrow morning's classroom, get words to come out of his mouth, or reenter any part of what had been, until a few hours ago, his normal life. Chloe said, "Then you make it sound like I'm some completely greedy bitch who wants to run through some guy's money, and that is so unfair. Money is money, okay? I mean it's not that I worship it. It's more like what it represents. Stability. Serious, serious . . . Have a real life. An actual adult, not some I'm still a kid so I can just play around. Children? Don't make me laugh. You can't take care of yourself. Or me. Or anything. Let alone, you know. An actual baby."

She was running down, as she always did eventually, losing the thread of language. They were only a few blocks away from home and if Jack could just find a parking space quickly enough, no easy thing this time of night, he wouldn't have to listen to much more of her.

As if she was again aware of his thought, as if alcohol gave her some spooky, direct-current access into his brain, she sat up straighter, appeared to get a second wind. "You know what your problem is? You think you're so *sensitive,* you never have to *do* anything, just hang

around looking all droopy and superior, Mr. Artist-in-Residence. Your
problem, one of them at least, is you think you're the only one in the
world who knows things. Feels things. But everybody's really writing
their own story, baby, writing it down some place you can't see. Me.
Everybody. You— Well looky here."

Jack saw it too. Three squad cars collected in the middle of their
block, flashers shooting red and blue panic into the darkness, a couple
of halogen spots washing the sidewalk with white glare. As they drew
closer Jack felt his skin register the cold knowledge that it was their
building the police were camped in front of.

He stopped the car on the street, left the engine running. "Stay here,"
he told Chloe, who only raised her eyebrows in perfect indifference to
whatever mayhem was going on at their house.

Jack jogged a little way up the sidewalk to the nearest cop. At least
there wasn't any ambulance. The cop was standing next to one of the
squads, talking into his shoulder mike. He was a middle-aged, slab-
faced guy and he looked annoyed at having his conversation interrupted. "You blind or just stupid? You can't come through this way."

"But I live here."

"Sure. Take a hike."

"Seriously. I live here. What happened?" Jack reached for his wallet,
presented his driver's license. Proof of residence. Beyond the cop's
hammy shoulder were more cops engaged in standing around, talking
to each other, at ease, like none of this was any big deal. Jack registered
the usual mild shock at the realization that those were actual guns hol-
stered at their sagging belts. The cop with his driver's license was taking his sweet time and still hadn't given Jack any clue as to what was
going on. Something to do with H.P.R.B., he guessed, or maybe that
was just what he hoped. They'd come to haul him off for the drugs,
most likely. Damned shame.

The cop, with Jack's license still in hand, turned his back and saun-
tered off to join his fellows. Jack was able to edge closer. The sidewalk
before their building's front door sparkled with glass nuggets, and the
door itself was splintered and shattered in a jagged jigsaw pattern.

"Well this is a fine howdy-do."

Chloe had come up next to him. "What did I tell you," she said. "Safe neighborhood, right."

"Get back in the car."

"Stop telling me what to do. What do you think, somebody forgot their key? Or we got ripped off?"

"I don't know yet, all right?"

"Wow, something you don't know the answer to. I want to make a note of the date."

The cop walked back to them. Chloe huddled up against Jack, as if she were cold or frightened. He wanted to strike her. The cop got himself an eyeful of Chloe, handed Jack's license over to him. "Which apartment's yours, sir?"

"Ours," said Chloe. "His and mine. First-floor front. Did you catch whoever did it?"

"Not yet, ma'am." The cop had manners now. "But we're on it. Let's go check your apartment. Watch your step here."

"Thank you, Officer. You know people always take the police for granted until they need them," said Chloe, laying it on with a trowel. The front door was propped open and they eyed the wreckage. Above and below the central emptiness, the glass shards formed a pattern like a shark's mouth. A lump of aggregate the size of two fists lay just inside. They stared at it as if it might cause some further trouble, take it upon itself to explode or levitate.

At his doorway Mr. Dandy was holding forth to yet another cop. When he saw Jack and Chloe, he turned to them, already in mid-sentence: "—believe this? I'm going out and get me a gun. Shotgun. Next time somebody comes around here that don't belong, they're gonna get what for."

Jack sidestepped him, checked the apartment door. The lock held, undamaged. "Give me your keys," he said to Chloe, who handed them over grudgingly. When he got the door open and turned on the entryway light, everything looked the way they'd left it. Computer, TV, stereo. The cop was behind him, and Chloe was behind the cop. "Seems fine," Jack said, and the cop said it was best to make absolutely

sure. Jack led the others in a procession through the rooms. He was trying to think just what else of value they owned, couldn't come up with
much. It was surpassing weird, having a cop marching through their
bedroom, but nothing should surprise him about this night by now.

When they reached the kitchen, Jack said, "Nothing's missing. Nobody's been in here."

Mr. Dandy, uninvited, had come in behind Chloe. "We're lucky we
wasn't murdered in our beds." It was as if some unclean phantom had
materialized in their kitchen. Mr. Dandy wore his usual old man's
pants, a dull, shiny green, hiked up too high and defeated at the knees.
A plaid shirt that seemed to be rotting away underneath the arms. He
was bending his head this way and that, he was actually *sniffing,* either
the room itself or Chloe, his inflamed, red-veined nose perched over
her bare arm.

Chloe was stuck between him and the cop, the cop trying to turn his
bulk around in the narrow kitchen doorway. She was giggling. "Oh,
excuse me. I don't know who that was, but excuse me."

As soon as they'd retreated to the dining room and cleared enough
of a path, Jack pushed past them to the front door. "Where are you
going?" Chloe called after him, her voice still swallowing down a laugh.

"To move the car."

He shut the apartment door behind him. He didn't want to have to
go back inside, although he knew nothing was ever that clear or simple, that he was only in the middle of things and with no end in sight.

In the lobby a workman from the board-up service was already un-
loading a sheet of plywood. The broken glass had been swept into a
pile. Jack had to give credit to people who dealt with emergencies on a
daily basis. They had the drill down cold. There was one cop still out
on the sidewalk, maybe the partner of the officer still inside. The rest
had taken themselves off to somewhere more urgent or interesting.
Jack stepped back out of the way of the workman just as H.P.R.B. and
Raggedy Ann approached on the sidewalk. He heard them in conversation with the cop, Raggedy Ann's squeal and Rich Brezak saying, "No
shit," then saying it again, and then a third time, with different inflec-

tions to indicate the different degrees of his amazement. A moment later they stepped into the lobby and stared at the heap of glass fragments as if trying to figure out where each piece had fit into the door.

Jack guessed they were stoned. That was always a safe guess. Their expressions were rubbery and unfocused, and they walked as if their feet were half a beat behind the rest of their bodies. "Hey man," Brezak said by way of a greeting. He still wore his hair in those yarn-wrapped braids, although the hair seemed to have worked loose into a layer of fuzz, so that his head resembled a large and unkempt spider. Raggedy Ann was treading delicately on the edge of the glass pile, enjoying the crunching sound it made beneath her boots.

"What a fucked-up mess," observed Brezak, in the tone of a disgusted property owner. The cop had followed them inside. Jack wondered if he'd caught the whiff of pot smoke that clung to the two of them, but then figured the cop wouldn't care. He only wanted to finish up his business and get back to watching cop-reality shows down at the precinct.

The cop was writing in a notebook. "Who else is upstairs, anybody?"

"This old lady. I don't think she speaks English."

"Nobody's home," said the cop, still scribbling. Jack debated sending him up to pound harder on Mrs. Lacagnina's door, make sure she was accounted for, then decided against it. She was probably better off oblivious and deaf.

"Who'd want to get in here anyway," said Raggedy Ann, disdainfully. "I mean, what's the big deal? What's there to steal from this bunch?" She seemed to be smirking at Jack as she said it, or maybe he was imagining it.

"Act of vandalism," said the cop. "You see it all the time. Punks don't need a reason to act like punks."

"I wouldn't break in here even for grins. This place is so nothing."

Rich Brezak said, "Yeah, right. You're made for better things. We through here?"

"Unless you got some other damage or theft, sure, you're through."

"I guess we should go make sure. Hey." Brezak got Raggedy Ann's attention and herded her toward the stairs. The girl gave Brezak one of her pouting, let's-have-instant-sex looks, and started up ahead of him. Brezak raised his eyebrows at Jack, in invitation to witness that he was about to get himself some, then followed the girl's lolling ass, step by step. A little bop in his step, a jaunty, stoned, soft shoe.

Jack stood for a moment, listening to Chloe's voice trilling behind the closed apartment door. "Excuse me," he said to the cop, who wasn't paying attention to him anyway, and walked quickly down the back hallway.

The yard was empty. That was only what he expected. There was a gate that led to the alley, and this was supposed to be kept latched. One more thing Brezak was sloppy about; when he did manage to get his garbage out, he was just as likely to leave the gate open. It was un-latched now. Jack listened, testing the silence. He felt stupid, self-consciously stupid, but he whispered, "Ivory?"

Small sound from the other side of the wall. Something shifting or scraping. He pushed the gate open and stepped into the alley's moon-scape of gravel and garbage and power lines. The girl was pressed flat against the fence. A security light from across the way turned her hair and skin so white they were nearly blue. Her eyes glittered, hard as marbles. He realized he had never seen her in daylight.

"What are you—" He stopped. "What did you do to your arm?"

She was holding it close to her chest and it was leaking black blood. "Nothing."

"Nothing hell."

"Leamme alone."

"I'm not going to bust you," he said to reassure her, and then was forced to wonder why he was not.

She said nothing. Although the night was warm and calm, there was a tremor in her shoulders and tight-clenched jaw. Her eyes were still pointed at him but the seeing had gone out of them. He had the sense that she was dangerous, that she might shriek or strike him out of pure reflex. But she was also a shivering child.

He began talking to her in a matter-of-fact, calming voice, about nothing at all, about the kids in the class he was teaching this week, how funny they were, how he actually did like teaching, or wanted to like it, and on good days you did, but on bad days you thought about how little they paid you to have a really bad day, and that's when the sourness began, although you could always lift yourself up with some bit of good feeling. Sometimes the kids were sweet almost in spite of themselves. When she'd finally stopped that high-voltage-wire shaking, he said, "Come on, this way," and started off down the alley. He saw that she wasn't moving from her spot against the fence. "The police are still out front, you want to wait until they get around to checking back here?"

She followed, but slowly. Jack was about to say something impatient when he remembered her bad leg. It was half a block to the end of the alley, another slow passage around the corner to where he hoped like hell nobody'd made off with his car. They hadn't. The taillights glowed and the engine chugged in the middle of the quiet street. The one squad car was still angled in front of the building's door, but even its flasher had been turned off. Party over.

"Get in," he told the girl, holding the passenger door, and she ducked under his arm and got herself inside double quick.

Once he'd gotten behind the wheel and put the car in gear and eased it past the apartment building—lights on, upstairs and down—Jack glanced over at her. It was a confusion to his eyes to see her there, in the space that was always Chloe's. He couldn't remember the last time he'd had another woman in his car. "How bad is your arm?"

"It's no big deal." She was wearing another of her long, hobbling skirts; she'd pulled it down as far as she could over her drawn-up knees, as if she might indeed be cold. He couldn't see her injured arm; she had it tucked away inside her denim shirt. When they reached the corner of Clark she said, "You can let me out here."

"Why here?"

"Because I don't want to bleed all over your car."

"If that arm was about to fall off, you'd still say it was no big deal, wouldn't you?"

"It's not falling off, okay?" She made a show of being exasperated, of sighing. It made her seem even younger, a kid acting uppity with a parent, but at least she was back to her usual smart-mouth self.

With one hand Jack rummaged behind him and came up with an old towel. "Wrap this around it, apply some pressure." Because he didn't want her to jump out of the car, he kept moving, turning south on Clark. "How about I take you to an emergency room."

"I don't like hospitals."

"That's not the point."

"It quit bleeding, see? Or it almost quit. If you want to take me any-place, you can take me home. Turn here."

She directed him south on Western Avenue, then on toward Hum-boldt Park, through neighborhoods where there was less and less good news, more and more beaten-down blocks of four flats and houses that might have been said to have seen better days, if those earlier days had been more hopeful in the first place. It wasn't one of the worst parts of the city, those were reserved for people like his students, but it was a good three or four notches down from where he lived. It was the kind of neighborhood Chloe wanted people to envision when she com-plained. He tried to think about Chloe but his mind veered away from her. There was a space of emptiness where she'd been, like the broken emptiness of the door.

He said, "What were you trying to do with that stunt anyway, were you drunk or high, what?"

"I bet you think that explains stuff. Being fucked up."

It unnerved him to realize that Chloe had said almost the same thing, that he seemed unable to escape her, or the rest of the bastard night. Everything had followed him here.

He hadn't answered back before, but he did now: "Yeah, I do. It makes people do things they're sorry for later."

"Well I'm not sorry."

He kept speaking in the same heavy, censorious tone, as if it was the only voice left to him. "I hope you enjoyed your little tantrum. I just want to point out, once more for the record, that the guy's really not worth it."

"Thanks."

"You don't have to do this to yourself. There are other guys out there. Ones who won't treat you like absolute shit."

She turned to look at him then. Streetlights slid over her face in a series of rapid white bars. She was going to say something about Chloe, he was sure of it, but no, she couldn't possibly know what had happened . . .

"Fuck you."

"Nice." It was a relief to him to be talking to her in this way, he was accustomed to it.

"Why do you care, huh? What do you know about me, nothing, there's all different ways of being fucked up. I wanted to break something, I wanted to pick up a rock and throw it, so I did. Maybe you're not that way but I am. Here. Turn here. I feel things I don't want to feel, so what, just leave me alone."

She had burst out with this string of words and now she came to the end of them, or maybe she didn't trust herself to keep speaking without losing control. There was a small fabric bag around her neck, a kind of homemade purse, and with her good hand she began to rummage around for her keys. Jack thought they were not really angry with each other. He might be only another sort of rock she wanted to throw. She was right, he didn't know her, as he no longer knew Chloe, or his own heart, or what miserable confusion had led him to this place. The street Ivory directed him to was occupied on one side by some sort of industrial concern, Lownes and Co., a nondescript name that told you nothing, a long, windowless sheet-metal building surrounded by cyclone fencing topped off with four canted rows of barbed wire, as if something precious was inside. There were a couple of tanker trucks parked in a lot behind the gates, and some vents and ductwork that might have held compressor or exhaust fans. Who knew what they made there, paint or industrial adhesives or ball bearings, some aspect of human enterprise with its own structures and economies and history that he would know nothing of, as he knew nothing of the world itself.

Ivory was leaning forward. "See that light? You can let me off there."

Jack pulled over. There was a narrow two-story building of some oddly painted brick, the paint the exact color of dried mud in a hot climate, a slit of a window or two in the expanse of ugly wall, so that it gave the impression of a fortress or a jail.

"You want your towel back? Because I can leave it here, or I can wash it and get it back to you."

"Let me see that arm."

She said no, but she didn't make any move to leave the car. Some exhaustion she'd been too stubborn to give in to until now. Jack cut the engine, got out, went around to her side and opened her door. He expected some further back talk or protest from her but she was quiet. When he peeled the towel away from her arm, when he got himself to look past the shock of the gaudy blood staining the towel and her shirt and even the skirt where she'd held the arm, he saw some long scratches, already beginning to mound up with welts, and one deeper, oozing wound where the glass had gouged her. Blood was still leaking from it in a slow, puddling stream.

"I think there might be some glass in it still." She sounded matter-of-fact, or maybe that too was fatigue.

Jack pressed the towel back into place. "Hold this," he directed. "Hold your arm up." He was genuinely alarmed now that he'd seen the extent of the bleeding. She should get to a doctor, but he doubted his ability to manage her to such an extent. He said, "I want to look at that in better light."

"Why? It's gross." But she got out of the car and hitched along ahead of him, to one side of the building and down a half flight of cement stairs, where she unlocked a door that opened into darkness.

Jack hung back until she'd turned on the light. "So this is where I live," Ivory said, stepping aside to let him in. "So it sucks."

They stood in a kitchen, a lamp dangling low over a small table. The lightbulb was covered with a Japanese paper globe, pale green with a pattern of painted bamboo. The rest of the room or rooms beyond were in deep shadow. Jack deliberately kept his eyes from them. He didn't want to know anything else sad about her.

"Do you have bandages, antiseptic? Anything like that?"

He waited while she stepped out of the circle of light. He heard her footsteps, then rummaging noises, then she was back, dumping things in a heap on the table. Jack told her to sit. He found paper towels, ran water in the sink, and began swabbing away at the dried blood. The cut was meaty and inflamed, perhaps three inches long. One end was deeply incised. With the paper towel he prodded, then extracted a kernel of glass and two fine slivers. There was still a great deal of blood. The blood smell carved a path through his nostrils and into his brain, making him languid. There was another scent beneath that, her musky hair and skin. He had to remind himself that she was a child, she was angry and damaged and it was only through a long series of accidents that he was here at all.

The air in the room was warm and heavy, but the girl's skin was cool to his touch. She was quiet and let him work. The forked vein at her wrist was hardly perceptible, as if everything had already drained from it. Her upturned hand was slight and dangling. He looked down on the crown of her head and the haphazard tangle of her hair, which the light turned to pale green straw. He was having trouble catching his breath. The blood, the closeness of the room, the growing wound of his own life, the green, underwater light—he thought he might faint, or embarrass himself in some even worse fashion.

He washed the cut with liquid soap, then swabbed it with hydrogen peroxide and squeezed out a line of antiseptic cream. He was relieved to be able to do a workmanlike job of it. The girl watched him. He saw her eyes and their sparse, childlike lashes following his hands. He pressed a gauze pad in place and was glad to see that the bleeding had slowed. But it was difficult to tape it down and keep the pressure on. The tape was of the cheapest, paper kind, and it turned sweaty and useless as he fumbled with it. "Here," the girl said, her voice just a breath above the silence. "Let me . . ."

She wrapped a layer of tape, then pulled a thin scarf from around her neck and laid it over that, indicating that he should use it as a bandage. He was clumsy here too, he was afraid of hurting her, getting the scarf too tight. Finally he managed it. They both stared down at the flimsy pink silk, waiting to see if it would hold the blood. She said, in the same low breath of a voice, "I think . . ."

She trailed off without finishing. "What?" Jack said, or tried to say. He had to clear his throat to get the rust and spit out of it, but before he could come up with words she was out of her chair, she was kneeling on the floor before him, her hands on his thighs, shoving him backward until he collided with the sink. Then she was reaching for his belt, unzipping him, his shock and alarm not keeping up with what was already *Jesus Christ* happening. He couldn't speak. His hands tried to dislodge her but he was still afraid of hurting her, still thinking that way, and she already had him out of his clothes, her mouth was around him and in spite of himself he was growing big, he was letting it happen.

Her mouth worked him slowly at first, more tongue than anything else. He groaned and reached down to grip her head on both sides, making her move faster. For a time he was afraid he wouldn't be able to come and then she found a steady, harder rhythm and everything changed and he was afraid he would come right away. The girl stopped for long enough to take a deep, ragged breath. His feeling ebbed and when she started in again he was able to hold off another minute more and then another and then it built again and there was no stopping it, oh crazy sad bad he was going to be sorry forever her hands and greedy wet mouth. He pushed hard into her and cried out and she swallowed him down.

He kept his eyes closed. His breath and blood and heart were still harsh and racing and a black fist of dread was squeezing the last bit of pleasure out of him. He was sore from her mouth, and sticky, and he fumbled to pull his clothes back together again.

When he did finally unseal his eyes, the girl was watching him from the other side of the table. The lamp on its cord was swinging, they must have bumped into it. The circle of green light wobbled. He felt seasick. He said, "Why did you do that?"

"Didn't you like it?"

"I didn't . . . God, what's the matter with you?"

"It was like, thank you."

He couldn't read her face in the shifting light. "Thank you . . ."

"For the ride and all."

"Jesus."

"So now we're even. It was okay, wasn't it? I tried to do it right. I bet you don't get it like that at home, do you?"

"That's not . . . Don't . . . ," he began, but a wave of sickness rose up in him, he was desperate to breathe some cleaner air, he refused to hear any more. He turned and found the door with his hands, fumbled the lock and stepped outside.

Then he was in his car, driving through streets that were as dark and blind and secret and sad as anyone's life, and in spite of everything he knew good and well that a part of him had wanted to throw a rock through glass.

Five

It was very early, not yet six. They had slept for only a few hours, and had already said some of what needed to be said. Chloe watched from the couch as Jack loaded bottles into a cardboard box. The three bottles still left of the good Shiraz. Half a bottle of white wine from the refrigerator. The last of the Galway Pipe port. Odds and ends of hard liquor, kept mostly for company. Remnant of a twelve-pack of Coors Light. Chloe stirred.

"I never drink beer."

"Doesn't matter. Clean break."

"Whatever you feel you need to do. I completely understand."

Chloe was wrapped in a quilt and only her head and bare feet were visible. Her skin was white and drawn. There were fine lines around her mouth and eyes, like cracks in porcelain. Overnight she looked ten years older. She was going to call in sick to work, but Jack was planning to teach his class. He didn't want to be here with her.

He carried the box outside, through the back gate and into the alley, where he left it for some lucky waste hauler or homeless person. Eight hours ago he had been standing in this very spot with the girl, but that was one more thought he was unable to hold in his bruised mind.

He walked back inside and past Chloe without speaking. He only wanted a shower and a chance to get to Starbucks before his long bus ride. The bathroom mirror was not his friend. His eyes were so dry and grainy that it hurt to close them.

Chloe stood outside the bathroom door. He sensed her there. "What?"

"I'm really sorry."

"I know."

"Please open the door."

"I have to get ready."

"Please."

Jack opened the door. Chloe was still wrapped in the quilt. "I didn't mean any of it. I don't even remember most of it."

"Then how do you know you didn't mean it?"

"Tell me you forgive me."

"I want to. I will. But give me a little time."

"Please, Jack. I can't stand this."

"Just let me take my shower, okay? And go to school and clear my head and get some sleep."

He closed the door. But when he'd stripped off his clothes and was standing beneath the running water, letting it pour over him, turning him into a creature that was all skin and no thought, he heard the door open again. Chloe pulled back the shower curtain and stepped in behind him. He felt her arms around his waist, her head against his back. He stood without moving. Her hands dropped and began searching for him. He turned, dislodging her.

"No, Chloe."

"God I've ruined everything."

"No you haven't. I just can't right now."

"You mean you don't want to."

He kissed the top of her head. Her eyelashes were wet from crying, and in her nakedness she was small and abject, like a disaster victim. He couldn't bear to think about making love to her. He felt as if his body might never be entirely his own again. "It'll be all right. We can talk later."

"I'll go to AA. A counselor. Tell me what to do. Tell me how I can fix things or I'll just start screaming."

"Why don't you go back to bed. Everything seems worse when you're this tired."

"You won't give me a break, will you? You're going to keep dragging this out."

"That's not it at all."

"Because you're the kind of person who makes judgments. You've already judged me."

"Now you're being ridiculous."

"Just say it. You hope I won't be here when you get back. Well maybe I won't be."

And then she was gone, stepping out of the shower and closing the bathroom door behind her. When Jack finished and went in to dress, she was lying in bed with her face turned toward the wall.

"Chloe?"

No answer. He knew she wasn't asleep, but it seemed easiest to pretend that she was.

The plywood over the front door blocked most of the light from the street. It made the lobby seem smaller and meaner, the stage for some crabbed and diminished drama. The air that met him outside was gray with haze, the humidity already thickening. His head felt as if it was stuffed with flannel. He looked around furtively, he half-expected to see the girl lying in wait for Brezak, or even for himself, anything seemed possible, any wrong or crazy thing.

But she wasn't there, thank God. He stood in line for his coffee and then stood in line for the bus and rode through the funky streets with the bus chugging its obscene exhaust and the bursts of radio noise that swam past them in traffic and the fat lady next to him shifting her weight from thigh to thigh and saying, Jesus, Jesus, but in a way that was conversational rather than vexed or prayerful. They traveled south on Ashland, crossing three expressways, under cement-damp viaducts or across overpasses that gave him dizzying views of roads tying themselves in concrete knots, and steady streams of cars. It was another hot day, or rather, the heat had never dissipated. Heat islands. That was what they called it when every brick and paved surface trapped and stored the air and the temperature kept building and old people too thrifty or timid to turn on air-conditioning or even open their windows were carried away in refrigerated coroners' vans. He reminded himself to check on Mrs. Lacagnina.

After a time Jack was the only white person on the bus. He was used to this by now, he even recognized one or two of the passengers. His head drooped and his eyes closed. He slept a little as the bus rocked and wheezed and carried him down the north-south spine of the city. He dreamed all the lives around him, *Jesus, Jesus,* as strangers jostled and coughed and conversed, he dreamed that his own life was simply one among many, like the cells of a single body. The dream consoled him. He felt for the first time that his troubles were nothing extraordinary: they were only his allotted portion of the world's troubles. When he opened his eyes and came to himself again, he was able to step into his day, his classroom, pick up his normal routine. He was still unhappy but his mind was more settled, and even as he called the roll and administered quizzes he was busy trying to work things through.

This morning had gone badly in all the ways he had expected it to go badly, with Chloe crying and threatening and wanting him to feel sorry for her. Whenever she was desperate, trapped in some misbehavior, she fought back in this way, tried to deflect the blame onto him. Jack had a foreboding that this too had something to do with alcohol, that much of her history and manner and very self might be intertwined with it and there was more dishonesty to her than he wanted to admit. He was deeply angry with her. The anger was deserved. Then in spite of himself he remembered Ivory, his body remembered her with a flood of sensations. He would have to forgive Chloe. He would have to forgive himself.

Chloe was going to have to stop drinking entirely. She had agreed as much. He would stop also, to show that this was something they were in together. At the moment that didn't seem like a sacrifice, but a relief and a penance. Perhaps things would never be restored to what they had been. You couldn't unsay what you'd said, unhear what you'd heard. You couldn't make broken glass whole again. But you could move forward. Love each other in spite of knowing the worst, or maybe because of it. That was what a marriage was, or should be.

During Jack's lunch period he tried to call her but there was no answer. Maybe she'd gone in to work after all, or she might have turned the phone off so she could sleep. He thought about trying her again before he started for home, but decided against it, and began his long trip back north in the slow late-afternoon traffic. When he reached his stop, he walked another two blocks to their favorite deli, where he bought chicken salad and onion rolls and ginger ale. At a sidewalk stand he picked up a plastic sleeve of yellow daisies. Peace offerings.

The front door had already been repaired with new glass. He took that as a good and hopeful sign. But Chloe wasn't in the apartment. She hadn't left him a note. Jack hardly expected that. He knew she intended to make him worry about her, and this was meant to be his punishment. It was somehow necessary to Chloe, to her sense of grievance, that he be punished. He tried calling her at work and got her voice mail. He listened to her brisk, sweet voice, that other Chloe who was neither angry nor estranged from him, and then he lay down in their bed and slept.

Jack opened his eyes to darkness. The key worked in the front-door lock and he heard the sounds of something lifting, scraping. Ivory? He almost spoke it aloud, but that shocked him fully awake. He rose up on one elbow and turned on the light.

Chloe walked the length of the hallway without looking in on him. He heard her in the kitchen. Light switch, refrigerator, running water. She would know he was here, would have seen his keys and briefcase as she came in. So they were still at war and nothing was over yet.

She was drinking a glass of water at the sink. Jack came up behind her and put his arms around her.

Chloe said, "I haven't been drinking. In case you're trying to smell it on me."

Jack stepped away from her. "Good. Fine. Way to go. Nice to see you too."

"Don't tell me you weren't thinking it."

"I wasn't. I'm not going to do that to you." He hoped that this was the truth. It was too easy to imagine things going the other way, the endless ugly round of accusations and denials.

This seemed to take some of the fight out of her. She put the glass down and rubbed at her eyes with the back of her hand. "I feel like absolute shit."

"Did you go into work?"

"Not until late. Then I stayed so I could catch up. I told them I had a dentist's appointment this morning. Beats saying sloppy drunk and hungover."

Jack supposed it was good for her to be making jokes about it, even bitter ones. They would have to find some way to talk about everything. The clock above the sink said almost nine. He realized he hadn't eaten since lunch. "You hungry?"

"A little. Yeah. Food. I remember food."

From the refrigerator Jack brought out the chicken salad and ginger ale, a jar of pickles and a wedge of yellow cheese. He sliced the onion rolls in half and set out plates and silverware on the kitchen table.

"Did you get all this? And the flowers? That was so sweet."

They sat down together and ate their supper, and it was almost as if their troubles had never happened, as if all it took to forget them was feeding a simple hunger. Chloe asked how school had been and he told her. And wasn't it hot, though it was supposed to be cooler tomorrow, and once more Jack had forgotten about Mrs. Lacagnina, which was understandable but made him feel that he'd compromised himself with good intentions, and then Chloe said, "I need to specifically apologize—"

"No you don't."

"You don't even know what I was going to say."

"Yes I do."

Chloe said, "Look at me. Please. The only reason I said all that about your writing—"

"You were drunk. I understand that."

"No, I mean sure I was drunk, but did you ever think maybe it's because I'm jealous?"

He hadn't thought that. He did look at her then.

"It was something I used to do, remember? Maybe you didn't really know me back then, maybe I wasn't even that good at it, but hey, I *wanted* to be good. And I gave up on it and you didn't and I'm just saying that sometimes it's hard for me to deal with."

"I didn't know it was that important to you."

"Well now you do. I mean okay, it's stupid to think I would have gotten very far with it—"

"It's not stupid at all. You're a terrifically verbal person. You can do anything you put your mind to."

Chloe regarded the half-finished sandwich on her plate as if it had tricked her into eating it. "You don't have to keep shining everything up like that."

"I'm not. I'm being factual. Writing just wasn't something you chose to pursue. You had other interests."

"So you wouldn't mind if I started up again. Writing."

She watched him swallow the surprise of this down. He said, "You don't need my permission."

"I know that. I just don't want it to seem like I'm going into competition with you."

It did seem like something of the sort, but of course he was not allowed to say this. "What is it you want to write?"

Chloe considered this, or seemed to, but Jack had a feeling that this was actually something rehearsed and calculated, a test of him in ways he did not yet understand. Since that morning she had regained her complexion and fixed her hair in some new way, a headful of black Gypsy curls, and she wore a white blouse he didn't remember seeing before, with embroidery set into the sleeves, and although he was used to a certain chameleonlike aspect of her beauty, how she could change her looks in this way, there was something uncanny about it. She said, "I haven't yet decided if it's going to be fiction or nonfiction."

Jack said, neutrally, "That's kind of an important thing to get straight from the beginning. Whether you're making things up or not."

She leaned over the table, suddenly animated. "No, see, it's definitely going to be autobiographical. Like a journal. A record of everything that's going on with me now, in terms of drinking and you and me and my goals and whatever else. I thought it would help me to make some changes." She waited while Jack nodded to signify that this was a good idea. "But I don't want to impose arbitrary factual limits on it. Because when you try to define 'fact' or 'truth,' the very words begin to negate themselves. There are different narratives implicit in every action and every relationship. Different ways in which language accommodates subjectivity, the intersection between self and other. There's one version of events that we all agree to validate. There are alternative narratives, what we believe happens, what we wish or fear would happen. That's what I'm interested in. That zone of ambiguity and disjointure."

She finished, a little out of breath, and it was Jack's turn to say something. "Wow. You have this all planned out."

"And that's bad?"

"No, not at all. You've obviously given this a lot of thought."

"Oh don't worry. It's not going to be one of those tell-alls. I bet there's some things you would never ever write about."

Christ yes. He shrugged, eloquently, he hoped.

"Well I'm the same way. Relax. And I'm gonna surprise you. I'm going to write a hell of a book. I've even got a title. 'Anesthesia.' Everything's going to center around the metaphor of pain, and pain killing, and of course that's one of the things that alcohol does. But the metaphor will be ironic. Because the reader is always a participant/voyeur in the narrative, and by implication, another inflicter of pain. I want the whole concept of authorship to become subversive."

"I never thought of it quite like that. The voyeur part." Jack was treading cautiously here. He didn't want to say that it sounded like more of the old, top-heavy grad school thinking. He was afraid that at some point Chloe would present him with a wrongheaded and hopeless piece of writing that he would have to read and respond to. But Chloe seemed so genuinely excited, so hopeful and energized, he didn't have the heart or the nerve to discourage her. "It's really good that you want to take something negative and deal with it creatively. I think it will be"—he hesitated slightly over the word, it felt false in his mouth—"empowering."

Chloe nodded. "Exactly. That's what I'm hoping. It's mostly this personal thing, so I don't know if anybody else would ever be interested in it, I mean want to publish it . . ."

She stopped, shrugged. "I know. Dumb idea. Publishing."

"Not dumb. You never know how far you can go with something when you're first starting out." In fact he thought it was nearly delusional of her to think about publishing. Chloe hadn't yet done any of the hard work of pushing words around on a page, didn't know how easy it was for writing to never get written. But in order to keep her from dissolving into another fit of self-doubt, he had to sound more upbeat than he really was. "I think you could end up with something really good."

"No you don't, but it's sweet of you to say it."

Then she laughed. "You really don't have a poker face, you know?"

"If you say so." He laughed along with her. Ha ha.

"It's okay, silly. You're just trying to be nice, I appreciate that. But I can tell every thought you think. That expression you have when you're trying to be really smooth? I love it. I bet that's what you looked like when you were five years old and told your mother you weren't the one who broke the lamp."

"I'm that bad, huh."

"Oh I don't blame you for being skeptical. I'm just starting out as a writer, what do I know?"

"I'm sorry if I was acting like the resident expert."

"Well that's what you are. But I'm going to give you a run for your money." Chloe smiled and reached across the table and touched her fist lightly to Jack's chin. "I can't believe how good I feel about this. About quitting drinking and getting started on the writing and being somebody who actually uses the right side of their brain for once. Not just Little Miss Business Plan. This morning I was in despair, I couldn't see my way out of this hole we'd dug, okay, I dug. I want to accept responsibility here. Then it's like it all came together, and I'm feeling so good and positive about you and me and please tell me you feel good too, because I really need to know that."

Her most beautiful smile. It teased the fullness of her mouth into a pure and perfect curve. Jack pressed the tip of one finger to her lips and said, "I do."

And because he meant it his face had no lie in it and Chloe tugged at his sleeve to get him to stand up from the table and they embraced there, swaying a little. Chloe's hands pressed against his waistband and for one panicked moment he remembered that other kitchen and what the girl had done to him and now he was afraid that his body, not his treacherous face, would give him away if she . . .

But Chloe drew back from him and pulled him toward the bedroom. Jack reached across the bed and turned off the lamp. He didn't trust himself to be seen in any way. In darkness he thought he might manage to convince them both, Chloe and himself, that love was something you could heal.

Afterward, Chloe's soft weight rested on top of him. His body, drained, exhausted, kept sinking into sleep, but his mind was still alert and shrill. No matter how hard he'd tried to push his way out of himself and into her, he had only succeeded for that one moment, now receding, the best you could do and never enough. Maybe there was nothing in life that was not conflicted and imperfect and wounded, love most of all, and he was no more of a fool or a liar, no more lonely, than anyone else who walked the earth.

He was still awake when the music in the kid's apartment ratcheted up from a growl into the forbidden zone. The air ducts vibrated, a faint, metallic humming, and the music itself was lost in the thudding bass. Jack was almost glad to have this excuse to get out of bed. The kid, at least, was someone you could depend on for consistency and unambiguous jerkdom. If he wasn't there to be despised and scorned, life would be that much less predictable.

Chloe was sound asleep and didn't stir when he eased her aside. How often had he done this very thing, roused himself out of bed to make the trip upstairs. It felt like a recurring dream, or maybe he should look at it as normal, whatever that had come to mean.

Once he was on the stairs he could make out the song, one of the jazzy, upbeat cuts, about the pleasures of smoking ganja. It was punctuated by the kid's voice expressing something enthusiastic. His words were smeared into the music so that it might have been either the kid or the singer saying he was gone down de road, mon, and feelin mighty fine.

Jack raised his fist to the door and pounded. After a long enough pause to irritate him, he heard locks unsnapping, and Brezak saying,

"Yeah, I know, I know," and the singer agreeing, and then the door opened. Brezak stepped aside as it swung inward. Dank, incense-tinged smoke escaped in an almost visible plume. Brezak was already working the remote that punched the volume down to the top end of the permissible range.

"It's cool," said Brezak, returning to the entryway and bobbing his chin at Jack. He had the kind of beard that made him look like he should be wearing underpants over his face. "Right before you showed up, I was thinking, Uh-oh, I better cut that down, my man Jack's gonna kick my ass. Am I psychic or what?"

From the passageway that led back to the kitchen and the bedroom, Ivory came toward them, her stumping gait tangling another of her long skirts as she walked. She entered the living room, waved briefly to Jack, and sat down on the couch to leaf through a magazine.

Jack said, "Yeah, psychic."

"And I bet you knew that I knew that you were coming. It's like we already had the whole conversation."

"Sure. Let's just not have it again tonight."

"Oh he's quick, my man Jack. Isn't he sharp?" He appealed to the girl, who hiked up her skirt and crossed her legs beneath her before she replied:

"Sharp as a major tack."

She was immersed in her magazine. One bare foot swung back and forth in a half arc, just visible at the hem of her skirt.

Brezak said, "He's a little uptight around the edges. But he can work on that. Right, honeybunch?"

"Right," said Ivory from the couch. Her hair fell over the magazine pages and she shook it aside.

Jack didn't like the way Brezak was looking at him, his eyebrows wiggling in some Groucho Marx–style leer, if Groucho was way stoned. Jack's skin went cold, wondering what Ivory had said to him. He had no trust in her discretion. He had no reason to trust her about anything. The idea of Brezak having such knowledge about him was unbearable.

"And don't worry about the music. We were just about to turn in."

"Sure," said Jack stupidly. He realized that Brezak was waiting for him to leave. "Good night, then."

The door closed. Jack started down the stairs, swearing weakly to himself. Somehow he'd gotten himself involved in the ongoing comic book saga of the kid's life. Somehow, hell: he knew exactly what he'd done, how he had bulled and blundered and refused to keep his distance from everything perverse and wrongheaded. Dirty little secret. He liked a taste of walking on the wild side. At least until he got caught at it. Why was the girl back here with Brezak, where was Raggedy Ann? How had she managed it, had she broken in again? Had she gotten around to telling him about that particular trick?

If part of what he felt was jealousy, and he had to admit he did, and if that shamed him, then it was only what he deserved.

By the time he reached his own apartment, he'd decided that bluffing it out was his only option. He didn't know for a fact that Ivory had said anything. He couldn't let nerves and paranoia get the best of him. Even if she had been telling tales to Brezak, he could deal with it. Stare the kid down or avoid him altogether. Nothing irrevocable had happened. Nothing of the sort would ever happen again, he would make sure of that. Things might all be working out, in some messy way. The girl and the kid. Him and Chloe. Status quo restored. Just a little less uptight around the edges.

He reentered his own bed, and the zone of warmth around Chloe, and the faint, unmistakable smell of sex that rose from her. The music upstairs was only a pulse now. He let it beat behind his closed eyes until his thoughts unraveled into sleep.

Whoever it was that forecast cooler weather had lied. It was the next morning, and good neighbor Jack stood at Mrs. Lacagnina's door, knocking away. The air in the upstairs hallways was so dizzy hot and thick, it took an effort to draw it into his lungs. Jack tried to hear if Mrs. Lacagnina's air conditioner was laboring away behind her door. Nothing. That wasn't a good sign. The units were old and undersized, and when the temperatures climbed this high, they only stirred the tepid air. Jack and Chloe had already replaced theirs. Maybe Mrs. Lacagnina's daughter could get her a new air conditioner, or at least get her to use the one she had.

Brezak's door was shut and no one within was awake, as far as Jack could tell. Fine with him. They were, officially, none of his business.

"Mrs. Lacagnina?" He knocked again. He remembered seeing her the day before yesterday. Or maybe the day before that. She'd traded her hideous black coat for an equally ancient and bunchy cardigan sweater, which she wore over a long cotton dress. White cotton socks, sandals, and a cabbage-rose print head scarf, tied underneath her chin. The sight of her had reminded him of something troubling, fairy-tale witches, perhaps, figures of fear and dowdy malice. But that was the crazy heat that made everything ugly and queer. It was the sixth straight day of temperatures in the high nineties. The sky was a blistered, sunless gray. Newspapers kept a tally of what were called heat-related deaths: twenty-four as of last night. There were times he missed California, where people died of normal things like getting shot. The city had declared a heat emergency and had opened cooling centers and urged people to check on the elderly and not think barmy thoughts such as how they resembled witches.

Fortunately (he supposed), there was no need to check on Mr. Dandy, who had taken to hanging around the lobby more often than was usual, mopping at his forehead with a plaid-bordered white handkerchief. Jack didn't think they sold handkerchiefs like that anymore. Mr. Dandy must have bought up a stock of them before they closed Montgomery Ward's. "Hot enough for you?" Mr. Dandy offered whenever anyone came in or out, and then you had to find something to say back to him, different sprightly versions of yes, it certainly was hot.

"Mrs. Lacagnina?"

Jack had to bawl it out. He tried not to think about Brezak and Ivory, tangled up in the wreckage of their bed, waking up and listening. Finally, he detected signs of life on the other side of Mrs. Lacagnina's door. She was running some sort of appliance, maybe an electric broom, that made a distant, whirring sound. So she was moving around in there. But he might stand there all day knocking without her hearing him.

Jack went back downstairs and returned with a pen and paper. In big block letters he wrote, HELLO! VERY HOT TODAY! HOW ARE YOU? YOUR NEIGHBOR, APT. 1-A.

He drew a crude sketch of a thermometer, at least that's what he meant it to be, with the mercury bubbling up to the top, and more exclamation points and zigzags surrounding it. Only then did Jack notice its unfortunate resemblance to a penis. He hoped Mrs. Lacagnina wouldn't take the wrong meaning and think he was inviting himself in for a hot time. He waited until the sound of the cleaning machine moved closer. He knelt down and worked the paper beneath the crack in the door, pushing it from side to side.

The electric noise stopped. Jack heard Mrs. Lacagnina take a step toward the door, then halt. He agitated the paper again. He wondered if her eyes were as bad as her hearing. Did she even know any English?

She stooped to pick up the paper. Jack heard the small, orthopedic sounds of her knees and spine creaking, and her slight shadow darkening the space beneath the door. Then the shadow withdrew. He wondered how long he ought to wait for a response. But it was only another few moments before the paper pushed beneath the door again. In pencil she had written, HOT NO GOOD. The letters had a sturdy look to them, as if she'd held the pencil in her fist and borne down.

Jack considered how to convey all the cautions about heat stroke and the like. Finally he wrote, AIR CONDITIONER? And sent the paper back her way.

He waited. Sweat collected behind his bare knees and made him pluck at his T-shirt to pull it away from his miserable skin. He had to wonder just how hot it was in Mrs. Lacagnina's apartment, which he imagined as decorated with crucifixes and gloomy sepia portraits of the lost Mr. Lacagnina. What did she do in there all day anyway? What did she hear inside her head, conversations from the past, replayed like old wax records? Or was the sound of deafness just blankness, roaring?

From behind the closed door, something chunked and hummed. Mrs. Lacagnina's air conditioner coming to life. The paper inched its way beneath the door again. She had crossed out words so it said, simply, GOOD.

If he did nothing else right today, at least he had done this. He made his way back downstairs, where Chloe was getting ready to leave for work. Her high heels made a bright, busy sound as she went back and forth between the rooms. The steam from her shower mixed with her scented shampoo and powder and cologne. It all made him happy, the commotion and the dense, perfumed air and waking up in bed with Chloe and knowing that he would wake up with her the next day and the next. And you never could tell where loving a woman might lead you, through just what fierce troubles, but he had to admit that here, this morning, was a very fine place. Chloe walked out of the kitchen with her coffee cup and laughed at him in his scruffy shorts and T-shirt. "You're a mess."

Jack regarded his bare, uncouth legs, his feet in grimy flip-flops. "Yeah. I guess I should change into a clean housedress."

"Funny guy." She was wearing a gray summer suit and a pink blouse. With her long legs and her elegant shoes, she made him think of some tall cool flower, an orchid, perhaps.

"Come here so I can defile you."

"Uh-uh." But she stood still as he drew her in with an arm around her shoulders, allowed him to kiss the smooth skin at her temple. He said, "How about if I groom myself all morning, then meet you somewhere for lunch?"

"Oh, I don't know. I mean, this might not be the best day for that. I'm still so behind from yesterday . . ."

He had known, even before she spoke, that she was going to say no. She said, "Sorry. Rain check?"

"Sure. No problem."

"Really, if they weren't riding us so hard about the damned market research . . ."

She sighed, to indicate exasperation. He figured that she was being protective of her work, her world of work. It was a place that she wanted to keep separate as much as possible from her life with him. He understood this, or told himself he did. Chloe could go into the office and be bright and competent and charming and not have to worry about all the sad-sack baggage of the last couple of days. She wouldn't want him showing up, intruding, a reminder of weakness and distress. She needed her space. Okay. It might hurt his feelings a little, but it was only a lunch. He said, "Maybe some other time."

"Absolutely. Count on it. As soon as—"

A woman shrieked and kept on shrieking, somewhere over their heads. Jack and Chloe looked at each other. "God," Jack said. The sound unstrung his nerves. "What are they—"

Rapid, thudding footsteps, and words in the shrieking now, Geddout, geddout, geddout, and more they couldn't hear, a confusion of voices, a muddy sound mixed up with slamming doors. Chloe handed the phone to Jack. "Call somebody, 911."

"I don't know . . ."

"What are you waiting for, he's killing her!"

"Just hold on." Jack unlocked their front door and stepped out into the lobby. From there the racket was less distinct. If it had happened late at night it might not have been so disturbing. But it was still early, not yet nine, they were never up that early, and then the shrieking started in again. Jack was halfway up the stairs when the kid's apartment door opened and crashed back into the wall behind it.

"Goddamn bitch!"

"Bitch yourself!"

By the time he reached the top of the steps, the two of them, Ivory and Raggedy Ann, were on the landing, going at each other in the clumsy, inexpert way that girls fought, slapping and shoving and tearing. Raggedy Ann was pushing into Ivory with her shoulders and hips. Ivory was trying to squeeze the pulp out of Raggedy Ann's face. Jack said, uselessly, "Hey, cut it out." They ignored him. He couldn't tell if they'd done any real damage yet, they were both red-faced and gasping and the sweat was rolling off them, streaking their hair and clothes, and their eyes and noses were running with tears and snot. He stepped in, tried to pull them apart. Girl hands filled the air, beating and flurrying. Where was Brezak anyway, why wasn't he here to keep his women in line? One of them was going to end up losing an eye or an ear, the kind of thing that happened when nobody knew how to fight.

"Cunt!"

"Fat-assed pig!"

Their bodies collided with his. He got one of Raggedy Ann's elbows in his ribs, hard. Pissed him off royally. They were still trying to get at each other, reach around him to grab and claw, middle of a goddamn catfight, Ivory kicking uselessly through her long skirt, the other girl either crying or attempting to spit, he couldn't tell.

"Nice threesome, dude."

It was Brezak, standing in his open doorway. He was wearing only a pair of blue-jean cutoffs that rode so low on his hips, you could see the column of hair rising up from his crotch. His chest was pale as a root. Smiling his wiseass smile. Jack had an urge to let go of the girls and give him a good face punching.

The girls quieted, waiting to see what would happen next. Ivory's small, underdrawn features were clenched up like a fist. Her eyes worked Jack over, a brief, poison glance that he didn't really take personally. He was only in her way, he even felt sorry for her, watching her try to read anything fond in Brezak's smirking face. One of Raggedy Ann's tattoos, a green-blue fish, was swimming up her breast and out of her torn shirt and her face was still bright pink and the meanness was still in her and anything might have happened then, any one or two of them clobbering the others, if Chloe hadn't called up from the foot of the stairs. "Jack?"

"Yeah."

"Are you all right up there? What in the world's going on?"

"I'm fine." He let go of the girls and they backed off, still sullen, but the fight had gone out of them that fast. They'd been shamed.

"Should I call someone?"

Jack peered over the banister, saw Chloe looking up at him, clean, dressed up, adult, disapproving, a creature from a different world. He said, "I don't think there's any need for that."

"I have to leave for work."

"Right down." He left the three of them there, didn't bother looking back. Chloe watched him descend, her face shaping questions.

"So what—"

Mr. Dandy's locks unsnapped and, before they could escape, Mr. Dandy himself was upon them. Something askew about his face. He'd put his dentures in hastily and they gapped and clicked. He tried to whisper, or stage-whisper, but the effort of keeping his teeth in his head made his voice come out in a windy roar: "Was they naked?"

Jack steered Chloe out the front door without answering. He was still breathing fast. One of them must have kicked or jabbed him from behind, although he couldn't remember it. His back felt wrenched. Chloe said, "Now tell me."

"It was the girls." He didn't want to tell her too much. He didn't want to talk about Ivory. So he just said, "The two girls fighting. I don't know what set it off."

"That is so tacky. What is wrong with those people. They're like some bad TV show. Can I take the car? I've got errands."

"Don't leave me here with them. I'm begging you."

Chloe punched him in the bicep and he made a show of pretending it hurt, when in fact it did hurt a little. It pissed him off to be so seriously out of shape. They walked toward Clark, past the new, security-gated town house that marked the high end of the neighborhood's aspirations. Across the street another house was slated for teardown. Another modish piece of architecture would rise up in its stead. Sooner or later their own building would be replaced with some updated version of itself. No more scruffy characters like the kid and his harem, no more tottering old people, hell, even he and Chloe would have to make an income jump or move on. He couldn't think that far ahead, he was still dazed by the fight and everything that had come before the fight. For the first time he considered that Ivory could have said something to Chloe, out of spite or meanness or simple perversity. He was sweating like a pig, he could smell himself. He looked around at the new construction, the evidence of progress, robust growth and civic health, and it made him uneasy. How mortal a building, a neighborhood, a city might be, things you took for granted, tall structures of brick and steel and stone torn up by the roots . . . Chloe said, "I know this is kind of a sore subject, but—"

Jack kept walking. Dread settled into the floating space that had been his thoughts. Chloe said, "Turn around. Is your elbow bleeding? I guess it's just scraped. Those she-devils. Look, maybe you don't want to do this anymore, but what if I stopped taking my birth control pills?"

Jack stopped walking. "Wow."

"I mean I still am. So last night was okay. Even if we decided to, I should still probably use something else for a month or two, you know, get all those hormones out of my system."

"Can I just keep saying wow?"

"Well sooner or later, wow yes or wow no."

They had reached the car. Chloe unlocked the driver's-side door, placed her purse and briefcase inside, made a point of adjusting her sunglasses so Jack would have time to speak. "Wow yes," he said, trying to make up in enthusiasm what he'd lost in spontaneity. "Yes, sure. Pitch them pills."

"They're gone. They're toast." Chloe beamed at him. Jack was trying to count back, how many hours ago had this been something he was excited about. His heart's desire. Chloe's smile flagged. "What?"

"Nothing. It's great."

"But *what*?"

"You're sure about this? Because last night you were so excited about writing."

"And I still am. You think I can't be pregnant and write at the same time? God. You make it sound like I'm going to be flat on my back in a dark room for nine months."

"Well sure you can do both." Jack attempted a judicious tone. He didn't want to appear to be trying to talk her out of anything. "It's just a lot to take on at once. Stopping drinking—"

"That's not something you *do*. It's something you don't do."

He had to squint through the sun to see Chloe. The light seemed to gild her in irrefutable logic. "Okay. Fine. But believe me, writing and any kind of a job are a definite handful."

"But that's exactly what I need right now. I need all sorts of creative—creative—I have to be productive, I can't be some worthless, okay, not worthless, but— Look. This book's gonna be huge for me. And a baby, nothing's huger than that. I can make it all work. Besides, I probably won't get pregnant right away. Most women don't."

There was something brittle about her enthusiasm. He felt it might exhaust itself too quickly, or turn in on itself if he wasn't careful. Jack tried again. "I wouldn't dream of holding you back. But please don't be so hard on yourself. You aren't worthless. You won't be no matter what happens." He stooped and kissed the top of her head. It smelled of shampoo and hot sunlight.

She looked up at him through her dark glasses. "You mean it? We can have a baby?"

"Just tell me when to pull the trigger."

She squealed and swatted at him. "You are so gross!" Then, her face slowing down, her voice going dull, "Do you think I'd be a bad mother?"

"Now why in the world would I think that."

"Because sometimes I'm a bad person. Yes. Don't just automatically tell me I'm not. I'm shallow and insecure and dishonest and I'm not all that nice to people or especially to you and you have to tell me you love me in spite of all that and you won't let me screw up our kid."

"Chloe, everybody thinks they're going to make mistakes as a parent. That's because everybody does. You'll be great." She was still looking up at him, eyes just visible behind her sunglasses, secret, watchful. Somewhere out there in the universe of words were the ones he needed to use. "I love you no matter what and I'm going to keep telling you that until you believe me, goddamn it."

Then she smiled and took off her sunglasses to dab at her eyes and Jack hugged and whispered and administered small kisses and got her into the car and grinned and waved until she was out of sight.

"Good grief," he said out loud.

He shuffled his way up the street for coffee and a newspaper. He sat at a corner table and read that the city was settling yet another lawsuit stemming from a police pursuit and shooting, this time of a citizen armed with a cell phone. The heat wave had not yet broken any records, it was only bumping up against the records, if that made anyone feel better. And Sammy Sosa had belted out another home run. All of it news he felt he could have written himself, before he even saw the headlines.

Then there was nothing else to do except go back home and hope the freak show had cleared out. This was supposed to be his day for writing. He wondered if he was going to be able to settle down to it anytime soon. He guessed if you were good enough, tough enough, you could just turn on the writing part of your brain and let it do its thing, rise above the crap of your daily life like some meditating Buddha.

When he reached the building's front door he was relieved to note the absence of blood trails. The lobby was quiet. No sound from up-stairs. He stood in his front room, letting the air-conditioning wash over him, and waited to see whether his body would take itself in some recognizable direction: bed, shower, desk. There was a knock at the door.

He opened it to find Rich Brezak standing there like the world's funkiest door-to-door salesman. "Hey, I need to talk to you."

"No you don't."

"I just wanted to tell you I'm sorry, man—"

"Fine. Go be sorry somewhere else."

"—and that if you got a thing going with one of those hens, I'm cool with that, but I hafta tell you—"

Jack got him inside and shut the door. "Watch your goddamn mouth."

"I thought your old lady went to work."

"You should still watch it."

The kid made a face that was just this side of sneering. Jack thought about throwing him out, but something cowardly was rising up in his throat, the familiar taste of dread. He settled for, "What do you want?"

"I just realized, I never been in your place before. Hey, sorry about this morning. Those chicks, who knew they'd go off like that? Tell you the truth, I'm sick of both of them. You okay, man? You look like shit."

The kid had put on a shirt and his hair was slicked back from a shower and at the moment he looked a good deal better groomed than Jack himself. Jack said, keeping his tone unfriendly, "Something on your mind?"

"My man Jack, I'm on your side here. You and me against the wacked-out bitches of the world. Meaning no disrespect to your very fine-looking old lady. Sorry! Sorry! Hey, Jack, if you're so sensitive, you gotta be a little more discreet, I'm here to tell you. Mind if I sit down?"

Defeated, Jack pointed to the couch. Brezak settled himself in it and crossed his bare and bony legs. Jack couldn't imagine any health food store wanting the guy to work there; he was pallid and undersized and he looked utterly resistant to vitamins. But there was also something whittled down and economical about him, like a cockroach, something just as persistent and unkillable. Brezak pulled a pipe and a lighter out of his shirt pocket, waggled it invitingly.

"I don't think so."

"Oh come on. Think of it as, like, combat pay. Don't tell me you're above it, I know better."

Oh come on. Jack shrugged and leaned forward as the kid fired up, then he took his turn. It would stink up the place. Chloe would raise hell. But he had all day to clear the air and besides, she was going to have to cut him a little slack. It was her turn to be on that end of things, wasn't it? He sucked in a mouthful of smoke and let it do its thing. Then another round. His brain began producing cartoons. The ceiling, with its whorls and lumps of paint, was a fascinating place. The kid's voice buzzed in his ear.

"You're a fiend, man."

Jack wanted to say no, he wasn't, but first he had to consider if he knew what "fiend" meant.

"A total pothead. Lookit you, stoned to the eyeballs. You gonna sit on that till it hatches?"

"Sorry." Jack fumbled the pipe and lighter back the kid's way. He decided to risk words. "Hey, Rich? There's nothing going on with me and . . ." He didn't want to say, the hens. He couldn't believe anyone actually said such a thing. "There's just nothing going on."

"Sure," said the kid cheerfully. He let his lungs empty out and

watched the smoke curl, then vanish in the draft from the air conditioner. "She's such a weird girl. You don't want to get mixed up in any of
her shit, I'm serious."

Jack ignored the way the kid had gone from the general to the spe-
cific, from sleazy suggestion to sleazy confidence, and now sleazy advice. The kid twinkled at him through the wavering smoke. "She has
kind of a thing for you, you know?"

"I don't think so," said Jack incautiously.

"Oh I think. Yes sir. She said you're 'serious.' That's her way of saying
hot."

Jack groaned. "What else did she say?"

"Not much. She told me you were over at her place the other night.
She was trying to make me jealous. That don't work on me, I just don't
have a hang-up about possession. Not people, things, nothing, it's part
of my belief system. I figure, whatever you got going on, that's your
deal."

By now Jack had left off staring at the ceiling and was staring at the
floor. There wasn't much use in denying or explaining. He was already
implicated. It was almost worse that the kid didn't seem to mind sharing his women, mind, hell, he wanted to offer them up and then hang
out and have nasty chats about it.

Jack said, "I love my wife. I don't know why I'm telling you, it's not
like you care, or it makes me any less of a—forget it."

"No, I hear you, my man Jack—"

"And quit calling me that, would you?"

"—which reminds me, that's another thing she said about you, she
thinks you're sensitive. Man, you are really screwed. 'Sensitive,' that's
like catnip to chicks. Hey, maybe she'll give me a break, transfer all her
weird obsessive shit to you."

"Sound of hollow laughter," muttered Jack, reaching for the pipe
again.

"Her name's really Irene."

Jack regarded him over the exhaled smoke. The kid's head pumped
up and down. "I swear to God. Irene Sosnowski. I guess I'd be changing my name too. Let me guess, she told you the leg story."

Jack shrugged. He didn't want to say or not say. It was distasteful to be discussing a woman in this way, part by part.

"Guy I know, he knows her folks. They're some kind of DPs, and they're more Polish than the pope. And get this, they're deaf and dumb! Yeah, in Polish and English both! Can you imagine? They have about eighteen kids. Nobody knows how to say, 'We got enough kids already.' Poor as shit. So there's this accident, little Irene gets mashed by a car, and afterward they're too deaf and dumb to keep taking her to the doctor like they should, or maybe they're too cheap, or maybe they take her to see some Polish witch doctor instead, who knows. They basically let her hip rot. Boy," the kid finished, running out of language himself. He shook his head in stoned amazement.

Jack said nothing. He was still trying to get his mind around the idea of Irene Sosnowski. The name fit her better than Ivory, which he'd never believed anyway. Irene Sosnowski, a girl with a name like a limp, and two strikes already against her. Jack didn't think he knew any Polish people, not actual ones. They'd been in short supply in Sherman Oaks. His father's Slavic ancestors were a generation back and a world away, Russian and Serbian, not Polish, and he supposed that made some sort of difference but he was too ignorant to know. Irene Sosnowski. She'd have brothers and sisters called Stan and Alvin, Bernice and Lillian, names that, like hers, were old before their time. The family would live on the bottom floor of some stoop-shouldered house, or one of those Chicago four flats that lined certain streets like rows of broken teeth. The older kids would always be in the process of moving out and the younger ones would hardly know them. They'd grow up waving and clapping to get their parents' attention, maybe learning sign language in Polish, all those consonants knotting their fingers.

Now he was imagining things again, a bad habit, making the world into a story, he should concentrate on what he knew for sure, which was that he was in shit up to his neck here. He closed his eyes. Maybe he and Chloe could move. He couldn't think of any other way to extricate himself. Maybe he could talk to Ivory, tell her—what? No more blow jobs, or if there were any, they didn't really count? That he loved his wife, and that was why he was seeking her out, to tell her so? Anything he said would be absurd or dishonest or both. He was still discomfited from his talk with Chloe. He was tired of words, the effort of wrangling and coaxing and explaining. He wanted to be deaf and dumb. Maybe the kid and his crew had it right. They yelled and screamed and fucked and fought and didn't try to cover it up with layers of talking, didn't try to pretend that one thing was its opposite, or that they didn't feel what they felt.

Jack roused himself, opened his eyes to see the kid sprawled out on the couch. The kid's hair was beginning to dry and portions of it were reasserting themselves, like an animal's fur bristling. The braids had gotten pretty sad by now. Only the ends were still plaited. The rest was all snarls and fuzz. He didn't want to think the two of them had anything in common. He didn't want to see himself as some older, better-financed version of the kid. He didn't want strange young girls brooding about him, or at least, he didn't think he did.

The kid stretched and scratched and grinned. He opened his mouth and words came out. Jack didn't hear them. They blew away like smoke in the roar of the air conditioner. Maybe he really was deaf and dumb now, or just too stoned to comprehend speech, or else he'd used up all the words in his head and nothing in his life made sense anymore.

Six

A week later, Jack and Chloe attended their first counseling session. They had expected to be nervous and they were. The counselor came highly recommended, in the discreet way that such recommendations were made. They were lucky she'd had a cancellation and could see them this quickly. Jack didn't like the idea much. What if she asked probing questions, took them to task for doing things wrong? But he kept this unworthy fear private. He told himself that the counselor was used to seeing people like him and Chloe, that she'd certainly seen much worse. Couples in every state of misery and disrepair came through her door on a regular basis. People who never should have been married in the first place, to each other or to anyone else. People who'd totaled their relationships. He and Chloe just needed a tune-up.

Chloe had made the appointment. She said she wanted a clean start, everything set right between them, to go along with the rest of her new clean-start life. Jack had tried, halfheartedly, to talk her out of it. "You don't have to do this if you don't want to. I think we're in a good place now. I think we've gotten through the worst."

It was true, they were both making an effort. They were, for the most part, happy. Chloe declared that she didn't miss drinking at all. She should have quit years ago. She slept better now, she had more energy. She'd bought a journal bound in beautiful marbled Italian paper and was busy taking notes for her book. Jack had been allowed to admire the perfect blankness of the thick cream-colored pages before she shut it away. Chloe talked less about things at work, which Jack thought was a good sign. The office creep apparently no longer in the picture. Nor had they seen or heard much from the crew upstairs, the kid or either of the girls. For the first time in a long while, nobody else in their marriage except themselves. And now, this counselor.

The counselor's name was Pat Rubin. Her office was in Oak Park, in a weathered brick building that also housed a drug-treatment program, a divorce lawyer, a collection bureau. A place you went in order to transact embarrassing business. The counselor said they were to call her Pat. A big woman, dressed in flowing blue-green draperies. She had a big jolly laugh that didn't seem in keeping with the circumstances of her clients. "Take a few deep breaths, guys. We're here to make you feel better, not worse."

They smiled brightly. Jack thought about reaching for Chloe's hand, but decided that would seem too much like putting on a show. He never liked the idea of someone else scrutinizing him, sizing him up, and here he was in exactly the sort of place where that was done. "So let's see," Pat Rubin said. "Somebody's got to go first."

"Her," said Jack.

"Why's that?" asked Pat. She really was a big woman. The loose clothes made it hard to tell exactly where she began and ended.

"So I don't get it wrong. That's just a joke. But I guess . . ." Both women were looking at him. "I guess there's no such thing as just a joke around here, is there?"

"Well, you said you wanted Chloe to begin, but in fact you're the one who's talking."

"Yeah. I am." Jack shut his face and sat back in his chair.

"Chloe?"

Chloe's hands were folded up in a tidy bundle. She still wore her office clothes, nylons, heels, a navy suit with a scallop of white at the neckline. Her hair pulled back in a twist. All business. She said, "We had some problems because I was drinking too much. That's one place to start."

"How does it feel, saying that?"

"Not terrific."

"Tell me about your drinking. Do you drink every day?"

"I actually quit drinking, so it's not an issue anymore. I'm trying to learn to handle job stress better, and deal with frustration in more appropriate ways. Jack's had to put up with a lot. I think he's still angry about it."

He hadn't expected that last. He looked over at Chloe, failed to catch her eye. Pat Rubin nodded in a way that indicated neither approval nor disapproval. Jack wondered if she'd ever been married herself. She was somewhere north of forty. She didn't wear a wedding ring, only a bracelet of clicking blue-green stones and some oversized silver costume rings. Hot-pink nail polish. He guessed she was one of those big women who chose to make a statement with how boldly they presented themselves. She was attractive in a flashy, retired-nightclub-singer sort of way, hell, she'd probably been married and divorced two, three, four times, an expert.

Now she said, "I'd like to get back to the drinking, Chloe. But let's give Jack his turn."

Jack planted his feet and flexed his knees, as if getting ready to take a charge. "Right. Good to go."

"You're not loving this, are you, Jack. Being here."

"That's very good. I'm betting you have a number of advanced degrees."

He'd meant it to come out funny, not sarcastic. After a measured pause, Pat Rubin said, "What are you so afraid I'm going to say?"

"Not you. It's what I might say."

Next to him Chloe made a small, audible breathing sound. Jack said, "Maybe it's not always a good idea to talk too much about things. Put names on problems. Because then you're always thinking about them. Like if a doctor tells you you've got cancer. All of a sudden everything's worse, because there's that name."

Chloe said, "That's a totally negative way to think. Marriage equals problems equals cancer equals death."

"If anything I say is going to be used against me, I don't want to keep talking."

Pat Rubin said, "Let me ask you this, whose idea was it to come see me?"

They did look at each other then, shrugged. Chloe said, "Mutual, I thought. I didn't expect Jack to operate in bad faith."

"Not bad faith. Fear. There's a difference."

Pat said to Jack, "Is it fair to say that change frightens you?"

"Yes."

"You'd rather go along in the same old just-getting-by way, instead of taking a chance on life getting better?"

"Yes."

"Care to say why?"

Jack only shrugged. Pat Rubin said, "What, you thought we weren't going to get into the good stuff? Okay, let's back off, take it slow. Let's—"

"I mean, are we here to solve problems, or so you can tell us we don't really have any?"

He hadn't planned on saying it. The words had squirmed out of him of their own accord. He swallowed, too late. Pat said, "Maybe you should tell me."

"Maybe that's your job."

Pat didn't look offended at that. She didn't look anything, except calmly interested. She was probably following some sort of therapist playbook where you checked off client reactions: anger, denial, defensiveness, check check check. Chloe said, "Jack can be very inflexible. I think he needs to work on that."

"Chloe wanted to come here so you can tell her that not having a drink for a week or two is all she has to do. It's not that simple. I think she's an alcoholic."

The room seemed to push away from him, as if he'd set off a bomb that scrubbed the air with deafening sound. So now he'd done it. Gotten into the good stuff.

Chloe said, "I wish I could say I stopped drinking a month or six months or a year ago, but I can't yet. It is so unfair of Jack to hold that against me, when there's not a thing I can do about it. So now he's calling me an alcoholic. That's his way of getting back at me."

Jack said nothing. He wanted to keep the taste and weight of silence in his mouth. Pat said, "Somebody has to tell me what happens when Chloe drinks."

"If Jack wants me to say what a drunken pig I was, okay. I was. But it wasn't like I was always so out of control. I could have one or two glasses of wine, leave it right there. Then other times, say I was trying to unwind from a really bad day, I just kept going."

"And then what?"

Chloe's turn to keep silent. Jack said, "She gets very emotional, and sometimes hostile."

"Hostile, how?"

This time neither of them spoke. Pat didn't seem impatient to move things along. She sat comfortably and let her gaze travel between the two of them. She was making some sort of point, Jack knew, but he didn't feel able to rise to the occasion, respond, perform, confess. He wondered how he'd managed to walk into this office thinking that he and Chloe were basically a happy couple, but the longer he sat here, the worse he felt. His eyes rested on the blue-green fabric of Pat's dress. He floated away, let the colors ease over him.

He roused himself when Chloe spoke. He wondered if he'd been staring at Pat's boobs or anything like that, dropped his eyes hastily. Chloe said, "I can't remember a lot of what I said. When I drank."

"Do you remember enough to agree with Jack's characterization, hostile?"

"We were both hostile."

"Jack?"

Some new fight Chloe was trying to pick, but he didn't want to fight back, couldn't will himself to. "I guess so."

"Physically? Verbally?"

"I would never hit Chloe. Christ."

"I wasn't assuming that. Does Chloe ever hit you?"

Jack shook his head, laughed a little. "No, she hasn't tried that yet."

Chloe said, "I don't think you should even joke about something like that. Besides, it never happened."

"I'm hearing something very interesting here. Jack says 'drinks,' Chloe says 'drank.' That tell you anything?"

They were dull children in front of a teacher. Teacher knew the answer, but she wanted to hear them say it. Chloe said, "Jack thinks it's going to keep happening. He thinks I'm going to keep drinking. Thanks for the vote of confidence."

"I just don't think we're out of the woods yet on that one."

It was the only thing he could come up with. Goddamn lame. He should either be properly furious at all the bad behavior Chloe had subjected him to, or he should properly forgive her. But he was equally balanced between resentments and cowardice. He looked to Pat Rubin, waiting for her to push him in one direction or the other. How quickly he, both of them, had come to depend on her to referee things, tell them who they really were. And she'd done it by simply sitting there and asking a few questions. He guessed she really was good. That, and he had always known there was something within himself that looked to women, depended on them, sought them out. Even in the face of his own fear and reluctance, Pat had won him over. Women were necessary to him as they might not be to other men, or maybe other men had to hide their needs behind jokes and complaints and sex talk. Men gathered in places that excluded women, bars, firehouses, sports teams, and the need in them twisted into a shape they could manage and diminish. And was he better or worse than they were, more or less of a man, because he could not do the same?

But those thoughts made him uncomfortable, and he concentrated instead on Chloe's slim foot in its elegant shoe, tapping out a syncopated rhythm on the carpet. So she was agitated also. Good.

Pat said, "In the time we have remaining," and Jack and Chloe came close to exchanging glances. They hadn't been aware of time, but in fact the session was close to over. Pat said they would concentrate on putting things back together now, giving them a road map, a plan, positive steps they could take. She didn't want them or anyone else walking out her door still in crisis. The word alarmed Jack. But maybe this was what a crisis was, what it felt like, and you never knew until you put a name on it.

Pat said, "Chloe, I'm going to recommend doing an alcohol assessment. We can handle that at a separate appointment. You shouldn't look on it as an accusation or a judgment or a threat. It's just a way of getting more information."

Chloe nodded. It would have been hard for her to do anything else. Not agreeing would make her look resistant and uncooperative, in other words, a lot like an alcoholic. But he knew, because he knew Chloe, that it was killing her not to argue back.

"And Jack, let's see if we can't get beyond the fear. The future is always an unknown. But you don't have to dread it."

His turn to nod. He wondered again what he must look like to Pat. A man in crisis, trying desperately not to be.

"What I'd like you both to do is tell me about a time when you felt something strongly positive about each other. A high-water mark. A happy memory."

Chloe said, "I had bronchitis last winter and Jack always got my prescriptions and fussed over me and took care of me. I was so sick. My lungs were like sandpaper. One night it was really bad, I could hardly breathe, and he didn't want to scare me, so he acted like he was kidding around, he said, 'You ever wonder how long it takes them to get an ambulance out when you call? Want to give it a shot, see how good they are?' I mean, I talked him out of the ambulance, we drove to the emergency room, but he was really . . ."

They did look at each other then, smiled, looked away, as if it was more embarrassing, more personal, to share good times than bad.

"Jack?"

"The first time I ever saw Chloe, she was sitting in a classroom wearing these crazy ripped-up jeans with black lace stockings underneath. And she got into a big fight with the professor and I kept thinking she was going to cry, but she didn't, she just kept slugging it out with him, and when class was over she walked out of there like a queen and I wrote bad poetry about her for weeks."

"You did not." Chloe smiling.

"Yup. Really bad."

"You should have seen Jack when he was a college kid," Chloe told Pat. "He was a *babe*. Those big blue eyes, and that California-guy long hair, and he was just so ready to grow up and stop being shy."

Jack allowed the two of them to give him fond, appraising looks. He didn't think he'd been a babe. He didn't even think he'd been shy.

Things seemed to be winding down. Pleasantries. Reminiscences. Jack supposed it had gone pretty well. He felt sluggish, he'd hoarded his energy to get through the session, and now he had none left. Nothing too bad had happened. The wheels hadn't come off. He'd said alcoholic but maybe that had to be said. Pat could talk to Chloe about drinking, or not drinking. He liked that better than the idea of her going to AA meetings, which would be populated by attractive, dissolute men who would get Chloe to feel sorry for them and invite her out for coffee, the better to feed her some line about how much the two of them had in common, mutual suffering of the sort her pain-in-the-ass husband could never understand, while he, Jack, would have to trail them to the coffee shop, lurk outside in the parking lot, confront the sorry mother-fucker and punch him out, get arrested, sued, go on probation, and wind up back in Pat's office for court-ordered counseling.

Pat said, "I want to make clear, these sessions aren't necessarily about fixing or saving your marriage."

Jack hadn't expected that, and from her suddenly rigid posture, nei-ther had Chloe. Pat said, "Don't worry, I'm not making a diagnosis here. It's what I say to all my clients. Counseling is about deciding what it is you want, both separately and as a couple. So that's going to be part of your homework. Determining goals, and identifying the behaviors that keep you from achieving them. Sorting out what would make you happy. No, don't tell me. Think about it for the next time."

Jack tried to look as if he was settling in for some serious, protracted thought. But he already knew what he wanted. To go back to that class-room and see Chloe all over again for the first time. And then to travel step by step through all the events of their life together, but this time to be better, kinder, wiser, stronger. It wasn't anything he could tell Pat, hell, it wasn't even possible. But it was his heart's truth.

Chloe said, "Umm, if it's all right to ask, how long do you think we'll have to keep coming? I mean, how messed up are we?"

She laughed, but it came out sad. Jack watched her folding and refolding her hands, gathering them up into a smaller and smaller bundle. What would Chloe say, what would make her happy? He didn't know. It was a lonely feeling.

Pat said, "That's not one of those clinical terms I like to use, messed up. But you want to know what I think, okay. I see two very intelligent, very verbal people. Which makes my job both easier and harder. Easier because we can discuss things with a high degree of complexity and comprehension. Harder because people like yourselves—young, attractive, bright, healthy, prosperous—tend to think they shouldn't have any serious problems. It's unfair, it's calamitous. It's not. It's just life. Sometimes it catches up to you."

Jack wondered if this was meant to be a comforting thought. He didn't find it so. Some voice he could no longer remember, saying the same thing about Chloe, how she always expected things to work out perfectly . . .

Pat was letting that one sink in. Jack was beginning to recognize a pattern or technique in the way she spoke, something subtle but measured, designed to get people to listen. She was good at this. She already knew things about them that they didn't themselves. Jack imagined coming back to Pat on his own, or maybe just running into her on the street or somewhere, asking her privately and urgently what she thought of him and Chloe, *how messed up were they?* But she was speaking again.

"As for appointments, I ask people to commit to a six-week period. Of course it can be extended, and of course I can't drag you here if you decide not to come. But that's my recommendation."

It was the end of June. Fourth of July was coming, and after that the heart of summer. Before Labor Day this might all be over. They could get some kind of diploma, be certified a functioning, happy marriage.

There was some awkwardness involved in getting themselves up and out of there. They didn't want to look too relieved, or as if they were fleeing, although they were. They shook hands with Pat, thanked her, made another appointment for next week, turned their back on the indirect lighting and soothing pastel walls and hardwood flooring and all the apparatus of expensive professional intervention. They stepped out of the well-kept doorway into the long summer evening's last sunlight. They didn't speak until they reached the car.

Chloe said, "Don't take this the wrong way, but boy I'd love a drink right now."

"I can definitely understand that."

"Not that I would."

"I know you wouldn't."

"I'm glad you said that. I'd hate to have to run right back inside and tell her we couldn't get out of the damned parking lot without another talking-to."

There was a Mexican restaurant they liked in Oak Park, an old-fashioned family place that displayed, without irony, sombreros and paper flowers and piñatas and *retablos* and holy candles, all the artifacts that in other restaurants now were meant as inside jokes. Jack and Chloe ordered a pitcher of iced tea and fajitas. Their usual was a pitcher of margaritas. The waiter brought the tea and poured out two glasses and they watched the condensation form and bead on their surfaces. A simple, predictable, observable phenomenon involving water vapor and temperature. Jack thought this must be what the world looked like to scientists. A rational place where the laws of physics and thermodynamics kept order. It was probably too late to decide to be a scientist.

The last time they'd been here was a few months ago, before the move to the city. They'd finished two pitchers of margaritas and giggled lewdly at each other through dinner. As soon as they got in the car, they'd put their hands on each other and Chloe had hiked her skirt up and rolled down her underpants and they might have done it right there in the parking lot if another car hadn't pulled into the lot, its radio blaring an old Beatles song, one of the silly ones, We all live in a yellow submarine, yellow submarine, yellow submarine, and it was too absurd, he couldn't keep his erection going. It was just as well. They could have hurt themselves trying or gotten stuck or some other idiocy. Instead they laughed themselves sick and somehow they managed to drive home, where they'd done it up right.

Good old drunk sex. Say what you would, it had its charms. And now there would be no more of it. Jack imagined Chloe was thinking of that time also, but she only raised her glass and drank and said, "This is good. I was really thirsty."

Jack drank also. "Yeah, it is good." He supposed it was, for iced tea. He told himself, severely, not to sulk. "So what did you think of her?"

"Oh, she's okay. I guess I'm a little disappointed she didn't have us do anything less, you know, obvious."

"Obvious?" Jack repeated, stalling. Nothing that happened had seemed obvious to him.

"You know, saying everything was about drinking. I really think that's a cop-out."

"Well . . ." He wanted to sound judicious, neither argumentative nor overly quick to agree. "I don't think it was just that. Anyway, it was only a first appointment. Getting our feet wet."

Chloe shrugged, seemed to lose interest. "At least something's getting wet. God, relax. I'm not going to drink but I have to be able to talk about it without you jumping out of your skin."

"Sorry."

"You're always sorry. It gets annoying."

"Double double sorry sorry." He raised his glass, saluted her.

"What are you—"

The waiter came by, set down a new basket of chips, and she was obliged to stop talking. "What?" Jack asked, when she didn't resume.

"Skip it."

"Come on, Chloe."

"What are you so afraid of? It drives me crazy when you do that, look at me like a damned whipped dog, you don't even realize it, do you? Just tell me what I'm doing that makes you like that."

"You didn't do anything. Or I mean we've both done things wrong over time, that's not the point. I guess I'm afraid . . ." The glass in front of him showed the imprint of his hand on its moist surface. Molecules, temperature, humidity: once you understood such things, the world might explain itself to you. But what if the glass were to turn green, its contents bubble and fizz and explode in your face? "I'm afraid you'll realize it's all been some kind of fluke or mistake, you ending up with me. That you made a bad decision."

The waiter returned, set their plates down with a flourish just as Chloe was saying, *Honestly.* Again she had to pause. Jack thought he understood why people had such conversations in public places. You needed interruptions and distractions so you could hear yourself both before and after you spoke. Chloe said, "That is so ridiculous."

Jack murmured that he was glad to hear it. Chloe said, "Honey. Look at me, please. Are you crying? Jack?"

He shook his head. His eyes and nose were thick with tears. He saw everything through their prism. It mortified him, he concentrated on keeping his face rigid so the tears would not spill over. Chloe reached across the table but he waved her hand away. "Just give me a minute."

"Honey, don't—"

He motioned for her to stop. If he just sat there, moment by moment, he thought he could get through it. And he did. He was spared having to mop his eyes or excuse himself to the rest room. It wasn't crying, it was simply condensation. But he could not have been more wretched, even as he went through the motions of recovering himself, shrugging and saying, I don't know what got into me there.

They settled down to their dinner. The food, as always, was excellent. Jack made a point of eating with good appetite. Chloe began a conversation about something that had happened at work, some minor event, minor complaint that was easy for Jack to sympathize with, impersonate disapproval or understanding, as called for, and then Chloe stopped speaking and he said, "I want to tell you . . ."

Chloe leaned forward encouragingly, although he could also read dread in her face, wondering what was to come next. For all her bright talk and the seeming confidence of her beauty, there had always been something skittish and frightened about her that might do damage without meaning to, and there was a limit to what he might expect of her, and he had known that from the first. He said, "Nobody is ever going to love you like I do. Whatever happens."

"I know that."

Then it was as if nothing else remained to be said, and they finished their meal without distress, and drove home. Jack was thinking that it was possible they could be happy, this new, sadder happiness that would be based on knowledge rather than hopeful ignorance. It was coming to terms, it was life catching up with you. People lived like that. Got on with it. As he should and would. But he was trying to remember if Pat Rubin had said "drink" or "drank."

In fact they ended up canceling their appointment with Pat. They had forgotten about Chloe's parents. The parents regularly issued invitations to their St. Louis home, and whenever possible Jack or sometimes Chloe or sometimes both cited work, the necessity of work, and stayed away. Now they were coming to Chicago. Oh boy, said Jack, Oh boy, said Chloe. Mr. and Mrs. Chase's marriage could best be described as loud. "They're too much," Chloe said. "Too much emotion and mess and melodrama. And they get the biggest kick out of themselves, that's almost the worst part. They think they're a stitch."

Jack was glad that Chloe complained about them. It meant he didn't have to. At their wedding reception, his new father-in-law danced with all the pretty girls. He announced that he'd paid for everything and was entitled to have some fun. In retaliation, Jack's new mother-in-law locked herself in the bridal limousine. Chloe and her sister and aunts trooped back and forth between the banquet hall and the parking lot, trying to placate and intercede. Finally Mr. Chase himself went outside to shout his bullying apologies through the closed windows. "Let me in, Allison, what, you think I'm going to run off with some nymph in her teens? You should be so lucky." Eventually he was granted entrance. The two of them emerged sometime later to dance a truly alarming tango of reconciliation. The wedding pictures showed the still-handsome Mr. and Mrs. Chase smiling, glazed with post-argument, married lust.

Now they were going to be in town for an extended weekend. They were staying at the Omni, where they could shop expensively on Michigan Avenue. Jack and Chloe had arranged a lot of exhausting sight-seeing. They would visit Navy Pier and the Shedd Aquarium and a Cubs game. They would lunch and dine and brunch. They'd take a tour of Chloe's office and gaze at the edifices of power and commerce. Mr. Chase had made his money in high-end real estate. He would have opinions about downtown's vacancy rates, about development and overbuilding and square footage. Mrs. Chase would have opinions about Mr. Chase. No one would be left guessing as to what they were. There were times when they were fine, amusing even, with their banter and sniping and theatrics. And they seemed to like Jack, in the middling, resigned way you could like a son-in-law. Mrs. Chase had Chloe's blue blue eyes, or rather, Chloe had hers. It was disconcerting to see them in that older, carefully maintained face. Mr. Chase had a full head of silver hair and the good looks of the fraternity president he had once been. He was gradually losing his hearing, but since he seldom listened to other people anyway, he remained cheerful about it. Jack found it easier to imagine them as Chloe's older, disreputable cousins than as her parents.

Jack and Chloe cleaned their apartment like fury. They bought flowers and throw cushions and new towels. "It really looks good," said Jack, surveying the finished result.

"It better." Chloe had been scrubbing out the kitchen cupboards, wearing shorts and an old Northwestern T-shirt. She looked grimy but fetching, like some warped *Playboy* feature, Girls of the Big Ten Get Dirty. Chloe's mother was not the sort who inspected kitchen cupboards, but Chloe knocking herself out was always part of the drill.

"No, I meant, this has turned into a nice place. You've made it something nice. Like Mrs. Palermo said. It's always the woman who makes the house a home."

"Mrs. who?"

"The old lady's daughter. I told you, she complimented the place up and down."

"I don't remember." Chloe brushed her hands on her shirt and took a swipe at the windowsill with a sponge. Jack bent and kissed the back of her neck, but Chloe wasn't having any of it. Waiting for her parents' arrival always made her irritable, although once they were actually on the premises, she'd relax and enjoy them, in a fond, exasperated fashion. But the parents weren't due for another twenty-four hours, and she was still distracted. Jack wanted her to see, in the splendid cleanliness and order of the apartment, in its pretty furnishings and well-loved objects, that they had accomplished something fine. He wanted her to take pride in it, take heart from it. Not that nice furniture or any of the rest of it was enough to validate a marriage, but it counted for something. He wanted Chloe to understand that. He wanted the rooms to be more eloquent than he was.

Mr. and Mrs. Chase were Ed and Allison. It had never occurred to Jack to call them anything else. "Ed, Allison," Jack said, pumping Ed's hand, presenting his jaw for Allison's kiss. They were meeting in the Omni's bar before they went out to dinner. Mr. and Mrs. Chase were established at a table by the window. From there you could look down to Michigan Avenue, which had been outfitted with a great deal of wrought-iron fencing and sidewalk flower planters. It was possible to imagine you were in Paris, that is, if you had never actually been to Paris. A waiter hovered. Mrs. Chase was drinking white wine, Mr. Chase gin and tonic. Mr. Chase announced that he was buying them a drink. Jack and Chloe ordered good old iced tea.

"Iced tea?" Mr. Chase looked as if this was a joke that needed to be explained to him.

"I'm not drinking," said Chloe. "It's a health thing. So how was your drive, any stinky construction?"

"Sweetheart, don't tell me," said Chloe's mother.

"Don't tell you what?"

"You're pregnant."

"I think I asked, how was your drive."

"Let me look at you." Her mother swiped at the tablecloth, peered underneath it. "Honey Bear, you're simply skin and bones!"

"I'm not pregnant, Mom. I just want some iced tea."

"Actually, I'm the one who's pregnant," said Jack. They all looked at him. "Skip it."

"Classy place," said Mr. Chase, looking up at the lounge's ceiling, which was high and painted like a sky, tender blue, with a lacework of golden clouds. "You're not pregnant. No grandpa. Boo hoo."

"Oh stop your stupid noise, there's plenty of time for that," said

Chloe's mother. "Thank God for modern birth control. Did you know the pill was first made widely available the year I was seventeen? I was fortunate in that respect. The drive up was fine, Honey Bear."

"I don't suppose you're ever going to stop calling me that."

"So, Jack." Mr. Chase, Ed, leaned toward him over the table, and Jack leaned gamely in turn. "Don't tell me you're still holding out hope for those Cubbies."

"They'll get it together by September," Jack said. "Wait and see. Sammy's just getting started."

"You're dreaming. You know the old joke? Cubs' schedule. Fold here."

Jack shook his head in rueful pretend agreement. He'd been to only one Cubs game in his life. He supposed it was too late to admit any such thing. It would have been akin to admitting he'd married Chloe under false pretenses. Ed went on to talk about the Cardinals, their superior lead-off hitter, their power pitching, their advantageous lineup. As with most hard-of-hearing people, it was easiest to just let him talk. All of Ed's enthusiasms were competitive. He was a middle-aged boy.

It was still alarming to Jack to realize that he had in-laws, and that he was now connected to these semi-strangers in certain inevitable ways. The future loomed. Jack would be the one who would convey Chloe to the emergency room when Ed had his heart attack or stroke. He'd fetch coffee and Kleenex, he'd be the one they'd count on to stay strong, that is, emotionally uninvolved. He'd help Allison sort through the insurance. He'd handle all the messier business of their declining lives. He'd confer with doctors, help select nursing homes, and when the time came, he would get them both properly underground. He'd take care of all the arrangements that Chloe and her younger sister would be too grief stricken to handle. No wonder parents looked askance at the men their daughters married. No wonder Ed made a point of bonding with him. There was a lot at stake.

Chloe and her mother were talking about Chloe's hair, and whether she should cut it. Hair was what they talked about instead of baseball. Allison Chase said, "I don't mean short short. More like, layers. Then

you could do more with it." She reached out and pushed a piece of
Chloe's hair behind her ear. "You're getting just a wee bit scraggly."

"Jack likes it long," said Chloe, and Jack tried to assume a manly,
proprietary look. He did like Chloe's hair long, but he knew very well
that she liked it long herself.

"Oh what does he know about professional women and making an
impression in the workplace. Too much hair is tarty. You don't want to
look like some stripper act, do you? You know, the ones where the girl
comes out in a business suit and starts peeling down?"

"Mom, that is so weird."

Ed said, "Now, Allison, no need to tell the kids about our little
games."

"Don't you just wish," said Allison, signaling the waiter for another
drink. Her own hair was cut chin length. Over time, Jack guessed to
cope with the graying, it had achieved a burnished, mid-blond tone
with metallic highlights. It now resembled something other than hair, a
space-age miracle fabric, perhaps.

"Ha ha," said Ed. "Let's have another here too. Mr. and Mrs. Lipton,
you good? What your mother isn't telling you, Chloe, is her enthusiasm for certain erotic—"

"Chloe," Allison announced. "Your real father was a war hero whose
life was tragically cut short at a young age. I've been waiting for the
right time to tell you."

Jack said, "We should probably think about dinner. It'll take us
about twenty minutes to get there, traffic and all."

"He's such a grown-up," her mother said to Chloe. "Really, he's so responsible. That must be why you married him."

"Partly," said Chloe, giving him a weary, comradely look. He knew
she appreciated his willingness to be the straight man and allow her
parents to carry on this way. He had to wonder how they behaved
when there was no one around to serve as an audience. They drank
too much, he believed that Chloe had either learned or inherited her
drinking problems from them. They had been loving but incomplete
parents, too childish and self-involved to be entirely attentive. Jack

supposed that Chloe's own scenes and dramatics were another habit, a way of competing with them for attention. They were careless about their words and behavior in ways that made Jack wince. But damned if they didn't seem happy together. They were a cartoon, a situation comedy, but they were happy.

The Cubs game was the next day, Friday. Jack was to meet Ed and Allison at their hotel and stop by Chloe's office before they made their way to Wrigley. Chloe had begged out of the ball game. She didn't pretend to be interested in such things, and besides, ditching work on a Friday afternoon was bad form for management trainees trying to exude the Right Stuff. After the game, they'd all meet back at the apartment for dinner, which would be casual. Burgers on the grill, potato salad, nothing that would lend itself to conversations about cooking skills, something Chloe was sensitive about. "Mom already thinks I'm some kind of kitchen slut because I buy bottled salad dressing. Fine. Let them eat burgers."

Jack took the bus downtown to the hotel. The day promised to be hot but not wilting. There was a fresh breeze off the lake and an actual blue sky instead of the usual cement-colored pall. Somewhere beyond his view, tourists were presented with the marvel of the lakefront, its layers of water, beach, green park, highway, and skyline, the best of the city served up like some grand dessert. Buckingham Fountain threw out its arcs and fans of bright water. Even the tame river had a sparkle to it. It was the finest summer day Chicago could offer, and Jack had to allow that there were worse things than heading out to the ballpark with the rest of the city's pleasure seekers.

Ed and Allison emerged from the hotel elevators wearing hats. Ed wore his Cardinals baseball cap as a joke (the Cubs were playing the Brewers, so Jack hoped it might escape notice), while Allison had selected a modish brimmed straw. They both wore khakis and polo shirts. Jack liked them for that, for dressing up together. In the cab over to Chloe's office, he sat in the back with Allison while Ed rode shotgun, his arm draped across the seat. High-rises turned the streets into shadowy canyons. Ed gave each block an appraising look and

asked Jack questions that he couldn't answer about property tax structures. Ed nodded in disappointment and swiveled around to face them.
"Chloe works too damned hard," he pronounced. "I don't see why she
can't come with us."

"Because she doesn't want to," said Allison. "Don't be pestering her,
besides, she has obligations."

"She has what?"

"A career."

"My daughter, the banker."

"Would it kill you to be supportive of her?"

"Who said I wasn't? It just takes some getting used to. When I was in
school, girls mostly got education degrees. Because they always need
teachers, right Jack? That way they had a little flexibility, and they
didn't have to knock themselves out working."

"She wants to distinguish herself," said Allison. "She has ambitions.
Come on, Ed, why don't you just walk around wearing a sign that says,
'I don't get it.'"

"Christ, she's already distinguished. She's beautiful, she's smart, she's
got Jack to keep her feet warm at night. Now, Jack, that didn't come out
right. What I meant was, she's not alone in the world."

It was a short cab ride, but by the end of it Jack was pretty sure where
he stood in the rankings.

Chloe met them downstairs in the lobby, smiling her best. "Hey,
guys, I have to have you sign in. How was the hotel? You sleep okay?"

"Fine and fine," said Ed. "Do you know you can order a fitness kit
from room service? They send up a jump rope, exercise mat, towel, and
a bottle of water. You think I'm making that up but I'm not."

"I like your suit," said Allison. "We should have dressed better to
come here, I don't know what I was thinking."

Chloe's office was on the ninth floor. The building's public side, its
facade and entrance, was grand enough, all the architecture money
could buy, but they stepped out of the elevator into a long, corporate
barracks of a room. Secretaries labored in a center row of cubicles;
hutchlike offices lined the outer walls. One of these was Chloe's. There

was nothing fancy about any of it, but that worked in its favor, as if everyone here was too engrossed in serious business to pay attention to their surroundings.

"Come on, I'll give you the cheap tour." Chloe led the way. Her parents followed and Jack brought up the rear. He hadn't been up here often, a time or two meeting her after work, but he already knew there wasn't much to see. Chloe was covering ground, smiling back over her shoulder to make sure the others kept up. People glanced at the little procession but no one greeted Chloe, nor she them. Jack watched the faces as she passed. Something in them seemed to close down, was even unfriendly. He gave thanks once again that he didn't work in the corporate world.

He hadn't been in the building since Chloe had all the problems with the junior-grade asshole who must be around here someplace. Jack made a point of glowering into every office they passed. Chloe had refused to tell him a name or any details, so he was free to imagine which one of these dressed-up punks liked talking sex with his wife. But it was almost lunch hour, there was a general emptying out as people began thinking about sandwiches and getting a good spot in the sun of the courtyard. And none of the men he saw looked either flashy enough or creepy enough to match his mental picture. He told himself to forget it, stop clawing at the itch. He didn't enjoy jealousy. He was too good at it.

Chloe reached her office and halted in the doorway like a museum guide. "There's really not that much to it." She shrugged. But Jack knew it meant something, a first office. A toehold on the ladder. Chloe took pride in it, even as she pretended hard not to. Ed should realize this. Ed could calculate to the inch just how much downtown office space was worth, what it meant to have walls that went all the way up to the ceiling. It was a standard-issue office with built-in desk and shelving. Chloe had explained to Jack that you did not decorate an office. Decorating was a girl thing. God forbid you should have a floral-printed Kleenex box holder or a cute poster. Chloe had made room for a coffee mug, and pictures in sterling-silver frames. (Chloe and Jack on

their honeymoon in New Orleans, Chloe's family assembled for Christmas.) Her raincoat hung on a peg. The rest of it could have been anyone's.

Chloe's mother said, "Your own little space. That's so wonderful."

"Mom."

Ed said, "It's an office, Allison, it's not anything to get mushy about."

"You're a big drip. He's really very proud of you, darling. We both
are."

"Easily impressed, aren't they?" Chloe remarked to Jack.

"She never could accept compliments," said Allison. "At least, not
from me. What do I know, I'm just the mother. A figure of fun."

Ed said, "So what exactly is it you do in here? If you don't mind me
asking."

"Different things. They move us around to work in all the bank's
areas, like a medical student doing an internship. We train in finance,
retail banking, sales and marketing, that's things like credit cards and
small and midsize businesses. Oh, and investments, and international
operations."

"I see," said Ed, just as if she'd answered his question.

A man looked in from the open doorway. "Knock knock." It was
Spence, Chloe's boss. Or rather, her boss's boss. Spence was the Vice
President in charge of something-or-other.

"Spence, come on in, I'd like you to meet my parents. Mom, Dad,
Jim Spencer."

Allison said, "We're on our way to the ball game." She indicated the
polo shirts, apologizing.

Spence shook hands with Ed. "A Cards fan, huh." Meaning the hat.
"Don't rub it in, buddy." Spence kissed Allison's hand, cornballing
around so it was funny. To Jack he said, "You have to quit coming up
here, you look too damned good." Jack liked Spence. Everybody liked
him. He was the good boss. "I can't have anybody prettier than me
around here." And this was funny because Spence was a big, well-
upholstered man who had no doubt once been slimmer, but not pretty.
He had a big high balding forehead, a graying mustache and beard that

were a triumph of precision barbering, and a big man's hearty laugh. "Chloe, you gotta mess him up a little."

"I do," said Chloe. "But he heals fast."

And just like that they were smiling, an easy, animated group, something they hadn't been able to achieve on their own. Jack wished he'd said something funny about Ed's hat himself.

"Did you tell your parents you're the star around here? She is. She sets the pace."

"Shucks," said Chloe.

"We were very lucky to get her. We try to treat her like a jewel and keep her polished."

"Cut it out, Spence, they'll think I'm paying you off." But Chloe looked happy. Contrary to what her mother had said, she did know how to accept compliments.

Spence was the one who made it a point to know all the trainees' names. He was very good at his job, he'd made a name for himself, moving from one institution to another, acquiring ever more hiring bonuses and stock options. Being successful was probably what allowed him the luxury of being nice. Spence said, "Chloe tell you about her award?"

"Chloe!"

"Mom, it's more like what you get for finishing probation."

"Well, it's a little more than that. She gets to go with us to New York next month for a junket. Not that we call it that. It's officially a week of off-site training. But we only take the top people in the class."

"I just found out, I was going to tell everyone tonight at dinner. Oh well."

Jack put an arm around her shoulders. "Congratulations."

"No huge fuss, okay?"

"Sort of huge."

Ed said, "Congratulations, baby," and Allison said that she never told them *anything*. It was a setup. Chloe had asked Spence to deliver her news for her. Jack was certain of it, though he couldn't think why, unless it was intended to impress the parents.

Spence asked Ed and Allison how long they were going to be in town, could he take them to lunch? It was too late for that, they were going to eat hot dogs at the ballpark. Spence probably figured on that. Still, it was nice of him to go through the motions. It was nice for Chloe's sake. Jack raised his eyebrows at her, winked, and she gave him a remote smile. She seemed anxious to move things along and sent them all on their way, probably before Ed and Allison could launch into another one of their picturesque arguments. It was his cue.

"Guys, we should probably get a move on."

Spence shook hands with everyone again. "You folks have yourself a time, now."

"Take care of our girl," said Ed, and Spence promised that he would.

Jack said, "Just don't keep her out too late tonight."

"Now that's the kind of thing I like to hear from a husband."

That was good for another laugh, then they made their way to the elevators. Jack looked back and saw Chloe and Spence already engrossed in serious conversation. Chloe frowned over a piece of computer printout. Back to work. It was an office, after all, not a place where wives, husbands, and sweethearts were meant to be hanging around.

In the cab on the way to Wrigley, Ed said, "Well. Well, well, well."

"I hope she'll be careful in New York," said Allison.

Jack said that Chloe worked really hard, it was good to see it starting to pay off for her. He told himself that he was not, goddamn it, going to begrudge her any of it. He was going to be supportive. The enlightened husband. The cab let them off a couple of blocks from Wrigley, and they joined the crowd sauntering in from the parking lots. It seemed to have gotten hotter out on the sidewalks. Four or five young men passed them, their heads shaved at the sides like marines. They wore shirts advertising different alcoholic beverages. They were loud and casually profane. Fucking this, fucking that. Jack stopped at a vendor and bought two Cubs hats.

"Here." He handed one to his father-in-law. "Do me a favor, wear it."

The seats were good seats. Just over first base, and close in. Chloe had procured them through someone at work. Jack got Ed and Allison settled and went to track down hot dogs. A beautiful day at the Friendly Confines. You didn't come to a Cubs game for the team, but because, by God, it was such a pretty place, ivy, mint-condition grass, the corny organist playing "Take Me Out to the Ball Game," and people singing along, bawling, really. What was bothering him wasn't Chloe's new success, or not entirely. Chloe hadn't wanted him there this morning. He had thought it was her parents that made her so distant and edgy, but it had been him.

Jack returned with the hot dogs just as they were finishing up "The Star-Spangled Banner." The singer was a guy who took singing seriously, somebody from a choir or maybe the Lyric Opera. He succeeded in making the national anthem into such a showpiece of trills and vibrato, everyone in the stadium must have felt secretly relieved that it couldn't be sung in any normal way. "Brewers, huh," said Ed, accepting his hot dog. "They're pretty lame, aren't they?"

"Yeah, but they always get inspired when they play here." Jack hoped not to get too involved in the play-by-play. He tried to remember something knowledgeable about the Brewers' starter. He was a left-hander. Jack offered this up. But Ed only nodded, looking thoughtful, and turned his head toward Jack, adjusting his cap to shade his face.

"You guys are okay, aren't you?"

"Sure," said Jack automatically. Then, "What are you talking about?"

"The two of you."

"Jesus, Ed. This is a ball game."

"Sometimes, it's nobody's fault, things just get off track."

Jack opened his mouth to say something, he didn't yet know what, but Ed raised a hand to wave him off. "Look, never mind, tell me to butt out."

"Ed, we're fine. Why do you . . ." Jack glanced across to Allison, on Ed's other side. She wasn't paying attention; she was having a hard time balancing her hot dog and her game program. "Are you talking about something Chloe said, or . . ."

"Ah hell, Jack, you're a good kid. I always thought that." Ed patted Jack's knee. Jack couldn't remember him ever doing such a thing. "Maybe someday you'll have a daughter, you'll understand how foolish you can get. You start thinking the world's an ocean, and everybody swimming in it is a shark. Forget I said anything. Play ball."

Ed raised his hands to his mouth like a megaphone and whooped along with the crowd. The Brewers batted first and stranded a runner on first. Then the Cubs were at bat and the Brewers' left-handed pitcher went into his windup. The batter hit a pop fly and everyone groaned and settled in for a long afternoon.

Jack stared straight ahead of him. What had he done or said to make Ed think of him as a shark? He watched the first two Cubs go down in order, one strikeout and an easy tag at first, pop fly. Sammy Sosa was up next. The crowd did its thing. "Sam-mee! Sam-mee!" You had to have somebody to get excited about on this team. Sammy waved and tipped his hat, took a few more massive chops of the bat for practice. He bulled his way to first with a long grounder. The batter after Sammy got on base but Sammy was forced out at second. People swore and hooted. It was all part of the show.

The teams traded places and the Cubs took the field. Kerry Wood was the starting pitcher today and that got the crowd going again. It meant there would be no prisoners. The seats were close in enough to see the players' features. Wood had his game face going. He scowled into his blond beard and threw a bullet, a dead-center strike. Then another. Then the catcher trotted out to the mound and everything slowed down. Ed hadn't meant him.

It wasn't some kid in the training group that Chloe had been talking about. It was Spence, and the fact that she hadn't mentioned anything lately meant it was still going on, and Chloe had lied about everything.

He didn't move. He didn't want his face to register any expression. Ed had seen it right away, sensed something. Good old Spence. Good old Spence was taking his wife to New York for a week. The performance this morning had been for his benefit. Chloe hadn't wanted to be the one to tell him. Maybe they weren't even going to New York, but somewhere sexier. Barbados, or wherever rich men went for such things.

Slow down. His head was pounding and his heart seemed to have dropped down deep inside him. Suspicion wasn't proof. He had a choice here. He could be a blind complacent fool or a paranoid fool. He felt the terrible pressure of having to decide what he should do. He tried to remember anything Chloe might have said about Spence. Spence was married himself and had children, well, that never stopped anybody. And her harassment story made a lot more sense if you substituted boss for coworker. A coworker wouldn't have any power over her, and none of the temptations of power. Jack saw again Spence's big, bearded face, his big, well-manicured hands, Chloe, naked, the hands touching her . . .

He refused to allow himself to think like this. It was pornographic. It wasn't fair to Chloe. She had told him about it, or at least she'd told him some version of it. Had she wanted him to do or say something more, had he failed some test? But she'd said she'd handled it, it was over. Christ, didn't he want to believe her?

The crowd roared and hooted. He'd lost track of the game, something had them excited. Allison was saying that one of the players was cute. Jack smirked along with Ed. Ha ha. His face had thickened, stiffened. He couldn't say anything to Chloe, do anything, while her parents were around. He felt a coward's relief.

"My *word*."

Jack looked up to see Allison glaring at somebody behind her. "What?" he asked, leaning across Ed.

"He spilled beer on me!"

Jack craned to see who it was in the seat behind her. A gap-toothed white guy in a black T-shirt and a porkpie hat. His face had a crumpled look to it, as if someone had squeezed it, hard, when he was still a baby. Knuckles blue with scribbled tattoos. His equally skanky girlfriend sat next to him. She was wearing one of those bra tops and shouldn't have been. Pork Pie raised his beer, shrugged. "Sorry, man. Accident."

Allison said, meaning to be overheard, "Honestly. Some people."

The world was full of scumbags. They came in all varieties. The Cubs were up again. No score. Jack hadn't missed anything. It was only the second inning. He was going to have to sit here and practice what he'd do, say, when he next saw Chloe. Smile. Make chitchat. Keep it zipped.

From the corner of his eye, Jack saw Pork Pie nudging his girlfriend, saw him tip his beer, deliberately, delicately, so that a thin stream landed on Allison's neck.

Jack was out of his seat even as Allison arched her back and felt at
her collar. He planted one foot next to Pork Pie's knee, leaned in to
keep him from getting to his feet. "What's the matter, asshole, game not
exciting enough for you?"

He'd caught Pork Pie by surprise, but he still had enough attitude to
come back at him. "Hey, get outta my face, man."

"Apologize to the lady."

"S'accident." He was cock-eyed drunk. Jack could smell it on him.

"No, accident is what must have made you so damn ugly."

"Fuck you, man."

"That's very original. Stunning, in fact."

Skank Girl put in her two cents' worth. "What is your major mal-
function, huh?"

People behind them were starting to shout at him to get out of the
way, sit down. Ed was saying, Jack? Jack? Reaching up to tug at Jack's
pants leg. "Apologize to the lady," Jack said again. Adrenaline was
making him shake. Just when you thought the universe was against
you, it presented you with a pure gift like this jackass.

"The bitch? She's—"

Jack tucked his head to protect it and drove his weight forward. He
got one hand on Pork Pie's throat, squeezed, swung with his free hand,
connected. Pork Pie's jaw felt like brick. Pork Pie unloaded a punch
that glanced off Jack's ribs. Jack hit him under his chin and felt the
man's teeth slam together. Pork Pie scrabbled at him with both hands,
but only feebly. Jack realized he'd hurt him, and that felt fucking fine,
he wanted to hurt him some more. Skank Girl was screaming and
pounding on Jack with her hard little knuckles and that might have
stung but Jack hardly registered it. He got in a good one on Pork Pie's
already smashed-ugly nose, heard something rip and pop that was either the nose or his own hand, he couldn't tell, but it was the nose that
bled. Noise reached him, people howling, cheering, either for him or
the team, and then his arms were seized from behind and he was wrestled backward.

Two security guards had hold of him and they hurt him more than
Pork Pie had, got him in a headlock and forced him down, then shoved

him to his feet and toted him off. Whoa, these guys were good. Another guard was hauling Pork Pie away. Jack was glad to see him stumble, his head lolling. Skank Girl was screaming that she was going to kill him, kill him, and Jack caught a glimpse of Ed and Allison holding on to each other, pictures of amazement wearing hats, before he was hustled up the stairs and down the ramp.

Then he was underneath the stadium in some sort of wire-mesh security cage with the two guards checking out his ID. They were big, solid men and they made it a point to take a long time with his license. Jack was just as glad Pork Pie wasn't here also. They'd probably had to clean him up.

"Some folks don't know how to enjoy a ball game."

Jack said nothing. His ear and neck hurt where they'd wrestled him, and his right hand was already swelling.

"Mister Orvich. You a lucky man."

Jack waited to be told how lucky he was.

"You didn't break nothing serious on Mister Hauser. And Mister Hauser, he intoxicated. So this is within our discretion, you understand? Whether or not we call CPD?"

"Yeah." They were screwing with him. They were either going to call the cops or they weren't, and for all he knew it was within their discretion to pound the shit out of him. The noise of the game reached him dimly, a subterranean roaring. The guards' faces were fixed and surly. They were loving this.

"Mister Orvich, you come here looking for a fight today?"

"No."

"Excuse me?"

"No sir."

"So why don't you tell me what all the ruckus about?"

"He was pouring beer on my mother-in-law."

They couldn't help it. They cracked up. They couldn't stop laughing.

"Mother-in-law."

"Boy is *too* wild."

"Go on, get out of here, man. Just go."

They handed him his license. They unlocked the cage and one of them led Jack to an exit, followed him out to make sure he left. "Mother-in-law," he said, shaking his head, still mirthful.

Jack wondered where Ed and Allison were, whether they'd stayed to watch the game or were looking for him right now. He didn't want to see them, or anyone, so he kept walking. His hand was, possibly, broken. It throbbed at the end of his arm. His knuckles looked like steak. To avoid seeing it he tucked it inside his shirt. His shirt was already bloody. He hadn't noticed until now. It looked like he'd been finger painting in the stuff. For all he knew there were other things wrong with him, his hair on fire, maybe. People were giving him sideways looks, well screw them and everybody else, except there was no one here he was allowed to hurt or hate, and he felt helpless and stupid but also, he had to admit, ready to do it all over again.

It took him more than an hour to walk home. There was nowhere else he could think to go, unless he wanted to march back up to Chloe's office and make some other kind of mess. When he let himself in, the message light on the answering machine was blinking epileptically. Jack ignored it and went to the kitchen to ice his hand. He was hoping now that it wasn't broken, that it was only the swelling making it so stiff. The phone rang again. He listened to Ed saying to please call them at the hotel as soon as he got in. He took off his shirt, went to throw it out, decided not to leave such a thing festering in the garbage beneath the kitchen sink, made a special trip out to the alley to dispose of it.

By the time Chloe and Ed and Allison arrived, he was making potato salad for dinner. His hand was going to be a problem for a while but he could manage. They walked in the front door calling for him, reached the kitchen and halted in the doorway. "Hey," he said.

"Are you all right?" Chloe asked.

"I'm fine. Did the Cubs win? Silly question."

"Jack!"

"I didn't start the grill yet because I didn't know when you'd get here."

"We spent all afternoon looking for you. We thought you were in the hospital. We thought you were in *jail*."

"Well I'm not. Sorry."

He wasn't looking at Chloe but he could tell she was bristling like a cat. Then she made a point of shutting it down, being ominously normal. "You should probably think about the coals."

"Check. How hungry is everybody?"

"Pretty hungry," said Ed.

"Oh, whenever it's ready," said Allison. "Don't feel you have to rush."

"We'll get it all on the rails," promised Jack. "Ready to move out."

"That's the ticket," said Ed.

By God, he liked his in-laws more and more. They were troopers. Whatever the program called for, they were game. Pretend the kids weren't throwing knives? No problem. They'd stopped and bought beer and wine. There was probably no way to keep them from doing such a thing. In any crisis short of nuclear attack, they would stop at a liquor store. It didn't seem like a big deal right now for Jack to help himself to a beer. His new, evil self.

Conversation took a little while to get airborne. There was talk about hamburger buns, about paper plates versus china. Allison said it had been nice to see where Chloe worked, it was all so downtown. Ed said it sounded like things were going awfully well for her, it sounded like she was tearing the place up. Chloe said she was still just a lowly trainee. Nobody was going to talk about the ball game.

"I've been thinking," said Jack. "What if I went along with you when you go to New York? See the sights. Paint the town."

"It's not a vacation, it's work."

Chloe was running water in the sink. Watching her, Jack couldn't tell anything.

"Oh, I'll stay out of your way. Besides, I bet it's not all work. I remember Spence said 'junket.' I've never been on a junket."

"He was being funny."

"He's a funny guy."

"It's not a trip that's set up for spouses. Not the airfare, not the hotel. Please don't be a butthead."

"I'm happy for you. I want to help you celebrate."

"Fine. Just not in New York."

He could have kept it up, made her keep saying no. Chloe was pretending to be only aggravated with him when she was actually furious. Ed and Allison looked as if they were watching a train wreck in progress. He didn't want to do this, at least not now. Anger only fueled you for so long, before it receded and left you sick at heart.

"Maybe I could go out there for a few days. Let's at least think about it. Where there's a will there's a way, you know? Do we have lighter fluid?"

The grill was set up in the backyard. Jack dumped charcoal out of a bag, poured on some liquid petroleum stink and set it ablaze. The yard faced west and caught the nearly horizontal evening sunlight, heavy and golden. A car rattled through the alley, trailing its blast and boom of amplified music. It was still a beautiful day. The back door was propped open and he saw Ed coming down the hallway to join him.

The last thing he wanted was another heart-to-heart, man-to-man with Ed. He wondered if the women had sent him to try and smooth things over. Perhaps you were allowed, in certain circumstances, to throw punches at a ball game. You were not allowed to skulk around the house acting like you were about to put your fist through a wall.

Ed stepped outside and made a point of looking around him approvingly. "This is a nice little spot. I bet you spend a lot of time out here in good weather."

"Not really."

"I don't believe that jerk. Then they wonder why attendance at games is way down. That's true. It's a trend nationwide."

"Still, you have to give their security points for a prompt, effective response."

"I shouldn't have said anything. MYOB."

"Nothing's your fault."

"This parent business never ends. That's all I can say for myself."

Mr. Dandy's back door opened. Mr. Dandy was one reason they did not spend time sitting in the yard. He was like mosquitoes, only louder. On this occasion Jack was glad to see him.

"Howdy-do, folks." Mr. Dandy advanced on them, sniffing the air as if to test for particulates. His skin was so white and pruney, he looked like he'd spent the summer buried in a pile of dead leaves. "Some nice evening."

Jack made introductions. Mr. Dandy lowered himself into a lawn chair and elevated his feet on a ledge. He wore sandals and thin white socks, an old man's concession to summer. "Lordy Lordy Lordy." He sighed and belched, getting comfortable. "So what's cookin' tonight?"

"Burgers," said Jack. "Nothing better."

"E. coli. That's what they put in beef nowadays. I quit eating it. I don't want to end up with worms."

Ed looked at Jack, eyebrows raised, for some clue as to how he should respond. Jack said nothing. The trick with Mr. Dandy was to let him blather on unchallenged. Ed didn't know that. "Well," Ed said, "that's why you cook it. To kill any contaminants."

Mr. Dandy dismissed this with a hiccup. "You can't cook out the mad cow disease. There's mad cow in Texas. The government doesn't tell you because the big ranchers give them money. That's why there's those Eat Beef commercials. Paid for with our taxes."

Ed said, "I think you've been watching too much *X-Files*."

"Ex-who?"

"Never mind."

"This your father?" Mr. Dandy asked Jack.

"Father-in-law."

"He talks like you. Peculiar."

"Thank you," said Jack.

"They fired my doctor. Whoever invented the HMO, he oughta be hung, then shot."

"Fired?"

"Won't pay for him anymore. He was a good doctor, I don't know what they had against him. Had a good-looking nurse too. Big knockers, careless about her buttons. You get as old as I am, you look forward to a thing like that."

Mr. Dandy didn't look very well, not that he was ever the picture of rosy good health. He was curving into himself like a question mark and there was a tremor to his hands that Jack hadn't noticed before. Mr.

Dandy said, "I got arthritis. I got the hard arteries. I got a soft spot in my one lung. I got the prostate." He turned toward Ed, studied him up and down. "You old enough for that yet? Prostate?"

Jack left them and went inside to get the burgers.

They sat at the dining room table eating dinner. By now they were all quiet with each other, they seemed to have agreed among themselves that there would be no more unpleasantness. Jack had left the burgers on for too long and they were crusty. No one complained. He guessed that he and Chloe would have some kind of blowup once her parents left. Or maybe not. They might just table it, give it a bye. That was one way people dealt, he guessed. Strategic silence. He remembered he'd advocated as much to Pat Rubin. He wondered if Pat had any kind of a hot line.

They were still eating when Jack and Chloe sighed, put down their forks, looked at each other. "Honestly," said Chloe. "I was beginning to hope he'd moved."

"What in the world is that?" Allison asked, staring at the ceiling. It seemed to visibly bulge at each concussive impact, although that didn't seem structurally possible.

Jack said, "The guy upstairs gets carried away once in a while. Be right back." He and Chloe managed to smile at each other, a faint, here-we-go-again smile, another fifteen rounds with Rasta Boy. Maybe the smile was only a kind of reflex, but he felt better for it.

The kid had the music cranked up as well. Bob Marley and the wailers wailed. It was like old times all right. Jack knocked. He could still hear the racket in the far room. Brezak must have invented some kind of giant floor-stamping machine. He knocked again. The door opened a narrow width and Ivory looked out.

She must have known it was him. Her face was ready for him. Sullen and belligerent. He couldn't think why she might be angry with him, except that everybody else was.

Even before Jack could speak, she said, "Yeah, yeah. I know. Richard," she shouted into the apartment. Brezak shouted back. The pounding stopped.

Jack said, "And if you could just . . ."

She turned and did something to drop the volume on the music. There were occasions when Jack thought that most of the problems of the world could be solved if you got rid of loud music.

Ivory reappeared at the door. "There. Happy now?"

Her mouth was held too tight and her eyes were trying their damnedest not to let anything past them and she was not angry with him, not really, she was only wounded, by her life and everything in it, sad girl whose sadness came out crooked. For the second time that day Jack allowed his body to speak for him. He reached for her, drew her in, kissed her hard on her hard mouth, took in the damp, human smell of her skin and hair, her shoulder blades thin and jutting against his arm. It was like holding a child, her bones were that meager, or a willful animal that might struggle dangerously, although she didn't try to pull away from him. He released her and stepped back. "Happy now," he said.

Her mouth was pink and inflamed from him. She rubbed the back of her hand across it, staring him down as the door closed.

Seven

Chloe had left for work and Jack was searching through the apartment for her journal.

He didn't bother feeling bad about it. If you were going to rummage in your wife's underwear drawer and the back of her closet and through her desk, if you got down on your hands and knees to look under the bed, inhale the scurf of rolling gray dust and poke among the rinds of some forgotten, calcified food item, you had to be resolute about shutting down your finer feelings.

He couldn't find the journal. He had to wonder if it was even here, if she might have taken it with her to the office. He had gotten it into his head to read what she wrote. He needed it to feed his unhappiness, keep it up and running.

After Chloe's parents left town, Jack said, "We need to talk about this New York thing."

"I don't think so."

"How many other people are going? Just curious."

"I have no idea. What's all this about, you don't trust me out of your sight? Because then we really do have problems."

He hadn't answered. Backed down. There was nothing to accuse her with except his own jealousy and ravening need. He didn't want to bring up Spence's name just to bait her. New York became a code word for everything unspoken between them. By now Jack wasn't even certain if he wanted to be proved right or wrong, a jilted husband or a crazy man. He wasn't sure if Chloe's journal would prove anything either, but he wanted to know what she wrote in secret. Pathetic, that he would have to read a book to know her heart and mind.

And then, just when he thought he had lost everything, Chloe would turn to him in bed and curl herself around him and they'd fuck, that was the word, hard and fast, and Chloe would whisper I want you, I want all of you, and there was something new and fevered between them that he would never get his fill of.

He stopped even pretending to work on his own writing. It no longer seemed possible to believe that the people he wrote about were real. Just as California had ceased to be a place he wanted to live, he didn't want to write about it anymore. He supposed he'd thought of James Joyce writing of Ireland from the Continent. California would be his Ireland. He would reveal and expose the country of his youth (its beautiful surfaces and shallow depths) with his gifts of silence, exile, and cunning. Except he wasn't Joyce. Funny how he hadn't noticed before.

In an attempt to salvage something from the novel, he spent several mornings making elaborate notes, diagrams of where the plot and characters might take him, complete with swooping arrows and exclamation points and interlocking circles. When he looked at these pages, it was apparent that he had been drawing, not writing.

He didn't say anything about this to Chloe. When she asked him how things were going, he said what he always did, that things were fine, not bad.

For the Fourth of July, some of the old Northwestern crowd, Reg and Fran among them, were coming into the city for the fireworks. They were all going to meet in Grant Park and find a good spot, smoke the dope that somebody still kept on hand, watch the electric sparks rain into the black water, add their stoned oohs and aahs to everyone else's. The night before, Jack said to Chloe, "You haven't had a drink in three weeks."

They were in bed, a non-sex night, the two of them lying quietly, loosely twined, before sleep. There was enough light from the street to outline the shape of the windows and Chloe's soft profile.

"Yay for me."

"Yes, yay. You should give yourself credit."

The sheet rustled as Chloe moved away, untangling herself. "It's not all that big a deal. A few weeks. You said so yourself."

"I only meant, you shouldn't expect to accomplish something that big instantly. But it is a big deal." Jack reached over and pinched her nose gently. "Dummy. I'm giving you positive reinforcement."

"I know."

Jack waited. He pinched her nose again. "You're supposed to say something nice now."

"I know that too. Okay. But sometimes I don't think I can ever be nice enough back to you. I feel like one of those Third World countries that can't ever get out of debt."

"You shouldn't turn every piece of good news into something you feel bad about."

"But I do. Because I can do it better than anything."

He had to stop himself from sighing audibly. She could go on and on like this. And Jack's job was to keep protesting and reassuring, in ways that were never effective but somehow necessary, that she was wrong about it all, she was not worthless, undeserving, and so on. He was the ambassador to a Third World country, a place with some desperate, inequitable, crippled government that would never really improve.

Jack said, "I don't even think you believe that about yourself. That you're some terrible human being. You're used to saying it, is all. It allowed you to have low expectations of yourself that can never be a source of disappointment. It's a defense mechanism."

"Thank you. For telling me how I really feel. I can never figure that part out."

"Well Christ, Chloe, if there's something you don't like about yourself, make some effort to change it. That's why I want to give you a lot of credit for not drinking. You're taking control. You're addressing a problem honestly and working toward a solution."

Chloe didn't answer, and his own words hung in the air, fatuous, glib, pompous, the distillation of a hundred slick magazine pages on Healthy Living. Chloe kept her silence. She was either thinking about what he'd said, or she was treating it with the unspoken contempt it deserved. He should apologize. She was probably waiting for him to do so. Somehow things had gotten all twisted around until he couldn't remember who had done the most wrong to whom.

Another space of silence passed. He touched Chloe's bare arm. "Is there anything you want to tell me?" he whispered. But by then she was asleep.

The Fourth of July weekend started out muggy and gray, a headache sky that made you squint and shield your eyes even in the absence of sun. Everyone watched the horizon, expecting the worst. After all, it was Chicago. By noon the first line of storms pushed in from the northwest. Long, ripping peals of thunder sounded. Lightning forked and danced. Picnickers in forest preserves ran for cover. A drilling rain followed. It soaked the patriotic bunting along parade routes in Northbrook and Skokie, it kept sailboats in the harbor and moved the backyard barbeques in Bridgeport inside. Then the rain passed away to the south and people tried to calculate how much clear air they'd have before the next batch of violent weather arrived. Because summer storms always seemed to arrive in platoons, fresh waves of electricity and lashing rain. If you watched from the roof of a very tall building (say, the Hancock, which might have been built for no other purpose), at any time you would see, out over the lake or down along the Indiana border, advancing or receding, the wall of blue-purple cloud that meant falling rain.

Everybody worried about the lakefront fireworks and how crummy it would be if they had to cancel. There was a rain date if they needed it, and somebody somewhere in the public events office would decide whether or not to be a giant killjoy. At six o'clock Chloe was on the phone to their friends who lived in Lincoln Park. A light, steady drizzle was falling. The television radar showed fist-sized patches of green rain near Rockford. It could go either way, disperse or settle into a downpour. The friends said they could still come over. Which meant taking the chance of being in traffic when the skies opened again, then hanging out on someone's apartment balcony or watching videos.

Chloe said Sure, they could still get together. It was clear no one had a lot of enthusiasm for plan B. Reg and Fran were coming to Jack and Chloe's place first, they were already on their way. Once they'd arrived, everyone would check the weather again, figure something out.

Jack very much hoped it would stop raining, and they would spend the evening in a group that would dilute the presence of Reg and Fran. It wasn't their fault that he didn't want to see them. After the infamous dinner, Chloe had called to apologize. Reg and Fran had been just terrific about everything, just super. They completely understood. They fell all over themselves to understand. It was, gee whiz, the kind of thing that could happen to anyone. Jack resented even their niceness. There was something craven about it.

It was raining harder when Reg and Fran showed up. "Who ordered this weather?" asked Reg, stamping his feet to dry them. He was wearing a shirt made out of a flag, different patches of oversized red white and blue stars and stripes, laid out so the stripes ran perpendicular and hectic.

Fran said, "It's so great to see you guys?" Giving it the rising inflection of a question. Jack imagined them in the car on the way here, discussing how to comport themselves. He felt sorry for them, and guilty about his own ill will. Nothing was their fault. They hadn't asked to witness someone else's misbehavior and humiliation. They didn't have to come here, try to smooth things over. Sometimes going through the motions of friendship was indistinguishable from real friendship.

There was the rain to talk about, and whether or not they should stay or go to Lincoln Park, whether and when they'd hear about the fireworks. Jack and Chloe served glasses of lemonade. Lemonade, now, that hit the spot. Reg and Fran were delighted with lemonade. They could have been offered beakers of O negative and that would have been fine too. Chloe maintained a detached, ironic smile, which Jack recognized as a defense against shame. She asked Fran to help her in the kitchen and the two of them trooped off. Jack wondered, not for the first time, if there were things Fran knew about his marriage that he himself did not.

Jack and Reg watched the rain pool along the sides of the street in shallow lakes. The overworked sewers were forcing water back out in plumes and sluices. "Good day for ducks," Reg offered.

"The ducks can have it."

"When I was a kid we used to go fishing up in Wisconsin every Fourth. My folks had a cabin and my aunt and uncle had one next door, so there's all us kids running around, swimming and scratching mosquito bites. We fished for crappie and bass. Had ourselves some big old fish frys. Bread em in cornmeal, cook em in bacon grease. Nothing better."

"You won't believe this, Reg, but I've never been fishing."

"Get outta here." The flag shirt made it seem as if Uncle Sam was giving him a look of national disbelief.

"Well we didn't exactly live on Lake Gitchigumee." No cousins or other kinfolk on the premises either. The Orloviches were a meager and dispersed clan.

"We gotta do something about that! Jack! We'll get you out on a bass boat with a high-test reel and some hungry bigmouths. You'll be in heaven! Any weekend. Just say the word."

Jack said thanks, it was something to think about. He envisioned a fishing trip with Reg. It would have its moments. The fishing would be all right. He and Reg would get by. Maybe they could trade dirty jokes. Find some conversational path that didn't reach the usual dead end. He tried to imagine asking Reg about married happiness. His imagination stopped right there. He wondered when he had last talked to anyone with ease, without withholding himself, hedging and guarding.

Reg took another melancholy look at the rain. He was probably measuring this holiday against the idylls of his youth. An early, rainy twilight was closing in. Jack turned on the radio to try and get the word on the fireworks. Fran and Chloe came back in with potato chips and dips and carrot sticks, and they killed a little more time wondering what to do for dinner, if anything was open, if it was worth getting wet to find out. Nobody wanted to go to Lincoln Park. Eventually Jack and Reg drove around until they found a Kentucky Fried Chicken and came back with buckets of chicken so heavily breaded they looked corrugated.

At eight o'clock the fireworks were officially canceled. Almost immediately the rain let up and the sky softened to a misty drizzle. "Well that's crummy," said Fran. "I guess I don't feel real patriotic."

Chloe said, "We could sing songs. We could do historical reenactments." She seemed to have settled on mirthless irony as her tone for the evening.

Or Reg and Fran could just go home, which was probably what they were waiting around politely to do. Jack willed them doorward. His brief flicker of affection toward them had not caught fire. He gave them credit for good intentions, he granted that they were loyal to the point of perversity, but in fact they bored him and always had. He was trying to keep his distance from Fran, who eyed him from time to time with moist sympathy. You want to fuck Fran, Chloe had accused him, although she hadn't said it again and gave no sign of remembering it. The truth was he both did and didn't want to fuck her. As a pure fantasy, some yummy, blond-furred, bottoms-up romp, sure. As an actuality, a walking talking human being with the capacity to cause him endless wreckage . . .

CRACKCRACKCRACK

"Whoa, what was that?" said Reg. Ever since the rain had slacked off, firecrackers had begun to go off at greater or lesser distances, an isolated pop or a fusillade of noise. One of these had sounded from the street right in front of them. As they looked out to see what was happening, a small, rocklike object arced past them from above, trailing a fizz of gray smoke. It landed on the sidewalk, fizzed and smoked a few seconds more, then CRACKCRACKCRACK, exploded. From somewhere overhead came the sound of applause and encouraging cheers.

Chloe said, "Tell me they are not doing that."

"I think they're up on the roof."

"Are those the guys you were talking about?" asked Reg. "Pretty wild."

"Call the police," directed Chloe.

"I'll go holler up at them."

"Jack, you could get hit by one of those things."

"Well go ahead and call the cops if you want, it's only going to take them about three hours to get here."

"I think we should just all stay inside." Chloe looked more peeved than worried about Jack getting himself exploded, but he knew she was stressed to begin with about the day. If he got himself beaned by a live cherry bomb, he assumed she'd feel bad.

"Look, I'll go out back, that should be safe enough."

"Be careful," said Fran, as if to balance out Chloe's irritation and to demonstrate her anxious concern for him. He had avoided hugging her when she arrived. She looked as if she might try to sneak one in now. Jack ducked out the door with a wave. He thought they were all secretly pleased to have this minor drama to enliven things.

From the backyard he could hear them clearly. There was music playing, and the smell of something charring on a grill, and voices. They'd managed to use the fire escape, a spidery zigzag metal thing, to haul themselves from the kid's kitchen window. "Hey!" Jack called. "Hey, Rich?"

They either couldn't hear him or didn't want to. Jack jumped, pulled the bottom rung of the ladder down, began a cautious ascent. He wondered how often, if at all, anyone inspected fire escapes. This one seemed barely code legal. When he reached the platform that was its terminus, he was still a good four feet below the roof. "Rich?"

A face peered over the edge, the young, pudgy girl he'd seen once on the stairs. She was wearing a white, abbreviated undershirt. Breasts on legs. The cotton fabric squeezed so much of her up and out, even looking at her was an indecent act. She said, "You have to get on top."

"What?"

"Up on the top rail."

There was an improvised stair made out of milk crates, and with it you could reach the railing and haul yourself up to roof level. The girl gave him a hand and Jack tried not to graze her anatomically well-defined nipples with his ascending head. He felt like Mr. Dandy. "Thanks," he said, once he got upright and clear.

"Wow, you're really tall."

"No, just an overachiever."

She walked away. Among the seven or eight people on the roof, Jack identified Rich Brezak, Ivory, and Raggedy Ann.

It was a flat roof with a raised, waist-high parapet of brick, so that it was possible to walk around on it without real caution. This was only a two-story building, but Jack had the sensation of entering some different air, like a bird or an urban astronaut. Neighboring buildings revealed themselves in new, peculiar angles. The sky opened up, the gridwork of wires pressed down. The roof's surface was some gritty, freckled, sandpaperlike substance. Housings for different mechanical items, heating vents, ducts, piping, were scattered around, a field of metal mushrooms. There was a chimney, crumbling brick by brick, marking a long-dead fireplace. Rain still glazed the metal surfaces and puddled along the roof's edges. Everyone was damp from the intermittent drizzle. Brezak looked as if he'd been wetted down to keep him fresh, like lettuce in a grocery store.

He and the rest of them were squatting over a cache of bottle rockets, flares, M-80s, Roman candles, and other less than legal entertainments, laid out in a clear plastic bag. Raggedy Ann leaned across Brezak's shoulder. Ivory crouched with her back against the chimney, fiddling with the boom box, seemingly untroubled by the other girl's presence. He would never understand these people. "Hey, Rich?"

"Don't tell me you're here to bitch. Itsa holiday."

"How about no more aerial bombardment. It's making people nervous."

"No problem. Those were just practice shots."

"Practice?" Jack the obliging straight man, as always.

"We got some big stuff here. Red white and blue, downtown-sized fun."

"Great. Try not to kill anybody. We have company."

"Bring em up, come watch the show. Somebody get this man a piña colada."

"No thanks." But Breast Girl was already pouring from a thermos, handing him a cup. In fact he wasn't anxious to go back downstairs and labor through another round of conversation where each remark landed like a bowling ball. At least up here he had no hosting responsibilities, and if it was a weird scene, it was at least weird and interesting. He took a drink of his piña colada. It tasted of summer and beaches. By now it was nearly dark, but they had distributed a number of cheap citronella candles at intervals along the parapet, shielded from the rain. The music was something not reggae, for once, it was bouncy and rapid-fire and while Jack could not say, on balance, that he liked it, there were parts of it he did. Ivory stood up from her crouch by the boom box and came to stand next to him.

"Happy Fourth."

"Same to you."

Not that she looked happy. But then, she never did. She said, "Act like you're telling me something really really funny."

Jack bent down to whisper into her humid ear. "This is about showing him how much you don't care what he does?"

"Something like that." She threw her head back and laughed, hahahaha.

"Then you shouldn't even be here."

"Hahahaha. What do you know."

"Men don't like being stalked and pursued."

"Yeah. Well that's not what I'm doing." Her eyes passed over Brezak and Raggedy Ann. They amused her.

"I'm just saying. Try a little harder not to try so hard. Keep him guessing."

"That how it works at your house?"

A veil of sudden rain blew across his face; he brushed it aside. She was such an odd, a freakish, even a dangerous girl, and perhaps that was why he could speak to her without certain kinds of caution. "Pretty much."

She smirked at him. Her pale limp hair snaked over her shoulders. She was wearing her usual floppy cottons. She was so without vanity as to seem unkempt. The things they had done together seemed unreal to him, a sexual complicity that had no place in his waking life. She was shaking her head, smiling, her face relaxed from its pretense of mirth. "What's your story?"

"What do you mean?"

"I mean, I know why I'm fucked up, but what the hell happened to you?"

Nothing, he started to say, pissed off that he'd left himself open to her peculiar sympathy. But wasn't that what he'd started off wanting, under the guise of feeling sorry for her, somebody to feel sorry for him, his lost lonely pitiful jerk self.

"Yo, Jack?" Reg's head appeared at the edge of the roof. They'd sent a second patrol after the first. "What's going on?"

"I found the party. Check it out."

Reg took it all in. The candles, the music, the grill, the promise of alcohol. "Well, let me go talk to the girls."

"Sure." He toasted Reg's retreating head with his drink. Ivory had walked away from him. She was helping with the food, gray pseudo-sausages and some sort of corn and tomato and mushroom combination wrapped up in aluminum foil. Jack watched Rich Brezak and two other delinquent types argue about the timing, trajectory, and throw weight of some of the heavier items in their arsenal. Raggedy Ann was rubbing against him like a cat. Jack found the thermos and poured another drink. All around them now, from other rooftops, from vacant lots, back porches, the unsecured territory of parks, a steady crackle and whine of fireworks sounded, some of them visible as clusters of white or red starbursts, or a tail of orange cinders on a concussion rocket. There was a smell of gunpowder and drifting smoke, there were voices everywhere in the darkness, hooting, cheering, a sense that anything might happen, the city taken over by fire or violence, just for the hell of it, in the name of having a good time.

Jack was halfway to an agreeable drunk when Chloe, Fran, and Reg climbed over the edge of the roof. He was surprised to see them. At the most he expected Reg, while the women stayed below and thought dark thoughts, said dark things. But here they all were, making their way cautiously across the uneven, puddled surface. Jack saw them in silhouette, backlit by the alley light. "Hey there," he said brightly. He thought Chloe was probably still mad at him, and now she was here to rip him a new one. She and Fran had their heads together, giggling, amused by something, maybe just the notion of being here. Okay, not mad.

"Hey yourself." Chloe sounded friendly for the first time that day. "So what have we here, the alternative Fourth of July?"

"Yeah. The kids are going to burn the place down, I thought we could watch." Jack observed them taking in the scene, the costume of Breast Girl, the various and striking configurations of hair—braided, shaved, fluorescently tinted. Rich Brezak got to his feet, removing Raggedy Ann from his person, and walked over to rummage in the cooler for a beer. "Rich, thanks for letting us, uh, hang out."

"It's your roof too, buddy. Help yourself to . . ." He waved a hand, indicating food, drink, sexual favors. "Come here, you got to see these."

Jack followed him over to the fireworks cache. A small, respectful crowd had gathered around it. Brezak said, "We got repeaters, candles, mortars, aerials. We got a Blazing Blast Furnace. Some Whistle Whirl comets. A Galactic Glitz. And a Battle of Khe Sahn."

"Well that's . . . Jesus Christ, where did you get this stuff? This isn't fireworks. It's ordnance."

"Internet," said Brezak. "I figure the small stuff, the candles and rockets, we can set off whenever we want. But once we get going with the heavy hitters, we gotta dump and run, cause some chickenshit'll call the law down on us."

Chickenshit Jack thought the kid had probably found his true vocation, as a tactician and guerilla commando, if only he had anything resembling a cause. He was cool and resolute, well provisioned, even organized. Whatever musky charisma kept the two girls fighting over him showed to good advantage as he consulted with one of his lieutenants over the fine points of the Airborne Mortar Kit. Raggedy Ann had draped herself over the kid's knees. Jack had lost sight of Ivory. It occurred to him, dimly, that he ought to keep track of her if only to steer her away from Chloe.

He surveyed the darkened rooftop, but couldn't sort anyone out among the moving shapes. He sensed a need for craft and strategy, without entirely being able to remember how he ought to proceed.

Somebody had fired up a joint. It wafted among the other burned smells. He located Chloe, finally, talking to Reg. And here was Ivory, a safe distance away, loitering near the fireworks. He took note of how amazingly stupid he'd been to have anything to do with her.

Chloe was wearing Jack's rain slicker. It came almost to her knees and with her bare legs it made her look as if she might have been wearing nothing underneath it. What if Spence, Spence and Chloe . . . He made himself follow the thought. What if Chloe's infidelity—Christ, what a word. You needed a word you could spit out of your mouth, like fuck. There probably was such a word but he couldn't think of it. Maybe whatever Chloe had done was just as accidental and detached and stupid as what he'd done, and didn't really count, except now he supposed he was only making excuses for himself.

Jack turned around and collided with Fran. "Whoa, sorry, sorry." He was flustered but Fran was laughing up at him.

"Silly. Watch where you're going."

"Sorry," he said again. Fran seemed to be blocking his way. Jack rearranged his face into jokey good humor. "You having fun yet?"

"Well they are a little, like Chloe said, alternative. But sure. Any old party in a storm."

"I get that. Funny."

"I'm just glad it quit raining."

"Yeah." Jack had stalled out conversationally. His head was full of rum and fumes and an idiot's rage.

Fran lowered her voice so that Jack was forced to bend down to hear her. "I want you to know, if you ever need to talk to somebody, give me a call."

"Talk about what?" he said, then backpedaling, "Thanks. But I don't think I'll need to bother you."

"Like you would ever be a bother. Not."

"Sure. Thanks anyway." He tried to make her disappear. Hocus pocus.

"I know I'm babbling. I love you guys. I consider both of you my friends. You're both precious to me."

Precious? Shit. He was alarmed on all fronts, what the hell was she suggesting, something about Chloe that everybody knew but him, and even as Fran plied him with concern she seemed to be offering up her big blond tits and pink-painted mouth and all the rest and how was he going to tear himself loose from the woman? Just then another round of firecrackers, loud ones, went off, and everyone turned to look at them. Jack pantomimed something to Fran that he hoped conveyed sincerity, regret, an urgent errand, and walked off to join Chloe.

She was still talking with Reg, only they had turned away from each other to register the firecracker noise. Jack made an effort to shrug off the alcohol, knew he was beyond making efforts. "Howdy, folks."

"I've been trying to hit on your woman." Reg not too sober himself. "But I'm not getting anywhere."

Had everyone gone loco tonight? Jack punched Reg in the arm. What a guy. He hadn't yet fixed on what he should say to Chloe so he turned back to the show. Brezak stood at the edge of the roof, overlooking the street. He had perfected a kind of one-handed lob, holding a lit firecracker at the top of the arc for what was probably an unsafe second or two for maximum cool effect. Then he let it fly. Oooh, said his audience. Oooh and oooh. Brezak took a bow.

"I thought he wasn't going to do that anymore," said Chloe. More commentary than disapproval, or at least it didn't sound as if she wanted Jack to do anything about it.

"I don't think it's going to go on much longer." They were setting up the bigger pieces along the edge of the brick parapet. The idea seemed to be a grand finale. At least the rain would probably keep anything from igniting. Raggedy Ann was standing at an admiring distance, Ivory just behind her, although they weren't conversing. Maybe they'd worked it all out, maybe it was like one of those leering TV shows where the guy or girl—that's what they were, guys and girls, certainly not men and women—had to choose between two dates, or sometimes even more than two, and you watched the show mostly so you could make fun of how shallow and nasty everyone was, but not entirely.

Jack turned around, but now Reg had disappeared. "Where'd Reg go?"

"To pee off the roof, I think."

"He wasn't really hitting on you, was he?"

"Oh, you know. Reg."

"Yeah." He could have made a joke about Fran, Oh, you know. Fran. But it wasn't the same thing, it wouldn't go over.

Chloe said, "I'm glad we wound up here. Our little group needed some loosening up."

"Things were bound to be tetchy. Nobody's fault."

Chloe didn't answer. Dead topic, by mutual agreement. Jack said, "If you want loose, I'd say this crew fills the bill." He indicated a pair of hair boys pretending, semi-seriously, to push each other off the roof.

"They're a bunch of lowlifes. And they should definitely keep their music turned down. But I guess they don't ever have to worry about behaving themselves."

"And that's a good thing?" The longer he kept on top of the conversation, the more he felt crafty, a successful drunk.

"I don't know. I guess there's times when it would be a relief to be, well, not them, but to stop even pretending I'm normal . . . Never mind. I'm not making sense. Anyway they're bottom feeders."

"Catfish," agreed Jack. He didn't want to take on the idea of normal, why Chloe might feel she wasn't. His sodden brain was busy contending with the surprise of Chloe saying what he himself felt, at least on occasion, that the kid and his ragtag household represented something one might envy. Lack of impulse control, maybe, all the childish, stupid, spiteful behaviors you condemned in other people and secretly allowed yourself.

Chloe drew the rain slicker close around her. It wasn't raining, technically, but rain seemed suspended in the air around them, along with the smoke and noise of the citywide celebration. Next week she was going to New York. They had stopped arguing about it, that is, Jack had stopped. "I borrowed your coat."

"No problem."

"It smells like you. Sort of like the sheets when you've been in bed for a long time."

"Thanks, I guess." She was giving him an affectionate look, so he supposed he passed the smell test.

"Everybody has their own scent. If we were dogs, we could be happy just hanging around sniffing each other."

The first of the major-league fireworks went into the sky, whump, traveled a long, whistling path, and burst into a chrysanthemum of gold glitter at the end of the block. People sucked in breath. The thing was huge. There were small towns that wouldn't mount shows with pieces this big. More explosions. A trail of red stars that went off like popcorn. A blue and white waterfall, small but elaborately staged, then whump whump, two more sunbursts of redgreenpurple, and a Roman candle that cartwheeled along the rooftop, sending out zigzags of flame.

Everyone screeched and ducked. That one had come a little too close for comfort. Jack, who was watching and cheering along with everyone else, had to wonder what might happen if Brezak launched his missiles into a power line, or a parked car. The pieces were going off too fast to allow for safety concerns. Brezak and one other boy galloped along the length of the roof, lighting fuses. The noise was terrific. Jack's ears went, not blank, because they were filled with reverb and stinging, high frequencies, but they weren't working the way ears were supposed to. A silver-green flare crisscrossed overhead with a mortar. Surely the kid couldn't keep this up much longer without getting very busted.

"Good morning, Vietnam."

The air shook with whistles and reports, white strobes and bursts, electric crackling. The Battle of Khe Sahn, Jack guessed. Chloe moved closer to him, trying to speak. Her words came to him with gaps in between them. " . . . shouldn't . . . worried."

Jack nodded. He was getting a little shouldn't and worried himself, he thought it might be time to head back downstairs. He located Reg, eating sausages and gaping skyward. Chloe waved across the roof to Fran, and Fran mouthed something back. Jack saw . . . He couldn't be sure what he'd seen. He was probably mistaken. By now he was whatever came right after drunk. It was dark, except for the occasional pyrotechnic flash. Even the street lamps were obscured by smoke so full of burnt particles, it settled into the back of your throat like paint. Now what the hell was happening?

Screaming and people flailing around. None of the apparatus in his head was working right, it took him a slow time to sort out this new commotion. It was a girl screaming. Chloe said, "Oh Jesus God." He still couldn't see right. Even when he moved closer and stared, there was some kind of shock filter in his brain that didn't allow for comprehension, the new smell of burning, the raw red glossy wet slick of flesh, the deep angry wound, extending from Raggedy Ann's waist to just below her arm. Something stringy, some part of her, flopped loose from her armpit.

She wasn't even the one screaming. She was still on her feet and her fingers kept plucking at the torn edges of her clothing as if that was the only thing wrong. Except that some of what had been torn was skin. Other people were telling her to lie down, lie down, but the girl's face was noncommittal, absorbed in the fussy task of trying to keep blood from soaking into her shirt. As if one cue, sirens began to sound.

Jack turned and herded Chloe away, toward the fire escape. "Go on down. Go with Reg and Fran." Chloe had a hand pressed to her mouth, as if she was about to lose her stomach. "Can you make it?"

Chloe nodded. She looked seasick. "Hurry up, get moving." He gave her a shove. The sirens had closed in on the street below and one of the girls was screaming down that they needed help, help. Jack watched Chloe take a shaky first step onto the fire escape as Reg reached up to steady her.

The injured girl was making a noise by now, a sound that would have been a scream if she'd had breath for it. It took the cops some little time to get themselves up to the roof, it took the paramedics longer, and until they arrived there wasn't much that could be done for her. Jack and anyone else who chose to look at her had to get used to the sight of the red mess in her side. The cops' flashlights exposed her left breast, tattooed now with both ink and blood. She found enough air to scream then, and her eyes rolled back whitely in her head, and while it was to turn out that she didn't die, at that moment it seemed very possible that she might.

Brezak was saying *Shit shit shit*. He'd tried to talk to the injured girl, soothe her, but she was beyond talking. He stood a little distance away, furiously smoking a cigarette. One of the other girls was crying. Jack didn't see Ivory. Some of the kids had run off before the cops came, and he guessed she was one of them. He couldn't get himself to move. He was still trying to work his mind around it all, understand just how bad things would get. Somebody had collected as many of the fireworks scraps and wrappers and unexploded pieces as they could when they hightailed it out of there. The cops took sour note of what was left.

"Whose party is this?" No answer. Brezak muttered something under his breath. "What's that?"

"Nothing."

"You the one with the fireworks?"

"Maybe you could get a goddamn ambulance here, huh?"

It seemed unsurprising that Brezak was angry. There were only so many emotions you might allow yourself if you were him.

"Maybe we could throw your stupid ass in jail and watch you spread some of that attitude around. Where did you get the fireworks?"

"Some guy brought them."

"And where did he get them?"

"Place in Indiana."

"Which guy?"

"I don't know him, he took off."

"Don't go anywhere," the cop told him. The ambulance was here, the paramedics were climbing up and hustling people out of their way and the girl screamed harder as soon as they touched her.

There was a consultation about how to get her down from the roof. The roof was going to make it a real piece of work, said one of the paramedics, chatting professionally with the cops. In the end they secured her to a backboard and lowered her head to toe, toe to head, all the way down, and by now they'd given her some kind of shot so that the sound she made was fainter, like a broken bagpipe.

Jack stopped the last of the paramedics, who was about to step onto the fire escape. "Is she going to be all right?"

"What the hell do you want me to say?"

Jack let him go. Everyone probably asked the same stupid question. The ambulance left. The cops took down names. It didn't look like anyone was going to jail on the spot. Brezak and some of the rest of them were in a hurry to get to the hospital. Jack knew that Chloe would be waiting for him, probably Reg and Fran too, and there was still more of this night he would have to get through. Rain blew in from the northwest, the last of the day's squalls, and turned the rooftop into a soggy territory of trash and diluting blood. Tomorrow's paper might give the event an inch or so of newsprint as a cautionary tale, a stupid, predictable accident engineered by people who had not believed that such accidents really happened. No one had suggested it was anything else.

Eight

Chloe wanted to be at the airport early. She always had to get to airports early, it was one of the things that Jack was resigned to. Her flight was at nine A.M., and they were on the road before seven. Chloe regarded the traffic on the Kennedy with grim intensity, as if everyone else was going to get there before she did. Jack said, "You know, the one thing about planes, they never take off early."

"Funny."

"I bet the others won't show up for an hour." Five of them were going on the same flight: Chloe, Spence, three of the trainees who Jack knew only by name.

"I don't mind waiting. I can get coffee."

It was true that she never minded waiting, and he was not to read anything into it.

O'Hare was one of those structures that came close to obliterating the natural world. The weather was always concrete, the weather was always traffic, exhaust, glass, and steel. The sky might be blue, as it was today, the sun bright and the breeze fresh, but once you entered the maze of access ramps, the only weather that really counted was On Time, Delayed, and Canceled. Jack threaded his way around to the United terminal, angled in to the curb among the cabs and heaps of disgorged luggage and surly security types making sure everyone kept moving. If you wanted to say a proper good-bye, you had to dawdle as you opened doors, stack and restack suitcases. Chloe was distracted, checking for her ticket and ID. It wasn't even seven-thirty. Jack waited for her to stop fussing.

"How about I call you when I get in."

"Sure. Whenever you get a chance."

"There's a reception tonight. An orientation. Then I guess we're all going out to dinner, so use the cell phone if you need to find me."

"Shouldn't have to."

"I wish you could come. I know you wanted to."

Smiling her best, blue-eyed smile. She was able to relax a little, now that she was finally here. She was able to be nice to him, now that she was almost rid of him.

"Maybe some other time. Enjoy the hell out of everything." Jack carried her suitcase to the curb, slid out the tote wheels and handle. "Knock 'em dead, kiddo."

They kissed, in the self-conscious, public way you kissed at airports, then Jack said, "Break clean," and Chloe stepped away from him, through the glass doors and into the terminal, looking back once to wave.

Jack waved too. He got into the car, edged out in traffic, threaded his way around the ramps and into the short-term parking lot. He found a space, locked the car after him, and walked back to the United terminal. Three days before he had booked a United flight to Detroit, then canceled it. The computer printout and his ID got him through security. He was carrying a backpack, which contained a new Discman and several of Chloe's favorite CDs. He did not intend for Chloe to see him, but if she did, he would say this was a present he had forgotten to give her.

He took the walkway through the United tunnel with its blinking light show and computer-generated chimes, wondered as always if they meant the place to be spooky or relaxing, a weird, outer-space send-off before you entrusted yourself to air travel. *Oh folly, folly:* what he was doing crossed some kind of line, he was aware of that, but he was not inclined to think about it now.

For a time he had tried to come up with a way he could follow Chloe to New York, then gave it up. He had thought about things like hidden microphones, video cameras, tracking devices, all the gizmos ever invented to snare a cheating heart, but that was laughable, he had no idea how to procure or manage such things. He'd found himself considering

wigs and false mustaches for sneaking around airports. That should
have been enough to shame him but it wasn't. Then he remembered
some minor Clint Eastwood movie where Clint was miscast as a master
of disguise. The disguises consisted mostly of Clint wearing a variety of
hats. If he was found out, Jack decided, it would be that much worse to
be wearing a wig or a silly hat.

At the top of the escalator he took a quick look left and right. The
gate for Chloe's flight was midway down the concourse. He set off on a
slow, careful path toward it, looking into all the cocktail lounges and
newstands and Starbucks. Even this early, the place swarmed with trav-
elers. The worst thing about O'Hare was not that it was miserably
crowded, rude, noisy, or inefficient—it was that and more—but how it
made you hate all of humanity. You could be pretty sure they were hat-
ing you right back.

Chloe wasn't in any of the places he checked. As he approached her
gate, he ducked into a bank of pay phones and pretended to dial. It was
still early for the New York flight. The ticket agent hadn't yet opened
up, and only a few people, none of them Chloe, sat waiting. He walked
past the gate, into the end-of-concourse hinterland of snack carts and
not much else, except for several gates jammed together in a round-
house. A troop of young Asian men, each carrying a navy blue JAL
flight bag, milled in front of a departing flight to Los Angeles. A janitor
in no particular hurry pushed a cleaning cart. Outside on the tarmac,
planes lumbered in and out of line. It might have been an elaborately
arranged stage setting designed to convince him that the rest of the
world was normal.

Jack reached the end of the concourse, scanned the seats, and dou-
bled back. Across the aisle he saw Chloe and Spence sitting at a table in
a snack bar.

He stopped dead and found a wall to shield him. They must have
just now sat down. They had paper cups of coffee and they were busy
stirring and blowing and taking cautious sips. Spence had purchased a
sweet roll. Jack could see them clearly enough but not hear them. He
watched Spence break off a piece of the roll, lift it to Chloe's mouth.
Two fingers supported her chin while Chloe's lips parted. She swal-

lowed the bit of roll, then leaned forward to lick the rest of the sugar from his fingertip.

He would fucking kill them both.

Although he was hidden from them, and although he was the one spying them out, he felt horribly visible. Anyone walking past would see murder shooting out of him in gaudy, radioactive flames. He was biting down hard on nothing, he made a conscious effort to unclench his jaw. Spence and Chloe were seated by a window. The splendid morning sun backlit Chloe's hair. She was wearing a black pants suit and a white blouse. Her colors, black and white. She'd always been vain about having the dramatic looks you needed to carry that off. When she had dressed this morning, she was dressing for Spence.

Good old Spence. Now he was covering Chloe's hand with his big executive paw and listening seriously as she explained how truly rotten it made her feel to be screwing around on her clueless dope of a husband. Spence nodded. He was a sensitive guy. He understood her deeply conflicted and nuanced feelings. They did her credit. He was calculating the hours until he'd be able to get into her pants.

If he were Clint Eastwood he would walk over, cool and tough, pull a gun, throw a punch.

Jack didn't move. He couldn't keep from watching them. He needed to hate them both for a while, breathe it in. He probably hated Spence less than he wanted to. After all, what man wouldn't want to fuck Chloe. He knew exactly how that tooth bit. How old was Spence anyway, sneaking up on fifty? Jowls. Going to fat. He looked in the mirror and saw himself too successfully disguised, as a middle-aged man packed into a suit. A guy who probably read, in secret, ads for weight-loss products and hair restorers. His dick gone as lazy as a trout in winter, rising only occasionally to take the missus's familiar bait. Doctors talking somberly of triglycerides and prostate and heart attack, heart attack, heart attack. Oh vicious irony, tragic fate, that a man could achieve the very pinnacle of worldly success, yet find himself looking down this dreary narrowing tunnel, bereft of youth, joy, vigor, passion, etc. Jack corrected himself. He did hate the whoreson prick.

Was it better or worse that his wife was fucking a fat old man? Better
than some muscle-bound walking penis? Was this all just some slimy
career move? He couldn't figure it any other way. Jack didn't doubt that
there'd been some of the pressuring Chloe had talked about, mixed in
with courtship. Promises, coaxing, negotiations. He wondered when,
officially, technically, their affair had begun. Probably back when Chloe
had stopped talking about it, when she said she'd settled it.

So now he knew otherwise, or thought he did, raging fool, skulking
behind a rack of luggage carts.

How long had he been standing there? Once more he felt visible and
self-conscious, but now there was shame in it. He guessed he'd been
there long enough for Chloe and Spence to finish their coffee. They
were getting up from their chairs. Nothing extraordinary in their manner now, they were simply people with a plane to catch, and Jack might
have believed he'd imagined everything except for the look on Spence's
face. Chloe was bending down to retrieve her carry-on. Spence stood
over her. Chloe didn't see him but Jack did. Spence looked happy. Not
just cheerful or content or at ease. Happy, even grateful. Love, hope,
the rebirth of everything that made life worth living. Got the knot in
his middle-aged pecker untied. Oh yes.

Chloe and Spence made their way to the gate and Jack trailed after
them. Up in some control room, security guards were watching TV
monitors, hoping to spot hot babes. Jack paused in front of the arrival
and departures boards and tried not to look like a terrorist. Chloe
headed for the ladies' room. Spence took her carry-on over to the gate.
Jack saw no sign of anyone else from the bank, no one there who
Spence seemed to know. He had to assume that part was a lie also, and
that the two of them were traveling alone. He bet they had first-class
tickets. Fringe benefit to whoring yourself.

When Spence's back was turned, Jack walked quickly past him to
the phones on the other side of the gate. From his hiding place he
watched Chloe emerge from the ladies' room. She passed within a few
yards of him. He heard her heels clicking and imagined, rather than
felt, the current of cool, displaced air in her wake. She took the seat

next to Spence and the two of them settled in to wait. Spence had a newspaper and they traded sections. Jack picked up the phone and dialed Chloe's cell number.

He observed the phone's ringing register on them, and Chloe reaching into her bag for it. Then her amplified, staticky voice in his ear. "Hello?"

"Hey there, beautiful."

"Jack? You're home already?"

He watched the show. The two of them mouthing questions. Christ. What does he want.

"Yeah, there was like, no traffic. So, you all squared away? You get your coffee?"

"What's going on?" Shifting the phone to her other ear. Forehead puckering, expression of impatience. Spence rattled his newspaper, detaching himself. You had to expect these little episodes of unseemliness. Husbands making pests of themselves.

"Nothing. Just wanted to call and tell you how much I'm going to miss you."

"That's nice. Me too."

"I don't want to bug you while you're in New York, I know you'll be busy and all, so I figured I'd better call now. Boy, a week seems like a really long time."

Jack was pleased to see that Chloe had lowered her head in some attempt at privacy. She said, "I know. But it'll go fast."

"When I say I'm going to miss you, you know what I mean, right? The old hubba hubba."

"Don't be obnoxious."

"Marital consortium. Hot cha cha."

"Are you drunk or something?"

Eloquent raised eyebrow from Spence.

"No, but listen, I've been thinking, maybe we've been taking things for granted in that department. Too much of a settled routine."

"Do we have to talk about this right now?"

"A little experimentation. Couldn't hurt. Hey, here's an idea. Phone sex."

"No."

"Come on. Just for fun. Get crazy."

"I'm going to hang up now."

"Fine, but then I'll just keep calling back. If a man can't talk dirty to his own wife—"

"I'm in an airport." Chloe stood up, paced. With her free hand she waved to Spence, waved him off. No big deal.

"So don't say anything. Just listen. Where's your sense of adventure? A mad caprice. I ever tell you that you have a great ass?"

Chloe sighed. They were announcing some flight and Jack heard it in both ears. He said, "Come on. Work with me here. I can get hard just thinking about your ass."

"Thank you."

"I'd like to spread your legs and tickle your pussy till it's wet. How'm I doing so far? Having any effect?"

Spence was motioning to Chloe, he wanted to ask her something. She walked over to him and covered the phone while she spoke. "What's that?" Jack asked.

"I wasn't talking to you, it was one of the guys."

"The guys are all there? Everybody rarin to go?"

"Are you finished yet?" She sat down next to Spence, opened her briefcase.

"Darlin, I'm just warming up. Stay in the moment here with me. I've got you butt naked and I'm playing with you, you know, finger-banging, and then I decide I want your nipples hard—"

"Jack, I'll have to talk to you later." Another off-mike conversation with Spence, who seemed to require something in Chloe's briefcase.

"Why, you're doing something really important now?" Spence leaned across Chloe to retrieve the needed paper. He took the opportunity to squeeze her thigh. The rogue.

"Now's not the time, okay?"

"But I'm just starting to hump you. The way you like it. You know, kind of teasing, so you have to ask—"

The phone clicked off. Jack watched Chloe put it away. Spence asked her something and she said, clearly, Nothing. Spence said—he couldn't guess what Spence might say. Something about the sad necessity of deceiving the injured parties? Or hubba hubba? Chloe smiled briefly and shook her head.

He could have gone up to them then, done the Clint Eastwood thing, watched their faces change. Instead he turned and walked back through the terminal and drove home.

The apartment had the feel of absence. It was a place that a woman had left. Damp towel in the bathroom, empty hanger parked on a doorknob. Her orange juice glass in the sink. The unmade bed. He lay down in the softened sheets, with their ghosts of bodily smells—what was it Chloe had said about the smell of sheets?—and tried to remember back to before his troubles began, his and Chloe's, but he couldn't follow the trail of events that far, nor find any sequence of thought or hope or action that might lead him there again.

He surprised himself by falling asleep, or rather, by waking up. It was almost noon. Chloe's plane had already landed in New York. Jack got up and poked around the kitchen. He was actually hungry, another surprise. He didn't feel good, or anything close to good, but his unhappiness was more matter-of-fact now, he found it easier to take up the weight of it. He made a sandwich and ate it at the kitchen table and sat there a long time, trying to keep his mind from dragging him around the same rutted track, like an ox dragging a millstone, the question of what he must do, do, do.

The only thing that mattered was to get Chloe back. The ox had produced an answer. The how of it was unimportant, as were her lies, the fact that she'd sold herself and made a fool of him. All that could be bargained away, if in the end he had Chloe. It didn't seem impossible. People got through things like this. He loved her. Love, sure, everybody knew what that meant, or thought they did, but who could have guessed it was a stone, a stone inside you, who could have guessed its weight. He wanted her back in spite of everything wrong or sad or lost that had happened, that was happening *right now*, but he couldn't let himself enter that track again, not yet.

Chloe didn't call him that day, or the day after. This meant he was being punished for his stunt on the phone. Jack stayed inside, sunk in himself. He considered calling her, inventing some excuse. He knew he wouldn't be able to go a whole week without talking to her. A part of him was curious to see how long he'd be able to hold out, and even what new, outlandish thing he might do next. Chloe called on the morning of the third day.

"How's it going out there?" Cheery tone. His heart was running laps.

"Fine. Busy. I've got a workshop that starts in a few minutes, so—"

"What kind of workshop?"

"It's on computer fraud."

"How to commit it, or how to catch it?"

"You know, you're not always as funny as you think you are."

"I'm not always trying to be funny."

"How about that business the other day, was that supposed to be funny?"

"No, not really going for funny. Writers, you know. Always trying to paint a picture with words."

"Because it was like getting raped over the phone. If you need to do things like that, find somebody who takes Visa and MasterCard."

"Sorry."

She was waiting for a better apology. Jack held his silence long enough to let her know it wasn't coming. In the background he heard the sounds of—a hotel lobby? Voices, chiming elevators? At least she'd put on her clothes and come downstairs to call him. He said, "So how's New York?"

"Fine."

"Yeah? That's great. How's Spence? I bet he's fine too."

"Everybody's okay."

"Something like this trip, I bet it really builds the old esprit de corps. Team-concept management, all that good stuff."

"This is so childish. You just can't get over me being here. You want me on a leash so you can keep yanking it."

"I'd say you were pretty unleashed these days."

"What? What the hell is that supposed to mean?"

He'd wanted to choke down his anger but he'd failed and now it was too late to be anything else but angry, so he goaded her, he wanted to see if she could turn everything she'd done into his fault, and here she was, coming through like a champ. He had an intuition, no, a twenty-four-carat gold-plated *certainty* that she was drinking again, sneaking drinks like she did the fucking. And because of the drinking, or as a part of it, everything would be turned inside out, guilt into accusations, lies into hotly defended positions. The truth had never been good enough for Chloe because she was never good enough for herself. The funniest damn thing about all this was how well he was coming to understand her.

He said, "All right, look." Stalling. He'd gone too far, too much was going off inside him, like Brezak's Fourth of July fireworks. If he opened his mouth anything might come out, a flamethrower, a dud. Now he only wanted to get off the phone before things got any worse. "I'm sorry this . . . New York business has been such a big issue."

"You're the one who made it an issue."

"Yes. I cop to that. But I think when you get back, we ought to set up another appointment."

"With . . ."

"I think we ought to keep seeing her. Or somebody." There had been only the one session. Something else had always come up.

"Or you could quit acting like a big jerk, which would be a lot cheaper. My workshop's starting, I have to go."

"How about I go ahead and make the appointment, we can talk about it when you get back. Because look, I've never been married before and I didn't practice for it but maybe you get to a place where it's not enough, two people in this little airtight cocoon called marriage, maybe you need to punch a hole in it once in a while, bring in a third party? Somebody to take the pressure off? I guess I can understand that."

Jack stopped talking. Chloe said, "Are you feeling all right? You sound funny."

"Let's forget funny."

"You know what I mean."

"I'm fine. I'm just as fine as everybody else."

"Maybe we should forget fine too for now."

"Agreed."

"Look, I really do have to go. But all right, sure, call and set something up."

"I love you."

"I love you too," said Chloe, hanging up. And maybe she did.

Four more days. He wanted to stop counting. There were probably drugs that were big and bad enough to make you lose four days, but Jack didn't know how to get his hands on them. Chloe had a prescription for Valium. He found them in the bathroom medicine cabinet. Weighed them in his hand. Vitamin V.

First he had to get past the mirror. Hey there, Mister Fool. He looked like crap. He hadn't yet shaved or showered and his mouth was full of dry paste. His hair was stiff and matted, his skin dank, his eyes looked cracked, like eggshells. Maybe he should ask Spence who his barber was, get himself spiffed up. He'd never been inclined to think much about his looks, he thought they were average to good. In any case they were what they were, and since he didn't think about them, he was defended against disappointments. But now he tried to see himself as others might, as a wife who was tired of him might.

A long face, long in the bones, like the rest of him. Forehead, jaw, nose, all the architecture carved out with a heavy hand. Eyes and mouth, his mother's, the sweetener in the mix. He used to fret that his long-lashed blue eyes and curved upper lip made him look girly. It had taken growing up to balance him out, give him the face of a man rather than a pretty boy. Yet what women always remarked on were the vestiges of that prettiness. Maybe Chloe had grown bored with one or the other aspects of his looks, the man's bones or the woman's sweetness, or maybe just the sameness of him, a movie she'd watched for the hundredth time.

In the end he put the Valium back without taking any. He ran water for a shower, shaved, cleaned up his act. Weakness wasn't going to get him anywhere with Chloe.

The ceiling was vibrating with reggae. Brezak had acquired a couple of new CDs—by now Jack was familiar with everything in his repertoire—and was in the process of playing them to death. The volume level this morning was borderline, Jack could have let it go, but he needed to be pissed off at someone besides himself, and so he made his way up to the second floor.

Twice since the Battle of Khe Sahn, he'd made a point of intercepting Brezak on the stairs to ask about the injured girl. Her name, he learned, was Vicki. On the first occasion Brezak held up his own knotty arm to demonstrate how much tissue the girl had lost. And she was going to need skin grafts for the worst of the burns, but the really great thing was that she was still on her parents' insurance.

"So she's going to come through this okay?"

Brezak said Yeah, he guessed. He seemed unduly chipper, long since recovered from his fit of angry guilt. Perhaps he was rendered upbeat by the insurance news, or to give him more credit, relieved that the girl had survived in the first place. "The arm's kind of tough, it means therapy and shit, but the rest, Vick figures she's gonna have some really cool scars."

Jack said he was glad to hear it. In the kid's circle, where skin was routinely inked and perforated, he might well imagine that scars were cool. He thought of dueling scars at Heidelberg before the First World War, decided not to offer that up.

Brezak said, "In this weird way, she was even lucky. One of those big suckers goes off in your face, you have, you know, monster face."

The next time Jack saw him, Brezak said the girl was out of the hospital now but taking it easy. Her parents were being major assholes, they wouldn't let him in to see her. Jack imagined this was probably what it had taken for them to reassert some sort of parental control. A daughter firebombed and partly disassembled.

Now, climbing the stairs, Jack assumed the girl was out of danger and it was appropriate to return to complaint mode. Although this music wasn't that bad, comparatively. It had a back beat that kicked, and the singer hit his high notes square on. My God, he was developing a critical taste for this stuff. He knocked, then pounded. "Rich?"

Feet crossing the floor. Through the closed door Ivory said, "He's not here."

Was he so square and clueless that these people were always going to take him by surprise? So it seemed. "Open up."

"I told you, he's not here."

"I want to talk to you."

"Go ahead."

"It's about Vicki."

"What about her?"

"Would you at least turn the damn music down?"

As if someone had put a lid on a pot, the singing grew tiny. Jack waited, but the door didn't open. "What are you afraid of?"

She worked the latch and opened the door just wide enough to give him a sour face. Jack said, "Were you one of those little girls who everybody kept saying how much prettier you'd be if you smiled more?"

"Fuck off."

"I heard she's going to be all right."

"Yeah, they already kicked her out of the hospital."

"That's a little harsh."

"Look, I don't have to pretend to like her, even if she got herself blown up." She'd twisted her front hair into a number of little braids. It wasn't really flattering; it made her look pop-eyed from the tightened skin. But it was the first gesture toward vanity he'd seen in her.

He said, "So how'd it happen, huh? How'd she get hit by that rocket?"

"Stupid people always wind up getting in the way."

They stared at each other. Jack said, "That's your final answer?"

"Look, I have stuff to do."

"I bet."

The door closed in his face. But half an hour later she was downstairs applying her knuckles to his apartment door. He opened it. "What was that crack supposed to mean?" she demanded.

"Which crack?"

"You know."

He did know. He opened the door wider and allowed her to step inside. Jack watched her take in the room with darting, rabbitlike glances. Even with his three days of nonhousekeeping, it was several cuts above anywhere she'd ever lived, he was pretty sure of that. She said, "Where's wifey?"

"At work." The short answer. "Her name is Chloe."

"Chloe. What kind of name is that?"

"Old-fashioned. Like Irene."

Her nearly lashless eyes flickered, but her face was more belligerent than startled. She wasn't giving an inch. Jack said, "I saw that business on the roof."

She shook her head. He thought this only meant she didn't want to hear any more. "What were you trying to do, kill her?"

"No."

"I saw you point a damn rocket at her." Bluffing now. He couldn't have sworn to it, in all the drifting smoke and rain vapor and drunken commotion and flash and sizzle. But he'd seen Ivory watching the other girl, crouching like a soldier on guard. Something about that rigid posture. A moment later the streak of fire and stinging air.

"Well I wasn't really trying to kill her."

He kept talking, trying to match her so-what tone, but he was deeply unsettled, he hadn't expected her to admit to it. "What were you going for, disfigurement?"

"You make it sound so yucky," she complained. "Besides, it really was sort of an accident."

"Sort of." He was having difficulty with this conversation. It seemed as unreal as a cartoon, cats chasing mice with sledgehammers, Wile E. Coyote treading air as he ran off the edge of a cliff. He saw again the girl's torn skin, the glossy blood. "Sort of doesn't work for me."

"Okay, I thought about it. How nice it would be if she went up in the air and came down like snow. I have to say, it crossed my mind. She's such a pig, I don't know why everybody's always on her side. See, you're doing it too."

"What happened."

"I was just thinking about it," she repeated patiently. "I don't know. My grandma used to say, 'Don't even pretend to do that,' when I was a kid and I got into fights with my brothers and sisters and told them I was going to push them down the stairs or poke their eye out with a stick. That always seemed so unfair, that you couldn't even pretend to do something really rancid."

"She lost part of her arm."

"Oh come on. It honestly was an accident. Those little rocket things just take off on you. Besides, she's going to be fine."

"You're crazy," he muttered. He shouldn't be listening to her.

"So what now, you going to rat me out?" She folded her arms and tilted her head back to look at him.

"Are you even a little bit sorry? Never mind. I guess it doesn't matter."

"God, Orlovich, you are such a girl."

"She could have died."

"Look, I didn't do it on purpose. It was scary. I never saw anybody messed up that bad." She did look sorry, or at least, she was trying to look sorry. "Are you going to tell Rich?"

"I have to think about this."

"Oh, great. Leave it all hanging over my head."

He was thinking about Spence. He wondered if he could take anything into his hand—gun, knife, club—and will himself to use it. Think about it long enough to call it pretending. "Hey, what are you doing?"

Ivory was standing in the dining room, peering down the hallway that led to the rest of the apartment. "Just seeing how the beautiful people live."

By the time he caught up with her, she was in the kitchen. "Boy are you guys slobs."

He hadn't done much cooking on his own, but the evidence of it was piled up on the countertop and in the sink. "I'm the only slob."

"What, she's got you doing the dishes? You are so whipped." Jack didn't answer. "Got your number, don't I."

"You don't know a thing about it."

She made one of her trademark smirking faces and limped past him as he stood in the doorway. She took a step into the bedroom. "How about in here, you keeping up with your chores?"

"Maybe you should leave now."

Instead she walked over to the bed and sat down on it, bounced. Jack had pulled the covers up so that technically the bed was made, although he hadn't bothered to do a good job and it had a slatternly, untidy look. He said, "What are you doing?" Although he knew. He already knew everything that was going to happen.

"How about I make you a deal."

"Don't talk like that."

"Like how, exactly?"

"Like a whore."

"Jeez, Orlovich. Don't tell me a nice boy like you knows how whores talk."

He couldn't remember her calling him by his last name, or any name, before today. It seemed like another whorish thing. He crossed the room and sat next to her on the bed. "I don't think this is a real good idea."

She patted his hand. "We're not exactly in the business of good ideas, are we?"

He let her ease him backward on the bed. He wondered if he was going to be able to go through with this. It wasn't so much a failure of the body that he feared, but a failure of the imagination. Ivory was touching him, kneading him through his clothes. His penis struggled to make its usual counterclockwise swing. Attaboy, Jack. Now he thought about Spence and Chloe, allowed them to come to the front of his mind. This he could imagine. Spence was on top of Chloe. He was fucking her raw with his fat, Viagra-engorged dick. Ivory worked to get him out of his clothes. She moved over him with her mouth and her hair grazed his skin. Then she took hold of him and the good old reliable machinery of arousal started up. But he wasn't entirely inside his body, or wasn't there alone, and among all the other reasons this was a bad idea, fucking shouldn't be about revenge.

Jack reached down and lifted the girl's head away from him so he could get to the drawer where they kept condoms. He closed his eyes and groped one-handed in the pile of empty wrappers.

"Hey."

It startled him that she'd spoken. He opened his eyes to see her pulling her shirt over her head. Her bra was made of something slight and stretchy and she stripped that off also. She had small, juvenile breasts tipped with strawberry. She said, "My leg's really gross. I can, you know, leave some of my clothes on if you want."

So far he hadn't been thinking of her body and its particulars. The question embarrassed him. "What do you usually do?"

"I *usually* wait until it's dark to do it the first time."

"I guess it's up to you."

She shrugged and stood up to manage her skirt and underpants. She kept the long skirt wadded up against one side of her when she lay back down. "Well come on," she said, mildly impatient.

He was having trouble with the condom. Somebody should invent a spray-on model. The longer he had to work and fumble at it, the more desperate the whole business seemed, less an exercise of lust than of engineering, and when he finally got himself ready and positioned himself over her on his hands and knees, he had to think again about Spence and Chloe, get himself raging before he could push into her.

It didn't last long, and he didn't try to do a good job of it. His body spasmed and everything left him, pleasure, thought, fury. The enormity of what he'd done was the only thing remaining.

And yet it was all perfectly matter-of-fact. Their bodies came unstuck with the usual hideous plumbing noises. Ivory covered herself with her clothes before he could do more than register the memory of her thin, child's body. Jack went into the bathroom to put his pants on. He felt dull and spent. He half-expected or hoped that she'd be gone by the time he returned, but she was stretched out on the bed, flexing her knee and then shaking the leg out again.

"She's not due home real soon, is she?"

"She's in New York." He hadn't meant to tell her. He hadn't meant to avoid using Chloe's name again, but so he did.

"I thought you said she was at work. Never mind. I'll go in a minute."

"Sure." He didn't want to lie down with her again so he stood looking into his closet, as if choosing a shirt.

"She's real beautiful."

He kept his back to her. "Thanks."

"I guess that's why you're so hung up on her." Jack turned around then and she held up her hand. "Okay, you don't want to talk about it. I'll go in a minute, I just have to do this stretching stuff so my hip doesn't cramp up."

"I'm sorry if I acted like a jerk about that."

"No biggie."

"I honestly wasn't even thinking about it."

She was straining to adjust something along the length of her right side. "Yeah, don't worry."

Jack found a shirt and put it on. He almost felt worse about the possibility that he'd hurt her feelings than about sleeping with her. So what was he trying to prove anyway? That he was a sensitive guy? That even if he engaged in joyless, get-even sex, he hadn't lost his innate human qualities?

Ivory swung her legs over the side of the bed. "Well I'd love to stay and chat, but I've gotta go to work."

Jack walked ahead of her to the front door. He opened it a crack to make sure Mr. Dandy wasn't prowling the lobby, kept it open to discourage any fond-farewell scene. Not that he needed to worry. Ivory stopped just short of the door and punched him lightly in the stomach. "What does it take to cheer you up, huh?"

He couldn't think of any equally jaunty way to reply. He only shrugged, as if to say he didn't know. Ivory said, "So we're square now? You're not gonna say anything to Rich?"

"I wasn't going to anyway."

Her braids had come loose and the escaped hair was damp and kinked, softening the line of her forehead. Her eyes widened and there was a moment when she was almost pretty, before her face twisted up again into a smirk. "So now he tells me," she remarked, as if to an invisible onlooker. Then, to Jack, "Have a nice day." She crossed the lobby and started up the stairs, waving her fingers over her shoulder, bye-bye.

Nine

When I was six years old, Mom entered me in a contest, Little Miss Sparkle. She sent my picture in and I was chosen to be a finalist. I forget, or maybe I never knew, what kind of promotion the contest was tied into. Chamber of Commerce? Diamonds? Cleaning products? I imagine a bunch of advertising men shuffling through the photo entries, saying rude things about all the little girls who didn't make the cut.

"What's a sparkle?" I asked Mom.

"Something bright and shiny. When you sparkle, you look like this." She made her smile big and white and hectic.

We were in the car, driving downtown. I was wearing my red velvet Christmas dress. Earlier my mother had told me to Hold Still and make a kissing mouth while she dabbed and dotted at my face. My mother's bathroom was like the laboratory of a wizard. There were lotions that smelled of coolness and flowers, and bath salts, chips of sea-foam glitter. There were colors in small glass bottles. I didn't know the names of them, but I imagined I could taste them, like fruits. When she was finished with me, she sighed, "There's my pretty girl," and turned me round toward the mirror so I could grin at my new, lurid face.

The rest I don't remember as well. I was very young, after all, and those memories are like watching a movie with gaps and sudden zooms in and out. Mom held my hand as I trotted beside her through a big shiny echoing space. A hotel lobby? There were other mothers and other little girls all frilled and painted up, and I stared at them. They were pink powder puffs and yellow sugarplum fairies and blue satin princesses. There was a stink of hairspray and cologne. There was a stage, and a man with a microphone talking loudly.

Then a light in my face and the man with the microphone squatting down to talk to me with his scary, unnatural enthusiasm, and my mother holding my hand and prodding me to answer. One little girl, one of the pink ones, wet her pants. There was a drumroll from the orchestra that suddenly materialized in my memory. "How about a big hand for our new Little Miss Sparkle!"

It wasn't me. It was a girl with bright auburn curls and her cheeks rouged up like apples. They went to put the crown on her—it was shiny, but I couldn't tell you if it was made of rhinestones or aluminum foil—and she began screaming and flailing around. A lot of the other little girls were crying too, either because they were disappointed at losing, or because crying seemed like the thing to do just then. One of the mothers was crying. I wasn't used to seeing grown-ups cry and it frightened me to see it, her face crumpling up like that.

I didn't cry. I hadn't yet figured out that this was about winning and losing, pretty and prettier than.

I think we're all born perfect. It's only later that we learn to be ugly, or stupid, or lazy, or whatever kind of crown other people put on our heads.

Little Miss Sparkle kept shrieking. She hit some notes that approached dog range. Her crown cartwheeled away. She ripped the tablecloth from a banquet table and sent the dishes flying. She stuck the knives in her hair. She swallowed broken glass and spit it out like bullets. People screamed and ducked. The man with the microphone made the mistake of coming too close. She bit off his finger and decorated her white lace tights with stipples of his blood. Her mother said, "Lucinda Ann Evans, if you can't take better care of your clothes, this is the last time I buy you anything nice."

In the car on the way home, Mom said, "Well. I'm sure if you'd won, you would have behaved yourself a lot better."

"Uh-huh."

She seemed to think I needed cheering up. "You know, it's a very special thing, what you got to do today."

"Uh-huh." I was kicking at the upholstered seat with my patent leather shoes. Maybe I looked disappointed, but I was lost in the wonderful thumping vibration I could make again and again.

"Sometimes they're looking for a certain type of girl. You just never know until you try. It's not your fault." But she gave the steering wheel a vicious jerk.

Everybody has their own kind of trouble growing up. This was just the flavor mine came in.

When we got home my dad said, in response to my mother's wriggling eyebrows, "Why, don't you look just beautiful, you look like a million bucks." His tone made me uneasy. He reminded me of the man with the microphone.

I rubbed at my face. The makeup felt greasy. I was glad when I could wash it off and change into my ordinary clothes. I was glad I was through with being pretty. It didn't seem like the sort of thing that made anybody very happy.

Ten

Chloe came back from New York and everything was the same as before, except that now they waited for the next thing to happen.

What? Chloe asked him. What is it? During a space of silence at the dinner table, or as they drove, or in bed before, during, or after sex. (Because they never stopped, even in their worst, angriest times, and this was either a sign of marital health, or of some relentless bodily imperative that had nothing to do with the two of them.) And Jack said, Nothing. Sometimes he was the one who asked, and Chloe the one who shrugged off the question and went on about her business. Nothing. Nothing. Jack hurt his mouth with smiling. His heart ticked, his brain spun. He wasn't fooling anyone, he felt like one of those clocks with a glass case, all his inner workings visible. But neither of them was ready for a showdown.

Jack stepped up his teaching schedule. It was easiest to spend less time at home. And the kids cheered him up, or at least distracted him. They were so fiercely contained in their own worlds, he had to take several steps out of himself just to meet them halfway. What did he know about being a black girlchild with her hair done up in a dozen bead-tipped braids, wearing a Baptist cross around her neck and a Starter jacket? What would it take for him to learn? What did he know about any childhood except the one he'd had? For that matter, how could he claim expertise in even his own life when it seemed to be galloping off in all directions. No wonder he'd stalled out as a writer. People thought you could just make everything up. But there were some things you had to know.

The kids made fun of his name. They giggled and put their heads close together and made him rhyme with itch and bitch. They called him Little Britches, they called him the Big O. He allowed some of this, although he insisted that to his face they at least attempt his name. And whenever he stumbled over Javier or Laquanda or some other name and they indignantly corrected him, he said, mildly, that it was a sign of respect to call people what they wished to be called. He made his point. He watched their expressions turn inward, visibly learning.

Maybe there were some things your own face wouldn't tell you; somebody else had to see it for you. These days when Jack looked in a mirror he leered and jigged and mugged, like the kids in his classroom when they knew they were being watched. And Chloe asked, Why are you making that weird face, and he said he didn't know what she meant, it was nothing.

In some universe of French farce, husbands and wives always had lovers, it was understood. They had elegant conversations about it. It was all very blithe and civilized.

Ivory hadn't come around, either upstairs or downstairs, or at least Jack hadn't seen her. It had been a couple of weeks now. Perhaps she was avoiding Brezak. Perhaps she was avoiding him. Whatever the reason, Jack was grateful. He had to wonder if he'd used her to strike back at Chloe, well of course he had. There were times he imagined himself saying to Chloe, You have somebody on the side, well so do I, now we're even. There were other times he thought Ivory was exactly what kept him from saying anything, from some simple, righteous vengeance. It was his own guilt, or maybe something even less worthy, a wish that he might have slept with some other, prettier girl, or maybe he was only a coward.

Then Chloe surprised him by suggesting they go away for a weekend.

"What exactly did you have in mind?" Jack asked. Feeling his way. He had no idea what this meant.

"As far north as we can get. You know. Piney woods. Mosquitoes. Birch-bark canoes. Taverns where they have stuffed deer heads and fish on the walls."

Jack thought briefly of Reg and his Wisconsin summers. He tried to match Chloe's bright, determined tone. "Doesn't really sound like your kind of vacation. The rustic stuff."

"Did I say rustic? No. More like, lodge. Lodge with a spa."

"What brought this on?"

"Well, I got to go to New York, but you really haven't had any kind of a trip . . ."

Careful not to look at each other. "So anyway," Chloe went on, her voice flattening a bit, downshifting, "I can only take a long weekend, I don't get any real vacation time this first year, so this is probably the best I can do. If that sounds like anything you'd enjoy . . ."

Jack wondered if Spence was going on vacation with his family somewhere, and Chloe felt aggrieved by it. Or was she going to break his damn-fool heart all over again, and take him back?

He opted for French farce. "You, me, and the bears. Sounds idyllic."

"Forget bears. Zero bears."

Chloe had looked up some places on-line. She had printouts, rate quotes. There were pictures of chalets and knotty-pine interiors, sunsets over glassy lakes, happy vacationers picking berries, building campfires, hauling trophy fish out of foaming rivers. There were wait-resses bearing trays of hearty north-woods fare, there was Paul Bunyan rendered in massive fiberglass. It was all a little corny, it all had the look of well-worn vacation country, generations of weary city families head-ing up to Minocqua or Lake Tomahawk. But what the hell. It was yel-low August and Chicago baked in its own sweaty juices. It was bound to be cooler somewhere else, and besides, his wife was asking him to go away with her.

They settled on a place with golf and tennis. Not that they really wanted to play golf or tennis, but it seemed a good socioeconomic indi-cator, just as water slides and go-carts suggested another kind of place. For extravagant credit card promises, they got a three-night reserva-tion. Jack picked Chloe up early from work on a Thursday and they stopped at a rest area north of the city so she could change into shorts and a T-shirt. They watched corn and bean fields give way to pasture,

hay fields, grazing black-and-white cows, red barns, the placid coun-
tryside of America's Dairyland. "Vacation," said Jack. "Vacation," said
Chloe.

Chloe rolled down her window and let her hair whip around her
face. "When's the last time we went away like this? Just for fun."

He had to think. "Honeymoon."

"You're kidding."

"Nope."

"New Orleans."

Jack nodded, keeping his eyes on the road. Chloe was silent as she
calculated. "I guess you're right. That's sad."

"All work, no play. Tragic consequences."

"What's that supposed to mean, tragic?"

"Nothing," he said heavily. "It was a witticism. An attempt."

"I don't want to spend all weekend talking about stuff, okay? I want
this to be a noncombat zone."

The highway signs promised places like Bear Creek, Shawano, Belle
Plaine. Clouds as white and puffy as a child's drawing hung in a
crayon-blue sky. The horizon began to close in with marching woods.
Jack wondered if Chloe had fallen asleep. But she stirred. "Did you
make an appointment with what's-her-name yet?"

"I thought you said noncombat zone."

"We aren't there yet."

"You're pretending not to remember her name because you don't
like her."

"Well, did you?"

"Not yet."

She yawned. "I don't know if I can do another of those sessions. I
think I'm through with all that sad-sack talk."

Jack said, "Well, I guess that's good. It could be good. Depending on
how you mean it."

He waited for her to answer but this time she really had fallen asleep.

The resort was a snazzy new log construction designed to evoke his-
toric lodges. Golf carts zipped over the last fairway. The parking lot was
full of prosperous vehicles. There was an actual lake in the near dis-

tance. Inside, the lobby was blond wood and timbers and chandeliers made of antlers. Their room was grandly oversized, with a balcony that offered a view of the shoreline. They felt hopeful, and then some.

They dropped their bags and went out to sit on the deck. A waitress came to take their drink orders. Chloe asked for club soda. She said, "Oh go ahead, get a beer or something. I'm tired of watching you not drink."

Jack ordered a Leinenkugel. It sounded like something you ought to drink in Wisconsin. He said, "Now, that's a lake."

"Very close to what I had in mind. Yes indeed."

The lake stretched out before them in a wide oval, gray at the dock just below where they sat, veined with blue and green farther out. The opposite shore was a third of a mile away. Toy houses lined the water's edge and forested hills rose above them. The far ends of the oval were lost in the trees. A single powerboat buzzed across the lake's surface. A tennis court not too far away sent out the friendly sounds of a ball traveling back and forth. The coming sunset filled the sky with stained-glass tints. It was as pretty a piece of cultivated nature as you could find within four hours' driving distance.

The waitress returned with their drinks. Jack said, "I have a question about bears."

"Just stay on the hiking trails and don't throw away any food."

She left and Chloe said, "That was actually a little more information than I needed."

They raised their glasses and drank to the bears, and then again to avoiding bears. The sunset deepened. Jack asked Chloe if she was hungry and she said she wanted to lie down for a little first.

"You feeling okay?"

"Kind of draggy. I am a drag. Sorry." There were patches of muddy skin beneath her eyes. When Chloe was overtired, her face took on a taut, stretched look, an unsettling skull-beneath-the-skin quality. "I think I just need a nap. Come get me when you want to eat."

"You need anything? Want me to come with?"

But Chloe told him to stay put, she was the official drag here. Jack ordered another beer. He watched the sun touch the western edge of the lake, fire the water into opal and gold. The deck, and the lounge behind it, filled up with people coming in from their golf games or antiquing tours or other organized fun. For the most part they were older than him and Chloe. The resort's prices were too steep for the young and struggling. The guests were Midwestern healthy, that is, well fed, sunburned, good-natured. They wore clothes that had been purchased specifically for vacations. Every one of them seemed to be in a fine mood. They were whooping it up. They were getting their money's worth. Jack had to keep reminding himself of where he was. It was all too disorienting, as if he'd ended up in somebody else's vacation by mistake.

After forty-five minutes he went back to the room to check on Chloe. She was curled up, asleep, the blanket pulled over her. The window curtains were drawn and the room was dim. He used the bathroom, came out, spoke her name. She didn't stir. She looked as if she'd fallen from some great height. Jack shut the room door behind him and went back to the lounge.

He sat at the bar and ordered a sandwich. The beer was making him feel thickheaded, so he switched to scotch. The sandwich came and he got busy with it.

"Fight?"

It was their waitress from earlier. She was standing next to him at the bar. "Excuse me?"

"You two have a fight?"

After a moment he said, "Not this time." He hadn't really noticed her before. She was older than him, mid-thirties perhaps, and she looked like she'd been a cocktail waitress all her life. Something thin, wiry, and worn down about her. Cigarettes-and-coffee skin. Pretty in spite of it. A band of green eyeliner along her upper lid, black below. Her eyelashes were shaggy. Red hair, chemical and overbright, but Jack thought it was probably meant to look dyed, it was red for fun, the same way people did hair pink or purple. Her name tag said Susie.

She said, "I know. None of my business." She raised one eyebrow, as if waiting for him to decide between baked potato or fries.

"Susie."

"That's me."

"You married, Susie?"

"Twice. I think I'm over it. Don't listen to me. I'm a girl with an attitude." There was Wisconsin in her voice, in the bleating *a*s and the upward twist she gave her sentences.

Jack turned on his bar stool and surveyed the room around him as a
conversational tactic, a way to look at something else besides her. "All
these people are happily married," he announced.

"You think? I could tell you some stories. Well. Back to work. I'm
sure glad you nice folks didn't have you a spat."

Jack watched her as she made the rounds of her tables. The resort
went in for middle-of-the-road sexiness when it came to uniforming
their servers. White ruffled blouses, cleavage available if you looked
hard enough, short black skirt with just a hint of dirndl. She moved
with a measured efficiency, picking up, putting down, dispensing chat,
smiles, change. He was trying to remember if he'd left her much of
a tip.

He finished his drink and his sandwich, paid his tab, and went back
to the room. Chloe didn't seem to have moved. Jack leaned down to
feel her cheek. She wasn't feverish, and her breathing was calm. You
couldn't really be angry with someone for falling asleep.

He went back out to the deck. By now the sky was completely dark.
The resort had illuminated their portion of the docks and shoreline
with small electric lanterns, so as not to be sued by guests who might
otherwise fall into the drink. There were a few lights visible on the
lake's far shore. A cool breeze was blowing. It smelled of lake damp and
pine. He turned his head so that he was facing only blackness: tree,
water, sky. Whatever else might happen, he was glad to be in this place
where you could have the illusion of peaceful nothingness.

After a minute Susie came out of the lounge to take his order. "I don't
need anything, thanks. Just getting some air."

"She didn't kick you out, did she?"

"She's sleeping. Catching up on her sleep."

"Glad to hear it. Saves a lot of trouble. Thought we'd have to find you a flop."

Jack took in her tough, serviceable little body, the jut of her hip as she balanced her tray, her watchful eyes in their rings of makeup. He said, "No need. Thanks."

"You come up here for the fishing? Golf? Just a little getaway? Quality time for the two of you? What's your name, hon?"

Jack told her. "Nice to meet you, Jack. Look, don't mind me. It's what I do for a living. Cocktail talk. Smart mouth. Cheer people up. A lot of guys go for it."

"I bet they do."

Her attention lifted from him to a table of golf buddies who were reaching the bottom of their glasses. "Well, don't sit out too late. We're not supposed to tell the guests, but sometimes those damn bears come right up on this porch, looking for something tasty."

"Thanks for the heads-up."

He watched her walk over to the golf buddies, jolly them up, watched them decide to stay for one more round. After a little while he got up and went back to the room, stripped off his clothes and lay beside Chloe in the strange bed. He couldn't give himself much credit for passing up something he didn't want in the first place, but at least he was capable of making a normal, adult decision.

Jack woke up to the sound of a running shower. He opened his eyes to the room's unfamiliar light and shadows. Chloe came out looking scrubbed and small in a white terry-cloth robe. "Oh. You're awake."

"How's Sleeping Beauty?"

"God. You must have thought I'd died on you."

"You slept right through dinner. I bet you're starved."

But when they were seated in the knotty-pine and gingham dining room, facing a menu that swam in syrup and butter and offered five different kinds of pancakes and four different kinds of pig, all Chloe wanted was juice and toast. "What," said Jack.

"Nothing."

"If you're sick . . ."

"No, I just don't feel like, whatever it is you got, moose-meat pie and spaghetti."

"Biscuits and gravy. Fine. Don't eat. Cheaper that way." Chloe still looked tired, out of sorts, and the last thing he wanted was to push her into some stupid argument for no reason. It brought home to him how very badly he wanted this small interlude where he could pretend that everything was well between them.

After breakfast they wandered along the lakefront. It was a clear, bright day with the wind from the north and it was possible to imagine that someday soon it might be autumn. They got in the car and took a tour of the local country, the roadside stands selling corn and white peaches and cherries and honey, the gift shops where you could buy ugly quilts and wood burnings and teddy bears and cheese, cheese, cheese. They ate lunch at a tavern that did indeed have deer heads and fish mounted on the wall, and rest rooms labeled Pointers and Setters, and Chloe had her appetite back now and ate a club sandwich and potato salad, and for a joke they put quarters in the jukebox and played all the polka songs, the ones with tubas and accordions. An old man at the bar, as dry and spry as a grasshopper, asked Chloe to dance. When she protested that she didn't know how, he took her hand and guided her up and down the plank floor, slow at first, then a merry, bouncing pace that made her gasp and wheeze with laughter. Jack watched the old man's face kindle with pleasure and he thought how it was a harmless kindness, in certain circumstances, to share your pretty wife.

The music ended and Chloe sat down, fanning herself and out of breath, and the old man clapped Jack on the shoulder and wanted to buy him a drink, and Jack said thanks, but they'd better get a move on. The old man told Chloe to come back sometime on her own, leave Junior at home, and everybody in the place got a good laugh out of that one.

They were still smiling when they got in the car, and Jack said, "Well, that was—"

"Look, there's something I have to tell you, and I don't know how else to do it except just say it."

His first thought was, Not now. Not this happy, high-water moment that would be taken away from him. He stared out the windshield and waited.

"I'm surprised you don't know already, I mean, it's right under your nose . . ." Jack turned toward her, shaping words. "I'm pregnant."

Then she said, "Say something."

Jack shook his head. "Incredible."

"Tell me you're happy."

"Sure." He started the car. "That's great. Yay us."

"Mornings are getting a little rough. That honestly happens. What? What is it?"

"Shell shock. Give me a minute." He turned onto the highway and headed back toward the lodge. "You're sure about this?"

"I did one of those tests. I guess I should go to a doctor to make sure. But I swear, I can tell. I feel all *fertile*." She waited for him to insert some enthusiasm.

"So when is all this . . . When?"

Chloe's expression grew avid. "You're supposed to count from your last period, but I know it's got to be a couple weeks after that, so July August September October November December January February March. Sometime in March."

Jack kept his eyes on the road and reached over to pat her hand. "Pretty amazing."

"Tell me you're okay with this."

"Sure I am."

Chloe settled back into her seat. "I know I didn't do a great job of telling you, but at least I got it out."

"Full disclosure. Yep."

"I took the test a week ago, but I sort of knew before then." The turnoff to the resort came up and she braced herself as Jack slowed and swung into it. "We've got like a million things to decide."

"Plenty of time for that." He found a parking space, shut the engine off. He kissed Chloe on the top of her head. He asked her what she felt like doing for the rest of the afternoon and she said maybe a massage. She was going to load up on all the pampering she could between now and March. Jack said he'd just hang out, maybe go buy cigars. They kissed again and he watched her walk across the lobby. You couldn't tell anything by looking, it was way too early for that.

When he was sure she'd gone to the spa, he went back to the room and lay down on the bed, but, unable to stay still, left again and went outside to wander the landscaped pathways that allowed for the illusion of walking through forest. He spent more than an hour there, and this time when he got back to the room, Chloe was there, reading a magazine.

"How was the massage?"

"Fantastic. I don't have a bone in my body."

"How about a boat ride? I saw where you can rent canoes. If you're up for it."

"You don't know how to paddle a canoe."

"Sure I do. I took a video course. Come on."

He was pulling her off the bed, and she squealed. "What, this minute?"

"Best time of day. No mosquitoes."

The canoes were green, broad beamed, sturdy, designed to be forgiving of amateur boatmen. The teenaged attendant gave them paddles and life vests, and had them sign a waiver releasing the resort from any responsibility in case of loss, injury, or drowning. Chloe wobbled and hesitated as she took her seat. "I don't know about this. I don't think I'm going to be much good at paddling."

"Relax, I'll drive." He pushed them away from the dock, labored to get into a rhythm, then found it, dipping cleanly from one side to the other. He could feel the muscles in his back, shoulders, arms, stretching and articulating. He tried to remember the last time he'd done anything physical, besides punching out the jerk in Wrigley Field. Maybe he should start going to a gym.

The breeze had died and the day had grown warm. Midges danced over the water's surface. Gold-edged clouds piled up on the western horizon. Chloe let a hand trail over the side of the canoe. Jack paddled them away from the lodge, toward the most thickly forested part of the shore. Trees closed in overhead. He drew the paddle up and allowed them to drift. It was silent, except for scraps of birdsong, very high and far away. Chloe, who had been half dozing, opened her eyes. "Rest break?"

"Yeah."

"I'm sorry I'm so lazy."

"I guess you've got a good excuse."

"It's not a nine-month illness. I'm going to be one of those super-healthy pregnant ladies. Prenatal aerobics. Wheat germ."

The lake barely lapped at the canoe. There was no current. The sky was blue porcelain. Jack said, "Whose is it?"

She didn't hear him, didn't understand at first. Her placid smile didn't change. Then she saw his face. "What?"

"Is it mine, or the other guy's?"

Even now he hoped to see something in her that would mean innocence. Her eyes flickered. They were as small and hard as grains. *"What?"*

"Doesn't work. Nope. Sorry."

"That's a horrible, horrible . . . I'm going to wait for you to apologize."

"This would be so much more convincing if I didn't already know."

"Jack. Stop this."

"I want to hear you say his name."

"Tell me what's the matter. Why you're doing this."

"Let's just sit right here and have us a talk."

Chloe looked at the shoreline, a hundred yards distant, the placid water, darker where the trees shadowed it. "All right, if you want to talk, let's go back to the room."

Jack held up both paddles, grinned, and shook his head.

"Are you crazy? Did you suddenly have some kind of brain event?"

She was beginning to cry. "Oh please," Jack said. "Could we just skip this part?"

Chloe wiped at her eyes with the back of her hand. "I want to get out of this boat."

"Canoe. I'm insisting on calling things by their right names today. Spade a spade."

"Jack, whatever's upsetting you, we can work it out."

"That's right. Paternity tests. Affidavits."

Her voice rose to a shriek. "Take me back or I'll jump, I'll jump."

Jack waited for the sound to reach its dead end. The trees and water gave back no echoes. "That's pretty much your only other option, but I don't think you'll do it."

Chloe hiccuped. "It's your baby."

"Possibly."

She made another sound, lower down in her throat.

Jack said, "I think you got chickenshit when you found out about this baby. Decided you'd better suck up to hubby. Clean up your act."

She was crying hard now, lifting her face to the sky so that tears streamed down her throat. Jack said, "Something like that? Huh? Come on, Chlo. Show some spunk."

"Why do you hate me?"

"This doesn't have to take all night. Up to you."

"You make me sound like a monster."

"You were scared, you didn't think you were going to get pregnant, or not this soon, while you were still fucking both of us—"

"Stop it."

"—because that's so messy. Have you told him yet? I think he deserves equal notification."

Chloe made some movement in her seat, trying to get farther away from him, it seemed, and the canoe rocked and pitched. She yelped and sat back down. "What do you want, what do you want me to do?"

"Tell me the truth, for once in your screwed-up life. God. I can't stand it that I love you. I really can't. It's like a character defect."

"It's your baby."

"And we know this why?"

"Because the other times I always—we always—used . . ."

He was aware of the sun beating down on the top of his head, the blinding reflections on the water.

"Used stuff. I was careful. I kept track. I'm sorry. I'm really really sorry."

Her sobbing quieted to a steady, keening sound.

"Say his name."

"Stop it."

"Or we could do it like charades. You know, one syllable, sounds like."

"This is a crappy way to behave, Jack. Whatever I've done, this is still crap. You never did anything wrong? You're perfect? You can hate me because you're perfect?"

"Yeah, perfect," he muttered.

"I want to go back now. You've humiliated me, that's what you wanted."

His head hurt from the light slicing the surface of the water. It was tearing at some root of him to continue, but he couldn't stop. "So what should we call the little nipper? Here's a suggestion. Hyphenated names."

Chloe screamed. The sound shook the birds into silence.

Another green canoe nudged around the corner of the forested point. Two people, Mom and Pop types, paddled toward them. Chloe said, "I'll scream again. I swear I will."

The canoe came closer. Cheery hellos traveled across the water. When they got within conversational distance, the man called, "They told us there was somebody else out here. Some great day, huh?"

"It is," said Jack. "Damn nice."

"But next time I'm going for a powerboat."

"Good call."

"Too much of a workout. Where you folks from?"

"Chicago."

"Hey, so are we!" the man wore a bucket-shaped canvas hat, and a pink shirt a couple of shades lighter than his sunburn. His wife was dumpling shaped with a nest of gray hair. They both radiated goodwill. "I guess they get most of their business from Chicago area. I said Chicago, but we actually live in Oak Park."

"Close enough," said Jack.

"Excuse me," said Chloe. "Could you take me back to the lodge?"

"Take you where, hon?"

"If you have room. If I could get in your boat."

"Canoe," Jack reminded her.

"For God's sake, leave me alone."

The couple's expressions had not so much changed as retreated. The man said, "Everything okay here?"

Jack said, "My wife's pregnant and we're trying to figure out who the father is."

Chloe said, "He's crazy and I need to get away from him. I need to get out of this boat."

"Actually," Jack said, "we're almost through here."

The two canoes bobbed and drifted in a pool of ripples. "Now look," said the man. "We're going right over there and sit tight while you folks settle your business."

"Thank you," Jack said.

"We'll be keeping an eye out. To make sure there's no funny stuff."

Jack shrugged. "It's a little late for that."

The couple fumbled with their paddles and chopped their way out to the center of the lake. Although they were some distance away, their voices carried across the water. The woman said, "Was he making a joke?"

The man said, "Don't let them see you looking at them, Barbara."

Chloe said, "Fine. Real class act. I have to go to the bathroom." She wasn't crying, but she looked blotchy and unwell. "This kind of stress isn't good for the baby."

"Please don't tell me that you're going to start using this baby to get you off the hook." But he picked up a paddle. "Just one more thing."

"Spence. It's Spence. Let's go now. Let's go do whatever comes next."

"Is that what you call him in bed? Spence? You guys are like the very zenith of romance."

"I'm not talking to you anymore."

The couple in the other canoe had gone on ahead of them and were standing on the dock, waiting. Their arms were folded and they glowered with righteousness. Jack guided the canoe up to the boat slip. The man bent down to help Chloe out. "Oh thank you," she said, her voice brave and quavering. The dumpling woman put an arm around Chloe and led her away, giving Jack a final look of curdled disgust.

Jack stepped out onto the dock, handed over the paddles, helped the attendant tie up the canoe. The other man was still standing on the dock. Jack brushed past him. "Hey," the man said.

Jack turned and waited. "I've been married twenty-seven years, and I've never raised a hand in anger to my wife."

"That's great. She ever fuck her boss?"

"What kind of way is that to talk." The man shook his head. His face under the canvas hat was red and wattled, like a furious rooster's.

He couldn't keep getting into fights with people who had nothing to do with his life. He walked away, toward the lodge. "Hey, I'm talking to you, mister," the man called after him. The sound dwindled behind him, anger going nowhere.

Chloe was probably in their room with the chain lock on. Crying strategically to the dumpling woman. On the phone to Spence. Jack skirted the lounge, wandered through the lobby, ducked downstairs to the fitness center. Two matrons chatted as they walked the treadmills. They gave him a look. Clearly he didn't belong here, or anywhere else.

He had his wallet on him, and the only set of car keys. He was tempted to get in the car and drive off and leave Chloe to find her own way home—with her new Oak Park friends, maybe—but he didn't want to give her any more ammunition against him. Already he had a sense of how everything might come to be his fault.

It was after five. When he went back to the lounge, it was filling up again with golfers and early diners. Susie was already at work, efficiently serving and clearing, trading jokes and tips. Jack saw her register his presence from across the room, smile at the old couple drinking whiskey sours, then turn her back to give him a view of her bending low over the table.

He sat down at the bar to wait for her. "You again," she said, balancing her tray and cocking her head to one side. Her brilliant red hair was fluffed up like feathers.

"Busy night?"

"Average. It's like a feedlot, except the cattle are happy."

"I need a favor," he said, and held her eye long enough for her to realize he was being serious. "I need a ride out of here."

She considered this. "Just you?"

"That's right."

"Where to?"

"Anywhere I can get a rental car."

"Hang on." She whisked away to pick up her drink orders. A television was on above the bar and Jack watched vapidly as somebody somewhere played golf. After a few minutes she came back. "If you can wait a couple hours, I'll drive you to Green Bay."

"Thanks. You're sure you have time? You won't get in trouble?"

"I'd say you're the one with the trouble around here."

He had a drink, and then another. The televised golf gave way to televised baseball. He paid his tab and walked outside, to the lake's edge. His back and arms were beginning to ache from the canoeing. In the locker room in the basement, he showered and cleaned himself up as best he could. He went up to the front desk, asked for an envelope, detached the car keys, and asked the clerk to make sure the lady in 202 got these in the morning, she was sleeping now and he didn't want to disturb her. Then he went back to the lounge to wait for Susie.

"Half a sec," she told him. "Meet me out by the parking lot." Jack nodded and went to stand at the edge of the front portico. It was too dark to see the lake, but he could hear its quiet voice, the sifting water. He walked around the back of the lodge and tried to make out which window might be Chloe's. He couldn't tell. It wasn't one of the important things anyway.

He returned to the front entrance and a few minutes later Susie came out. She'd changed into jeans and a sleeveless black shirt and high-heeled sandals that made clopping sounds on the wooden steps. She lifted her chin to look up at him. "Ready?"

"I appreciate this. And I hope you'll let me at least pay you for gas." His wallet was still fat with twenty-dollar bills, the big withdrawal for vacation fun.

Susie fished in her handbag for cigarettes, lit one, and started off down the rows of cars. "If that makes you feel better about things."

Maybe he shouldn't have mentioned money, he was insulting her. The true dismalness of his situation was beginning to come home to

him. He reached out and touched her arm to stay her. "I just don't want
to take advantage."

"You're not. I know what taken advantage feels like. Yes I do."

"I don't think I can stand to have anybody else mad at me right now."

"Hey, do I look mad? How often do I get to go off with a handsome
stranger? Relax." She turned her head to the side to breathe out smoke.
The security light overhead turned her hair living pink. "I'm the part
you don't have to worry about."

"You're a nice girl."

"Girl," she said, shrugging, but she smiled and allowed him to take a
step toward her, slide his arm around her bare shoulders, draw her up
for a kiss. He tasted smoke and face powder and whatever perfume-
smelling perfume she'd just applied. He was touched that she'd done
that, primped for him.

Headlights swept over them, a car pulling in. They blinked but didn't
move apart. The car parked a few yards away. The man and woman from
the canoe got out and took their time looking Jack over. They were
dressed up for dinner. Jack had an impression of seersucker, white jack-
ets, handbags.

"You take the cake, buddy," the man said. "You are a genuine work
of art."

The wife said, "I rebuke you. I rebuke you in the name of Jesus."

She and her husband walked away. Susie stepped out of Jack's flaccid
embrace. "Do you know them?"

"Sort of."

"This anything you want to talk about?"

"Not really."

"Boy, you do need to get out of here." She stepped on her cigarette
and led him to the far end of the parking lot. Her car was a new-model
undersized sedan. Susie unlocked his door. "Go ahead and put that
seat all the way back. Still not much legroom."

"I'll manage." Jack shoehorned himself in. Susie started the car,
flipped the radio on. Country station.

"Unless you don't want any tunes."

"No, it's fine." The lodge slid across the rearview mirror and was

gone. The car's headlights turned the dark road ghostly. The radio was
on low, a friendly, twangy voice. He was driving away from Chloe and
that bubble of blood growing inside her that might or might not be his
child, a child that already felt lost to him. He turned to Susie. "You have
any kids?"

"Two. My girl's fifteen, my boy's eleven."

As he was wondering if he should ask about the children's father, or
fathers, she said, "It's just us three. Their dad's not around. And we're
glad he's not. How about you?"

"What?"

"You have kids?"

"No."

"Well if you ever do, try not to be a total dick to them."

The road spun away beneath them. The small car, its darkness and
motion and tiny electric dashboard voices, seemed like a place for
telling secrets. But they were too far down in him. Instead he asked,
"How far to Green Bay?"

"About an hour to the airport. That's where the rentals are. Relax,
enjoy the ride."

"I'm sorry I'm not better company. More entertaining."

"So far, honey, you've been good clean fun."

He must have slept. His head rolled back. When he opened his eyes,
he saw highway, traffic. "We're almost there," Susie told him. "I let you
sleep, you looked like you needed it."

"I guess." For the first moment he hadn't remembered where he was
or why, and then once he did he tried to trace his way back to the one
moment or event that had brought him here, but it was like a river with
no true source. His head hurt, his eyes were having trouble sorting out
the revolving lights and shadows the car's speed produced. Chloe was
an hour away now. Child in a pink womb room.

There was a sign for the airport. Susie slowed to take the exit. She
said, "Are you a spiritual person?"

"Spiritual?"

"I don't mean church. More like forces in the universe more powerful than we are. Do you believe in those?"

"Yeah. Gravity." His mouth was dry. He wondered if he was becoming ill.

"No, silly." She reached over and slapped at his knee. It stung. "Things like coincidence, fate. We don't know each other at all. But here we are, having this *moment*."

"We are that."

"And it's not even sex. Just this connection. Even if we never see each other again. That's what I mean. Spiritual. We have a spiritual connection now."

"I'm glad I got to know you a little."

"You wouldn't guess I'm that kind of person, but I believe in past lives, tarot, ESP, all that stuff. Go on, tell me you think it's all a bunch of hooey."

He thought it was all a bunch of hooey. "No, it's interesting."

The airport's fences and runway lights and tower came into view. "I've got this feeling about you, Mister Troubled Mind. Intuition. I'm very intuitive. Want to hear it?"

"Sure."

"Nothing's ever gonna be quite the same for you from now on." She pulled up to the curb. "Because now you're not the same."

They kissed again over the gearshift, and then Jack got out and watched her taillights drop down a chute made of darkness.

All the rental-car counters were closed. The airport itself looked closed. At the baggage carousel, a single plaid suitcase circled on the belt. It hadn't occurred to him to call ahead, or that small airports went to sleep after ten. There was a traveler's aid office, locked, and in front of it a padded bench that offered the closest thing to comfort. Jack stretched out on it, hoping he'd be overlooked or left alone. He closed his eyes and entered a blue, floating space that had snatches of sleep in it. From time to time he sat up, thinking that no time had passed, and it would be black night and fluorescent glare and metal shadows forever.

At five A.M. a teenaged boy in a white shirt and tie unlocked the counter at Budget. Jack handed over his license and credit card and came away with car keys. He drove south on the interstate to Manitowoc and then Milwaukee, watching the sky lighten and the lake dip in and out of view. By the time he reached the northern suburbs, it was fully light. He turned on the news radio for its hopped-up energy of talk and ads and sports, and so he came to his own street, his own block, and walked in his front door on what was to all appearances a normal Saturday morning.

He lay down in bed and cried for perhaps the second time in his adult life. He slept until close to noon, showered, ate, then hurried to get his packing done. Although he knew it was unlikely that Chloe would start for home immediately—she might have them dragging the lake, she might even stay for the final night of their reservation—he very much wanted to get away before she returned.

In the end he didn't take much, just enough to let her know that he was gone. Clothes, some books, the computer. No one was around as he made trips back and forth to the rental car. Once everything was loaded he closed the front door and stepped out into the street. There was a smell of hot sun, and the rising vapors of exhaust. He had no idea where he was going. He looked up at that portion of skyline available to him, its rooftops and cross-hatched wires and billboards and receding hazy vistas and thought how easy it would be to drive off into the shouldering, anonymous traffic and disappear forever.

Eleven

I was sitting by myself at a party when the Drink came up to me. "I know you," he said. "You're a friend of what's-his-name."

"No I'm not."

"Sure you are, cupcake. You know who I'm talking about, don't you? That guy who hangs with those other guys? I'm tight with all of them. I get around."

I didn't say anything. I thought he was a jerk. I waited for him to get the hint and go away. But the Drink leaned in close to peer into my face. "It won't work."

"What?"

"The princess act. Wearing kind of thin."

I should have gotten up and left right then. Anybody else would have. But I just had to hear more bad news.

"May I sit down?" he asked, sitting down. "I think this should be a private conversation. Let's not spread it around. But you're kind of a sad case, Betty Lou."

"That's not my name."

"Course it's not. I'm funnin' with you. Nobody else does that, do they? They all think you're too stuck up."

"I'm not stuck up. I'm not any kind of princess either."

The Drink shook his head. "Now now. Better you don't interrupt. I have so got you figured, girlie. What a scared little chickenshit you really are. How every time you go somewhere, your chicken heart thinks everybody's watching you and waiting for you to screw up. Which they are, by the way. Everybody loves to see a hotshot, a snob, somebody who thinks they're better than the average dirtbag, get taken down a peg or two. It makes them feel better about themselves. Levels the playing field. Democracy in action."

"I don't understand why they're so mean."

"Because they never get past your gorgeous puss. Not"—he gave me another stare down—"that I haven't seen better. And honestly, I'm not sure how well you're gonna hold up over time. It's all in the cheekbones."

"I don't have to listen to this."

"Relax, girlie. I'm your friend."

"I don't have any friends." I hadn't meant to say that. It just came out.

"Boo hoo."

"I'm alone. I'm always alone."

"Not anymore you aren't," said the Drink. He took my hand. "I'm your friend who's got your number."

The Drink and I started hanging out. He could be pretty good company. He had a wicked sense of humor. He knew how to push people's buttons. Knew their weak spots. Good, mean fun. When you went out with the Drink, you could float above the surface of things, up where everything seemed amusing. And if we ever got a little carried away (damage inflicted on self or others), the Drink told me, Hey, what did it matter. Life was a big, honking joke, a game with crooked rules, and nothing was important enough to take seriously, least of all me.

Then one day I told the Drink I thought we were spending too much time together. People were starting to talk. We needed to cool it, give each other some space. He sulked. He could sulk like a champ. "What, all of a sudden you don't need me around? I get the bum's rush?"

"We just have to be more discreet."

"You think you're too good for me. Honey I'm here to tell you, you ain't."

"That's not it."

"Sure it is. You think you can flimflam the flimflam man? Little self-improvement campaign going on here? Wasted effort. Who else is going to put up with your weak shit except me?"

"We've had some good times," I said. Which was more of my weak shit, and he knew it.

"Those good times are over," he said, walking away. "But we ain't over."

Oh dearie me. What a sad story. Is there any such thing as sympathy for a drunk? Anything I could tell you? The skin-crawling sickness of the morning after, the hole you've dug for yourself just a little deeper. And since you're never going to be able to climb out of it anyway, you might as well do some interior decorating. Hang a few curtains. Stock the fridge. This is where you live and who you are. Everything else is a lie.

And after a hard day of lying, of pretending you're the person everyone thinks you are (Chloe the Wonder Daughter, or the Solid-Gold Bitch, or the Wife Who Won't Behave), isn't it a relief to come home and put your feet up? To sink back into the bottom of the hole, its familiar contours and seepage and smells, and close your eyes?

In the darkness the Drink says, "Whatever happens, no one's ever going to love you like I do."

And I don't even have to speak the words to say them: "I know."

Twelve

On Wednesday afternoon Chloe left her office building a little after five-thirty and walked briskly down LaSalle to Wabash. She crossed the street and stood on the northeast corner to wait for a north-bound bus. It was another day of heat funk, ozone action, glare burning on every glass and metal surface. That year it would stay hot long after people were tired of it, into a parched October. Grass in the parks crisped like shredded wheat. ComEd kept cranking juice to air conditioners and praying the grids stayed up. The lake was a blue mirage of coolness.

Chloe wore her lightest summer suit, the gray. She carried a black briefcase and a slim black handbag. She was part of the purposeful going-home crowd, everyone weary and irritated and trying not to show it. The bus arrived in its own wind of exhaust and grit. Chloe got on and walked halfway down the aisle, balancing, swaying slightly, until she found a seat. The bus left the downtown precincts and bumped its way north to Clark. Chloe got off at her stop and walked the three blocks to the apartment, and by now there was a lagging, dragging quality to her walk, as if the weight or the heat of the day had finally worn her down.

At dusk her bedroom light went on. The rest of the apartment stayed dark. Upstairs, Brezak's shrouded windows began to glow. Just before the streetlights came on, a flock of dingy city birds, starlings, rose up chattering from someone's backyard, like pepper thrown into the sky.

A little after ten the bedroom light went out.

Jack started the car and pulled away from his spot at the curb. It was the same rental car he'd acquired in Green Bay. No one here would rec-

ognize it. Chloe wouldn't recognize it. He had spent the last three days
following her as she came and went. He'd missed her return from Wisconsin. On one of his drive-bys their car wasn't present; the next time it
was. That disappointed him. He'd wanted to know the exact minute
she walked in to find him gone.

On Monday morning (and Tuesday and Wednesday mornings), Jack
waited at the Dunkin Donuts across from the bus stop for Chloe to appear, walking alone, the first sight of her face and small shoulders. At
evening rush hour he circled the city block that contained her building, desperate to be there when she came out, gunning the engine,
swearing death to anyone in his way. He cruised ahead of her bus, cut
through alleys to position himself to spy on her. He identified those
parking spaces which, come nighttime, afforded the best view of the
apartment windows. If he was lucky enough to find one, he parked and
shut off the engine and settled in, sometimes for hours. There were
times when he thought that people passing, people who lived facing
the street, were taking notice of him, and then he started the car and
drove off. He traced different patterns through the side streets, always
bringing him within view of the apartment. It was amazing how
quickly you could get good at this sort of thing. Yo ho! He was a pro. A
pirate of the intersections.

The first two nights he'd been on his own he'd paid for a room in a
midtown businessman's hotel, a utilitarian box with an air conditioner
that roared on and roared off at regular intervals. On Monday he visited
his broker, cashed in one of the Treasury bills, and set up a checking account at a new bank. He moved himself and his tatty belongings into a
furnished month-by-month rental, a third-floor apartment in an Edgewater building that looked like a crime scene waiting to happen. Jack
didn't mind. It was close enough to his old neighborhood to suit his
purposes.

Except that his purposes changed from day to screwed-up day, or
sometimes hourly. He was afraid he'd kill Chloe and Spence if he saw
them together. He was afraid he wouldn't kill them, would settle for offering up some really cutting remarks. He wanted to frighten Chloe
and humiliate and punish her and then he wanted to forgive her and

take her back again. He wanted to be a father to his child. He wanted
the child to have never happened. His life both waking and sleeping
had become a wheel that burned and turned and made a circuit of
everything he felt, but always came back to rest on rage. He bought
some cheap kitchenware and a lamp and a shower curtain for his new
apartment. It felt like furnishing a prison cell.

Each day (Monday, Tuesday, Wednesday), once he knew Chloe was
at work, he went back to the apartment and entered it. Already it
seemed like a kind of museum, a place where a marriage had happened.
He opened the mailbox and extracted anything that was his. He took a
few things he didn't think Chloe would notice: an extra can opener,
lightbulbs, an old set of sheets. He prowled the rooms, looking for bodily secrets on refrigerator shelves and in the bathroom wastebasket.
There were vitamins he didn't remember on the kitchen counter. On her
bedside table, a paperback book, *The Physician's Guide to Pregnancy.*
Within it were pictures of babies in different stages of being unborn.
Tadpole, fish, space alien. It wasn't a real baby yet. It hadn't yet taken
root in his mind.

On Thursday he opened the apartment door to find one of the dining
room chairs set in the entryway like a barricade. On the seat was an envelope with his name on it, written in Chloe's pretty handwriting.

"The jig is up," Jack said aloud. He sat down on the couch with it.
Chloe had written:

Jack:

*I know you've been here. Sooner or later we have to talk. I under-
stand that you're upset and you have issues*

"Issues," said Jack to his invisible witness. "Buddy, we are lousy with
issues."

*but we have to think about the baby. We can't afford to be selfish.
Please call me here or at work, or just let me know you're all right.*

Chloe

"Selfish," Jack told the witness. "Now there's an interesting word choice." But he went to the desk and picked up the phone. He wanted to talk to her, even if it didn't go well. He'd been too long without talking. Words were beginning to back up in him, go sour from disuse.

Before he tried Chloe's work number, it occurred to him to press redial. The phone buzzed and a woman answered, "Mr. Spencer's office."

Jack hung up. He stood for a moment, watching an eddy of dust drift and settle in a shaft of sun.

There were still plenty of his clothes in the bedroom closet, clothes he hadn't wanted to bother with. He chose a white dress shirt and a pair of old khakis. Unfolded them and laid them out on his side of the bed. Arms bent at the elbows, legs in an attitude of casual repose. A scarecrow. The husband who wasn't there.

He hurried to leave before he could change his mind and put the clothes away. It was one more childish, spiteful thing. And he was, by God, going to keep right on doing them.

He'd just stepped out into the lobby and pulled the door shut behind him when he heard feet on the stairs above his head, *Crap,* too late to make it out the front door or unlock the apartment. A pair of legs came into view. They wore teal blue capri pants and straw sandals. A moment later the upper, teal blue half of Mrs. Palermo appeared.

"Is that you?" she said. "Wait, don't tell me. Jack."

"That's right."

"Thank God. I can still remember a name once in a while."

"Sure." Then, because she wasn't going away, "How've you been?"

"Oh I'm fine. But Mom's not so hot. Her blood's bad."

Jack waited for that to make sense. Nothing came to him.

"It's her heart. It's not pumping enough oxygen into the blood, or not pumping fast enough, one of those."

"Is that, I mean it sounds . . ." It was harder than he would have thought to talk. He was rusty.

"She needs a thingamafotchie. Pacemaker. That's the next big fight. You say 'operation,' she acts like you're measuring her for a shroud." Mrs. Palermo had been rummaging one-handed in her tapestry bag, for cigarettes, Jack guessed. Now she stopped, moved a step closer. In the watery light of the lobby, Jack had an impression of teal blue lipstick, though he knew that couldn't be so. She said, "You feeling all right?"

"Me?" He spoke as if there might be some other self standing next to him. "Fine."

"You look, I don't know. Shady."

"I'm shady?" He tried to make a joke of it.

"Shaky, honey. I said shaky. Like you're coming down with something."

Jack allowed as how he might be feeling a little off. He was relieved not to be accused of shadiness, just as he'd been relieved when Mrs. Palermo had turned out not to be Ivory. But now that was dissipating and the clamor of his life was reasserting himself and he was anxious to be gone. "Well . . ."

"I don't know what I'm going to do about her. Maybe find her a Sicilian doctor. A *deaf* Sicilian doctor so they have even more in common. Somebody to make her understand . . ."

Mrs. Palermo shook her head. Beneath the black, teased carapace of her hair Jack could see her white scalp. Her voice thickened. "She's the only mother I'll ever have."

"Sure. It's tough."

"My goddamn brother. I guess he'll come to the funeral."

"Of course he will," said Jack idiotically. He felt both unable to leave the spot where he stood and unable to stay, leaden, itchy, complicated, undone by the simple fact of someone else's trouble. He'd stalled out, forgotten what it was you did or said in any such human episode. He might have kept standing there like a man doing a bad imitation of a mime if Mrs. Palermo hadn't sighed, finally found her cigarettes, shrugged.

"It's in God's hands. What else can you do."

"Amen," said Jack, hoping he sounded reverent instead of snippy.

Mrs. Palermo didn't seem to notice one way or the other. "Look, I have to go. I actually have this whole other house I live in, and three kids, and a husband, and a refrigerator that needs filling. You still have my number, don't you? Call me if you notice anything. Anything at all."

"I honestly don't see that much of your mother." Unless he wanted to add her to his stalking list.

She waved this off. "It's still a help." She'd gotten past her emotion, turned brisk again. "I'll be back in a couple days."

"Could I ask you . . . Does she still talk about your father?" His face burned. He should have kept on not talking. "I was just wondering."

"Oh, once in a while. Usually when I'm doing something she doesn't like." Mrs. Palermo held up her cigarette. "Dad doesn't approve of me smoking. So I've been told. Who knows. Somewhere inside her head, the way she lives makes sense. I have to run, my son's got an acupuncture appointment for his pitcher's elbow. Don't laugh. That stuff really works."

Jack said good-bye and loitered for a moment near the mailboxes so as not to have to walk outside with her. When he did open the door, he took two steps on the sidewalk and came face-to-face with Ivory.

He almost yelped, swallowed it down. She recovered herself more quickly. "Well look who's here," she said, one eyebrow raised in sophisticated mock astonishment.

Jack considered saying Sure, I live here, a non-joke she wouldn't get anyway, settled for Yeah, uh-huh. She peered up at him. "You look seriously crapped out."

By now he'd even run out of monosyllables. Ivory continued. "What's with the not shaving? And the hair?"

He wasn't aware there was anything wrong with his hair. She reached up and tugged at it. "A little scruffy."

He didn't want anyone touching him. He said, "I guess I need cleaning up."

"More like you need to be run through a car wash."

She was giving him a merry look. Jack supposed he should be grateful that he apparently looked like shit. It provided a topic of conversation when they might otherwise have had to consider different matters. Then Ivory's gaze shifted to high beam. Jack turned away.

She said, "What. What is it."

And he was supposed to say, Nothing. He couldn't get his mouth around it. He felt like some ungainly, flightless bird, too stupid to run, speak, save himself. He shook his head. Every part of him shook.

Ivory said, "Come on, let's get out of here." Jack looked down at his feet. They seemed far away. "What did you do, murder somebody? Let's go."

If she noticed that his car was different she didn't say anything, only asked, "You okay to drive?"

"Yes, Christ," he muttered, trying to nudge out of the parking space. He was jammed in, had to shift from drive to reverse, reverse to drive, gaining an inch at a time, bumper grinding against bumper, stopping for oncoming traffic. The tires locked up and he had to start all over and maybe he wasn't okay to drive but it was too late to say so now. Ivory wasn't offering up commentary, just sitting with her knees drawn up and her skirt tented over them, as before, looking out the passenger window as if there was something absorbing out there, and he was grateful for her silence, even as her very presence unnerved him.

Finally he managed it, achieved forward motion. For the ten minutes it took him to get to Edgewater neither of them spoke, and when Jack parked the car Ivory said only, "What's this place?"

"Where I live now."

She held her tongue, noticing everything. The grimed, barred windows, the pile of pee-stained newspapers, the tilting, funhouse staircase. When they reached the third-floor landing Jack opened the series of locks designed to inconvenience everyone except burglars. Ivory followed him inside. There was a living room/kitchen combination with a table and chairs, a sad couch, and a coffee table. Jack waited for her to say something snide about it. The place begged for sarcasm.

But she only limped over to the couch and fell back on it. A small cloud of dandrufflike particles rose from the cushions. "Killer stairs."

"Oh. Sorry." He hadn't considered the stairs and her leg. It shamed him that he hadn't thought of it.

"Got anything to drink around here?"

Jack's meager refrigerator produced a bottle of iced tea. He split it between two glasses. He didn't want to sit next to her on the couch. That would have brought them too close. He drew up one of the dinky kitchen chairs. Ivory said, "You all right now? I thought you were having some kind of fit."

He drank his tea, wished there was more of it. "I'm fine."

"Except for living in a shithole you're fine."

"It's a long story."

"I bet it's not, Orlovich. I bet it's real short and to the point."

"Don't call me that. Jack. My name's Jack."

"Excuse me, *Jack*. You going to tell me? She kick you out?"

"I don't really want to talk about it."

"Sure you do. You're about to bust wanting to talk about it."

She wiggled her eyebrows, pale little stubs, blond caterpillars. She was slouched inside her clothes. He found it difficult to look directly at her, remember the thin, damaged body beneath those cotton layers, the further trouble he'd made for himself. But because of that shared trouble, she was the only person he could tell.

"She was screwing around on me. I found out a while back. Or I wasn't sure. I called her on it. I made her admit it."

The eyebrows reached the top of their arc and stayed up. "Who's the guy?"

"Her big fat sack of shit boss."

"That is so bogus."

"Do you know what that word really means? Or are you just using it to mean something else?"

"Whatever, don't tell me the worst problem you have right now is *vocabulary*. So what did you do, did you do anything to her?"

"We had a fight. What do you mean, do anything? Like try and blow her up? Christ."

"Hey."

"That's almost funny. No, it is funny. Fucking hilarious."

"No it's not."

Jack shook his head. He didn't want to say any more. He didn't want to think about what his face must look like.

"Hey, come here."

She scooted forward to the edge of the couch, wrapped her legs, in their long skirting, around his knees. Well why not. Why the hell not. He hitched himself toward her on the kitchen chair, bent over to bring his face close to hers. Her energetic mouth and tongue sought him out. This time he wanted it to be about something besides spite and bad feeling. He owed that much to her, and to himself.

They were in the bedroom. Jack had already undressed and kicked his clothes into a corner of the uncarpeted floor, the girl had, as before, bundled her big skirt around her leg and was waiting for him, her arms over her head, flattening her child's breasts still further, when Jack said, "I can't do this."

"I'd say you can." She meant his erection.

"No condoms."

She sighed. "Some bachelor pad this is. Look, it's all right without them."

"No it's not."

"I honestly don't have anything vile. And you could pull out beforehand. It'll work."

"No."

She propped herself up on one elbow, leaned over him so the limp fringe of her hair grazed his throat. "You want me to take care of you?"

He nodded and closed his eyes. It was not possible to pretend that none of this was happening.

When she had finished with him and his breathing was rolling downhill and his heart was once more beating back inside his chest, he opened his eyes and said, "Good Lord."

"That was all right, then?"

"More than all right. Good Lord."

This seemed to please her. She wrapped herself in the stiff, cheap blanket that still smelled of its plastic packaging, and hiked herself up to lie next to him. "See? Don't I know how to cheer you up?"

"Yeah. Look—"

She wouldn't let him apologize. "It's all right. Some other time. I don't mind. It's nice to know there's one thing I'm good at."

"You shouldn't run yourself down like that."

"Well gee, Your Highness. I'll try harder to keep those laughs coming."

Through the opened window came the filtered sounds of distant street repair, jackhammering and the thunder of heavy equipment. Some previous tenant had left a Japanese-style paper lantern over the ceiling light fixture. It was pale green with a bamboo pattern. Only now did he realize it was the same lantern that hung in Ivory's kitchen and had thrown its green light over a scene much like this one. This struck him as meaningful, one of those weird little cosmic interstices that had to be significant in some way he hadn't yet figured out. He said, "Chloe's pregnant."

"You're kidding."

"Those laughs just keep on coming."

"So . . ."

"I don't know if it's mine. She says it is. Yeah. Like I can trust her on that."

Ivory was silent. He'd been whining. He could hear the echo of his own weak, aggrieved voice. How much more worthless could he be. Then Ivory put her hands on either side of his face and kissed him.

He was embarrassed. When he could, he broke the kiss and leaned back and patted her hair. He was a big whiny baby with too many delicate scruples to even fuck properly. He said, "You're sweet."

"No I'm not. But I'm a hell of a good sport."

"I couldn't take a chance, doing it without something. You understand? Not another baby. Not now."

"Well that wouldn't be one of my top-ten things either, Mr. Sperm."

They laughed a little at this. It felt amazingly like any normal couple, laughing in bed. Then Ivory said, "You aren't really going to keep living here, are you?"

"It didn't seem like a good idea to hang around the house. Under the circumstances."

"No, I mean *this* place." She waved a hand to indicate the yellowish-buff paint, the color of an ugly dog, the sagging plastic flophouse curtains. He kept waiting for her to notice the paper lantern, but she gave no sign. "This is like a complete dump. Not your kind of scene."

"Maybe it is now. Maybe I'm a down-in-the-dumps kind of guy."
He thought that might be the truth. He'd thought of himself as someone able, even entitled (by virtue of intelligence, upbringing, education), to pick and choose among various favored futures. There had
been assumptions. He would work, marry, live here or there, explore
the world's pleasures, break only those laws that impeded his minor
vices. He would never have to live in a room like this, do any of the
things he'd done.

Ivory was rustling around beneath the blanket, pulling on her
clothes. "I have to get going. I told Rich I'd come by this afternoon."

Jack had managed not to be thinking about Brezak. He didn't really
feel jealous—how twisted would that be—but it was another embar-
rassment. "Sure. I'll run you back over there."

"Go ahead. Say it."

"What?"

"He's a world-class dirtbag."

"Glad we got that settled." He began casting about on the floor for
his own clothes. He'd forgotten how graceless and awful it could be,
struggling to get dressed in front of a woman before you knew each
other well enough to feel easy about it. Or you might never know each
other well enough.

Ivory was making better progress. She was already dressed and sitting up and slicking her hair back. In spite of the heat, she wore her full
complement of garments. An undershirt in a camouflage pattern. Jack
hadn't remarked on it before. He wondered if it was a fad or if she just
wore it for ugliness's sake. Over that, a black cotton shirt with long
sleeves, and over that a denim vest. A long, olive-drab skirt that looked
like something the army might issue, if soldiers wore skirts.

He touched her shoulder. "Is your leg all right?"

"Not a prob, Bob."

"I'm sorry about the stairs."

She bent over to tie her shoes and her words came out labored. "Just
don't—move to a—high-rise."

"I wanted to say, your leg isn't a big deal to me. I'm not squeamish.
You don't have to keep hiding it."

She straightened, looked back at him over her raised shoulder so he
saw only a portion of her face, a triangle of nose and narrowed eye. "It's
not a big deal to me either. It's more like, you get into the habit of hiding things."

Oh, thank you." Mrs. Jim Spencer smiled as Jack held the door of the
Dominick's open for her. He said, pleasantly, that she was welcome. He
watched her choose a cart, set her handbag in the basket and extract
from it a shopping list written on pale gray paper. Jack followed in
her wake as she rolled toward the produce department. He'd forgotten
just how large and gleaming and well supplied these suburban grocery palaces could be. Here were kumquats, baby lettuces, snow peas,
peaches so ripe and fragrant each was packaged in its own nest of
molded plastic and shredded excelsior.

Jack felt conspicuous. A solitary, list-less man, wandering, at ten in
the morning, among the chatelaines. At least he'd spruced himself up
some. Ivory had been right. He'd looked like a molting vulture. So he'd
gotten a haircut, shaved and combed, and dressed himself in clean and
unremarkable clothes. It was that easy to impersonate a normal citizen.
He might be taken for an idle, ne'er-do-well son, or if he was lucky, a
self-employed entrepreneurial whiz kid.

Mrs. Jim cruised the citrus, selected a grapefruit. She was nobody
Jack would have picked out of a crowd. She had short, brown-going-
gray hair cut with thick bangs, like a child's. A forehead that puckered
easily as she contemplated filet beans versus spinach. She looked as if
she'd been fretting about things like vegetables for years. Short, snub
nose, remnants of prettiness. A body like a snowman's, one bundle of
flesh set on top of another. An aggrieved and deceived wife, though she
probably didn't know it yet. Jack didn't automatically feel sorry for her.
She was a dope, just like he was.

Jack detoured around her, turned left, and walked unhurriedly
down the store's main aisle. The deli offered marinated steaks, stuffed
baked potatoes prestuffed and prebaked, artfully butterflied shrimp,
slabs of red tuna garnished to a fare-thee-well. He stopped and pre-

tended interest. He wasn't sure what, if anything, he was going to do about Mrs. Jim. He hadn't counted on her. She was a bonus.

He'd looked up Spence's name on the Internet. It was part of his ravening need to know everything he could, which he recognized as a substitute for actually being able to do anything effective. Once he had the address mapped out, he didn't even pretend he wasn't going to go there.

He chose a weekday. He didn't want to encounter Spence, not on this trip. This was just reconnaissance, a side mission. He took his car to the car wash as part of his effort to look clean and bland. It was the third week he'd had the car. He kept calling Budget and extending the rental. He didn't even ask how much it was going to cost him. He'd grown reckless about a lot of things and money was one of them. He cashed in another T-bill. He didn't sign up for the substitute teaching pool. He had no idea how he was going to support himself, didn't much think about it. It was part of his new, dangerous-to-self-and-others life.

Spence's suburb was the kind of place where people bought not just lots, but acreage. They kept horses in the backyard and all the things that went along with horses. They owned carriage houses, guest houses, pool houses. The place that Spence called home wasn't even one of the larger piles of real estate, although it was impressive enough. A white-washed brick colonial, set well back from the curving street. The long driveway arced between stands of late-summer pink roses. Three-car garage. Chimneys, two of them. Fish pond with a small, spurting fountain. Jack wondered why any man who already possessed as much as Jim Spencer had to have Chloe also.

Jack drove past the house once, then backtracked and allowed himself one more pass. He was mindful of private security forces and vigilant neighbors, and besides, there was really nothing to see here. Just as he reached the crest of the mild hill before the house, he spotted a green Dodge minivan pulling out of the Spencer driveway.

Now here he was, shadowing Mrs. S., gleaning the possibly useful information that the Spencer household used margarine rather than butter. And that they relied heavily on frozen entrées. Bored, Jack left the store and went outside to wait in the parking lot. It had been a mistake to think that there was anything interesting or compelling about people like Spence. They thought they were living in some movie, a major-studio release with a thrilling sound track and moments of high drama and just that hint of corn. But they were ordinary. Behaving badly didn't change that.

Eventually Mrs. Jim emerged, pushing a cart full of plastic sacks. Jack wondered, without real curiosity, if the Spencers had what could be called a good marriage, aside from the occasional discreet infidelity. He wondered if Spence had done this sort of thing before. If Mr. and Mrs. Jim still took any comfort in each other. If Mrs. Jim suspected, felt the shadow of Chloe's presence. He would have bet money she didn't know anything outright. Otherwise she wouldn't be so placidly crossing turkey bacon and Egg Beaters off her list and worrying about Mr. Jim's cholesterol.

The idea came to him as he watched her load up the minivan and depart. He watched its stately progress out of the parking lot and into traffic. He waited forty minutes. Time enough for her to reach home, unload, maybe stick the meat and dairy in the fridge and leave the rest for later, brew a cup of tea and sit down with her new *Better Homes and Gardens*. He went back inside the Dominick's and from one of the pay phones in the entryway dialed the Spencers' home number.

She answered on the third ring. "Hello?"

"Is this Mrs. James Spencer?"

"Who's calling?" Edge of sharpness, no doubt wondering if he was a telemarketer.

"Mrs. Spencer, you don't know me but my name is Jack Orlovich. My wife works at the bank with your husband." Pause to let her consider this. "If I could have just a minute of your time? I should say, my wife's just starting out at the bank, she just got her M.B.A. and she's a trainee. And there's a problem—a situation—that I'm not sure how to handle. I've tried calling Mr. Spencer at the office but I can't ever seem to get through. Could I explain it to you? I really am sorry to bother you, but it's kind of delicate . . ."

His best shot at sounding awkward and sincere. And with just enough of a hook in it to make her alarmed or curious or both. He

waited. Imagined her looking around, annoyed, at the heaps of proven-
der she ought to be shelving. "What did you say your name was?"

"Jack Orlovich. My wife is Chloe. Chloe Chase." He dropped the
name into the calm water of Mrs. Jim's awareness. Something done that
couldn't be undone. "She's crazy about her job. Just loves it. She thinks
the world of Mr. Spencer. That's all I ever hear, Spence this, Spence that.
And I'm worried . . . I'm sorry, I just know she'd kill me for telling you
this. We just found out we're going to have a baby. Our first."

"Oh. Congratulations." Flatly. "That's very nice. What does—"

"She's afraid it's going to hurt her career. You know. Discrimination.
Mommy tracking. I tell her she shouldn't worry, there are laws, but she
just goes on and on."

Mrs. Jim made a sound of neutral assent. Jack wondered if it had
been the best thing to say to her, Mommy tracking, if it could be
worked around into some kind of reflected insult. Too late now. He
plunged ahead. "What I was hoping— Oh boy, Chloe would have my
hide if she knew I was talking to you. I mean, we haven't even told our
parents yet. If you could maybe ask your husband—without using any
names, just hypothetically—if she has anything to worry about, career
wise. I want to tell her she's just being paranoid. I don't want her to
overwork herself because she feels she has to prove a point. She already
puts in so many late nights at the office. And that trip in July, you
know, the big deal where they all went to New York. I just don't want
her to do a lot more business travel like that. A whole week away from
home. That can't be good for the baby."

There was a space of black, electronic silence. Jack let it ripen for a
few beats, then he said, "I could give you my phone number. Or maybe
you'd prefer I call you back. Either way."

"Who are you?" Her voice had roughened.

"Jack Orlovich. Funny name, huh? Kid isn't going to thank me. I really would appreciate anything you could do. Any little talk you and
Mr. Spencer might manage to have. I know, I'm probably worried for
nothing. I'm just so psyched about this baby, I want everything to be
perfect. You have kids, don't you? Chloe said—"

But she had hung up. Jack replaced the receiver and walked back to the parking lot. Once he was in the car he said aloud, "Bombs away." He didn't know what would come of the depth charge he'd just dumped into the Spencers' lives. Maybe nothing. Maybe Mrs. Jim would swallow her distress, let it ride. She might not care what her husband was up to as long as he paid the outlandish mortgage, maybe, for similar reasons, she couldn't afford to care.

Jack steered himself cityward. The malls and cul-de-sacs receded, replaced by the pale tollway landscape. It was wickedness, what he'd done. No other word for it. Yup. But if Mrs. Jim took up the cause—if she confronted Spence, demanded to know, forced him to give up Chloe—then it would be worth serving his time in hell. Because then he would get Chloe back.

He sped down the highway, turned the radio up loud to an oldies station, sang along to "Brown Sugar," backing Mick up with some funky, low-down wails. It was a little scary, the things that put him in a good mood these days.

Thirteen

Pat Rubin's office looked different in early morning light. Less a place for confession and trauma, more businesslike. Or maybe that was Pat herself, who was regarding Jack with a certain professional wariness. He'd talked his way into coming in before her regular appointments. Insisted he had to see her. Careful not to sound menacing or impolite, nobody you'd make go through a metal detector. Still. Pat said, "You're sure about this. The other man."

"Oh yes. Not in dispute."

"And the pregnancy."

"Yeah. That's bonus points."

"I'm sorry."

"When she sat here and told you how hard she wanted to work on the marriage, it was going on right then. Hot and heavy."

"You know, I see people in crisis all the time. There seems to be an inexhaustible amount of pain in the world. It never gets less."

Jack said, "The crisis is over. This is the postmortem. The accident reconstruction."

Pat gave him a measuring look. She was wearing lavender today, another flowing caftan. Her hair was piled up and held in place by a silver and mother-of-pearl clip set front and center. It made her resemble something out of *Star Trek*, the queen of some alien TV planet. She said, "Perhaps you should tell me where you want to go from here. What you want to focus on."

"Getting my wife back."

"Have you talked with Chloe about a reconciliation?"

Jack shook his head. "We haven't done a lot of talking."

"That would be a good place to start."

"Fine. Tell me what to say."

Pat's fingernails were painted silver today. They made her big fingers look like butter knives. Jack watched them tap against the desk's surface. He liked feeling that he might be throwing her off stride, making her run through her repertoire of responses, cautious about him. The last time he was in this office he'd been such a girl. Pat said, "I think you should prepare for other possibilities."

"No."

"There isn't any magic abracadabra here. It's a process. And it may or may not turn out the way you want."

"All due respect to the counseling profession, but if you can't give me something I can use, I'd say it's a real crock-of-shit racket."

He was sure he'd gone too far. Pat would rise up in a billowing lavender cloud and throw him out. Not bodily. With some galactic-force ray. But she didn't allow herself to show anger. She was, as everybody said, a pro. "All right. Here's the deal. I can give you an assessment, based on my very limited contact with the two of you."

"Deal."

"Then I'm going to strongly suggest you visit a medical doctor, or a clinician who can prescribe medication. Antianxiety drugs. Not because I disapprove of your rudeness and belligerence, although I do. But because they won't help you with Chloe."

Jack ducked his head to acknowledge that she might have a point. Even if he had no intention of getting a prescription, dosing himself into drooling calm. He said, "I wanted to keep coming back here. Working things out. She was the one who said no."

"That's because of the drinking. She didn't want to be called on it. I don't doubt that she's alcoholic. And just in case you're interested, which you aren't, there are any number of support groups and informational readings at your disposal."

"Thanks. I think I already know the basics."

"Maybe. Living with it doesn't mean you completely understand it. There's a basic dishonesty that's a component of alcoholism. What we call denial. Alcoholics aren't con artists because they're evil, devious people. It's because they're conning themselves. The disease affects behavior, memory, judgment. The whole package."

"So what are you saying, it's a symptom of alcoholism to screw your boss?"

"She's sick. Unless she gets into recovery, there's no happy ending."

"This is the best you can do? Drunks tell lies? Wow. Breaking news."

"The best I can do right now is try and talk you through—"

"Every time she opened her mouth, it was to lie. So I should go back and ask her not to? That's brilliant. I'm in awe."

"Jack."

"You ever think maybe this whole talk-therapy deal is oversold? I mean, here's you and everybody like you, sitting in cushy offices and saying all the right things, and people walk out of here with a head full of all the right words and pick up where they left off, treating each other like beasts. I'm a writer. Did we get around to telling you that? It was one of the things Chloe used to berate me for when she was drunk, being a bad writer. Well maybe I am, or was, who cares. But it was something I thought mattered. Words. Now they're just more crap on the crap heap."

Pat didn't speak. The silence stretched. After a time Jack said, "Okay, I get it. I'm sorry. I'm just at the end of some kind of rope here."

"Don't give up on words yet, Jack. They can work for you."

"Yeah." He felt a fool. He should be getting used to that by now, but he wasn't.

"Anything else you wanted to address?"

"Yes. Here's a question for you. Are you surprised? I mean, when we walked out of your office that time, did you say to yourself, 'Wow, these kids are really fucked'?"

Pat shook her head. Her face looked worn. Jack had a sense of what a truly crummy start her day was getting off to, thanks to him. She said, "No. But I thought you were more committed to the marriage than she was."

He wasn't prepared to hear it, even though he knew it was true. It shocked him, how much he could be hurt in this new, fresh place. He managed, "Why? Because of the drinking?"

"Not entirely. Because when I asked you both for a happy memory, hers was all about you doing things for her. How much you were willing to do for her. You're still doing things for her. Everything you're putting yourself through. It's all for her."

After a moment Jack said, "I apologize. I know I've been giving you a hard time."

Pat smiled. "Ah, you never laid a glove on me." But she looked weary. Jack liked her for that, for letting him see it in her.

He said, "I guess I didn't really expect you to fix this for me. I've been going a little crazy. But Christ Jesus. I don't know any other way to be in love. If it doesn't drive you crazy, how do you know it's love?"

Pat held up her silver fingernails to indicate she didn't know.

Jack called Chloe that night. He sat on his saggy bed and dialed from his recently acquired cell phone. A cell phone wasn't a big deal, didn't commit you to living anywhere.

Jack listened to the phone purring. Chloe answered on the fourth ring, just before the machine picked up. "Hello?"

"Guess who?" He hadn't meant to start off like that, flippant. Nerves. "Can we talk?"

"Talk about what?" He imagined her standing in the living room. The water lilies floating behind her.

"How are you feeling?"

"What do you want, Jack."

"Come on. I want to know how you are. With the baby and all."

Chloe didn't say anything. Maybe she was weighing just how long she could carry on being sullen and aggrieved before some of it started coming back her way. She said, "Not terrific. Mornings aren't good. They say it gets easier. You're missing a lot of real quality throwing-up time."

"Have you been to a doctor?"

"Next week."

A silence. Jack said, "I want to see you."

"What was that stunt with the clothes, huh? I turned on the light and just about jumped out of my skin. It was creepy. And stupid. I don't like you prowling around here when I'm not home."

"Anything else I've done wrong lately?"

"All right," Chloe said. "All right."

The silence ticked. He wasn't going to start in apologizing, "Can we meet somewhere?"

"The last time I saw you, you were holding me hostage on a boat."

"Canoe."

"*God.*"

"Sorry." He'd said it in spite of himself. It had an ashy taste.

As if that was what she had been waiting to hear, she agreed to meet him for coffee the next day, Saturday. "I'm just doing decaf these days. It's another big thrill."

When he hung up, Jack left his apartment and drove to the old neighborhood. He hadn't intended to go there, in fact he'd decided he was behaving stupidly, dangerously, and should stay away, but of course it did not surprise him to be ignoring his own good advice. He parked down the street and walked through the alley to the yard gate, found it locked, circled back to the street where he observed the drawn curtains in the living room and bedroom. A light was on in the kitchen. He edged between the two buildings for a closer look.

He could see only a portion of the refrigerator, and the high shelf where they kept an enameled tea canister and two fancy wedding-present wineglasses, the kind you couldn't really drink from. These were particularly strange; they were made in the shape of fish, fish reclining on their tails and gaping openmouthed. The tails were the stems, the mouths the bowls, so that drinking from one would give you the impression of kissing a fish. They'd kept them as a joke. He couldn't remember who they were from. He remembered the living room of their old apartment, Chloe shrieking as they emerged from the bridal wrapping paper, Jack saying something about the thank-you note, and then a little later they'd made love on their knees, Chloe astride him. Or maybe that had been some other time. Things you thought you'd never forget, playing hide-and-seek in the neon maze of your brain. He tried to remember the last time he and Chloe had made love. And he knew he could recall it but he didn't want to visit it just yet. He couldn't stand the thought of last, last time. As he watched, the kitchen window went dark.

He was meeting Chloe at three o'clock. She'd said mornings were out, you know, that morning thing. Jack couldn't help thinking she'd chosen three because there was no possibility of turning it into a meal and lingering. It felt, weirdly, as if they were back to dating, as if he was courting her all over again. Somehow he'd lost whatever advantage her bad behavior entitled him to.

Chloe was fifteen minutes late. Maybe that was another power play on her part but he let it pass. She wore jeans and a white shirt and carried an oversized red straw shoulder bag. People in the shop took note of her. Jack watched them watch her. It was like spotting a hummingbird. You had to keep your eyes on it until it was out of sight, or you remembered not to stare at strangers.

Jack stood up when she reached the table, leaned over, and kissed her on the cheek. His own power play. She wasn't expecting it, had to produce a smile. "Hi."

"Hi. What would you like?"

"A decaf cappuccino."

Jack went to the counter to order it. Bolted, really. He'd underestimated the effect seeing her would have on him. The coffee he'd drunk was roaring through his nerves like a truck on an expressway.

When he brought her coffee to the table, he said, "Here you go," and watched her curl her fingers around the cup, warming them. She didn't look pregnant yet, he guessed it was still too early for that. If anything, she looked a little thinner. She'd done careful work with her makeup but there were dark circles beneath her eyes and her face retained that taut, skull-like quality. He said, "Rough morning?"

"Rough night. Oh well. The wages of sin." She shrugged.

Jack imagined himself sitting up with Chloe, massaging her neck, massaging her feet, bringing her soda crackers and ginger ale. The old habit of pleasing her. Pat had that one nailed. But wasn't that what a marriage meant? You did things for each other.

Pat said, "You're still doing things for her."

"Come on. It works both ways. It's not the kind of thing you can quantify."

"Quantify?"

Jack looked up at Chloe, confused. She said, "You said 'quantify.'"

He felt stupid. He couldn't remember saying anything. "Just mumbling."

Chloe nodded. Polite. Not that interested anyway. Probably bored. Jack said, "It's good to see you."

"I guess we had to start somewhere," she said vaguely. She took a sip of her coffee, set the cup down again. "Hot."

"I'm glad to see you're watching what you eat."

"You mean, am I drinking again."

"That's not what I said."

"But it's what you meant."

He didn't answer. Maybe it had been what he meant. He didn't know.

"You don't believe me about anything anymore, fine, but that's the truth."

"Con job," said Pat.

"*What?*"

"Nothing." The caffeine rolled through him, its sloshy tides.

"Don't say 'nothing.' I heard you. Con job! Is that what you think of me?"

"This is so weird."

"Because if that's the way—"

"No, no, I went back to see Pat, you know? Pat . . ." It embarrassed him not to remember her last name. " . . . anyway, now it's like I can't stop her from talking."

"That's not funny either."

He tried to say he didn't mean to be funny. When he opened his mouth, no sound came out.

"What is wrong with you?"

Pat said, "No happy ending."

"Jack, stop this."

He slumped over the table and buried his head in his arms. This wasn't how he'd meant things to go at all.

Noise buzzed in his ears. Coffee-shop voices. He tried not to hear them. Then Chloe was talking. She tugged at his arm. She wanted him to look at her but he couldn't. She wanted him to stand up, walk. Well okay. He kept his eyes on his shuffling feet.

Once they were outside his head cleared a little. "Wow. That was so . . ." The sun made him squint. He felt the heat of the sidewalk through his shoes. "I guess I spaced out back there."

"You think?" She sounded exasperated.

"Sorry." He closed his eyes and waited for her to leave. The sun crept in behind his eyelids, a muddy red-orange. A space of time passed. He didn't know how long. It was measured in sunlight.

Chloe was still there. She said, "What's the deal with you?"

"It's hard seeing you when I know you're going to go away again."

"Would you look at me?" He opened his eyes. Chloe's face was skeptical. Her not-taking-any-shit expression. "How did you get here?"

Jack had driven, but he had just enough craftiness left in him to say, "Bus." He didn't want her to see his car.

"Do you want a ride? You look shot."

"Thanks. Sure." He felt as if he'd just awakened from anesthesia, or perhaps as if he'd been thoroughly beaten up. He followed Chloe along the sidewalk, trying not to bump into her.

"Where are you staying anyway, or is that some big secret?"

"No, it's just . . . a place."

"Glad we got that cleared up."

It felt strange to be in the passenger seat with Chloe driving. He could tell she'd moved the seat up and changed the mirrors. It was her car now. "Where to?"

Jack told her to go north on Ashland. The tired sun beat down. The sidewalks bled hot tar. Billboards offered YOUR PRODUCT OR SERVICE AD-VERTISED HERE. A dozen empty semi trailers were parked in a fenced-off

lot, like cows in a pasture. A storefront advertised VIENNA BEEF
AND POLISH. There were times and places in Chicago that nothing you
rested your eyes on was soft or easy. Chloe said, "Why did you go to see
Pat?"

He didn't want to be reminded of that. It seemed like another failure.
"Just to talk." That sounded pathetic, as if he couldn't get anyone else
to talk to him. He added, dryly, "I had some issues."

"Should I be worried about you?"

Jack thought about should. He said, "You're riding high in April,
shot down in May."

"What?"

"Sinatra. 'That's Life.' No. You should not worry about me."

Chloe braked at the next light, put her turn signal on. Jack looked
over at her. She said, "Let's just go back home, okay? Could we try
this?"

"Sure." He didn't know what she meant, try this, but his heart leaped
up. It was sobering to think that his weakness might accomplish what
all his rage could not.

They didn't speak much until they were at the apartment's front
door. Jack laughed. It came out lopsided. He said, "This place."

"What about it?" Chloe unlocked the street door and they stepped
into the lobby, its familiar, coffee-colored light and anciently dirty tile
floor.

It didn't feel like home anymore. It was an arena where gladiators
clashed and lions gnawed human bones. He wanted to say they should
leave here, break the lease and go someplace they could change their
luck. Clean start. He said, "Nothing."

Once they were inside Chloe said, "Go on, lie down. You look like a
stray dog."

"Dog," Jack said, by way of protest. But he went into the bedroom
and sank into the mattress, face in the pillows. He heard Chloe moving
around the room, closing the blinds, turning on a fan so that cool air
blew across him. He felt the bed give way under her slight weight and
he reached out for her.

Chloe drew in close to him and he turned onto his side and they kissed and he tasted the coffee she'd drunk and also something cooler, toothpaste, probably, and then beneath it all, just her.

She whispered, "I don't think we should do anything, you know, the baby . . ."

"Oh, sure." He rolled away, put a little space between them, stilled his hands. It was strange to think that there was a baby in the bed with them. He gave Chloe a loose hug that he tried to make nonsexual. "This is nice, though."

"Mm-hm."

Her body moved closer to his by degrees, turning as he turned. The old pattern of their nights together. Jack felt himself falling into sleep the way you fell into a tunnel or a well. He said, "I love you," and sent the words back through layers of sleep and darkness.

Jack woke up fast, as if from a sound or a touch, but there was no echo in his ears and Chloe wasn't there. It was still daylight. His body felt stiff, deeply aching. He took a moment to register this room that both was and was not his.

He rolled over, groaned at that portion of his spine that didn't want to move with him. Smell of coffee. He made a stop in the bathroom. He could hear Chloe moving around in the kitchen. Told himself not to be such a chickenshit, quit hiding.

The kitchen was flooded with light. Chloe turned around from the sink, smiled at him. "Good morning."

"Morning?"

"Yes, goofball, you slept, what, fourteen hours."

"No way." Among all the large and small shocks of the last few weeks this one struck him as absurd, unnecessary.

"I let you sleep. I figured you needed it."

Jack found a mug, occupied himself with pouring coffee. He wanted to kiss her good morning but was unsure about how to start up all over, touch her. "It's decaf," Chloe warned.

"That's okay. I think I poisoned myself with caffeine yesterday."

"With something," Chloe agreed. She was wearing shorts and a white oxford shirt with the sleeves rolled up to the elbows. She never tanned much, didn't have the skin for it. Even now in late September there was only the faintest tint of sun to her bare legs.

Jack said, "I feel like the guy in *2001*, who wakes up on Jupiter and keeps turning into all these different ages."

"Do you think you could stop saying weird things?"

But she was smiling, and Jack believed she must know what he meant. How he kept waking up in different worlds, one where his heart broke, one where Chloe loved him all over again. The enameled tea canister, the wineglasses in the shape of fish; here they were, just as he'd seen them before, or not really as before, because now he was inside with them.

Jack said, "How are you . . ." He didn't yet have a way to talk about the baby. He didn't even have a way to feel about it. "You know, the morning thing?"

"A little better today. I think I'm more into heartburn now."

It was a fine, bright, Sunday morning. There was a newspaper to get through, and a plate of toast, and orange juice. After a little while Jack went into the living room and turned on the television to watch the news shows. Dressed-up men sat behind desks and moved their mouths like puppets. It was more *Space Odyssey* stuff and soon he stopped trying to focus on it. On the wall the water lilies floated in their blue-violet pool. There was a dusty outline on the desk where the computer had been. And there were gaps in the bookshelves where he'd taken books. It could all be put back. It would look exactly the same as before.

Chloe came in and sat down on the chair across from him. She looked at the television. "What's this?"

"Some guys. I don't know."

They sat, intent on the television. Chloe said, "Should we get started? Do you want to talk?"

"Not really."

"We have to."

"Not yet."

She didn't understand. Jack said, "Let's not say a lot of things that get us all worked up again. Let's just go back to the way it was."

"I need to tell you. What it was and what it wasn't."

"I don't need to hear it."

"It didn't start out to be—"

Jack put a finger to his lips and shook his head.

"Please can we talk about the baby. You're going to keep all this inside and stew over it and then you'll throw it all in my face."

"No, Chloe."

"You can't be anything less than a father. Or if you can't, I need to know now."

On the television screen, the puppet men moved their mouths. They talked about politics and war. Their knowledge was profound and deeply rooted, their reasoning subtle, their ideas grave. It exhausted Jack to think of all the effort that went into such heavy, heavy words. He said, "I will be a father to this child. I won't ever throw anything in your face. Come here."

Chloe got up to sit next to him on the couch. Jack put his arms around her and held her close. He felt her heart beating through his own chest. He wondered if the baby had a heart yet, if it was something you could hear with careful listening.

Over the next few days Jack stripped his rental place down to its ugly bones. He left the kitchenware he'd purchased for the next poor slob who came along. He restored the computer and everything else to its rightful place. He took the car back to Budget and signed off on the charges without looking at the receipt. There was still a lethargy in him. His head felt thick and clogged, his muscles had come unstrung. His body was catching up with the long distress of his mind. The weather changed overnight to autumn, or the first sign of it, a spell of gray, chill rain. Jack slept long and hard. Chloe often called him from work. He knew this was a kind of demonstration on her part, meant to prove something, but he was glad of it.

They didn't mention Spence. Steered right around his name. That part was like some Victorian melodrama, an actor declaiming on a stage: his name shall never again pass my lips, and so on. But maybe that would feel different in time. A lot of things would. In the spring the baby would be here. Everything would change.

Jack had planned on going with Chloe to her first doctor's appointment, but that morning he woke up with a wheezing cough. Chloe brought him a cup of tea. "Stay put. You're not going anywhere today."

"But I'm the one who needs the doctor."

"Go back to sleep."

After she left Jack drank some of the tea. It was an herbal potion that made him feel genuinely invalided. He wasn't entirely unhappy to miss Chloe's doctor visit. He had the normal male squeamishness about the mechanics of all this, how a woman's body turned itself into a factory made up of bleeding, swollen parts.

He fell back to sleep for a time. When he woke up again he showered, dressed, stared out the windows at the unpromising gray sky. Over his head the kid's stereo was cranked up a notch or two past acceptable volume.

All in all they'd been quieter than usual lately, and Jack was glad. He hadn't wanted to think about Brezak or Ivory or any of the mess that went along with thinking of them. His cough seemed a little better now that he was upright. He made the bed so he'd be less tempted to get back in it, cleaned the bathroom, and took out the trash. On the way back, Mr. Dandy, who must have heard him, was lying in wait outside his apartment door.

Mr. Dandy looked even more frayed and ancient than usual. He seemed to be disappearing inside his clothes. His liver-spotted hands flapped. "You hear that racket?" Mr. Dandy's breath carried unpleasant reminders of his digestive processes.

Jack said, unnecessarily, that he heard it. Mr. Dandy hooked one hand over Jack's elbow in a death grip. "I got half a mind to turn the gun on them."

"You don't have a gun."

"Says you."

"That's right." The door to Mr. Dandy's apartment stood open. Jack saw a vista of brown upholstery, wallpaper gone shiny from bodies rubbing against it, a whiff of the same unfresh combustion that emanated from Mr. Dandy. Jack said, "If I thought you really had a gun, I'd come in and take it away from you. Go back in, turn on the television.

Or get some earplugs. I don't like it any better than you, but just deal with it."

"They practice abominations."

"Good for them."

"Used to shoot rats on the railroad. We had rats big as cats. Hell, bigger. They get into the grain cars. Big as damn ponies."

Jack pried Mr. Dandy's hand from his arm. "Go back inside. Chill."

"Used to be guys who that was their whole job, rat catcher. Go around and shoot all the punks."

Jack left him standing there. He thought the old man was addled.

Back in his own apartment, the noise from upstairs was well above the level where he would have felt justified in complaining, but he wasn't in the mood to take it on. He thought it best to stay away from them, get into the habit of disengagement. He guessed he'd have to talk to Ivory eventually. He needed to put an official stop to what they'd never, officially, been doing. He wasn't looking forward to that. There was an unease in him that he couldn't talk himself out of, the certainty that he'd behaved badly toward her, no matter that she was a hell of a good sport. There would be no way to feel right or easy about it. He and Chloe should get a new place as soon as possible. Whether from cowardice or simple self-preservation, there would be another end to things.

He heard some commotion on the stairs. Brezak's voice. Jack couldn't make out the words, but the tone was unpleasant. Laconic, jeering, snide. Classic Brezak. Another voice, which Jack identified with some dismay as Mr. Dandy's. He moved to the front door, cracked it open, ready to intervene if he had to.

"Wow, you just made a mistake. You have me confused with somebody who gives a shit what you think. Tell you what, how about I give you a dime and you can go call somebody who gives a shit."

Mr. Dandy's shrill and furious voice broke in over Brezak's words. "Shut your nasty trap! You and your nigger music! I don't have to hear cussin too!"

"Yeah, like nigger's the coolest. What's your problem, man, maybe you should take your racist ass back down—"

"You punks are worse'n niggers! That's right! Worse!"

Brezak laughed his donkey's laugh. "Oh, that one hurts."

"You don't turn that noise down, I call the police! They'll settle your hash!"

"Sure, go ahead. I'll call whoever it is picks up senile old—"

"Pervert! Queer!"

"What, now I'm queer? Make up your mind, man."

There was a sound like snoring, though Jack knew it wasn't that, and then a confusion of noise, Brezak saying "Hey," in a normal conversational tone, and something heavy and graceless landing again and again, and Jack stepped out into the lobby to see a white and untidy doll, except it was Mr. Dandy, arms and legs and flopping neck, thump down the stairs and come to rest at an impossible, ugly angle, one foot caught in the banister, head on the bottom step.

Jack ran to him. Brezak was still at the top of the stairs, looking down as Jack looked up. "What did you do to him?"

"Nothing! I swear! He just fell over, he had some kind of fit."

Jack knelt next to Mr. Dandy's head. A purple sack of blood, like a balloon, had formed beneath the skin behind one ear. His eyes were half open and his dentures had come loose and gotten mixed up with his bleeding tongue. "Call 911, go!"

Brezak disappeared back into his apartment. Jack tried to check Mr. Dandy for breathing, pulse. If there was breath in him, it was somewhere deep inside. And Mr. Dandy's skin was so thin and loose, Jack's fingers couldn't get a purchase, feel anything beneath it. There was no way to untangle him, start CPR or anything else, without risking some new injury. Jack reached into Mr. Dandy's mouth, tried to unfurl his tongue, clear his airway. "Can you hear me? Mr. Dandy?"

One of Mr. Dandy's eyes fluttered open, roved from side to side, unseeing. The pupil was black and exploded looking.

Brezak ran downstairs, followed by Ivory, moving slower. Brezak said, "He was schizting out. Acting weird. Not that he isn't always weird."

"Shut up, Rich. Did you call, huh? Let's focus here."

Brezak muttered that of course he had called. One side of his face looked crumpled, as if he'd been sleeping on it. His hair had been newly electrified into a halo of fuzz.

Ivory said, "I'll go watch for the ambulance," and limped and hobbled to the front door. Jack and Brezak crouched uselessly over Mr. Dandy. There was quiet now, and a sense that something more ought to be happening. Mr. Dandy hiccuped, swallowed, and his tongue righted itself.

"So he's not dead," said Brezak. "That's good."

"You're a sensitive guy. Anybody ever tell you that?"

"No, I meant, if he was dead, his last words would've been *pervert* and *queer.*"

A little while later the paramedic unit arrived with their sirens and crackling radios, latex gloves, and matter-of-fact urgencies. Jack and the others watched as Mr. Dandy was extracted from the banister, stabilized, righted, and packaged for transport. Jack was shocked by how dead the old man looked even though he might, technically, be alive. The paramedics had opened his shirt and hiked up one pants leg and displayed queasy amounts of Mr. Dandy. He hadn't opened his eyes again, nor shown any signs of coming around. The paramedics were almost too efficient. Jack thought there ought to be more tragedy and mess involved, an old railroader or two to mourn, an old Irish wife to throw a shawl over her head and wail.

They were taking Mr. Dandy to the closest trauma center. Jack fetched his wallet and keys. Brezak and Ivory had disappeared upstairs, but once Jack reached the sidewalk, Ivory came out after him. "Where are you going?"

"The hospital."

"I want to come too."

He couldn't think of any reason to tell her no, except that his shame made him uncomfortable around her. He waited for her to catch up. When they reached the car he opened the door for her and she bundled herself inside.

It was still raining, scattered drops that smeared the windshield when Jack ran the wipers. He had to switch over from air-conditioning to defrost. The vent filled the car with stale metallic heat and he quickly turned it down. They didn't speak until Jack had pulled out into traffic. Ivory said, "I didn't think you were friends with him."

"I'm not. I just think somebody ought to be there."

She considered this. Without looking directly at her Jack was aware of her profile, the slight bulge of her forehead, unemphatic eyebrows, chapped and bitten lips. She said, "Do you think he's going to die?"

"I don't think he looked very good." The car ahead of him braked and its taillights flared in the damp air. Red light refracted through the blurred windshield. The ambulance was long out of sight. Jack thought he heard its siren up ahead, but that could have been some other ambulance carrying some other used-up old man.

Ivory said, "He isn't a nice person. Even if he's dead."

"Maybe he used to be nicer. Maybe he just lived too long unhappy."

Ivory didn't answer and they drove the rest of the way in silence.

At the ER desk Jack asked about Mr. Dandy. The clerk waved a clipboard at him and asked about insurance. Jack said he didn't know, he wasn't family. He didn't think there was any family. "He was a veteran," Jack added. As if that might help explain anything. The clerk told him to take a seat. She was the kind of clerk who would tell you to take a seat even if you presented yourself with a detached limb or flesh-eating bacteria.

Ivory was already sitting on one of the molded plastic chairs, looking through a magazine. The chairs were bolted together in a kind of pod, so that you couldn't move them closer together or farther apart. Jack thought they communicated something about the state of modern American health care. He sat down next to Ivory, who must have seen it in his face that there was nothing to report. Jack craned to see the magazine. It was called *Family Practice,* and featured a cover story on pediatric eczema. He looked around him. Like most emergency rooms, there didn't seem to be any real sense of emergency. A troop of children ran shrieking laps around the chairs. An elderly couple dozed next to a thin mother nursing a thin baby. A man dabbed a handkerchief to his ulcerated neck. Jack felt his throat begin to ache and his head thicken.

There was a sense of contagion in the place, of germs wafting through ventilation ducts, viruses mutating beneath the stink of pine cleaner. He thought briefly of Reg and his purified air.

Jack stood and walked to the corridor, which led back to the treatment rooms, trying to see what was happening. Nothing was visible except a row of gurneys, and a woman in peach-colored scrubs moving unhurriedly down the hall. Mr. Dandy was back there somewhere, being inflated with oxygen, injected, rewired. Jack crossed the room to the lobby, used his cell phone to dial Chloe's and then the apartment. He left messages at both numbers explaining what had happened. She was supposed to call him after her appointment. He didn't want to hear about the baby with any taint of Mr. Dandy to mar things. It wasn't so much selfishness, although there was some of that. It would simply feel like bad luck.

He sat down again next to Ivory and set himself to wait. It was a long stretch of waiting. They seemed to have joined some doleful class of people whose job it was to be ignored by institutions. Ivory put down her magazine. "Did you tell your wife?"

"What?"

"Tell her about the old man. That's who you called, right?"

Jack made some halfhearted noise. Ivory's face kindled. "Oh wow. You thought I meant—"

"Yeah."

"Relax."

"Relaxing it up here, boss."

"Sure you are. Hey, I know you worked things out with her. I know you're back in the house. That's great. True love winning out and all."

He couldn't tell if she was mocking him. "Thank you."

"Because once in a while life ought to have a big fat happy ending. Somebody's life. I've read books."

"I'm sorry if you're angry."

"I'm not angry. I'm providing analysis. Color commentary."

Although no one seemed to be paying attention to them, Jack lowered his head and bent toward her to try and keep things private. "I want you to be happy too. There's no reason you can't."

She waved this away. "Girls like me are in some other book. That's why we have to specialize in fucking. It's like, the coin of the realm for us. Isn't this an interesting conversation to be having in an emergency room?"

"It is."

"Oh don't look that way, what are you, scared? Of me? Well maybe you should be. Or somebody should. I'm a little crazy, don't you think?"

She was beaming at him, nodding, as if impatient for him to get a really good joke. Jack said, "Sure. You're crazy."

"More than a little."

"As a bedbug."

"A giant bedbug. With superpowers."

"Whatever makes you happy."

But that fast, her mood changed. "Ecstatic," she said flatly.

"A giant, mutant, radioactive bedbug," Jack said, trying to play along, jolly her up again. But Ivory bent toward him, close enough to whisper. Her breath tickled his ear, hot, like the car heater.

"Remind me to show you something."

Flick of warm wet tongue, and then she was back to her magazine.

"Anyone here for Dandy?"

Jack got to his feet. A short man in blue scrubs and tennis shoes beckoned. His ID badge said Dr. Gold. Dr. Gold had a cautious look. He began by saying, "I'm sorry." Jack thought it was likely that Dr. Gold had experience with people who did not respond to bad news in a rational manner.

Jack said, "I was kind of expecting it." He amended himself, tried to sound less goddamn casual. "He fell really hard."

"It was a massive brain event. I expect that's what made him fall."

"Brain event?"

"Stroke. For all practical purposes, he was probably dead before he hit the ground."

Jack said nothing. Dr. Gold went on to talk about clots, and the medications used to break up clots, and the medications for relieving intercranial swelling. About ventilation. All the thorough and heroic measures that had been applied to Mr. Dandy, to no avail. The doctor was a youngish man, not much older than Jack himself, although his hair was thinning and his skin had a damp, crumbly texture from too many long hours spent in the hospital pesthouse. Dr. Gold stopped himself in midsymptom. "I'm sorry, I just assumed . . . Was he your father?"

"No. He lived next door."

"Oh, is there someone we ought to call? Wife?"

"He was a lifelong bachelor." Jack thought back to the first time they'd met Mr. Dandy, he and Chloe, that day in the lobby. A dozen feet from the bottom of the staircase where, for all practical purposes, the old man had washed up dead.

"Are there family members?"

Jack said he didn't think so, at least, he didn't know of anyone. Dr. Gold's eyebrows drew themselves together, considering this. Jack understood that this was a new problem. He said, "What do you do if there's nobody?"

"The coroner's office takes over. There's an investigation. To find any assets, insurance, prepaid burial, that sort of thing. Meanwhile, we keep him here."

"Maybe I could take a look around. See if there's anything, you know, papers . . ."

Dr. Gold nodded encouragingly. Jack was beginning to realize he might not yet be done with Mr. Dandy, that he was in danger of inheriting him as you might inherit a truckload of water-damaged furniture. He asked, "Did he ever wake up?"

Dr. Gold shook his head. "Lights out. Never knew what hit him." Jack knew that this was meant to be reassuring. Pervert. Queer.

Jack thanked him. For your time, Doctor. For giving it the old college try. For providing Mr. Dandy shelf space. They shook hands. Dr. Gold gave Jack a card, a coroner's office he could call in case he came up with anything. Jack thanked him again and made his way back to Ivory.

She was still poring over her ratty magazine, though by now it hardly seemed worth pretending she was reading it. Without looking up she asked, "So is he dead, or what?"

"Yes. He's dead."

She put the magazine down, stood up, and limped her way to the exit. Jack followed. When they reached the car, she said, "He was Catholic, wasn't he?"

"Well he was Irish. Sure. I guess."

"Somebody should light a candle for him. Have a mass said. That's what you do. I could go back to my folks' old church."

He didn't know what to make of this. "If you want to."

"Because it's like you said, somebody should do something." She had to wait for Jack to unlock the door, then for both of them to get in the car. She continued. "I know you think I'm some totally horrible person, but I'm not."

"That's not what I think." He maneuvered the car out of the parking lot and into the rain-clogged traffic.

"Or that I'm just some stupid kid you don't have to take seriously."

"Why don't you stop trying to tell me what I think."

"Okay, then you tell me."

"I think . . . I don't know. I can't decide if you hate me or just hate yourself."

She let that one hang out there for a time. Then she said, "Well. I don't hate you."

They were silent until they reached the recognizable boundaries of the neighborhood, the Polish bakery, the storefront that rented Hindi videos, then the newer, yupped-up enterprises that sold trendier ethnic fare (tapas, Thai) to nonethnics. Ivory started up again in a fast, animated voice. "I'm thinking about leaving town pretty soon. Yeah. I have these friends. They're going to Florida to start a club. Tampa, Florida. They said I can go with. I'm seriously, seriously considering it."

"A club, what do you mean? Book club? Stamp collecting?"

"A *music* club. God you are so dense."

"I knew what you meant. It was a joke. Lighten up."

She gave him a severe look from behind the pale fringe of her hair.

She seemed to find him not funny. "You know even in winter, you can go to the beach there? It would be very cool to be getting a tan when everybody back home was freezing their asses off. All I have to do is pack a few things."

"Sure. Whatever would make you happy."

"Oh, so now we're back to happy again."

Once they reached the building, Jack went in to check the phone messages and try Chloe again. She hadn't called and he still couldn't reach her. He assumed that Ivory had gone back to Brezak's. But when he came out into the lobby, she was sitting on the stairs, a fastidious distance from where Mr. Dandy had landed. "Locked out," she said, before Jack could ask.

"You can go home."

She shrugged. "Raining." Her eyes followed him as he walked past. "Whatcha doing?"

"I have to . . ." He didn't feel like explaining himself to her. He stood at Mr. Dandy's door and tried the knob. It nudged open and he stepped inside. The air was close and brown. Brown light from the brown windows. Brown carpet, brown couch, brown ghost of Mr. Dandy.

"You ripping him off?"

Ivory had come up behind him. Jack registered the thought that she could move quietly enough when she wished to. He didn't answer her but crossed the room to a hutch that gave some evidence of being used as a desk. There was a phone, and a laminated list of fire and emergency numbers provided by a drugstore. Crossword puzzle book, receipts, bills, pizza flyers, coupons, nothing you'd mistake for an asset. A box of Fannie Mae turtles, half full of their empty paper shells, last touched by a dead man's hand.

Ivory walked a little way into the room. "This place is a total dump."

Jack opened the hall closet. A collection of old-man coats, bulky plaids and wools. A pair of insulated coveralls, ancient galoshes, and winter hats. And propped up in the back, a blue steel, double-barreled shotgun.

"Jesus Christ."

Ivory came to stand next to him. "Is that thing real?"

With caution, Jack drew it out of the surrounding skirts of the coats. There was a red box of shells set next to it on the closet floor. Jack broke the barrel, peered through it. The shell chamber was empty but still he kept his hands a respectful distance from the trigger. "Yeah, it's real."

"Where does an old coot like him get a *shotgun*?"

"Where does anybody get guns?" But Jack had to wonder how the hell he'd managed it. Bus trip? Shop by phone? Or was it another relic of his railroad days?

"Like he was ever going to shoot anything."

"A few hours ago he was talking about shooting you and your boyfriend. I thought he was just bullshitting. Lucky for you he took his header down the stairs first."

She rolled her eyes at this, but Jack could tell it rattled her, as it did him. His lungs convulsed and he coughed painfully. The ancient dust of the place was getting to him. He put the shotgun back and shut the closet door. Overhead Mrs. Lacagnina started up her vacuum cleaner, pushed it back and forth, without mercy, over the same piece of floor.

Mr. Dandy's kitchen looked as if it had never seen a green vegetable. Yellow grease painted the wall behind the stove. The remains of his breakfast eggs were still in the sink. Mr. Dandy's bathroom, with its lineup of jars and vials and poultices devoted to Mr. Dandy's ailments, was better left unexplored. The bedroom was painted a deep, lurid blue. He'd made his bed, drawn up the sheets and the Najavo blanket that served as a spread.

Ivory hitched herself over, tested the mattress with one hand. "This is a dead man's bed."

Jack left her there and went back into the dining room. There was a framed picture of Jesus praying, done in the languid, romantic style, Jesus as matinee idol, light emanating from his face. Tucked in the frame, a collection of holy cards Jack didn't bother examining. He moved on to a china cupboard. Behind its glass shelves were some ornate, silver-topped tankards, a ceremonial-looking soup tureen, a set of dinky rose-printed china that must have belonged to some unimaginable female relative of Mr. Dandy. A black-and-white photograph of three grinning young men standing before a background of pine forest. Jack recognized Mr. Dandy from the nose and jaw. He was the one in the middle, with his arms around the others, a full head of (possibly red) hair, and somewhere beyond the borders of the picture, a railroad to run.

The dining room table was covered with a lace-printed vinyl cloth. Books and papers were heaped on it, and Jack sat down to go through them. Much of it was devoted to Mr. Dandy's Medicare coverage. He sifted through phone bills and dentist's bills and any number of paper scraps that scattered like moths whenever he lifted a layer of documents. He was losing heart for his chore. There was something horrible about it. A life reduced to these dirty leavings.

But in the end it didn't take him very long to find what he was looking for, a brown cardboard accordion file with Mr. Dandy's slapdash handwriting on the front: Imp. Documents. Jack thumbed through it without extracting any of it. More dead paper. Envelopes from the Brotherhood of Railroad Engineeers. Pension? Insurance? Someone else could decide.

Mrs. Lacagnina's vacuum shut off and Jack drew the elastic over the file, snagged Mr. Dandy's house key from its hook on the wall, just in case he had to come back for anything. Ivory still had not reappeared. He called back to her from the doorway. "I'm leaving. You probably should too."

Her voice was muffled. He couldn't hear what she replied. He said, "Well, lock the door on your way out."

"Come here a minute." Clearer now, as if she'd freed her head from some obstruction.

"What for?"

"Just come here for a minute. See something."

He didn't like to think what she might have unearthed in there. His chest ached and he felt feverish. He stood in the hallway, reluctant to enter the bedroom. "I really have to get home."

"One second. It's important."

She was lying on the bed, her clothes in a heap on the floor. The blue walls made her nakedness appear as if she'd been recovered from deep water, a drowning victim. Before he could speak she said, "You don't have to do anything. I just want you to look. Can you see from there? You can come closer. This is the only time I'm doing this."

He took a few steps toward her, stopped. Her arms were at her side. Her bare feet curled over the edge of the Navajo blanket. Her triangle of pubic hair was blond, with a tint of pink. Her hip, the bad one, was thin and sunken, like a shallow bowl. There was a knobby mass, strapped with muscle, where her leg bone joined it. The leg itself was a pale stick, wider at the knee than the thigh. It was hard to imagine how the contraption worked, bore weight, moved her forward.

Her eyes seemed bluer in the blue gloom. They were fixed on his face. She said, "I told you. Pretty funky."

Jack didn't want to think what his face was showing. He found himself shaking his head, no, but what did that mean, no, except that he was ashamed of his own shock.

He started to speak but she stopped him with a jerk of her head on the pillow. The pillow was sunken. It bore the imprint of the dead man's head, the long habit of its shape and weight. "Don't say a thing. Just look and then you should leave. I can tell you didn't think it was this bad. But this is me. You didn't know. I couldn't even make a list of all the things you don't know. This is what somebody who loves you looks like. Now I want you to go."

Fourteen

The doctor shined his light inside me. "Well well. What have we here."

My feet were up in the stirrups and there was a sheet draped over my knees like a tent. It was the posture recommended for excavations.

The doctor wore a miner's helmet with a headlamp attached in front. "Now you may feel some discomfort," he warned me.

I yelped when I felt him burrowing in. Discomfort. They had their nerve, doctors, talking like that. He was walking around inside me now, tapping the walls with his infernal tools. I said, "Are you looking for anything in particular?"

His voice was distant, underground. "Evidence."

I gritted my teeth. My nose tickled. I thought if I sneezed I might achoo him out of there, but that would be rude.

Finally he reemerged, puffing and blowing and brushing dust from his shoulders. "Very interesting."

"What?" I didn't like the sound of "interesting." It was another doctor word they used to sneak the bad news in sideways.

"Somebody's left a rubber doll in there."

"That's ridiculous."

"Perhaps, but those are the lab results."

"Is it a boy or a girl?"

"It's choosing not to commit at this time."

I was beginning to feel this doctor was a quack. I said, "None of this is very helpful. I was thinking it was a real, actual baby."

"That's a common misunderstanding. They aren't real until later, when you get more used to the idea."

"I was pretty sure I already was." I was getting frustrated. What good were all the miracles of modern medicine, all the wonder drugs and super scans, if all you got out of it was a fake baby?

The doctor told me to sit up, get dressed. He busied himself with his prescription pad. "I'm going to start you on peanut butter and jelly sandwiches, see if we can't put some weight on you."

"I guess I have to get used to the idea of being fat."

The doctor's pen stopped scratching. He looked me over with his doctor eyes. He had a long history of being smarter than everybody else, you could tell. It was something he took for granted. "Not fat. Normal, healthy, weight gain."

"All right," I said. "Sure. Bring it on."

"Diet. Exercise. Vitamins. Lots of rest. The whole nine yards."

"Roger that. Total health."

"That means—"

"I stopped drinking. Way back before."

I expected him to give me some kind of lecture. They never pass up a chance, believe me. Instead he looked up at all his framed diplomas and certificates, the things that allowed him to ask a lot of nosy questions or tell other people what to do. I could see myself reflected in the glass. He said, "Have you ever been totally honest about anything in your entire life?"

"Not really. Or not for very long." He took me by surprise, I guess that's how he pulled that answer out of me.

"So you've quit drinking except for—"

I told him I didn't appreciate him taking that tone, that I was offended. The doctor wasn't watching me, only my reflection in the glass of the frames. He said, "Your baby wants to be born."

That's when I started crying. Maybe he thought it was just part of an act. And yes I'd done that sort of thing before, cried because there was some advantage in it. But he was a woman's doctor, he'd seen his share of crying women, and I wanted to believe he could tell the difference. That there was nothing sadder than the thought of a baby trusting me to get it into the world, let alone be its mother.

The doctor let me go on awhile, then he pushed the Kleenex box at me. He said, "You must not think I'm unsympathetic. But unfortunately, I see this sort of thing all the time. People telling themselves they're making a fresh start. Out with the old me, in with the new. They make decisions, resolutions, promises. You know, husbands, babies, that sort of thing. And maybe it even works for a while. But you're still the same sad girl, aren't you? Let's shut down the waterworks now. You aren't fooling anybody but yourself."

Fifteen

Chloe said it must have been horrible. The man dying right in front of him. She couldn't imagine. Jack said it wasn't that kind of dying, the way it was in movies. No agony or death rattle or the soul escaping the body. But yes, it had been sort of horrible. He didn't feel like talking about Mr. Dandy, or anything else that had happened. He'd called the coroner's office, done his duty about the paperwork, and now he lay propped up in bed. Fever ran through him like a live electric wire. He coughed his foggy cough. He felt as if he had narrowly escaped some engulfing catastrophe, a roiling wind or flood that had walked right up to him, stared him down, and then retreated. He asked Chloe what had gone on at her doctor's appointment.

"It was fine. Very routine. We're going to have a perfectly healthy something-or-other."

"Do they do tests, what?"

"Half a sec." Chloe went into the bathroom, opened cabinets, ran water. She came back with a thermometer and shook it down. "Open wide."

"Why don't we have one of those digital thermometers?"

"These are more accurate. Open."

Jack wriggled his tongue around the glass tube, concentrated on trying to work a little air around it. He imagined the end of the thermometer bulging red and then exploding, like a cartoon. Chloe sat on the bed beside him. "They do blood tests. Poke around. No biggie."

"On-grm?"

"They do sonograms later. If you decide you want one, or there's some reason for it. He wants me to gain more weight. The doctor. He wants me to pig out. Get ready for the new sow me."

Jack said "Nnhh," by which he meant she would never look like a sow, and it was probably a good idea for her to eat a little more. "Nngry?" he added.

Chloe shook her head. "I've still got the queasies. The pigging-out part probably comes later. Quit trying to talk."

So he quit. He watched Chloe do her Big Nurse impersonation, folded arms and tapping foot and mock glare. She wasn't really a nurse. He wasn't fooled. Jack smiled a thermometer smile. The doctor told the nurse to eat more. Chloe hadn't filled out any. The skin of her face was still too tight. She was nothing but hard, sharp angles: shoulder blades, kneecaps, collarbone. He would pack the refrigerator with butter and cream cheese and pastrami sandwiches and what was it she didn't say that was making her thin? If he had gone to the doctor's appointment with her, would everything today have unhappened? Mr. Dandy still be alive? Never seen the girl's sad nakedness? Chloe popped the thermometer out of his mouth and announced he had a temperature of a hundred and one.

Jack slept, but his arms and legs were both heavy and restless and kept flopping like fish, startling him awake. His head fired and hummed. He was convinced that someone else was in the bed with him, that Chloe had discovered him and Ivory in bed together. The terrible nakedness of that leg, the part of it that was only bone papered over with skin. He had never meant for her to love him like a fever burning anything it touched.

Then it was dark and Chloe was getting into bed with him. Jack woke up long enough to ascertain that this was real. She wouldn't let him kiss her, pushed his mouth away from hers. "I don't want your germs. Go back to sleep." She said that Mr. Dandy's name was now Mr. Bones. Mr. Dandy grinned and nodded. His false teeth chattered like a windup toy.

Jack woke up needing to pee. He had no sense of time. He might have slept for one hour or for ten. Chloe lay on her side, curled away from him. In the bathroom Jack swallowed two aspirins and ran cold water over his hangdog face. There was no sound from the upstairs apartment. He couldn't remember hearing them since he'd gotten home from the hospital, and that seemed odd, even wrong. He stayed very still, listening at the bathroom vent. "Ivory?" But nothing whispered back to him. He wouldn't know what to say to her anyway. She hadn't wanted him to say anything. She hadn't wanted to hear him say he didn't love her back.

He slept again. Woke up to the discreet sound of the front door closing, Chloe leaving for work.

After a while he hauled himself out of bed, coughed up some lingering crud, and stood in a hot shower. The fever had broken but he felt light-headed, weak. Almost exactly twenty-four hours ago he'd been doing exactly the same thing, showering, dressing, standing in the front room listening to Mr. Dandy and Brezak.

He went out into the lobby. Nobody there, nothing stirred. It didn't feel haunted as much as lonesome. He went back inside and tried to call Chloe, got her voice mail. "Hey, it's me. Sorry I missed you. Call when you get this."

Almost as soon as he put the phone down it rang. He picked it up again. "Hey, gorgeous."

Silence. Then a strange woman's voice, low pitched, with a rasp in it. "Gorgeous. I like that."

"I'm sorry, I thought . . . Sorry."

"Well I'm not." She laughed. "Keep it coming."

"Sorry, who is this?"

"Jack Orlovich, right?"

"Do I know you?"

"Yes and no. Don't hang up. This is about your whore of a wife. Yeah. You got it now?"

The fever had drained out of him. Everything was cold. "Yeah, I got it."

"That was some stunt. Did you get a big kick out of it? You and the whore?"

"It was just me. I know it wasn't funny."

Mrs. Jim Spencer said, "I'll tell you what's funny. You thinking you know one thing about my life. My family's life. Don't hang up on me or I will find a way to put you personally in shit soup up to your neck. I'd like to hear you say that part. That you don't know anything about me."

"I don't know anything about you."

She said, "Orlovich. You're right, an unusual name. Distinctive."

"Thank you."

"I wouldn't just yet."

Jack held the phone to his ear but didn't speak. It held all the bad news in the world, that roiling, cresting wave.

Mrs. Jim Spencer breathed a big gusty sigh. It was probably meant to sound theatrical, but Jack thought it conveyed something genuine in spite of herself, weariness or heartache. "Is she really pregnant? Or was that another part of your song and dance?"

"She's pregnant."

"Is it Jim's baby?"

"She says it's mine."

"Well hey. Glad that's settled." When Jack didn't speak, she went on. "I think I met her once. Long, black hair. Frisky. Shakes her ass in your face. That her?"

Jack said it was. Mrs. Jim Spencer said, "So I guess we should be pals, you know, the wronged parties and all, but I don't think I like you very much, Orlovich. Why did you call me, huh? Why did you want me to know. I didn't, by the way. Thanks."

Jack thought she might have been drinking. He said, "I wanted you to help break it up. It was a stupid thing to do. I'm sorry. I just wanted her back. I'm sorry I put you through all this for nothing."

"I wouldn't call it nothing."

"Not nothing. Right. But I hope you and your husband can move on. Put the pieces back together. Get on with your lives. That's what we're trying to do."

"Oh boy."

"Again, I'm really, really—"

"And here I thought I was dumb."

She was laughing, a loopy, sniggering laugh. If it wasn't drinking, it was something else, pills maybe, the kind of pills suburban doctors dispensed to unhappy wives. "Oh *honey*. What do you look like? Are you one of those very handsome, not too bright guys?"

"I beg your pardon."

"Because if you think this is all ancient history, if you think it's really over—"

"Shut up. Just shut the fuck up."

The phone clicked and the line went dead. He put the receiver back. A moment later it rang again. He answered. "What."

"Wow," Chloe said. "I guess you're feeling better."

"Yeah."

"You were out like a light when I left. I thought I should just let you sleep."

"Good idea."

"Got a big day planned?"

"Nope. Taking it easy. You?"

"The usual rat race. There must be something I like about this job. Oh yeah, the money. I have to run. I may be a little late tonight. Anything I can bring you, in case you don't get out?"

Jack said he couldn't think of anything. They said good-bye and he put the phone back. It was only a couple of minutes before it rang again. "Hello?"

"Sorry," said Mrs. Jim Spencer. "I shouldn't have hung up on you. I often find myself making impulsive decisions these days. Anyway. In the spirit of sharing information—"

"If you want to say something, just say it."

"There are people who specialize in this sort of thing, you know? Right in the yellow pages. Professional. Discreet. What day is this?"

"Thursday."

"That's right. Thursday. The day I take our youngest daughter to ice-skating practice. You wouldn't know that. It wouldn't interest you. My boring life. In fact let's skip it. Because nothing about me would be the slightest bit . . ."

"What about Thursdays?"

" . . . for years and years . . ."

When she stopped talking Jack said, "Hey. You there?"

"What do you want?" He heard her breathing, slow and leaking air.

"What's your name? Huh? Tell me your name."

"Marianne."

"Don't wuss out on me, Marianne. Come on. Thursdays."

She sighed. "Oh boy. What time is it getting to be? You know how when you waste time in the morning and then you're behind all day? Or maybe you don't."

Jack didn't want to risk her zoning out again. "What were you going to tell me?"

"Eventually I believe I'll get to the point where I don't care what either of them do. I think that will be healthy."

"Marianne."

"Maybe it's better if you pretend I never called. And I can pretend you never called me. Even steven. Because really, in a hundred years, what will it matter? Not even a hundred. Fifty. Not even fifty. More like—"

"If you tell me, I'll go after them. That's what you want, isn't it? That's why you called. You want to dish out some pain and you can't do it yourself. All this crap about rising above things and taking the long view. Who you think you're talking to? Tell me where they are."

After a while she said, "What would you do if I told you?"

"Don't know that yet."

"I don't want him hurt."

"Sure you do. You just don't want to be the one in charge. I'm not making promises. Chance you take."

"I can't."

"You know you're going to tell me. Once you get through with your fragile-crackpot routine. You knew it when you called. Come on, Marianne. Self-respect's a bitch, ain't it?"

She said, "Do you have something you can write with?"

She gave him a Gold Coast address. "It's somebody's apartment. I don't know when they get there. Sometime in the afternoon."

"All right," Jack said. "All right." She was talking once more when he hung up the phone. It rang again but by then he had stopped paying attention to it.

He found Mr. Dandy's key, walked through the lobby and let himself in. The same brown air and staleness in the dead man's rooms. He fished the gun out of the hall closet and wrapped it in Mr. Dandy's musty raincoat. Scooped up the box of shells. There was still no one about in the lobby. Just as well. The bundle looked like a shotgun wearing a raincoat. It was a little past ten in the morning.

Jack laid the shotgun on the couch in his own living room and sat down across from it. His head was vacant but twitching with static, like a television turned on with no signal. He felt the wavering strangeness the fever had left behind. How unusual it was to have a dead body in the shape of a gun on his couch. At any moment he expected Chloe to come in and scold him for his foolishness. He must have fallen asleep. The clock on the desk said noon. He didn't remember sleeping but nothing else made sense. He tried to think where the car was parked. It was a long block away, it would never do to walk the shotgun all that distance. Put a hat on it, maybe, and pretend it was a friend who'd dropped by for a visit.

In the end he drove the car into the alley behind the house and went through the backyard. He shoved the shotgun into the trunk and put the box of shells under the front seat. He couldn't quite get the hang of driving. It felt like an amusement-park ride. The streets rushed at him through the windshield. Then he took a wrong turn and wound up heading north on the Inner Drive, swore at himself, tried to turn around, found nothing but one-ways that carried him farther and farther from the lake. He'd get there too late, or not at all, never know, stay crazy forever.

A horn sounded and a truck flew by in front of him. That put the top of his head back on, made him concentrate on his driving. At any given moment in Chicago, how many of its citizens were out on the roads stoned, drunk, hallucinating, murderous? They could have one of those call-in radio shows just for loonies. Hey there, this is Ed on the Eisenhower, how's it going? And this is Sammy on the South Side, it's a great day to be out here loaded for bear, bouncing through intersections like a pinball, mowing down the sidewalks, hey there, Sad Sack Jack, let's just keep on keeping it real.

Finally he got himself turned around, swung onto Lake Shore Drive. A clear day with the sun stinging his eyes. Driving the Drive always felt like being part of a parade, like you should be waving from an open convertible. He couldn't stop thinking stupid thoughts. There was another moment of mad panic when he thought he'd lost the piece of paper with the address, before he found it fallen down by the brake pedal.

He slowed when he got closer to the high-rent district. Here were modish buildings of red brick or creamy stone, tall windows swagged with draperies, wrought-iron balconies, fussy bits of brass and gilt on the front doors. Who the hell lived in these places? The widows of furniture kings and pharmaceutical emperors. Trust funders, real estate magnates. At least one close friend of Jim Spencer, guy who wouldn't mind if you drank his liquor and fucked on his bedsheets, what were pals for? The lake was the blue front yard for this neighborhood. They owned it in a way that other people couldn't. Why was it always money with Chloe? His whore of a wife. He was looking for her on every corner. He almost drove past the building itself.

It was whitewashed brick with an awning set out over the sidewalk. There were evergreens carved into bulbs and some spindly trees given space amid the concrete. One of the widows, hatted, exercised a Pomeranian on a leash. No one else was visible. Behind the stately windows multiple adulteries might be in progress in different, imaginative ways, but the street's public face was one of genteel boredom.

Jack parked beneath a sign telling him not to. Now what. Oh crying crap. He had an actual shotgun in the trunk. He who'd never fired a gun in his life. There was something funny about it, if he could find anyone to tell. The old woman and the Pomeranian tottered past him. Jack hunched down in the seat and got ready to withstand her scrutiny, but she didn't seem to see him. Cataracts? Or a lifetime of urban indifference? Maybe you really could unload a shotgun on a residential street without anyone noticing or sounding an alarm.

Scenes began to play out in his head. He broke down a door to find Chloe and Spence naked and scrabbling and Chloe screamed and they tried to cover themselves while Chloe got some words out, coaxing him, appealing for calm, forgiveness, a chance to explain. He brought the shotgun up to his chin and pulled the trigger and the kick of the thing would be tremendous, it would practically knock him over and Chloe would scream again, and the blood was a bright fountain and he fired once more, and what happened to a body when you did that, tore it apart in all the places it wasn't meant to tear and Christ no.

He wasn't and couldn't. And yet he was and could. If he found Chloe in the apartment upstairs he would be that man, whether or not he committed murder. He would become lost, crazed, unrecognizable.

But the longer he sat on the quiet street with nothing happening, the less likely any of it—Chloe, Spence, murder—began to seem. It occurred to him that Marianne Spencer was making it all up. She was playing him, getting him back for the evil of his phone call. She could have picked an address out of the phone book for all he knew. She was wacked out, jealous, she hated Chloe too and she'd found this new and nasty plan to stir up trouble between them.

He constructed the logic of this carefully, testing it step by step, and determined it sound. The sense of it asserted itself. Chloe wasn't betraying him. He'd been too willing to believe it, based on his own paranoia and the talk of a woman he'd never met. And the only thing he'd have to do to prove, or disprove, it all, to reclaim himself, step back from that brink, was to find the apartment number he'd been given, apologize to whoever lived there, be on his way. It seemed like such a clean, pure moment, this perfectly balanced instant before it would be decided if he was to remain himself, or cross over forever.

Then he roused himself, got out of the car, took one of the shotgun shells out of its box beneath the car seat, and slipped it into the pocket of his jacket.

He wished he had a package or a bouquet or some other prop to tuck under his arm as he stood in front of the buzzers listing the apartment numbers and their occupants. Apartment 2-N was someone named Hundley, which meant nothing to him. Jack pressed the buzzer and thought too late about what he might say into the intercom, but there was no need. He heard the electronic click of the front door unhitching.

The lobby was the kind that made a pretense of welcoming you into an actual parlor. There was a fireplace and a mantel with a gold-and-scrolled ticking clock set between two candlesticks. White marble floor, armchairs and a coffee table with a fan of magazines, potted plants. He chose the stairs over the elevator. Thick gray carpet underfoot. Light streaming in from the arched windows. He climbed two flights of stairs. The doors he passed were silent. Windows dozed behind them.

At apartment 2-N he stood to one side of the door, out of range of the peephole. He tried to listen. Indistinct, muffled sound, and even that was something he might have imagined. Blood beat and popped in his ears and his heart roared. He put his knuckles to the door and knocked.

It opened inward and Spence stepped into the space. Spence recognized him, tried to push the door shut, but Jack gave it all his weight and sent it crashing into him. Spence staggered backward and Jack slammed the door behind him and where was Chloe, rooms and rooms in this place, very classy, leather furniture and genuine Art on the walls, unseemly to be knocking over the lamps when he tackled the other man, drove hard into his pudding gut. Spence didn't go down but he was off balance, couldn't get his feet underneath him. Jack put him in a headlock. Sounds were coming out of Spence, not words, just the concussion of air jarred loose. Spence's teeth and jowls and thick neck were jammed up against Jack's ear and Jack couldn't wrestle himself enough space to really hurt him, it was all shoving and butting heads until Jack got his knees braced, found enough purchase to put some force behind his fists and a clear field of vision to hate him properly, and it was as if every crazy sad mad day he'd lived through had only been preparation for this.

"Where is she?"

Spence didn't speak. Maybe couldn't. His mouth was full of blood. "Where is she?" It infuriated him not to get an answer, even as he kept his hands working, kept him from talking. It went on and on. Or no. It was all over quickly. Or maybe something fast kept happening over and over again. Spence tried to cover his head with his arms. He crumpled over on all fours. Jack hauled him up by his tie, kicked his knees out from under him. Spence sprawled facedown. His mouth left blood kisses on the white carpet.

Jack left him there, ran down a corridor, bruised himself on walls and door frames, bedroom bathroom kitchen bedroom again, all empty, and then it came to him that of course Chloe wasn't there. Spence had been waiting for her, had buzzed Jack in because he'd thought it was Chloe.

Spence had rolled over on his back. He swallowed some of the blood, then heaved and vomited it back up. His shirt had come out of his pants and exposed a roll of white belly. He looked like something large and bloody and newly butchered. Jack went to the front door, opened it, took a careful look and listen. The building still slept. He closed the door again, turned back to Spence. "When is she supposed to get here?"

Spence's face was mottled white and red. His eyes were squeezed shut. His mouth made shapes. "Oh come on," Jack said. "Don't tell me you're giving up this easy."

"Heart." Shallow whisper.

"What?"

"I think I'm having a heart attack."

"Bullshit you are."

Spence clawed at his chest, tried to get free of his necktie, turned his head to one side and vomited more bloody soup. Jack stood over him. "Heart attack? No kidding. This your first?"

Spence writhed and arched his back so hard that his head cracked on the floor.

"That a yes?"

"911."

"Excuse me?"

"Call 911."

"I don't think so."

When Spence opened his mouth, the blood formed strings in the hinges. He was pale now, blue-white pallor. The blood from his mouth and nose made a Halloween mask of his face. Sweat was rolling off him, soaking his shirt. "So when is Chloe coming?" Spence got himself up on one elbow, propped himself against the couch. "If I were you, I'd say."

"There's a meeting. After." Sitting up seemed to ease him, or maybe some spasm had passed. "I need an ambulance."

"Do you know I saw a man die just yesterday? Isn't that an amazing coincidence?"

"Christ's sake. Call. We can settle this later."

"No, I think now's a good time."

"This is murder."

"Not technically."

Spence's head drooped, and he sucked in air so hard he gagged. "My kids."

"Mine too. Which is another thing we could talk about. Whether you're the one who impregnated my wife."

Spence raised his head, looked at him through meaty swollen eyes. Said something, or tried to.

"Didn't catch that."

"Chloe pregnant?"

"Don't play dumb."

"Didn't."

"Didn't what, Jimbo? Stick it in her?"

"She didn't tell me."

Jack felt the bruises and throbbing places in his own body that he hadn't been aware of until now. He thought about Chloe and Spence. What they told and didn't tell each other, what they did instead of talking.

Spence tried to hitch himself across the floor to a phone sitting on an end table. Jack picked up the receiver, pocketed it. His fingers closed around the shotgun shell. He said, "There's this question of just how many lies we got going here, yours and hers. Not sure what to believe."

"I didn't know. I swear."

"Yeah, but you'd say anything right about now, wouldn't you. You look like shit, man. Seriously."

Spence mopped at his face with his shirt sleeve. Then the explosion in his chest set off another aftershock and he bent over. When he came to he said, "If I'd known . . ." He stopped, hoarding breath. "I wouldn't have . . ." He raised a hand, indicated—the apartment? The affair itself? "We never meant to hurt you."

"Well shoot. I do mean to hurt you. That's what it's all about."

"Give me the phone."

"You do this kind of thing on a regular basis? Cruise the office talent? Little afternoon training sessions?"

"No."

"Convince me you're telling the truth and I might give you the phone."

"Once before."

"Once. Heck. That hardly even counts."

"I love Chloe."

Jack bent down close enough to Spence to smell him, the mix of blood, ammonia, and aftershave. "I'll sure tell her. In case you don't make it."

Spence's nose was leaking fresh blood. He no longer resembled the corporate top dog, the man at ease with kings and commoners, smiling and joking to demonstrate his human side even as he presided over the intricacies of Big Money. The change had the same shock value as newsreels of cities after wartime bombings.

Jack said, "You want to know something funny? Or more like really ironic? I don't think I love her. Not anymore. Because you can't keep taking it and taking it. The things she's done. I don't just mean doing the nasty with you, Jimbo, though you're certainly implicated. More like . . ." He stopped. It embarrassed him to be explaining himself to Spence. Yet there was really no one else he could tell. "Anyway." He shrugged. "She pushed it and pushed it and here we are. You and me."

Spence didn't speak. Jack fingered the shell in his pocket. He liked the feel of it, its shape and weight. It reminded him of a child's stubby pencil. He hadn't meant to start talking again. But he was aware that he hadn't yet explained himself properly, gone about it right. He thought he could have told Ivory, but she was gone. He'd let her go, for good or ill. "I guess what I mean is, you start out loving a woman and if it goes wrong, if it turns into some spectacular, ball-busting flameout, like . . ." It was Jack's turn to wave a hand. The hand blurred, the walls breathed, he was—the technical term for it—fucked up. "Well, it ain't love after that. It's whatever you get when you keep it around too long. Like milk going bad. And then when you know she's a drunk and a liar and a whore and you still . . ."

Jack stopped. He hated the sound of his voice. Its weak and whiny edge. As if even killing a man wouldn't keep him from being pitiful and aggrieved.

Spence spoke as if he had a mouthful of gravel. "They'll find you. Police."

"Maybe. Or maybe I'm just another one of those unknown intruders." Police weren't anything he could get his mind around right now. Police were something on television. "By the way, I got the address from your wife. If you do pull through this, you might want to bring home flowers."

"Last chance."

"Oh, I don't know much about these medical things. You might be able to hang on for a good long while yet. Depends on, is this your basic 'massive heart attack,' like guys your age seem to—"

"Last chance for you. Not do this."

"We're about out of chances here. You might have noticed."

"Kill me kill you."

For a moment he wasn't even sure Spence had said anything. His ears filled with a drumming sound, like water from a high-pressure hose. He shook his head clear. "I don't think you're in a position to kill anybody, sport."

"You kill you."

"Shut up, man."

Spence looked bad. Not as bad as Mr. Dandy maybe, but Mr. Dandy had already been dead. If he stayed he was going to have to watch that part. He should just go. He kept expecting to hear the buzzer, Chloe.

He'd let her in and walk away. Leave the front door open, let her find Spence, scream, see what her lying self had accomplished. What it all came down to. A busted heart and a face turned to gristle. He wished it was over. The whole stupid woeful deal. His own stupid life. He pulled the phone out of his pocket. The shell too. Balanced them. Guess which hand?

Spence watched him from the floor. His tongue protruded, thick and dry looking. Jack went into the kitchen, ran water in a glass, came back and squatted down next to Spence, put the glass to his mouth. Spence drank. The water in the glass came away tinted pink. Spence's eyes bulged. He should go now. Let it all be over. Jack said, "Look at it this way. If I hadn't come along, you probably would have blown out your heart valves in the middle of sex. Very embarrassing."

Spence didn't answer. Jack wished he hadn't said anything. His words were all spite and cheap shots, when he'd meant them to come out cold and righteous. He'd lost some advantage. He'd already lost Chloe. When she'd walked out of the house this morning, she'd still been his wife, and now she wasn't, whether she knew it yet or not.

Jack eased himself down on the floor next to Spence. His legs felt weak, either from the ebb of adrenaline or the last pulse of fever. Spence took no notice of him. His eyes were closed. Maybe he was already dead. No, there was air in him still. It visibly inflated his throat and chest. Waxy goose bumps stood out on the skin of his arms. Jack wondered what time it was, how long since Spence had been stricken. When you had a heart attack, you were supposed to take an aspirin, he remembered, although he'd never been sure why. Spence loved Chloe. He said so. If he died, no one would be left to love her.

He tried to remember loving Chloe. He had to reach deep down for it. That beautiful, aggravating girl who'd walked out of a classroom without once looking his way. He hadn't loved her then but he'd wanted to. He'd made a space for her in his imagination and the actual woman had come to occupy it little by little.

It was a space he'd ripped wide open. He tried to picture it, a room like a heart or a heart like a room, something you could close off. "Hey," he said to Spence. "You still here?"

Spence didn't answer. A pulse skittered in his temple, a rabbit twitching. He wondered if Chloe loved Spence, if they told each other that, I love you love you love you too. He tried to hurt himself with thinking it but nothing came. There was an end to everything. Jack picked up the phone, pressed 911, told the dispatcher that an ambulance was needed and where.

He put the phone back in its cradle, set the lamps and the furniture to rights. Spence was still breathing, eyes closed, dreaming of pain. Jack waited until he heard sirens. When the buzzer sounded he pressed the release. He stepped outside to the hallway, leaving the apartment door open, and took the elevator down. Through the metal cage and shaft he heard the commotion of feet on the stairs, voices and radio chatter, weirdly close and echoing but invisible, like ghosts.

The paramedics had left the front door propped open. Chloe was just then stepping beneath the awning. Jack saw her before she saw him. When she'd left this morning he'd been asleep. She wore her black suit with a white blouse. The awning lit her with filtered sunlight. There was a moment when he was able to take her in, her pretty, blooming mouth, the way her eyebrows worked as she considered the ambulance, how she stood up tall and straight in her high heels, as if there would always be someone to watch her.

She saw Jack and yelped, a tiny sound that extinguished itself. Jack brushed past her. The street was still quiet. No crowd, idle or curious or alarmed, had gathered to see what the ambulance was about. It was as if this kind of thing happened every day.

Afterward

From California, Jack checked the *Tribune* obituaries on-line. Spence's wasn't among them. That was how Jack knew he had not died. He didn't try to find out anything else, and no other news reached him. Nobody came after him with an arrest warrant. They must have been glad to see the last of him, and left it at that.

He'd flown into LAX and called his parents from the airport. "Taking a few personal-leave days," he told them. He didn't offer to explain any further and he must have looked so alarming that they didn't press him. He slept for most of three days in his old bedroom with its book-shelves of boys' adventure books and closet full of swampy tennis shoes. On the third day his mother asked him, with painful tact, how much longer he thought he'd be staying. Jack said he didn't know. He called an old high school friend in Huntington Beach and arranged to move into his spare room.

The friend got him a job at the same place he worked, a small firm that produced and sold industrial videos. Jack learned the basics of production costs and inventory, rewrote brochures, did a little sales repping. It wasn't a job he'd imagined himself doing, but then, he had not been able to imagine most jobs. After work he and his friend and one or two others from the office might go out for beers, or else they went home and watched Lakers games or rented movies.

The longer Jack went through the motions of a normal, undesperate life, the more outlandish the last few months seemed. He didn't speak much about his marriage and for the most part his friends behaved as if he'd been gone on a not very interesting vacation. They knew that most married people got divorced eventually. His friends were casual about work and serious about fun, about music and skiing and mountain climbing and working out. This cheerful pursuit of shallowness as an end in itself was something Jack had always professed to hate about California life, but now he appreciated its ease.

He bought a three-year-old Jeep Grand Cherokee and spent his weekends driving the coast. Once he and his friends went to Mexico, fished and surfed and built bonfires on the beach. The moon turned the sand blue-white and the ocean to crumpled silver. Jack, drunk, tried to call Chloe but the call wouldn't go through. He spoke to the rolling ocean instead, told Chloe how he was through with her, with loving her, he'd come out on the other side of it and soon it would no longer be necessary for him to want to tell her so.

There was a conversation with his parents. He said nothing about Spence and nothing about the baby. He told them that he and Chloe had been having problems and had come to a parting of the ways. Jack's father, no doubt cautioned in advance by his mother, said only that he'd never thought it was a good idea to marry so young. As if marriage was a kind of complicated toy, subject to breakage. His father called a lawyer friend who found a lawyer in Chicago, and Jack filed for divorce on the grounds of irreconcilable differences.

Then Chloe got a lawyer also and there was a period when the lawyers shuffled procedures back and forth between them. Jack was impatient for that part to be settled. He wanted to sign off. He removed his name from the apartment's telephone and ComEd accounts. He closed out any funds he had in the Chicago banks. He traded his Illinois driver's license for a California one. Those were the easy things. Then the child would be divided into portions by some Cook County Solomon, and a court would tell him when and where to be a father.

The week after New Year's Jack took a couple days off from work and flew into O'Hare. He had been gone almost exactly three months. There were arrangements to make about retrieving the rest of his belongings. There would be more of the signing off. The lawyers had set up a meeting between him and Chloe to get the machinery of the divorce in order.

The day was blue and clear, with a steady, mortifying wind off the lake, crunchy snow underfoot, tire tracks turning from slush to rutted ice and back again. Jack met his lawyer for the first time. The lawyer dispensed some professional sympathy and said that they were awkward, these sessions, but they almost always went better than people feared. Jack said the last time he'd seen his wife he'd just finished beating up her boyfriend, and the lawyer said those circumstances were not as unusual as he might think.

The meeting was at the office of Chloe's lawyer and they took a cab across town. The cab sped along Lower Wacker, down among the roots of skyscrapers, and surfaced near Union Station. Jack watched the shouldering crowds and the winter sun picking out the glass and chrome and the horizon opening up to the west where the expressway and the railroad tracks ran. It was the city that had refused to love him. Its bulk and ugliness and energy wearied him. Of course this had been one of his mistakes, to confuse a city with a woman, and now he had lost them both.

At the lawyer's office they were shown into a conference room. Jack's lawyer said, "Sunny California. We'll have you back there in a twinkling." Jack sneered. He hated being the recipient of charitable small talk.

They stood when the door opened. Chloe's lawyer was a woman. There was a kind of rightness about that, a team of angry women taking him on. Everyone but Jack and Chloe shook hands. Even as Jack's lawyer began talking, Jack was aware that the man was attempting to signal him. Except for one blind and dumb glance at Chloe Jack had not looked at her, but now he raised his head from his study of the polished table and regarded her. She sat at a little distance from the rest of them, and as far as she could get from Jack in the small room, but without much effort he could see her entirely as she sat. She was not pregnant in any visible way.

Jack turned to his lawyer, tried to indicate his own confusion. The lawyer had been prepped to talk about medical expenses and custody and visitation, and now he was gamely launching into his backup script about the division of property. Chloe's lawyer responded with her own speech. Chloe didn't look at anyone. The lawyers kept up their

choreographed call and response. The room revolved in minute incre-
ments as the earth tracked and spun. Jack felt a moment of black, dizzy
nausea, as if gravity had loosened its hold. Was she really going to say
nothing?

"Jack?"

His lawyer was smiling at him, his head cocked vivaciously. He was
waiting for some answer. "I'm sorry," Jack said, and the lawyer repeated his question. Was such and such acceptable? Jack said that it
was. The lawyer was a winking, gibbering fool. No he wasn't. He was
hurrying things along as best he could, now that there was no need to
parse babies. Then Chloe's lawyer asked her a question and Chloe
turned her head, considering it. Her face was puffy around the eyes and
jawline. Or maybe it was the white sunlight that made the outlines of
everything bleached and uncertain.

He could tell from the tone and timbre of the voices that they were
drawing to some conclusion. He sensed another bout of handshaking
coming on. Just as they were all getting ready to push their chairs back
from the table, he said, "I'd like to ask Chloe if she'd stay and talk with
me in private."

The lawyers pricked up their ears, in a mannerly fashion. Chloe
studied Jack. Her look was so opaque, she might have been wearing
sunglasses. "Five minutes," she said.

The lawyers cleared out. Jack let a beat of silence pass. "What happened?"

"A lot."

"Did you have an abortion?"

"It figures you'd want to believe the ugliest possible thing about me."

"Did you?"

"I miscarried at seventeen weeks."

Whatever he might have said, he found himself unable to say. Chloe
went on. "Maybe it's just as well. I bet you would have hated it just for
being mine."

"No."

Chloe gave him another flat stare. "The doctor said there was probably something wrong with it. That's usually why you lose a baby. Any-

way." She let her hands turn palms downward, a cup of sunlight emptying.

A child would have tied him to her forever. In spite of everything, he'd wanted that. He said, "I'm sorry."

"Sorry for what part, exactly?"

"For you. For the baby. Come on."

"What you did to Spence was inhumane."

"And what Spence did to me was pretty fucking raw."

"God, I hate it when you talk like that. You've turned into a total thug."

"Yeah, I guess I have. Good work."

"Not everything's my fault, Jack."

Now that he'd grown more used to looking at her directly, he was able to scrutinize her. He hadn't been mistaken. Her face was fuller, looser. A downward turn to her mouth, the slightest suggestion of gravity. Maybe no one but himself would have noticed. He'd studied Chloe's face the way an art collector studied a painting. She saw him staring. "What?"

"Nothing." And because Chloe would know it wasn't nothing, he said foolishly, "How's Spence?"

"Why do you ask, so you can go try to finish him off?"

"Not everything's my fault either," he reminded her.

"He's fine. He's going back to work in a couple of weeks. He's in a cardio rehab program. There's a special diet, stress tests, and monitoring."

"I bet you signed the office get-well card."

"Not that it's any of your business, but we're getting married. After both the divorces are final."

Because he had only this peevish, hateful voice left to him, Jack said, "Congratulations. Usually, the heart attack sends them back to the wife."

"I know you think I'm a horrible person and Spence is a horrible person and we deserve each other. But we really are happy. It's like all the sad, awful things that happened brought us closer." Chloe reached beneath her chair for her handbag. She gathered it to her and folded her hands on top, as if waiting for permission to leave. "You can go over and get your things anytime. I don't live there anymore. Use the lawyer's address if you need to correspond with me."

He was through with talking. "Fine."

When Jack didn't say anything else, she stood up, actually smiled. "I'm glad this part is over."

He supposed she meant the legal session, but she might just as easily have been talking about Jack himself. He opened the door of the conference room for her and they walked together down the corridor. Chloe said, "You're back in Los Angeles?"

"That's right."

She was almost friendly, now that she was finished with him. "Oh my God, I meant to tell you. Fran and Reg. They're splitting up."

"Yeah?" Because it seemed he was obliged to express interest, he added, "How come?"

"You won't guess in a million years. Fran found all this gay porn and gay chat room stuff on Reg's computer. He had this whole secret life. Now honestly, did you ever have the faintest suspicion?"

"Nope. Never saw it coming."

"He claims he's bi, he's equally attracted to men and to women. I don't even want to know how that works! Fran's devastated. She's in a support group. I guess you'd *need* one. Reg moved to Boys' Town. Can you even imagine it? Reg making the scene at a leather bar? Isn't that too wild?"

"Wild."

"I guess Fran's available now." She actually nudged him in the ribs.

"Reg too."

Chloe giggled. "You're awful." Then she checked herself, turned more polite and conversational. "So, are you getting some writing done out there?"

"Just working."

"Oh, I bet you'll get back to it, now you're in California again. Because it has to be so much easier, writing about a place when you're actually there."

They were almost to the bank of elevators at the end of the corridor. Jack knew she meant to leave him there, shake hands or even kiss him.

He stopped walking. Chloe realized it a couple of paces later, halted and looked back at him. He said, "Please don't blow me off being charming like you do everybody else."

She sighed. "I was trying to be pleasant."

"Don't. Not if it takes an effort."

"I'm sorry you think I can't be nice to you without being insincere."

"I stopped writing. I won't be doing it anymore. That's not your fault. I would have figured it out sooner or later."

He could see Chloe puzzling over this, not only what he'd said, but whether she ought to involve herself. "But it's what you've always wanted to do."

"Things change. As we see."

"What about your book?"

"A lot of books never get written."

"I don't understand. You have so much talent. You really do, I hope you don't think I'm saying that for some devious reason."

"Talent's only part of writing. It's either something you have in you or you don't."

Jack didn't offer anything else, and after a moment Chloe said, "Well . . ."

He pressed the elevator's call button. Chloe waited with him, and when the car came she gave him a kiss on the cheek and said, Take care, and Jack said, You too, and he stepped inside and the door closed and he rode down twelve floors, down and down and down, wishing he could lift himself up with some ironic, buoyant thought. Chloe was what he'd had inside him. She'd been the only extraordinary thing about him. His outsized love and outsized fury. Now he would be like anyone else, shrunk down to normal, made up of itches and exasperations and, in time, he supposed, his share of some purely normal happiness.

He took a cab back to the garage where he'd left his rental car. The lawyer was expecting him, but Jack thought they'd both be relieved if he didn't show up. Instead he drove north, past all the landmarks and intersections he'd taken care to learn so that he could feel he truly lived here. It was the first time he'd seen his old street, his block, in winter weather. The curbs were heaped and churned with old snow that in places had turned the color of Coca-Cola. To park, you let the frozen tracks grab hold of your tires and slide you into a space. Every car was scummed with layers of dried salt.

He had to park two blocks away. The wind made his eyes and nose stream. The Hawk, that was the name people gave to the Chicago wind. Someone told him that, way back when he'd first arrived at Northwestern. And he'd made a point of remembering it, working it into conversation. But did anyone still say it? He wasn't sure. Maybe it was outdated even back then, a piece of old slang that only reached someone like him when it was already used up. No matter how he'd tried, he had never really belonged here.

The heat had been turned down in the apartment. Nothing was untidy or out of place, but the cold made it unwelcoming. Chloe had cleared out her closet and desk and other items Jack had to remember by their absence. The Monet water lilies were gone, and the area rugs. She'd left the TV and VCR and stereo. He assumed that Spence had better ones.

Jack set to work. He made a pile of the winter clothing he would no longer need, set it aside for Goodwill. He disassembled the computer and stereo components. He'd have to call the lawyer and find out which one of them owned the furniture. Tomorrow he'd come back with movers, have them box up his books and anything else he wanted to ship. He hauled bags of unwanted things out to the trash. The backyard was full of oddly shaped snow-covered lumps, like the bodies of Arctic explorers.

He was sorting through the bathroom shelves when he heard, unmistakably, the sound of a baby crying from upstairs. It went on for a time, then ceased. Someone flushed a toilet overhead.

Jack went out into the lobby. He'd assumed that Brezak wasn't home, and counted himself lucky. Now he saw that new names were on Brezak's mailbox. J. DESOTO, M. DESOTO. A nice young couple with a baby.

So Brezak had gone, or maybe he'd finally been thrown out, and was living his dirty, disorganized life somewhere else. Jack had to remind himself that these were rentals, he shouldn't be surprised when people moved on. Piece by piece his own life here would be erased. He wondered if Ivory had made it to Florida, if she was on a beach with the hot sun freckling her skin, rubbing suntan lotion on her withered leg, daring people to stare. He knew this was a sentimental thought and she deserved better from him. She had made it possible for him to imagine the different shapes and ways of loving, its cruelties and extravagances, how someone might desire men and women equally, or reach the very end point of desire.

Someone named Rogers had taken over Mr. Dandy's apartment. Jack and Chloe's names were still on their mailbox. Jack used his key to open it, pulled out some old pizza flyers. They were damp and shredded, as if something had been making a nest in there. Mrs. Lacagnina's name was still in place. Who would have thought she'd outlast everyone else.

Jack had pulled his car up to the front door to load suitcases when Mrs. Lacagnina herself came out, dragging her grocery cart. Jack waved. He wondered if she'd find it strange that he'd returned, then he wondered if she'd even noticed he was gone.

Mrs. Lacagnina didn't wave back. She stared at him with no sign of recognition, but Jack thought her face might be so hardened by age and deafness that it no longer recorded actual expressions. Jack opened the passenger door of the car, tried to convey his willingness to escort her to the grocery. He wanted to believe that in spite of everything, he might still be a person who was kind to old ladies.

Mrs. Lacagnina regarded Jack, then surveyed the sidewalk between her and the corner. It was only haphazardly shoveled, with a layer of glaze that could send you straight to the nursing home with a broken hip. Mrs. Lacagnina allowed Jack to help her over the snowy curb and into the car. He put the grocery trolley in the backseat and took his place behind the wheel.

Mrs. Lacagnina's feet, in black galoshes that reminded Jack of pony hooves, were exactly level with the floor mats. She had a new coat—her daughter must have argued mightily to get the old one off her back—with fur at the cuffs and collar, but she still wore the same fringed headscarf knotted beneath her chin. He imagined her heart keeping its own stubborn, syncopated time. She stared straight ahead as if Jack were a chauffeur.

A new problem presented itself. Did Mrs. Lacagnina shop at the Jewel, which was closest, or the Dominick's, a little farther on, or at some ancient corner store known only to Sicilian widows? How could you hope to pantomime the range of choices? There was nothing in the car to write with. Jack raised a hand to flag her attention, and when she turned to him he did his best to convey *Where to?*, quizzical eyebrows, shoulders up, hands agitating the steering wheel.

Mrs. Lacagnina gave him back a series of signals he did not understand, since none of them seemed to convey the name of a grocery chain. He shook his head, and Mrs. Lacagnina repeated herself, a bit of animation, even of theatrical disbelief, entering into her performance: *What's the matter, Mr. Handsome, is the only part of that head you ever use the outside?* When she showed him for the third time he finally got it. The vast horizon, the skipping waves, the hand to her heart, the sign of the cross.

On the way he stopped and got them both coffee, guessing she took hers black and sweet. She held her cup carefully in her gloved hands. Jack drove to Hollywood Beach, nudged the nose of the rental car past the leavings of the snowplows, as close as he could get to the beach and the lake itself. Even on a day like this there were a few underdressed-looking joggers bounding along on the walking path, exhaling frozen clouds. Wind shook the car and sent waves thick with ice slapping against the concrete seawall.

Farther out, the lake had a gloss to it from the low winter sun, a path of watery shine. Mrs. Lacagnina settled herself into her fur collar, lifted her coffee to her lips but didn't drink. She seemed content to sit there in the small space of comfort that the car provided, and Jack thought they might stay there awhile longer. He would have liked to ask about her husband. He would have liked to tell her about Chloe. It was the same story, really, for both of them. *One day a boat went out on the water and never returned.* And all you would have to do was write it down.

About the Author

JEAN THOMPSON is the author of *Who Do You Love,* a 1999 National Book Award finalist for fiction, and *Wide Blue Yonder,* a *New York Times* Notable Book for 2002. A recipient of fellowships from the National Endowment for the Arts and the Guggenheim Foundation, she lives in Urbana, Illinois.